SHIELD AND WORTHY SINNER

ENERGY OF MAGIC
BOOK EIGHT

J.E. NEAL

Copyright © 2023 by J.E. Neal

All rights reserved.

No part of this book may be reproduced in any form or by any electronic or mechanical means, including information storage and retrieval systems, without written permission from the author, except for the use of brief quotations in a book review.

To the people who inspire me on a daily basis with their kindness. You have magic souls and you share that with the world.
Thank you

CONTENTS

CHAPTER 1

RECKLESS DETERMINATION

DAN VINDICO

Dan's breath came up short as he watched Fionna cup her hand. Heat danced in a veined orange glow that orbed between her fingers. She turned her hand and ran it over the pani popo, the coconut bread her father had prepared at her request, a delicious native dish from her island, Kauai.

Her long brunette hair hung in loose waves down her back. Dan's eyes tracked down the silky tresses until they landed on what had to be the world's finest ass.

She shifted as she continued to heat the bread that was to be served with coffee for dessert. His jeans tugged, and his cock threatened to sever the zipper of its own accord.

With a quick glance toward the living room, Dan rolled his eyes in annoyance and debate. He moved to her and wrapped his massive arms around her waist. He caged her between himself and the counter where she was working.

Satisfied for a moment, he smiled as she leaned her head back on his shoulder. "I was hoping I could get a little of that heat, Ms. Styler. I'm hungry."

He cupped his own hand and sent his energy rhythms through her arms. His need pulsed and ached, and she could feel it all. Quickly deciding to continue his coercion, he forced his shield out from his pores and surrounded her in the very essence of his fierce love and ultimate protection. The air around them tinged a brilliant green from his shield.

She gave him that wickedly virtuous grin that drove him insane with need. "We have guests, Chief Vindico."

Dan huffed in her ear. "That was not my idea. Our guests need to leave. Like I said, I'm hungry."

She spun and her grin morphed to the smile that warmed the dark recesses of his soul. "And I just fed you dinner." She waggled her eyebrows flirtatiously.

"Dinner was great, but that's not what I'm hungry for. I want my dessert."

"We're having pani popo," she continued to taunt him.

"I'm losing it, baby. I need you, and…" He let his index finger trace down the low V-neck sweater just over the top tender swells of her luscious tits.

He cupped her right breast. Her breaths came quicker. She glanced back toward the living room to make certain their guests weren't coming to find them and to remind herself why she should make him stop.

He had no interest in their guests or in stopping, so he continued to ply her. He could just make out the strain of her nipple against his hand through her sweater.

He leaned and let a low moan echo in her ear. "You're wet. I can tell. And swollen so tight you ache. You need me to make it better, baby doll. You know you do."

"Dan," his name quaked from her lips.

A deep, chastising chuckle had Dan jerking his hand away and Fionna gasping for breath.

Garrett Haydenshire shook his head at Dan as he set two plates and his glass in the sink. "Shall I kick out the two newest officers that you hired and invited over to spell out what exactly they'll be doing on the task force while Fi fed us all dinner tonight, or would you like to leash Dan Jr. there and not take her on the countertop while we're all here?"

2

Dan rolled his eyes. He'd wondered if he'd somehow pissed Fionna off when she'd insisted that they were hosting a dinner party, not only for Chase Barron and Trent McCoy but also for Garrett.

Barron had secured Dan and Fionna adjoining rooms at The Venetian hotel for the Summation challenge where Fionna and her teammates were competing. He'd made certain that Dan and Fionna had access to one another without anyone being the wiser.

Barron had phoned Dan the day he and Fionna returned home from Vegas. He'd decided to shoot for the moon and to immediately call in the favor Dan owed him for securing the rooms.

The memories of Vegas made Dan uneasy again. He wanted a life with her more than he wanted to draw his next breath. He wanted to put a ring on her finger and meet her at the end of an aisle. No one was more surprised by that information than he was.

How he'd managed to convince her of his love and to move her into his house without anyone knowing they were together was orchestrated with more tactical defense than he used when he executed search and rescues with Iodex, the fiercest peacekeeping police force in the Gifted Realm, which he captained.

He was the highest-trained officer in the entire Realm. He'd put more criminals behind bars than anyone before him. He was damn good at most everything that had to do with law enforcement. He always got his man, but what he wanted now was his woman.

Until he managed to end Dominic Wretchkinsides and his band of low-life thugs, he couldn't really have her because no one could know they were together.

He wasn't a pompous kid anymore. He no longer believed that his wit, his muscles, and his will could save her from a man like Wretchkinsides. It hadn't saved Amelia, and Dan refused to bury the only woman who could save him from the hell he'd lived through since he'd buried his fiancée ten years before.

"Come on, you two," Fionna commanded. Dan relieved her of the coffee carafe and followed her back into the dining room. Barron and McCoy both offered him polite smiles.

Dan lamented this dinner all over again. He wasn't accustomed to showing his men such polite formalities. Fionna had insisted that since they were moving from Vegas and coming to work for Dan and Garrett, that they at least welcome them to DC and to the Elite forces.

Chase Barron was an outstanding officer with several meritorious promotions who'd graduated top of his class at Faraday, the Gifted academy in Arizona. With just a little bit of interrogation, Dan had determined that Barron's girlfriend, who was not Gifted, was planning on gaining her master's degree in Special Education at George Washington.

She'd made this announcement the day after Barron had purchased an engagement ring. He'd held off asking her to marry him. He didn't want her to give up her dream of attending George Washington for him.

Since the university wasn't far from the Pentagon, joining the Elite forces and the Wretchkinsides task force meant that Barron could keep doing what he loved and be with the girl he was crazy about on a regular basis. It also meant that Dan now had two additional officers to aid him in his quest to end the Interfeci for good.

The Crown Governor, Garrett's father, had immediately approved the budget additions for new officers much to Dan's delight.

Barron's partner from Vegas, Trenton McCoy, had been part of the bargaining for moving Barron up to Elite. Although he worked differently than Barron, together they made a great team. Dan was even more excited about McCoy joining the team than Barron.

Barron was thorough. He dotted every i and crossed every t, but McCoy was riskier. He made damn sure the job got done even if he had to bend the rules to accomplish his task. That was a man Dan could get behind, not that Barron wouldn't make an excellent addition as well. After all, he'd had balls enough to up and ask for an appointment to Elite after securing the hotel rooms.

"So Neva, you said that you start classes next week?" Fionna put everyone at ease. She smiled at Barron's newly minted fiancée and poured coffee for everyone. Dan couldn't keep his eyes off Fionna. She was perfection.

"Yeah, I'm hoping we can go tour the campus tomorrow, so I have some clue how to get around." Always keenly aware of everything around him, Dan noted Neva reaching for Barron's hand. He wasn't certain if she was uncomfortable, nervous, or just shy.

McCoy looked bored with talk of higher education. He turned to Dan after a long draw of his coffee that he appeared to deeply appreciate. "You ever think about expanding the task force to the major hubs where the Interfeci have guys? We used to take down three or four gambling rings or drug runners a month in Vegas."

Dan was impressed with the question. "I've considered it, but it's not worth it. Wretchkinsides runs a very tight top end and a loose bottom. The top guys are skilled, vicious, and what they know would land them in Coriolis for the rest of their lives.

"The guys he's got out in Vegas, Miami, New York, Atlanta, Dallas, and everywhere else are nothing more than a quick way to get him more cash. They don't know anything, and they're trained to pick up and leave in a hurry with barely enough background to hold them anywhere. They aren't worth it. He changes them out too often. I want Nic and the top ten, and I plan to get them all this year. I'm sick to death of chasing down leads that go nowhere."

McCoy nodded his agreement, but fear tugged at the curves of Fionna's face. Dan watched her delicate neck contract in a harsh swallow. She didn't always care for his occasionally reckless determination.

He laced his fingers through hers. She drew from him, and he fought not to groan and order everyone from his home. Their energy coupled readily. They were meant to be together. The overwhelming sensation of her pulling his rhythms into her own made him ache. Nothing made him weak, nothing but her.

"Dan's a little eager in case you missed that." Garrett tried to bring a little levity to the room at large.

Everyone chuckled, but Dan just rolled his eyes. No one else had to live with the death that robbed him of breath, and he refused to live without the life force Fionna offered him.

"Well, I can't wait to get started." McCoy looked almost as eager as Dan felt.

Barron shook his head. "If it involves taking down a bad guy, Trent's all in. He still plays cops and robbers in his apartment."

The laughter continued. Dan shot McCoy a smirk. The reddening of his face said that Barron's teasing wasn't far from the truth.

CHAPTER 2

INTRODUCTIONS

"If I promise to be wearing this when you get home, will you leave at five?" Fionna drawled flirtatiously.

"Oh, hell yeah, baby," Dan assured her. He laved her mouth with a drawing kiss and let his hands caress over her body. He took several long minutes to remind himself yet again of everything he was working for.

She'd pouted adorably when he'd slipped from the bed long before six to work out, but after his explanation that he wanted so desperately to be finished with Wretchkinsides so that he could focus on nothing but her and the two of them together, she'd given him his smile—sleepy, sexy, and oh so sweet.

She'd even extracted herself from the bed and pulled on the white dress shirt he'd worn the night before. She'd left it unbuttoned so it hung deliciously off her exposed curves as she walked him to the front door to see him off before she crawled back under the covers he'd warmed for her before he left.

Images of Fionna's beautiful, naked body tucked up in his bed and memories of all they'd done when he'd finally ordered their guests from their home the night before drove him. He flew into the Iodex parking deck and raced to his desk. The imagery was all he needed to dive into the hacked emails Fitzroy, the Captain of French Iodex, had sent over.

She was all that mattered, and he was going to get her. Wretchkinsides, the Interfeci, and every other thing that set to do her harm because of him could go straight to hell. His thoughts and his energy converged in another single image. Wretchkinsides a fallen, broken entity of cruelty caught in a fierce blaze while Dan fanned the flames.

～

A few minutes later, Dan heard Logan Haydenshire huff in annoyance, "So, this is Iodex."

Dan headed out of his office and smiled at Logan, who was escorting his father-in-law, Lucas Nguyen, the Premier of Australia's son, Crown Governor Haydenshire, and Mrs. Haydenshire into the Iodex office.

Governor Haydenshire had the hand of one of his twins in each of his own. The Haydenshires both looked rather exhausted.

Lucas Nguyen was, in fact, a foreign dignitary, so Dan stepped forward to shake his hand. "Welcome, Mr. Nguyen."

He wondered how long he would have to play nice before he could put Rainer and Logan to work.

"Chief Vindico, this is quite an impressive operation you have here," Lucas complimented.

Dan took in Logan's air of disdain for his father-in-law. With a slight chuckle, he smiled. "We make it work."

"I turned fuh-ree," Keaton announced excitedly to Dan. He held up four fingers and made Dan laugh.

"I heard about that. Happy Birthday, little man." Dan scrubbed Keaton's head. The twins' birthday was right after Christmas, and the entire Realm had been made aware of the Crown Governor's youngest children turning three in all of the papers.

Keaton jerked his hand out of his father's and extended both of his arms up to Dan. "Where's Ni-on-na?"

While letting the momentary panic work through him, Dan

hoisted him into his arms. He reminded himself that the three-year-old Haydenshire twins had no dealings with nefarious criminals and therefore wouldn't spill the beans on the fact that Dan had fallen madly in love. Keaton had developed quite a crush on Fionna, something Dan understood only too well.

"Fi's at home. She's still in bed." He grinned at Keaton.

"Make her to get up." Keaton shrugged his shoulders. He furrowed his brow and stared at Dan like awakening Fionna was the obvious answer to Keaton's perceived problem that she wasn't there to play with him.

Everyone chuckled as Dan shook his head. "She's tired, buddy. We need to let her sleep."

"Why?" Keaton demanded.

"I don't think three is old enough to hear that explanation," Logan teased. Dan shot Logan a smirk and tried not to laugh.

Suddenly, Keaton grasped Dan's jaw with both of his pudgy little hands. "Do you know why Mommy stomach is huge *huge?*" he emphasized.

"Uh." Dan cringed as he tried desperately to think of an answer to that question.

"Keaton," Governor Haydenshire scolded, "Mommy is having a baby, remember?"

"I know dat!" Keaton scowled at his father. Turning back to Dan, he narrowed his little hazel eyes. "I to know how baby sisa got in Mommy's tummy!" He glared at Dan as if trying to catch him in a lie.

Mrs. Haydenshire covered her face. "He keeps asking everyone that," she whimpered.

"Me too." Henry seemed to decide that Dan might hold the answer to their question.

"Uh," Dan glanced at Logan for help. "Stork?"

"God," Governor Haydenshire supplied. Dan began to regain his equilibrium. "God put the baby in Mommy's tummy, Keaton. We talked about this." Governor Haydenshire looked very weary of the conversation.

"No!" Keaton screeched. "I no like it! Take it out!" he demanded of Dan as he pointed to his mother's extremely protruded stomach.

Mrs. Haydenshire took over, much to Dan's relief. "Keaton, we have to let baby Abigail come out and see us whenever she's ready, and she isn't ready yet."

"She's boring." Keaton crossed his arms over his chest and kicked his legs until Dan set him back on the floor.

With a quick glance at his watch, Rainer Lawson breathed a visible sigh of relief as he reached his desk. It wasn't yet eight.

"Wainer!" Henry rushed toward his future brother-in-law. He looked thrilled that he'd arrived.

"Hey, buddy." Rainer lifted Henry up in his arms that were now much more muscular since Dan had been working him out for the last few months that he'd been an Elite officer.

Henry gave Dan an extremely disappointed gaze. "He no no how da baby got in Mommy ee-ver."

Rainer laughed. "They asked you too?"

"Yep." Dan tried not to shudder.

Governor Haydenshire shook his head. "Let's continue our tour of the Senate, and we'll see who else the twins can make extremely uncomfortable."

"I'll be back," Logan assured Dan. He looked like he'd far rather stay and work than take his father-in-law on a tour of the American Gifted Senate.

Dan assumed the early morning tour was due to the fact that the Haydenshires and all of Iodex were trying very hard to keep Adeline's royal heritage a secret until her trial in two days' time.

As soon as Wretchkinsides learned of her wealth and status, she would become an appealing target for kidnapping, and the Premier's son, Adeline's father, was the linchpin in proving her innocence.

"Take your time," Dan said insincerely as he returned to his office.

~

Logan Haydenshire

"If your mother can learn to put up with your grandpa, then you can learn to deal with Lucas." Governor Haydenshire's eyes tracked Logan as he paced in his office after Lucas had gone back to the farm with Mrs. Haydenshire and the twins.

"He's driving Ad crazy with all of his wanting to buy her things and wanting her to experience things."

"He loves her, and he feels badly he wasn't there for her growing up. He wants to do things for her and *with* her now." Governor Haydenshire restated something Logan had become very accustomed to hearing over the past week and a half that his father-in-law had been visiting from Australia.

"He's been walking the farm looking for building sites for our new house." Logan wanted to scream. Lucas had been rather insistent that Logan and Adeline should build a much larger home on the farm.

Governor Haydenshire chuckled and shook his head. "He's going back to the other side of the world Friday. Try to be patient."

"There is nothing wrong with our house. Adeline loves our house. It's the first place she's ever really felt safe. He wants her to live in some big mansion. But it's not like it matters. As soon as Wretchkinsides finds out who her father is, she won't really be safe anywhere." Logan finally allowed the real reason he was so thoroughly annoyed with Lucas to surface.

"If you let fear rule your life, you've already lost. If Lucas doesn't testify Wednesday, then Adeline will never practice medicine anywhere. Are you going to let Dominic Wretchkinsides take that away from your wife, or are you going to look inside yourself and find the strength to help Dan, and Rainer, and Garrett, and all of them,"— he gestured toward the Iodex side of the Senate—"end Dominic Wretchkinsides?"

Logan drew a steadying breath and tried to think of an argument for his father's reasoning. It was a task he'd been trying since he was Keaton and Henry's age. He hadn't yet succeeded by the age of twenty-one.

"Courage isn't the ability to stand in a place without fear, Logan. Courage is looking fear in the eye and telling it to get the hell out of your way because you have something you need to do."

"I know that," Logan sighed.

"Now, a little advice from your old man," the governor quipped wryly. "You'll find, if you'll stop whining about your father-in-law's extended visit, you have a nice day here at the office with your friends and coworkers. There are occasionally reasons people enjoy work other than the paycheck they bring home. Besides being fulfilling and what you were put on earth to do, it can also serve as an eight-hour break from your in-laws."

Governor Haydenshire gave his customary smirk as Logan chuckled his agreement.

CHAPTER 3

STAIRWAY TO HEAVEN

"Come on, baby. Please just relax. Let's have dinner, just you and me. No Lucas, none of his staff, no Mom and Dad, no one but us," Logan pled on Tuesday night as he watched Adeline pull off her scrubs and slip into a pair of tight jeans and a sweater. She was a disaster—a stunningly beautiful disaster.

She'd been so nervous about the trial the next day and about Lucas making his involvement in her life known, not only to the Realm but to the Non-Gifted world as well, that she'd been sick when she'd gotten home from work.

"Was Lucas upset?" Her teeth clamped down on her bottom lip. Deep concern tensed in her rhythms. Logan tried to determine how much to tell her and how much to bend the truth.

"I explained to him that I wanted to take you out to get your mind off everything. He was okay with it." Logan stumbled over the last few words.

Lucas's visit to Haydenshire farm had been eventful. Keaton had asked him repeatedly how his new baby sister had come to be in Mrs. Haydenshire's stomach.

Lucas had been informed by Logan's mother, rather tersely, that she changed the linens on the beds on Fridays and only on Fridays, unless someone was sick. She'd continued her polite rant by stating that she didn't particularly care if the serving staff at the Australian palace changed the sheets every other day, she wasn't doing that and wouldn't allow the two servants who had traveled with Lucas to do it either.

He'd gotten in a screaming match with Logan and Governor Haydenshire when Lucas had been spying on Logan and Adeline in the living room of the farmhouse on Christmas day. Logan had flirted with his wife, and after he'd swatted her backside, he'd pulled her in his lap and had run his hands over several other places.

Lucas had gone on and on about how disrespectful that was, not only to Adeline but to him and to the Haydenshires as well, and that it was a completely inappropriate thing to do on a formal holiday when the Haydenshires were entertaining foreign guests.

After Adeline had defended Logan to her father and insisted that she'd enjoyed his flirting, she'd dissolved in a puddle of tears. Her confession and standing up to her father had taken every bit of her resolve.

She and Logan had returned to the guesthouse long before anyone else left the farmhouse and long before they'd gotten Christmas dinner.

Emily and Rainer had brought each of them plates heaping with food later that night. Lucas seemed to have been under the impression that Adeline would be spending the majority of her time with him.

He'd repeatedly asked why she worked such long shifts at the hospital and insinuated that because she was married to one of the Crown Governor's sons that her work should be done on a volunteer basis.

The entire way the Haydenshires existed, their lack of pomp and circumstance, and the fact that though Logan's father was the Crown Governor he still didn't believe himself to be anything more than a servant of the Realm truly baffled Lucas.

He'd been raised one of the Australian Premier's sons in a palace and was admired and respected by the Australian Realm, not for his actions, but by luck of his birth. The entire concept chafed Logan's shield.

He'd attempted to shield Adeline from the stress of her father as much as he was able. He'd planned their night out alone with a great deal of finesse. He was taking her to one of their favorite restaurants, the pizza place where they'd gone on their first date. He'd decided to try to give her an evening with just a little bit of their past. He hoped that taking her back to a time and place when life wasn't quite so complicated might give her a chance to breathe and relax, if only for a few hours.

Adeline pulled her brush through her long, silky, black hair. Logan was momentarily entranced by its sway.

Setting the brush down on their dresser, she spun and flew to Logan with her chin trembling again. Logan wrapped his long, muscled arms around her tightly. "I'm right here, baby, and I will take care of you. I'm not going to let anything bad happen to you, ever." He'd made that vow adamantly. He must've said those words a hundred times that day alone.

She nodded against him, but she didn't really believe his promise. Truthfully, besides Logan's testimony at her trial the next morning, he had very little power over whether or not she would be able to continue practicing medicine.

If she was found guilty of possession or use of drugs, that would be the end of her career. Whether Governor Haydenshire could keep her out of jail or not, he couldn't force Georgetown Hospital to break their long-term policy, no matter how trumped up the charges were.

"Come on, sweetheart. Let's just get out of here for a little while. We'll get our mind off everything. I just want to be with you, and,"— Logan kissed the top of her head—"truthfully, I'm probably just gonna keep saying random, stupid shit until I get you to laugh for me." He let her infectious giggle soothe his soul.

"You always make me laugh. You're the best thing that's ever happened to me." She continued to cling to him.

"Well, that works, because you're the greatest thing in my whole world. Nothing matters to me but you."

Adeline pulled away from him and gazed into his eyes. "I know you're kind of stressed out about Lucas, and Wretchkinsides finding out, and everything, and I know this is really probably very stupid."

Logan furrowed his brow as she went on.

She shrugged. "I'm kind of excited that I get to be with you so much more now that you're gonna take me to work and pick me up to keep me safe. I know that's silly."

"I'm excited too, baby. If there wasn't a deranged, psychopathic murderer, backed by an entire criminal organization involved, I'd be thrilled." Logan sighed.

"I decided not to think about that part. Besides, you and Rainer are going to catch him, and then we'll all be safe."

"Vindico has the whole damn force trying. It's not just the task force anymore. We're just not getting very far."

"But you will. I know you will." Adeline seemed to have no doubt in Logan's abilities. He would never deserve someone who loved him like she did. He hugged her tight.

"You ready to go?" He wanted to get out of the house, away from the trial, Wretchkinsides, and away from the Australian Royal Family. He wanted just a little while to let the world slip away. He needed the two of them to exist alone together.

∼

Crown Governor Stephen Haydenshire

"Are you sure Lillian's up to this? I don't want her going to any trouble on my account." Jack Stariff sounded quite concerned as they slowly meandered from the barn, where all of the cars were parked, to the farmhouse kitchen.

Stephen sighed. "I asked her four times if she wanted me to cook or pick something up. She insisted that cooking is one of the only things that distracts her from worrying." Truthfully, he wasn't certain she was up to a dinner with Jack and Lucas. "I guess we'll see. She does seem happier now that she's able to be up and around a little. I try to keep her from doing too much. Her mom and the kids have been coming by and helping out constantly. I've offered a dozen times to hire her some help, but she doesn't want it. When the twins were born, she ended up firing the maids and then yelling at me."

Jack chuckled. "And how's our newest baby girl?" he asked as they crested the porch.

"No one seems to be able to tell us exactly. She shows some signs of Gifted energy, but she also shows signs of having Down Syndrome. None of the tests are conclusive, and they upset Lillian. I don't want her to have any more done."

It tore him apart to think of what his precious little girl might be going through and what was happening to his wife all at the hands of Roberto Vasquez. How could he have let one of Wretchkinsides's men get that close to Lillian? He'd never forgive himself. He couldn't help Abigail yet, so keeping his wife from tears had become his single-focused goal.

"Lill tries not to think about it," Stephen warned.

Jack nodded his understanding that he was not to ask her about the baby's health.

"I'll be glad to get this trial behind us, and truthfully for her to stop playing hostess to the Premier's son. I want her to relax."

Opening the side entrance to his home, Stephen smiled and let the peace it always brought him wash through his weary soul.

Lillian gave him his smile, that half grin with the twinkle in her sky-blue eyes that he'd always known held the secrets to the entire universe. It was the very smile that had him turned inside out from the moment he'd first laid his eyes on her.

They'd gone to a school formal at the academy. The following Monday, her car had broken down in the student parking lot. Always eager to spend more time with her, he'd offered to drive her home. He'd never forget Lillian Anderson giving him that mischievous, all-knowing grin with the sparkle in her eye as she nodded and climbed up in his truck.

The F-100 had been ancient then, yet his father had made him work until he'd earned enough to pay current market value for it. He'd had to earn enough to pay for the car, the insurance for a year, and enough for six months of gasoline.

Stephen had been thrilled to give the money to his father once he'd amassed the required amount. His dad had handed him the keys to the truck and then put all of the money in a savings account for Stephen.

He eased into the kitchen and closed the door behind Jack. Lillian was at the stove, and the twins were in the living room watching TV. "Hey, honey, how are you feeling?" He brushed a kiss on his wife's cheek. He had to ask. He had to know.

"I'm fine." She was growing weary of his constant checking. "Jack, I was in a chicken and dumpling mood. I hope that's all right?" She shared a different smile with Jack, the one she reserved for the people she cared for deeply but who weren't Stephen.

"I've never been fed anything here that I wouldn't hold up to the finest restaurants in DC. If you made 'em, I'm eating them." He lifted her hand and kissed it in true Jack Stariff fashion.

She laughed and shook her head before she turned and slowly stirred the pot on the stove again.

"Hi da-yee." Henry extended his hands up to the governor.

"Were you a good boy for Mommy today?" Stephen hoisted Henry into the air and grinned at him.

"Will and Book came ober, and Keaton and me colored Wily Ana," Henry explained with a great deal of exuberance.

Stephen's heart sank as Jack began laughing. "What?" Stephen demanded of his youngest son.

Lillian sighed. "They found magic markers in Emily's old room. Thankfully, our daughter-in-law is still speaking to us."

"We do not color people, Henry. Only paper, you know that." Stephen couldn't help but wonder if any of his children ever really listened to him.

"Do you remember when Garrett and Levi finger-painted Cal?" Lillian chuckled as Stephen nodded and joined in her laughter.

He set Henry back down so he could return to his television show and let his gaze travel back to his wife.

His mind returned to her climbing up into his truck all those years ago, with her long blonde hair whipped out behind her, wearing a denim mini skirt that he'd definitely wanted to unbutton.

She'd had on high peep-toe heels that made her legs look like they went on for miles. When he'd offered her his hand to step up into the truck, her skirt had been short enough to show off the top of her inner thigh.

18

He'd lost the ability to breathe or to form coherent sentences for several long minutes after catching the glimpse of what he still considered to be the stairway to heaven.

"Making Love Out of Nothing at All" was on the radio.

"I love this song," she'd announced and turned up the radio that Stephen had added to the truck.

She'd sung along as they left the campus and kept giving him that impish grin that said she was either hell on heels or a heavenly angel come to earth to rescue him from his miserable existence without her, but that he was going to have to hold on tight if he wanted to figure out which. As it turned out, she was the perfect combination of both, and he'd known then and there she was the one.

After coming back to the present for just a moment, he took her all in. The sight of her standing, smiling at him, swollen full of his child still took his breath away. After all of these years and all eleven of their children, his heart still skipped several beats whenever he gazed at her and what their love had produced.

His thoughts turned to Will. Stephen replayed the scene of her standing in the bathroom of his tiny studio apartment crying. It was one week to her graduation, three weeks to their wedding, and she was two weeks late. She'd sobbed, and he'd held her tight, letting her ruin one of his only good shirts while swearing to her that he would take care of her and the baby. He'd promised that she didn't have to be afraid, that he would never let anything bad happen to her.

It had been the utterings of a twenty-two-year-old fool. Though he'd meant every single word he'd repeated to her, he was too pompous and too arrogant to ever understand that there were things in the world he couldn't protect her from, no matter how much he loved and adored her.

Will had come one week late, and they'd told everyone that he was a couple of weeks early. They'd assured her parents and his that they'd conceived on their honeymoon. They now knew no one had believed them.

He shook himself from his abstraction and smiled at her, still just as in love with Lillian Anderson as he was on that sunny, spring afternoon when his life had finally found its purpose.

"Where's Lucas?" He tried not to sound as weary as he felt. Lillian chuckled as she beamed at him. She could read him like a book, and she knew he was rather tired of sharing his home with Adeline's father and his serving staff.

"He gave Fred and Oliver the evening off, so it was my understanding that Logan loaned the Accord to the two of them. They wanted to go into DC to see a show, I believe. Anyway, Logan did that right after he infuriated his father-in-law yet again by informing him that he was taking Adeline out for the evening and that Lucas wasn't invited."

The story alone seemed to exhaust her. Stephen grimaced.

"Good for Logan," Jack quipped just before helping himself to a banana from the fruit bowl on the large center island.

"Hungry, Jack?" Stephen laughed.

"It's almost ready. Don't ruin your supper," Lillian reprimanded Jack just like she reprimanded the boys and Emily.

"Yes, ma'am," Jack answered with his mouth full of banana.

"Lucas said he needed a bit of a break, and he retired to his room around five. I'll see if he wants to join us for dinner in a few minutes."

Jack swallowed down his bite of banana before he spoke this time. "I do need to go over with him one more time what he needs to do tomorrow at the trial."

"He'll be down, I'm sure. I think everyone involved is just a little stressed," Stephen offered. Lillian nodded her adamant agreement.

CHAPTER 4

THE PAST, THE PRESENT, THE FUTURE

Lucas made his appearance as Stephen was fixing drinks. He'd insisted that his wife take her seat and that he would bring everything to the table.

"Keaton, Henry, come wash your hands and eat," he called into the living room. The twins sprinted into the kitchen, almost toppling Lucas over in their haste.

"Sorry." Stephen tried to remind himself that his home was probably extremely overwhelming to a man who'd been raised by servants in a castle.

"Oh, I've gotten rather used to it," Lucas assured him with an air of disdain.

Anger crackled Stephen's fraying nerves. He narrowed his eyes. "Good," he quipped as he carried the water and tea pitchers to the table.

After hoisting the boys into their booster seats, buckling them in, and scooting their chairs forward, Jack served the twins piping hot bowls of chicken and dumplings. He took the liberty of casting and lowering the temperature for them so they wouldn't burn their mouths. He seemed just as determined as Stephen that Lillian not go to any more trouble.

"Eat the carrots not just the dumplings," Lillian reminded the boys, who looked disappointed but nodded their agreement.

"Carrots make you strong wike Gar-wet," Henry informed Jack.

With a beaming grin at Henry, Jack assured him that carrots would make him strong like all of his big brothers.

"I'm not sure I can withstand another Garrett." Lillian gave Stephen another one of his grins as they shared the moment of intimacy over the raising of their wildest child together.

Stephen took Lillian's hand under the table. He squeezed it in an unspoken gesture to assure her that no matter what, he would be with her. He might not be able to keep anything bad from ever happening to the very reason for his existence, but if she had to walk through hell, as they had many times since that Monday afternoon when he'd driven her home, then he would walk right beside her and hold her tight until they made it to the other side.

"All right, Mr. Nguyen, I don't want to keep Stephen and Lillian up late tonight, so do you have any questions for me about tomorrow?" Jack urged politely. "By the way, Lillian, this is delicious." He gestured to his bowl.

Lucas's brow knitted. "Don't Logan and Adeline need to be here to go over the trial?"

Jack and Stephen shared a quick, annoyed glance. "Truthfully, I asked Logan to plan something to help get Adeline's mind off the trial for the evening. She tends to get very nervous and forget everything she's supposed to say. I'm certain you've noticed when she's with Logan, her entire world seems right. Of the great loves of our time, I'd have to say they're following in Stephen and Lillian's footsteps." Jack raised his glass of tea in a toast to the Haydenshires. They chuckled and accepted the toast.

~

Logan Haydenshire

"It was adorable. I think I fell in love with you right then." Adeline laughed hysterically.

Logan shook his head. She'd just retold the story of him dumping a full glass of tea in Rainer's lap the first time he'd asked her to eat over at his house.

"Remember the first time I asked you if you wanted to go walk around the lake?" he recalled with a sheepish grin.

Adeline beamed, and her laughter continued. Her quiet, infectious giggling righted every single thing in his world. "I remember you trying to walk the dock and me not letting you."

Logan feigned disappointment. "Yeah, me too. I cried myself to sleep that night."

She cracked up again and shook her head at him. "You were so nervous."

"Well, Rainer had been feeling my sister up for years. I thought I was behind."

"I eventually let you."

"Yeah, you did." Logan waggled his eyebrows and gave her a cocky smirk.

They were tucked up in the back booth of Alfredo's, the pizza joint just a few blocks from Venton Academy. They were in the very booth they'd sat in on their first date where Logan had spent two hours trying to get more than three words out of Adeline.

She'd eventually loosened up when he'd asked her what she wanted to do after graduation. He'd listened intently to her telling him how she wanted to take extra classes and graduate with honors because she wanted to be a medio and to get away from her mother. How she'd wanted to make her own money so she never had to depend on anyone ever again.

"That sounds kind of lonely," Logan had stated concernedly.

She'd considered that for a long minute. "Being lonely is better than living with someone who wishes you never existed."

Logan hadn't really believed then that her mother wished she didn't exist. But a few weeks later when he'd asked her to be his girlfriend, he began to understand.

He showed up at her apartment one morning to drive her to school and met Candy. She was coming off whatever she'd taken the night before and was screeching at Adeline because their cable had been turned off again.

Adeline had been trying to explain that the money for the television had been spent paying the heating bill.

Candy had attempted to backhand Adeline, but Logan had stepped in. He'd caught her hand and stared her down. The very same scenario had repeated itself numerous times in their lengthy dating relationship.

Adeline had been thoroughly embarrassed, but she had no other way to get to school, so she'd gotten in Logan's car and he'd driven her out to Great Falls Park. It was the first time she'd ever skipped school. He recalled her initial terror. They'd sat in the Accord, and then out in one of the hidden-away pavilions along the hiking trails, and they'd talked about her mother, her life, a few of the things that had happened to her, and how they'd discovered that she was Gifted.

Logan had refused to take her back to the apartment that afternoon. He'd taken her to the farm instead. She'd spent the weekend with them, sleeping in Emily's room.

That day she'd offered Logan a whole lot more than walking the dock. He'd felt sick as he recalled her shame and her terror as she made the offer, thinking that staying on the farm and eating three meals a day for three days straight must've meant that he expected repayment of some kind.

He'd assured her that she owed him nothing, and that if they ever had sex that it would be because they were in love and committed to one another, not because he'd invited her to stay at his family's home. And it certainly wouldn't happen when they'd only been dating for one month.

Right then and there, Logan had been determined not to move their relationship to that level until he was absolutely certain she felt loved, safe, and secure.

Truthfully, though he'd been thoroughly disappointed that she wasn't quite sure about letting him feel her up the night on the dock, the fact that she'd had the courage to turn him down had relieved him.

It was the first time he felt like maybe he was going to be able to convince her that her body was hers, and that they should decide together when to take their relationship beyond a few heated kisses and make-out sessions. It was the first time he realized that she believed he respected and loved her enough to wait.

"This was a really great idea." Adeline's sweet voice carried Logan back to the present. He beamed at her.

"Asking you out was a really great idea."

She bit her lip and gazed up at him. "I liked you for a long time before you asked me out," she confessed.

"I told you I saw you that night at orientation, and I was done for. It just took me a little time to work up the courage to talk to you."

"You asked me to eat lunch with you, and Rainer, and Connor that week."

Logan nodded. He couldn't stand the way Mitchell O'Ryan and all of his friends used to call Adeline horrible names and try and trip her in the dining hall because she didn't have a name or a family crest.

"I was so glad Emily was as nice as all of your brothers, because only having friends that were guys was kind of weird," she confessed. Logan laughed again.

When push came to shove, Rainer and all of his brothers had toed the line, just as he'd known they would. Eventually, most people stopped picking on Adeline because they didn't want to tangle with the Haydenshire boys.

Logan and Adeline's sub-freshman year, only Will, Garrett, and Levi had already graduated, meaning that Cal, Patrick, Connor, Logan, and Rainer kept constant watch over Adeline.

They reminisced and laughed as they finished off the pizza and several glasses of Dr Pepper. Logan paid and waited on Adeline to use the restroom and then escorted his wife back out to the truck.

"Are we going home?" She didn't seem ready for their evening to be over. They both wanted to ignore the world just a little longer.

"Not yet." Logan climbed in the driver's seat.

A delighted grin lit her entire face. Her onyx eyes sparkled in the moonlight. "Where are we going?"

"I have a few surprises up my sleeve."

The grin remained fixed on her delicate features. "Are we going to go make out in the old physics labs again?" The laughter continued as they recalled all of the times they'd done just that.

"I thought about that, but then I came up with something a little better."

He steered the truck onto the interstate. He held her hand in his. He was certain she would figure out where he was taking her as soon as he exited, but he reveled in her curious expression as she gazed at him with all of the love and adoration he felt for her.

"Logan," she whispered after several minutes of amicable silence. His name was so quiet it was almost lost in the hum of the engine.

"What, baby?"

"I decided while I was at work today that if for some reason everything doesn't quite work out the way I'd like for it to tomorrow, that everything will still be okay." Her tone shattered his heart.

"Ad…" He started to reassure her yet again, to tell her that everything would work out.

"And I know that everything will be okay no matter what happens because I have you." Her whispered tone turned haggard.

"Always," Logan agreed, though he was determined she would win the trial, and not only would she continue her medical career, but her mother would no longer have any hold over Adeline.

The complexities of the trial tumbled over and over in his head as he drove. It was not a standard trial, and it was one he knew very little about. Both the court systems of the Gifted and Non-Gifted Realms were reeling over the trial. Neither had any idea how to handle it. It was rare for the Realms to collide in a legal battle. The Gifted Constitution was clear though. The Gifted were not allowed to lord their gifts over the Non-Gifted, and therefore the trial was taking place in their court.

His father had been one of the governors of the Gifted Realm for Logan's entire life. He'd witnessed numerous trials, but this was going to take place where his family had no favor.

The charges were against her mother. The drugs found in the apartment the night Adeline had been attacked brought about her mother's arrest. Candy's lies that the drugs were Adeline's had sent both justice systems spinning.

It was all very convoluted, and truthfully, Logan didn't understand how this had all happened. If Candy convinced the courts that the drugs were Adeline's, she would walk away a free woman. Adeline would lose her job immediately, and would then have to stand trial again to plead her own innocence against the drug charges. More investigations would happen. The entire thing was completely ridiculous.

But if Candy was found not guilty, Adeline would lose her job, the one thing that meant almost as much to her as he did.

She'd worked so hard. She'd been through so much at the hands of her mother. She'd studied endlessly and had proven herself over and over again at Georgetown. Being a Gifted obstetrics medio was all she'd ever wanted to be.

Logan's mind became more resolute. If Candy walked, Logan would quit his job at Iodex. He would leave his family, his best friend, his entire life. He would walk away from the task force that held everything he'd strived for since he'd fully come into his own Gifted protective powers. He would leave it all behind and move her to Australia.

Her father could guarantee her a job in any hospital where she wanted to work. Logan would give up his entire life for her. He'd even live in that stupid castle if that meant that she could do what she loved.

Cal's joking smirk and kind brown eyes flashed in his mind and cinched his vocal cords. His big brother. God, there were so many conversations Logan wished they'd had. There were so many questions he wished he'd asked Cal before....

Logan wanted to end Wretchkinsides, end the Interfeci, and he wanted to watch Vladimir Pravus burn for brutally murdering his brother, but if he had to, he would walk away before any of that, and he would do it all for her.

Adeline's grin spread ear to ear as Logan took the Route 193 exit. He'd been driving in a trance, so her gasp jerked him abruptly from his abstraction.

"Logan." She beamed at him.

He chuckled and squeezed her hand. "I might've slipped a bunch of quilts and blankets in the back of the truck along with a few sweatshirts."

He made the left at the sign for Great Falls Park and laughed. "I mean, if you think it's okay we go parking for a little while, Mrs. Haydenshire?"

"Well, maybe just this once, but I don't know about letting you walk the dock," she declared, just before cracking herself up.

She was the cutest thing he'd ever seen. Logan mocked disdain. "Uh, I don't think so, baby. Those are mine, and I get to play with them whenever I want."

"Is that so?" she challenged with a great deal of sass.

"Yes it is, and there are a few other things that are mine as well, but I'll show you those later."

"You just wait until I tell your dad what you tried to get me to do in a parked car," Adeline feigned objection, but was unable to hide her delighted grin.

Logan cracked up. "Yeah, well, I'm pretty sure my parents might've made Will in a parked car, so I'm not sure he can really say much."

With another few turns, Logan pulled the truck into an alcove well off the main trail. He shifted the truck into park and turned to gaze at his wife.

"So, baby, you wanna see the truck bed?" He waggled his eyebrows, making Adeline giggle again.

"What if I get cold?"

"I'll keep you warm. Don't worry."

Adeline leapt out of the cab. Logan followed and helped her climb up in the bed. He spread out the numerous quilts he'd packed until there was a soft place for them to lie and gaze at the stars.

After pulling his warmest Ioses sweatshirt over her head, he lay down and cradled her on his chest. She arranged another few quilts over them. Together they casted the blankets with heat.

"Are you warm enough, baby?"

"I'm perfect." She tucked her head under his chin. Everything in their world fell into perfect accord as he turned on his side and brushed his hand over her face.

"I love you so much." He felt her rhythms and her energy begin to fly.

"I love you too."

"Hey, Mrs. Haydenshire," he whispered in the darkness, "I'm gonna kiss you now."

"I was hoping you would."

With that, Logan leaned and slowly brought his lips to hers. He mated their mouths, tracing her with his tongue until he was sweeping it slowly through her mouth, feeling her energy fill his soul and restore the restless, plaguing murmurs of his mind.

CHAPTER 5

PROMISES AND REGRETS

CROWN GOVERNOR STEPHEN HAYDENSHIRE

After thanking Jack for doing the dishes while he'd put the twins to bed so that Lillian could sit and have a cup of tea in peace, Stephen waved goodbye to Jack. With a deep sigh, he poured himself a little brandy and offered some to Lucas.

"Yes, thank you, Governor." Lucas seemed extremely nervous. He'd been on Lillian's nerves for the past week, and she didn't appear to have any further reservoirs of patience available at the moment. An idea formed in Stephen's mind.

"You know, I got in the habit of taking long walks around the lake when the boys were growing up because one of them typically had some girl out on the dock trying to get to second base, but I've discovered that it was actually extremely restorative and good exercise. Would you care to join me?" He gestured Lucas toward the back door.

Lillian gave him another one of those grins that said if he'd keep Lucas out of the house and let her have some quiet respite to think, she'd make certain he was rewarded for his efforts.

Stephen's heart sped back from its weary exhaustion. His trousers still tugged whenever she gave him the look that said the most astonishing pleasures of the entire earth would be his that evening.

My God, he would never deserve her or what she so willingly gave him.

Lucas gave a hesitant nod. He tried to hide his eye roll as he glanced from Stephen to Lillian. "I suppose, sure."

Stephen swallowed down raw need, and they grabbed their coats to saunter out into the chilly night air.

A few deep, restorative breaths settled him. He inhaled the pine-soaked scent of the winter Virginian night as he stalked toward the lake.

"I'm surprised Logan and Adeline haven't returned," Lucas stated fretfully.

Stephen fought an eye roll of his own. "They're twenty-one years old. They have jobs, pay their own bills, and they're happily married. I don't get to give them a curfew anymore."

For a moment, he tried to put himself into Lucas's shoes. To have discovered that you'd had a child, a daughter, twenty-one years before with a woman you'd only met once in your life.

"I don't really suppose anyone ever gave Adeline a curfew," Lucas lamented.

"At some point you have to let your kids stay out all night long and then have to get up and work the next day. Trust me, it doesn't take long for them to figure out that a few hours in bed might have been worth it."

"You never imposed a curfew when she lived with you either then?"

"She stayed with us many weekends before she officially moved in. When she was our guest, she was always in the house with Emily or Logan. A curfew wasn't necessary. They were always on the farm. She lived here for the very few weeks it took Logan and Rainer to rebuild the house they live in now, the one that makes that sweet girl beam every time she pulls in the driveway. I won't lie to you and assure you that there weren't a few nights that I knew of that Logan didn't sneak her into his room and into his bed. But they were just about to move in together, and as they'd already made that commitment to one another, I didn't say too much about it other than to request that they not, knowing perfectly well that they would anyway."

"I don't understand why Logan is so opposed to me paying for a new home for them. I certainly understand they want to stay on the farm, but you have to see that she is an Australian Realm Princess. I'm certain they have a great deal of nostalgia for their first home, but it really isn't suitable for her." Lucas's demands were growing terse in his worry and his exhaustion.

Stephen drew a long sip of his brandy. He let the warm liquid course through his veins. "Just be careful that you're not attempting to build Adeline a castle out of your own guilt."

Lucas huffed but said nothing, so Stephen continued. "When Lillian and I married, we lived in a studio apartment not far from the Senate. It had one room," he recalled with a smile. "I was working with Joseph Lawson, Regis Carrington, and several other men to get the constitution written to ensure that the Realm never took over the Non-Gifted people and that the Gifted worked for the betterment of the Realm itself, to make them stop taking away rights just to fatten their wallets. But at the time, I was just a Senteon aide. I barely made enough to feed us and pay our rent.

"My futon had more holes than cloth, and only one burner of the stove actually worked without having to be casted. Joseph didn't manage to get the Constitution ratified and the entire Senate reworked until she was pregnant with Levi. When I was elected, I got a rather substantial pay raise, and we bought this property. When the house was finally finished and we were ready to move, Lillian sobbed. She didn't want to leave the apartment because that was her castle. It was where she fixed us dinner and where we made our oldest sons. I tend to think that home is wherever you want to be when you want the rest of the world to go away for a little while.

"It's where you feel safe and secure, and Adeline feels that when she's in the guest house." He willed Lucas to really hear what he was saying. "You could build her a mansion, and if I thought that's what she really wanted, I'd give you the land. But if it's not a place where she feels safe, where she can exist outside of the world, where she can draw a deep breath, and fall into my son's arms then it won't ever be her home."

They continued their slow progress around the vast lake. "I am sorry, Governor. I know that my presence has been an inconvenience for you and your lovely wife. I'd hoped to get to know my daughter better, though she still seems to push me away at every turn."

"You're certainly not an inconvenience. You're welcome here anytime, just like I told you when I spoke with you on the phone in Sydney, but I also told you that you might get lost in the crowd. We have ten children and one on the way. I'm trying to run the Realm to the best of my ability. I'm trying to keep all of my children heading the direction they need to travel, even the ones I didn't have a hand in making." He chuckled wryly as he thought of Rainer and of Adeline and of Daniel Vindico, at least for the moment. "I'm sorry you've been disappointed in your stay, but Adeline has tried. You have to see that."

"She'd far rather be with Logan. I suppose that shouldn't surprise me. I'd just hoped I could have a little of her time while I was here."

"Adeline's a twenty-one-year-old newlywed. Now, I'm not certain how old you were when you married, but can you recall a time when you preferred to be with your father as opposed to your wife at any point in the first few years of your marriage?"

Finally cracking just a little of the hardened shell he'd donned upon his arrival at Haydenshire farm, Lucas chuckled. "No, I suppose not."

"Adeline isn't only an Australian Realm Princess. She's Logan's princess, and that is a role she's much more comfortable playing. I had to learn with my own baby girl, you don't get to be her prince. Logan does."

They made the turn on the far end of the lake and walked slowly back toward the house. It took virtually no provocation to turn Stephen's thoughts back to his wife and that smile she'd given them as they'd left. "The kids will be by here in a little while. I wouldn't mind taking my wife on a drive tonight myself." Maybe letting Lucas in, instead of keeping him thwarted, would serve them all.

"Adeline and Logan will offer to stay and make certain the twins don't wake up. Why don't you stay up with them? Have some tea and a conversation. But you'll get a lot more out of both of them if they don't feel like you're trying to change who they are, who they think they want to be, and the life they've decided to live."

Lucas continued his silence for several long minutes as they eased around the well-worn path. The water's gentle lap on the shores filled the momentary silence.

"If I may, Governor Haydenshire," he challenged suddenly, "you're the Crown Governor of the American Realm. If you wanted to take your wife on a drive, as you put it, then you could anytime, if you would allow yourself and your wife the slight luxury of perhaps employing a nanny, or night-nurse, and some household assistance."

Stephen forced himself to take a moment to will away his temper. He understood the insinuation. "You're certainly not the first person to think that. I always find it interesting that the people who seem to know the very least about us seem to have the most to say about our lives.

"Lillian doesn't want help from anyone that doesn't know our family and that we don't share an intimate bond with. That makes her uncomfortable.

"Over the years, I've heard a great deal about what our salary could afford us from the talking heads of the Realm. But it doesn't matter how much money we make, if I'm not making her happy then I don't want any of it. That smile I get from her when I come home and find my kids running around, raising the rafters with their laughter and love, that's all that matters to me." He took another long sip of his brandy.

"If my wife wants help, then I'm the one that's going to help because each and every one of that wild brood, I helped her make. And the woman sitting in that house waiting on us to get back because she wants to go out for a drive with me—which you can be damn sure is why I'm taking her out for one—she's what makes my whole life worth living. She doesn't want nannies. She wants precisely what we have, and if that ever changes, you can be certain I'll move heaven and earth to give her whatever she wants. But it will never be a servant or a staff."

"So if Logan and Adeline don't make an appearance this evening, who will take care of your twins while you and Mrs. Haydenshire go out?"

Stephen was well versed in dealing with people who tried to trap him with his own words. He shook his head and fought an eye roll. "If they choose not to come by here, which would shock me, then Lillian and I will stay home. There's nothing wrong with not getting what you want when you want it. Nothing wrong with having to work a little. The longer you wait and the harder you work for something, the more you appreciate it."

Lucas's scowl reminded Stephen of his own children.

"You just informed me that your wife wants to go for a drive with you. Clearly, she'd like a little time alone, some of your attention. Are you going to defer that for your work ethic and patience as well?"

"If Lillian wants to be alone with me, if Lillian needs anything at all from me, then that's precisely what she'll get. But it may not always be just the way we thought it would work out because sometimes the curve in the road leads us to an even better place.

"Lillian and I have given our resolve, our education, our tears, all of our effort, and, hell, sometimes even our own blood to the children we brought into this world, and though they don't always do just what I'd like them to do, they have always done right by us.

"I believe you were here when Brooke and Will were over this afternoon. They didn't come by to see you or to let Lillian enjoy her granddaughter, although I'm certain that's why they told her they were here. They came by after Will took off early to let Lillian take a nap while they took care of the twins. And tomorrow my children will be at Adeline's trial because they love your daughter, and they love her not only for the phenomenal woman that she is, but they love her because Logan loves her, and that's what family does.

"And after the trial, you mark my words, every one of them will be up at the house to take care of Lillian because she's always taken care of them. So I don't need a staff of people that make my wife miserable. We have family that no matter what crazy thing they've done, they make her happy." He let just a few of his favorite images of their lives over the past thirty plus years run quickly through his mind.

"It would be easier," was Lucas's last-ditch effort to make his point.

"The best things in life are never easy, and building a relationship with your daughter isn't going to be either."

"Well, that's certainly proven quite true," Lucas sighed. "She forgets how easily I can read her energy. I know I do nothing but make her uncomfortable."

Suddenly feeling genuinely sorry for Lucas, Stephen turned that realization over in his mind as they made the turn by the dock.

"Logan, like his old man and most of his older brothers, at twenty-one, is very much of the opinion that he has the world figured out." He gained a genuine chuckle from Lucas.

"Adeline, who's lived a great deal more life than Logan in the last twenty-one years, knows that she doesn't have the answers to much of anything, but she is so much in love with my son that she is fully convinced that Logan can always set her world to rights no matter what. So, if you want Adeline, you can't attack Logan. Nothing will drive her away faster than that. Simmer down a little. If you want Adeline's attention, you have to go through Logan, as frustrating as I know that is for you. You've got to stop thinking that you need to come in and fix her life when she doesn't consider any part of it to be broken, save her mother.

"And tomorrow, you're going to get your chance to step up and save her from something Logan couldn't, but you have to understand that to Adeline, Logan hung the moon and every single one of those stars up there all for her. And I'll tell you this, if Adeline asked Logan for the moon, I think he'd try his damnedest to climb up and get it for her.

"Look, there they come now." Stephen pointed to the headlights of Logan's new truck coming up the gravel drive headed to the barn.

Instead of going back in the house, Stephen and Lucas headed toward the truck. Logan was helping Adeline step down, and she was beaming at him when they reached the barn.

Logan was giving his wife looks that said he'd have much preferred to take her back to the guesthouse and right on to bed. Stephen tried to hide his chuckle as Logan and Adeline walked hand in hand toward them.

"Did you two have fun?" Lucas sounded genuinely interested in their evening. Stephen nodded his encouragement.

"Yes, sir." Absolute thrill sang in Adeline's tone. "Logan took me to the pizza place where we went on our first date, and then..." She halted abruptly, and Stephen could no longer hide his laughter. Lucas's brow furrowed. "Well, we just drove around a little," she lied, and she didn't do it well as she blushed. Logan valiantly tried not to join in his father's laughter.

"We just thought we would stop by and tell you good night," she changed tactic quickly.

"Actually, I'd kind of like to take your mom out for a little while. Would you two mind staying? The twins are already down for the night," Stephen requested.

"Oh sure," Adeline agreed, but Logan looked disappointed. They all meandered toward the house.

"Longer you wait, the better it'll be." Stephen slapped Logan on the back.

"Uh-huh, waited years, Dad, years." Logan gave his father a goading grin. He'd stepped back and allowed Lucas to walk beside Adeline.

They entered the kitchen, and Lillian stood from the window seat at the large kitchen table. "Brooke made some of my peanut butter bars this afternoon if you're hungry," she informed Logan and Adeline, who both dove toward the cake plate that had stacks of the bars inside.

"Would you like one, Lucas? They're amazing," Adeline offered sweetly.

"Certainly. Thank you, sweetheart." Lucas gazed at his daughter.

"Milk?" Logan held up the carton he'd pulled from the fridge. Lucas nodded his acceptance.

Lillian put away the cookbooks she'd been flipping through as she'd worked on the grocery list for the next week.

Stephen took her hand and let his gaze travel from those beautiful blue eyes, down over the swells of her ample breasts, not quite as full and lifted as they'd been on their first date more than thirty-five years ago, but always beautiful and so damned distracting they made his mouth water. His eyes continued their journey over her very swollen midsection before he took in her lush hips. Unable to help himself, he ran his hand over Abigail's bump. She rolled in her mother's stomach as soon as she sensed the weight of his hand.

Stephen decided to take that as a sign that she would be fine somehow, some way.

"Wanna go for a drive? The truck hasn't been cranked in a while. It could use a good run." He watched her broad grin spread across her beautiful face.

"Sure." She pulled on her cardigan.

"You two behave." Logan's quip made Adeline giggle.

"Might grab a few of the quilts in the back of your truck, son." Stephen teased.

He guided his wife out to the barn and helped her step up into the old truck. She required a bit more help at seven months pregnant with his little girl than she had that Monday afternoon in the parking lot, but he still didn't think he'd ever seen anything more beautiful.

As he moved to the driver's side door, he thought about all that had happened in that truck. Their first kiss, the first time he'd gotten a little carried away and unbuttoned her shirt. He'd backed off, but she'd pulled off her bra there in an alcove in Great Falls Park, lit only by the light of the moon, and he'd been done for. The drive up to that ridiculous hotel on their wedding night when she was so furious she'd refused to utter a single word to him. The drive to Georgetown when she'd finally gone into labor with Will.

Cranking the truck and giving it gas to keep it running, Stephen shifted into reverse and told his wife how much he loved and adored her as she slid across the bench seat and laid her head on his shoulder. He kissed the top of her head, then opened the glove box and pulled out the old cassette of

"Making Love Out of Nothing at All" by Air Supply. He pushed it into the player and cupped his hand to cast it so that it would play.

~

They drove the back fields and talked about Lucas and Adeline, the trial and Logan, Rainer and Emily's upcoming wedding, and the new baby. As they neared the guesthouse, she brought up Daniel and Fionna. They discussed what might be in store for them.

Stephen drove well past the guesthouse and pulled into the

farthest field from the house under one of the many massive oak trees.

"I love that you always know when I want to come out here." Lillian sighed as he shifted the truck into park and wrapped her up in his arms.

"I have gotten to know you pretty well in the last few years, I'd say."

Her soft curves jostled as she laughed against him, but her rhythm strains were tense and weary.

"Stephen," she choked, and his heart fissured.

"What's wrong, sweetheart?"

"Abigail will be all right? We'll be able to take care of her. Please just say that we will." Tears rolled down her cheeks as she shuddered against him.

Stephen steadfastly wiped away her tears. "Abigail Hope Haydenshire will be just exactly the way she is supposed to be, and we will take care of her just like all of the others. I will be right there every step of the way. I won't let you down. You don't have to do this by yourself." He tried to modulate his own voice. It sounded distant and choked. He didn't want to frighten her more.

"I know." She tried to swallow back her emotions. With a deep inhale of his shirt and his musk, she lifted her head. "Do you remember when I finally told you I was pregnant with Will?" She seemed terrified that he'd somehow forgotten.

He chuckled. "I remember it well. I'll never forget any of the times you told me we were having a baby. And the time or two that I told you."

A small smile eased the worry from Lillian's face as they recalled the morning they'd managed to make love tucked away in their bedroom while Will and Garrett fixed cereal for their siblings and let them eat in the living room in front of the television.

When Lillian had been under him with their bodies intertwined existing as one, he'd watched her fevered, swollen breasts dance all for him as he took her reverently. Her body had glowed. Her waist was just a little larger than it had been a week before.

Her long, thick blonde hair cascaded out over his pillow and caught the glint of the early morning sun through their windows. Those sky-blue eyes closed in the ecstasy he brought her, her body nursing away every frustration as she'd enveloped him completely. Her rhythms were always so nurturing and so responsive to his own when his seed grew inside of her.

They'd gotten so lost in the magic and the passion they made together that he hadn't commented until she'd begrudgingly extracted herself from their afterglow to throw on her robe and answer the timid knock at their door.

"You're pregnant again, sweetheart." He'd forced his body upright and caught her hand as she slipped on her robe. He'd pulled her close again and had run his hand under the robe from her breasts over her belly. "You're always so beautiful, but my god, when you're pregnant, you take my breath away."

She'd cried then too. Tears of joy mixed with a hint of panic due to the fact that she was so busy with their current brood she hadn't noticed all of the telltale signs. Logan had been born seven and a half months later.

"But with Will, I was so terrified. We didn't have any money, and I wasn't sure you wanted a baby so soon." She began her confession again. "You wrapped your arms around me, and I knew it really was going to be okay. I knew that you really would always take care of me."

He kissed her forehead tenderly. "And we made it through Will, and then quite a few others, and then we adopted Rainer, and we're going to make it through Miss Abigail too, sweetheart. Together."

She nodded against his chest. "Just keep telling me that for the next few weeks."

"Every day," he whispered.

They talked and reminisced. He kept up constant reassurances that he would be right beside her no matter what life brought their way.

He laid his hands tenderly on her round belly and felt his little girl kick and move languidly inside of Lillian when she felt the reverberations of his deep voice and the soothing pulses of his energy.

Several minutes later, he managed to get his wife to stop talking and to stop worrying. He persuaded her to stop doing anything at all but feeling his hands on her skin and his hungry lips on her beautiful mouth, her slender neck, and points beyond.

Logan and Adeline saw the truck pull into the barn, and they headed out. They seemed eager to get home.

"Mrs. Haydenshire," Adeline remembered suddenly, "would you mind if I borrowed that sewing book again. I messed up the ruffle on the blanket I was trying to make for the baby."

"Of course. Come with me. I'll get it for you, or I can help you with the ruffle." Lillian guided her back to the porch.

Just before she followed Adeline into the kitchen, Lillian turned and gave Stephen another sexy grin that said for him not to linger, that there were a few other things she'd like him to take care of before they drifted off to sleep in each other's arms.

Stephen's breaths quickened. His body stirred. Blood surged through his veins. His hands ached to feel the heat of her skin again. His muscles tensed in anticipation. He gave her the same cocky smirk he'd given her when he'd talked her into coming back to his apartment after that Summation challenge, a year or so after they'd begun dating.

"I'll be right there," he vowed, making Logan roll his eyes.

"Can I talk to you for a second, Dad, please?"

CHAPTER 6

PARENTS AND CHILDREN

"Of course, son. Anytime, you know that."

He'd been momentarily distracted by his wife, and it took Stephen a minute to realize that Logan was coming apart at the seams. He ran his hands through his hair. His energy was frantic.

"Dad, I swore to her that I'd never let anything bad happen to her. Please, please don't let her lose her job. You're the Crown Governor. You're the freaking most powerful man in the world! Just please."

Emotion settled thickly in Stephen's throat. He put his hand on his son's shoulder to steady him. "Don't ever promise her that again, not ever."

"What? Why?"

Stephen tried to think of a way to fill his son's head with wisdom and understanding that would take him half a lifetime to really get. "Because that's not a promise you can keep, son. Just promise her that no matter what happens you'll be with her. Promise her that you'll never leave her, that she's never alone. But don't promise her that you won't let anything bad happen. Never promise that." He felt the raw pain he knew his son was experiencing.

"She knows all of that."

"Tell her. Tell her over and over again. Whether she knows it or not, just keep telling her. And promise her that no matter how many pieces everything falls into that you will be there to help her put it back together stronger than it was before. Promise her."

Adeline reappeared carrying one of Lillian's old sewing books.

"Okay, I will," Logan agreed in a terrified plea as he took her hand and led her home.

~

Logan Haydenshire

The phone gave a shrill alarm at 6:00, and Logan switched it off. Neither he nor Adeline were asleep anyway. She cringed into him. Her energy spun in knots of terror that rose under her skin like jagged knives.

"Hey," Logan soothed, "no matter what, I will be right there the whole time." He carefully followed his father's advice. She nodded against him as he held her. They needed to get going. They were supposed to be in the Non-Gifted courthouse at 7:15 to meet Mr. Stariff.

"I just want this day to be over with," her voice trembled.

They showered and donned the clothes Mr. Stariff had instructed them to wear. Logan guided Adeline into the kitchen, where Emily and Rainer were making breakfast and smiling at them nervously. Adeline's steps held the cadence of a death march.

"I made pancakes," Emily offered sweetly.

"Thanks, sis." Logan took a plate, complete with sausage and syrup.

"Miss Adeline." Rainer offered her an identical plate with a kind smile.

"I'm sorry. I just don't think I can eat."

A knock sounded on the door. Adeline winced every time knuckles rapped against the steel. With a quick furrow of his brow, Rainer answered it.

Lucas stepped into the kitchen. "I thought maybe I'd come see you before we leave." He studied Adeline with concerned glances.

She forced a slight smile. "That was sweet of you."

"Pancakes?" Rainer gestured to the batch Emily was taking off the griddle.

"No, thank you. I don't think I could eat anything." A genuine smile of understanding eased the tense worry that had sharpened Adeline's features. "Little nervous, dear?" Lucas took the seat beside Adeline, leaving Rainer and Emily to eat at the counter.

Adeline nodded and reached for Logan's hand. He let the pancakes fill him while he supplied her with calming energy. "How about a Dr Pepper, baby?" Logan thought the enhanced soda might give Adeline a little energy and might soothe her stomach.

"Thank you." She nodded as Rainer handed one to her.

"Lucas?" he offered.

"Sure, I suppose." Lucas didn't look like having Dr Pepper for breakfast was something he was particularly accustomed to.

"I think I'll just take my book with me in case we have to wait or something." Adeline rushed back to the bedroom.

For most of her life, books had always been Adeline's security blanket. Logan had understood that they were really getting somewhere in their relationship the night she left her book at home and clung to him instead.

Since she'd been able to check books out for free from the library, Candy could never find anything wrong with Adeline's obsessive reading as it cost them no money. She often escaped the cold cruel world of her childhood by drowning herself in far grander worlds created by her favorite authors. She read of fierce heroines and planned her own escape.

Logan had never cared much for reading. He'd spent his childhood playing outside in any available capacity, but he'd always enjoyed watching Adeline devour books. They delighted her.

After they'd been dating a few months, he would frequently buy her books as small reminders of his love. He brought them to her like some guys brought their girlfriends flowers.

Tears of overwhelming gratitude would prick her eyes whenever he presented her with a new one. It was like he was somehow touching a part of her heart that she'd never let another person see.

When he had returned to her mother's apartment after Adeline had been attacked to bring her things to the farmhouse, the relatively small collection of books that Logan had purchased for Adeline had been one of the first things Candy had destroyed. They'd been what Adeline had sobbed over for hours, despite Logan, Governor Haydenshire, and Rainer's offers to buy her duplicates.

"Truthfully, I'm not certain if I'm more nervous about meeting her mother again or about the outcome of the trial," Lucas admitted.

"Candy's a real piece of work, trust me," Logan spat as Rainer and Emily nodded their agreement.

A few minutes later, Logan was loading Adeline and her father into his truck and driving into downtown Arlington while Adeline clung fiercely to his hand. Logan decided that reminding her of everything she already knew might be helpful. He tried to calm her rhythms with his own.

"So you know everything Jack's gonna ask you, and you know all of the drug tests came back negative. This is going to be fine."

"All but one." Adeline looked nauseous as she pointed out the hitch in the plan. "And all of those pictures from that party." Her head dropped with each word she spoke. They seemed to crucify her.

"You'd just had surgery, love. Certainly any jury in the world will understand that you had pain medication because you were in pain," Lucas tried to reassure her.

Logan gave him an appreciative smile in the rearview mirror, but truthfully, no one knew what the jury would decide. It all depended on Candy's lawyer's ability to vilify Adeline.

"But I don't know what her lawyer might ask me," was her next terror-filled statement.

Her was the kindest term Adeline had used for her mother in the past few weeks, Logan thought with a slight grin. She needed that fight today more than ever before.

"Jack's the best lawyer in the Realm, baby. He'll be all over him if he tries to pull anything."

Logan circled around the block several times before locating a place to park. He wrapped his arm around Adeline as they made their way into the old Arlington courthouse.

Stariff met them in the vast entry hall. If Adeline squeezed the book in her hands any harder, she was going to leave fingerprints in the binding. Logan began rubbing her arm. He tried to keep her cradled against him.

Fierce determination set Jack Stariff's jaw and shoulders. He looked somewhat concerned over Adeline's obvious nerves but not dissuaded.

"All right, we'll just step in here until it's time to begin." Jack guided Lucas, Logan, and Adeline to a small waiting room outside one of the courtrooms. "This trial is unlike any I've ever been involved in, and I plan to use that to my advantage."

"Uh…how is that an advantage?" Adeline squeaked.

"Because your mother's lawyer has never been in this situation either. The Realms don't often collide," he explained. "Lucas, I want you to stay in here until the last possible second. I want you to make a dramatic appearance in the courtroom with Adeline. It should be immediately apparent who you are."

Logan agreed. So much of Adeline's physical makeup came from him. She even matched a few of his mannerisms.

Logan was going to have to go and sit with everyone giving testimony on Adeline's behalf, so this was Lucas's chance. He was going to have to be Adeline's stronghold until they were taken into the trial.

A knock sounded on the door, and tears began to leak silently down Adeline's delicate face. She knew it was time for Logan to go. He hugged her tight.

"I'll be right behind you. You can do this, and I will be there the entire time. I love you so much. Let's just get this behind us, and tonight we'll celebrate."

She shivered in his arms. Logan shot Lucas pleading looks.

Lucas stepped in readily. "Let him go, sweetheart. You have so many people that love and care about you, and he has to go join them so we can all defend you. I'll be right here with you."

Adeline nodded and with tear-filled eyes and a trembling chin, she fell into her father's arms, letting him soothe her. Lucas was visibly overwhelmed as he cradled her and promised that everything would be all right.

Vicious nausea knotted Logan's stomach. He deeply regretted the pancakes he'd eaten. He was certain his body and his heart might actually be severed from one another as he left Adeline under Jack's insistence and traveled into the courtroom.

CHAPTER 7
OPENING STATEMENTS

His father stood as Logan approached the bench seating for the witnesses. Vindico did as well. They both offered him consoling pats on the back as he took the seat beside Rainer.

"She'll be fine as soon as they bring her in here and she can see you." His best friend knew why Logan looked like he was going to be violently ill.

Fionna offered Logan her kind, soothing smile from the benched area set aside for spectators. It was nice of her to come. Vindico was a lucky guy. Logan wondered if his boss really appreciated what kind of woman he'd been handed when he was given a second chance at life and at love.

Logan smiled at Patrick and Lucy, Will, Levi, Sarah, and Connor who were seated with Fionna. Brooke was watching the twins and Lily Ana at the farmhouse, as Mrs. Haydenshire was seated on the witness benches next to the governor.

Logan noted her air of determination as she moved to him and gave him a hug. With an overwhelming sense of love and of what his family meant to him, Logan smiled as Tad and Nathan slid into one of the bench seats behind his brothers. They were followed by Logan's Nana and Paps.

Nana gave Logan her sweet, reassuring smile. His grandfather gave him the wink he gave all of his grandchildren whenever they needed a little encouragement.

As Logan glanced toward Vindico, the air took on an icy chill. The hair on the back of his neck stood. Vindico's massive body pulled taut. His chiseled muscles seemed to visibly throb. His eyes were narrowed hatefully.

Following the path of his rancor, Logan's eyes landed on Paulo Ramirez, Candy's pimp and one of Wretchkinsides's mid-level thugs.

If Candy was arrested and sentenced per Adeline's testimony, he would be arrested as well, to stand trial later. Logan noted two Non-Elite Iodex officers who had followed Ramirez in. They'd been sent to make certain that if things didn't go his way, he wouldn't be making any quick getaways.

An ominous hush fell over the room as a rather short, beady-eyed, mustached man dressed in a cheap suit guided Candy Parker into her seat.

Logan wanted to vomit as he took in his mother-in-law. She was dressed in what he supposed must have been her attempt at a conservative dress suit.

She'd missed the mark slightly as the suit she'd picked was an odd seafoam green color, and the skirt appeared to be made of plastic. It was also so short that when she sat down everyone would be able to see most everything.

After seeing Adeline with her father for the past few weeks, Logan was struck again by how little she resembled Candy.

Candy gave Logan a sneering scowl. She was smacking bubble gum. Logan assumed it was because she couldn't smoke. When her lawyer suggested that she spit it out, she pulled it from her mouth and handed it to him.

Governor Haydenshire looked appalled as Rainer and Logan gave each other horrified grimaces.

"Unbelievable," Rainer whispered as Logan nodded his agreement.

Candy's baleful glare turned back to Logan who gave her a confident smile. Rainer chuckled under his breath, but then Candy shot Logan a bird discreetly. Her lawyer's eyes goggled as Logan shook his head.

After glancing nervously at Governor Haydenshire, her lawyer began a heated conversation with her in threatening whispers.

Well, he clearly knows who my dad is, Logan thought wryly. Emily was fit to be tied after seeing the gesture, but Rainer calmed her down by reminding her that Candy was effectively digging her own grave.

~

Dan Vindico

Dear God, could this be any more ridiculous? If Dan rolled his eyes once more they were likely to lodge upward against his skull. He'd been putting criminals behind bars for the last decade, and he'd never witnessed someone so desperate and impudent as Adeline's mother. His biceps tensed again. She seemed to have bathed in every available cliché.

So Nic obviously doesn't give a shit about the outcome of this. He sent her a lackey lawyer. Ramirez has obviously been moved so far down the Interfeci chain he no longer matters. This trial isn't going to do a damn thing. We're all going to sit here and defend a perfectly innocent woman who has no business being in a courtroom at all. And the way they managed to make one trial pending on the other isn't even legal. Dan tried to remind himself that there was no real precedent for this, and that both of the Realms were figuring it out as they went. But Adeline Haydenshire belonged at Georgetown Hospital, not sitting in a courtroom.

The fact that Dan, and most of his top officers, were going to sit there and be dragged through every scenario Wretchkinsides's stooge lawyer could come up with to try to turn the charges back on Adeline, instead of actually working and nailing Wretchkinsides and every ridiculous excuse for human waste who worked for him, pissed Dan off royally.

His eyes and his body sought Fionna. She gave him a quick, discreet smile as she scooted farther down the bench where she'd found a seat.

She was probably trying to get away from Ramirez. The dark energy he possessed had to be affecting her. Dan's heart ached. How many times was he going to have to drag her into situations where she would be exposed to that level of evil?

Dan's mind shifted slightly. He wondered what she was picking up on. If he'd summoned black, then Ramirez had committed far more crimes for Nic than Dan was aware. He'd either committed a murder by pulling the life-giving energy from another human or he was a rapist.

His heart sped and rattled against his rib cage. He longed to go to Fionna, to take her away from all of this. Her color seemed to be holding. She was smiling and speaking to Logan's grandparents, but she was drawing measured breaths. She pulled her wool wrap tighter around her. He assumed she was trying to block the chilling energy from her exceptionally strong Receiver strains. Being able to pick up on every strain of emotional energy made her incredibly powerful, but in the presence of dark energy, it also made her weak.

Dan saw Garrett watching her closely as well. She was holding her own. Ramirez was a criminal, no doubt, but he clearly hadn't summoned black or she would have shown signs of that.

The memory of freezing-cold snow dripping down his neck while he'd scrubbed the vomit off her beautiful face on Christmas Eve sent another icy chill through Dan.

He should never have taken her out to Felsink Prison to get his sister out of jail. He should never have done any number of the things he'd done to and with Fionna Styler.

The doubt crept back in whenever she was away from him. She deserved someone who she could openly admit to dating. Someone who could be seen with her, take her places, hold her hand, and buy her things. She deserved to be treated like the princess she was.

She deserved someone so much better than he would ever be, but my God, he loved her. Every single thing about her set his world on fire. His sun rose and his moon set by her. He wanted no part of a life without her in it.

Determination rooted in his veins once again. End Wretchkinsides, get her. The mantra echoed through his mind and sizzled down his spine. It set in his chiseled musculature, swirled in his gut, pounded with the determined beats of his heart, etched his soul, and tensed readily and constantly in his shield.

~

Logan Haydenshire

A minute later, Jack marched confidently into the courtroom while shooting Candy glares that had her suddenly looking rather concerned. Adeline followed Stariff inside. Her eyes sought Logan's. A small smile formed on her lips as soon as she saw him.

Lucas had his arm around her in a tender, fatherly embrace. He slid her chair out for her and took the seat beside her, placing her between himself and Stariff. All eyes went to Candy as she took him in. Looking at him there, seated beside Adeline, even if she hadn't seen him in twenty-two years, there was no mistaking who he was.

Well aware he was being gawked at, Lucas seemed to be happy to put on a show. He patted Adeline's hand and then very slowly turned an abhorrent, hate-filled scowl to Candy Parker.

Her lawyer's mouth hung open in shock. He'd been supplied a list of people bringing witness against Candy, but just as Jack had assured Logan and Adeline, he'd added her father's name under the names of medios and Gifted nurses from the hospital. Lucas Nguyen's name had meant very little to either Candy or her lawyer until that moment.

Jack shot her lawyer a cocky grin, and Candy began to pout. She crossed her arms over her chest, which was on full display in the tacky suit.

She returned to her previous task of glaring at Logan since Adeline adamantly refused to even look her direction.

"Is she gonna do that all damn day?" Rainer returned Candy's glare on Logan's behalf.

"She can glare at me all she wants, but if she looks at Adeline like that, I might just come over this railing," Logan growled under his breath.

"Yeah, well, you won't be the only one," Rainer pledged his undying allegiance.

"I hate her. I absolutely hate her, and I don't hate anyone," Emily spat furiously. Logan and Rainer chuckled at her adamancy.

"All rise," the bailiff's bellowed call shook through Logan.

Upon seeing Lucas, Candy had popped another piece of chewing gum in her mouth and was chomping away. The judge entered and gave a respectful nod to Governor Haydenshire. Governor Haydenshire returned the discreet gesture.

With one quick lift of his brow and the firm set of his jaw, he let the judge know that it would remain to be seen as to whether or not this particular Non-Gifted judge would ultimately gain the respect of the Crown Governor.

The jury filed in. Logan studied them. It was still difficult for him to fully wrap his head around.

They all existed on the same planet, in the same country, in the same towns, but Logan lived in a world where the ultimate decisions on laws, and on criminal behavior and punishment, lay with the Senteon and ultimately with the governing board. Six men and women who Logan knew to be good, honest, faithful, intelligent people, at least now that Peterson was no longer serving.

Though he did understand the way the Non-Gifted judicial system worked, he wondered if placing the fate of his wife in the hands of people who knew nothing about her could really be called a fair trial.

"Be seated," the judge, who appeared to be about his father's age with a kind dark face, ordered the room at large. "All right," he glanced over the paperwork on his bench. "So today's trial will be a little different." He didn't linger on that. "We are hearing the trial of Miss Jayda Hestia Parker, who's been brought up on charges of possession, use of illegal substances, and misuse of legal prescriptive drugs, per an entered testimony on behalf of her daughter, Mrs. Adeline Marie Haydenshire. But Miss Parker has entered counter-testimony stating that the substances found in her apartment on the night of June first belonged to Mrs. Haydenshire. Is that correct, gentlemen?" the judge drawled to Jack and Candy's lawyer.

"Uh 'scuse me," Candy attempted to flirt with the judge as she smacked her gum and batted her eyelashes. Lucas looked horrified, as did the judge. "You can call me Candy—all the boys do—and her name ain't Haydenshire, it's Parker."

Fury flared in Logan's shield. His hands clenched tightly into fists.

"No one asked you to speak, Miss Parker," the judge reprimanded. "Unless you'd like to be charged with contempt, kindly keep your mouth shut unless you've been directed otherwise. I have a marriage license here. It seems your daughter, Adeline, was wed to the Crown Gov..."—he choked and then cleared his throat—"to Senator Haydenshire's son, Logan, at the beginning of last month. She legally changed her last name to Haydenshire. It is interesting to me that you were unaware of your daughter's nuptials. However, I will be calling you Miss Parker, and you may refer to me as your honor or as Judge Phillips, should the opportunity for you to speak come up again."

Senator. So that's how the governors were addressed in the Non-Gifted legal system. Logan supposed that gave them authority without giving away their powers or their real titles.

Candy rolled her eyes at the judge. She looked thoroughly put out. Her lawyer shuddered and wiped his brow with a handkerchief he pulled from his pocket.

"Now, if the jury is ready, we'll begin opening statements with you, Mr. Snyder," he gestured his head toward Candy's lawyer. Logan's heart began to hammer. Emily tucked her arm through his as she tried to calm him down, but his shield had set internally, and he couldn't let her in.

His body shifted oddly. It was a strange sensation, one he'd felt only a few times before. His own shield attempted to leave his body altogether in order to cover Adeline.

She gave him a tender smile. Terror haunted her eyes as Logan returned the gesture. His shield spun. The smile was all he could offer her. But in that moment, Logan watched Lucas take her hand in his. She drew from her father, a motion which seemed to make Lucas's entire world settle.

Candy's lawyer began, "Ladies and gentlemen of the jury, this is a story that the courts see far too often. A troubled teen in a bad situation reaches out to drugs, legal and illegal, desperate for attention. Her mother, abandoned by the child's father before she was even born, in desperation to be with her child, to connect with her and try to lead her back, gets caught up in the same addictive storm and begins using herself." Snyder shook his head in mock sorrow.

Lucas looked like if given half a chance he would choke not only Candy but her lawyer as well.

Jack shook his head in warning to Lucas as tears leaked down Adeline's face. Fury erupted from somewhere deep inside of Logan. Vindico and Rainer's hands both planted firmly on his shoulders pushing him down, and he realized that he'd leaned to stand.

"My client, young, pregnant, and all alone, turned to prostitution in an effort to provide her beloved daughter with some kind of life that she saw no other way of giving her."

Lucas rolled his eyes in abject disdain.

"Today, I believe we will see that it isn't Miss Parker who needs to serve time, it is Mrs. Haydenshire who showed so little regard for her own mother and the many, many sacrifices she made for Adeline growing up, to the point that she wasn't even informed of her daughter's marriage."

To Logan's utter astonishment, the jury was visibly eating up his lies.

"Thank you, your honor," Snyder choked, still feigning sorrow.

Logan was quite certain he was going to vomit.

CHAPTER 8
WITNESS

Jack stood, nodded to the judge, and then moved to the jury. "Ladies and gentlemen of the jury, you've just been spun a story with so many holes in it, I'm quite certain if you used it for a blanket you'd freeze to death." He caught the jury's attention quickly.

"In this world where the lines between right and wrong tend to blur so easily, and one person's opinion is never the same as the other, I think there are a few things we can all agree on. I don't believe any of us could place our hands on that Bible and vow that abuse to a child is ever allowable, nor do any of us believe that starving a child when there are people offering to help at every corner is an acceptable option," Jack huffed.

"Let me tell you what else isn't okay," he demanded. "It was not okay that the first time Mr. Logan Haydenshire, my client's husband, went to pick Adeline up from her home when they were just beginning their college careers," he used the Non-Gifted wording for education with ease, "for him to have to physically halt Miss Parker from back-handing Adeline."

Logan watched the men's faces on the jury begin to glare at Candy.

"Why was she so upset with Adeline, you ask? Cable had been turned off again. See, Adeline had begun paying the household bills at the age of ten, and I have copies of her handwriting on the bills she paid when she was in the fourth grade. So when Adeline, at the age of eighteen, used the money she earned waiting tables to pay the gas bill so they would have heat and hot water, but didn't have enough to pay the cable, her mother got angry and attempted to strike Adeline." His furious growl moved the entire courtroom.

"The next logical thing I'll ask you to consider is what happened to Adeline when Logan wasn't there to step in on her behalf? I have numerous reports from doctors and teachers throughout Adeline's childhood that all reported suspected abuse, but when counselors and case workers stepped in, Adeline was terrified to tell them what really happened to her. Something I'm certain this court has experienced before. I do, however, have a report from a children's hospital from the time Adeline was seen when she was four years of age. Her mother had jerked her shoulder and elbow out of socket because Adeline attempted to admire a doll in a drugstore. Numerous patrons at the store, including the pharmacist and the pharmacy techs, reported the incident. She couldn't hide from that one, it seemed."

The jury began to shake their heads.

"On her graduation night from Venton Academy,"—Jack smiled at the deeply impressed gazes from the members of the jury—"Adeline was concerned about her mother. She'd been certain that, though her mother had never attended any function of any kind throughout her childhood or adolescence, certainly her mother would come to graduation where she was awarded high honors and a degree in pre-med. When her mother didn't show, Adeline went home to make certain she was all right.

"She walked in on Miss Parker offering her services to two gentlemen who proceeded to attack Adeline. She managed to escape, but when Logan located Adeline and police were sent to the apartment, arresting one man and Miss Parker and finding copious amounts of illegal drugs, Miss Parker cooked up the story that the drugs were Adeline's." Jack shot a glare to Candy.

"Today, I'll be proving to you that not only is Adeline a victim in this entire ordeal, but that we, as citizens of this country, sorely let Mrs. Haydenshire down. We should be ashamed of how we allowed her to exist. And if you really want justice to be served, you will put not only her mother but her mother's dealer behind bars. Give peace to Adeline and her adoring husband, because peace certainly wasn't something that the wealthiest, most powerful land in the world offered her every single night of her terror-filled childhood.

"Because the only time that precious girl,"—he held his hand out to Adeline—"has ever been under the influence of any kind of illegal substance was when she was in utero. In answer to Mr. Snyder's ridiculous story that Miss Parker used to be closer to her daughter, I do have the documentation proving that when Adeline was born she was immediately treated for addiction to methamphetamines and barbiturates. Judging by the look on my client's face, it doesn't appear to me that Miss Parker's use of illegal drugs while she was pregnant brought them any closer to one another."

Two women on the jury glared at Candy, and she was visibly enraged. Lucas looked physically ill as what life had been for his daughter began to settle in his psyche.

"Your honor," Jack nodded to the judge.

The judge drew a deep breath. "Mr. Snyder, you may call your first witness."

"I'd like to call my client, Miss Candy Parker, to the stand."

Candy stood and rearranged her scowl into an impish grin. She let he hips sway wildly as she made her way to the stand. Every male in the room rolled their eyes as they watched her.

She was sworn in, and Logan issued a silent prayer that everything would work the way it was supposed to.

"Miss Parker, please tell the court your age when you conceived and the circumstances surrounding your pregnancy with Adeline." Snyder gave Candy a sorrowful gaze.

Lucas leaned forward to glare at Candy.

She looked flustered as she began, "Well, a lady never tells her age, but I was young. It took me several months to realize I was pregnant. I don't gain weight, so…" She shrugged with a triumphant curl of her lips. "By the time I went to one of those clinic things 'cause I had a stomach ache, they told me I was going to be having Addy in just a few months." She stated this as if not realizing that you were pregnant would bring her sympathy.

"I wasn't really sure who her daddy was. You know, I tend to get all of the boys' attention, so..." she announced proudly as Logan shook his head and shared an astonished glance with Rainer. He couldn't believe she'd said that on the stand.

"Candy, could you please tell the court about your and Adeline's relationship when she was growing up?"

This ought to be good, Logan thought wryly.

"She was kind of a bratty kid. You know, always wanting something, always had her head stuck in a book, complaining all the time, always hanging around when I needed to have people over."

Adeline's brow furrowed.

"Then she went off to that academy she got accepted to and met him." She threw her garish red fingernails toward Logan. Her face lit. She seemed to suddenly remember what she was supposed to be telling the jury. "If you ask me, he's the one that got her into the stuff she was using. I was always telling her he was a bad influence."

The accusations she'd thrown his way didn't bring about the same fury that the ones made toward Adeline did. He met Candy's glare and waited on Jack to start asking questions.

"Did you discuss Adeline's drug use with her?" Snyder drawled.

"Objection, your honor!" Jack leapt up, bared his teeth, and glared at Candy. "That question assumes facts the evidence does not support."

Judge Phillips nodded. "Sustained."

Snyder looked thoroughly disappointed, but he moved on.

"Candy, please tell the jury what you feel happened on the night that you were taken into custody."

"Objection, narrative." Jack rolled his eyes, letting everyone know he felt Candy's lawyer might need another few years in law school.

"Mr. Snyder, do you have any further allowable questions?" It seemed Judge Phillips's patience was wearing rapidly thin.

Snyder narrowed his eyes. He worked his jaw and tried once more. "Miss Parker, could you tell the court why you were arrested?"

Everyone turned to Jack who held his hands up, inviting the question.

"I was arrested 'cause Addy came home when she wasn't supposed to, and him and his dad got involved and called the police." She pointed back to Logan. Adeline bristled with a slight shudder. She hated being called Addy, especially by her mother.

With a sigh, Snyder moved back to his files. He seemed to decide that any other questions he might've had, Jack was going to shoot down, so he drew an audible breath. "No further questions, your honor."

Judge Phillips shifted his gaze to Jack. "Your witness."

Jack gave Candy a polite smile. "Miss Parker, you stated that you were unaware of your pregnancy with Adeline until you were nearing your last trimester, is that correct?"

"Yeah," Candy agreed hesitantly.

Logan wasn't certain if the word trimester had thrown her or if she was averse to agreeing with Jack on any point.

"I personally have never had a baby," he said, drawing slight grins from the courtroom, "but it was my understanding that there are several telltale signs of pregnancy, the most common being the absence of the female menstrual cycle. Did you not experience this symptom?"

"I didn't really keep up with it. I kinda figured it went away 'cause I didn't need it. That way I could work more," she explained to gasps from several jury members. Her lawyer's face twisted in horror.

Jack didn't look surprised. "So you held a job that you couldn't perform when you were menstruating?" He feigned confusion.

"Objection, relevance," Snyder fumed.

"That question does seem relevant. Your defense is that Miss Parker turned to prostitution in an effort to raise her child," the judge huffed. "Continue, Mr. Stariff."

Jack nodded for Candy to continue. "Well, uh…" She finally began to realize what she'd just admitted. "Kind of."

Jack cocked his jaw to the side. "Kind of? Miss Parker, were you a prostitute before you conceived and gave birth to Adeline? I will remind you that you are under oath."

"Well, a girl's gotta eat, and it's not like I was hurting anyone."

Logan finally allowed his lungs to fill with air. Maybe this was going to work just the way Jack had promised. Maybe his father's warning was unnecessary. Maybe he could keep his promise that he wouldn't let anything bad happen to her. This was all going to be fine.

His mother-in-law was an idiot of epic proportion, and she was going to be her own undoing.

Adeline would be able to practice medicine, and life was going to turn out just the way it was supposed to. The thoughts pacified the hysteria that had set in from the moment Vindico had showed up at the farmhouse to inform them that Adeline was going to have to stand trial.

"Did you use drugs while you were pregnant, Miss Parker?" Stariff demanded, quickly taking Candy off guard.

"Not once they told me," she insisted, not aware that she'd just made Jack's day.

"Interesting, because according to numerous neonatal experts, the drugs that were in Adeline's system when she was born would have to have been ingested by you within two weeks of her birth. Care to rethink that last answer?"

"Well, I didn't know that she was gonna use 'em while she was in there," Candy sneered, as if Adeline had stolen something from her before birth.

Stunned disbelief etched every face in the courtroom, and Logan watched Adeline's head fall in shame. His heart ached for his wife, but the only emotion he could access was elation. No jury in their right mind would believe the drugs were really Adeline's. Candy was a lunatic.

Lucas didn't seem to share Logan's delight. He squeezed her hand again and offered her loving gazes as Jack went on.

"Miss Parker, you may not have been aware of this, but these,"— Jack moved back to the files beside Adeline and held up a thick folder—"are all of the medical tests performed on Adeline while she attended Venton Academy. It is one of the toughest schools in the country. They have extremely high standards. Each and every student that attends Venton, which I will point out is where my client and her husband met and fell in love as he attended the academy as well, must pass a full drug screening several times each year. If a student is caught using, they are immediately sent to a drug rehab and must repeat the year of school. Venton is not a place for drugs, and that has been the policy of the school for many, many years.

"Adeline passed every single drug test she was given while attending the academy from the age of fifteen to twenty-one, as did her husband, Logan. Adeline also agreed to broadscale drug tests as soon as she was arrested on drug charges. Four hair samples were taken. As the jury can see, Mrs. Haydenshire has very long hair. Drug use at any time in the last several years would have shown on the tests. They never found any evidence of illegal substances in her system, so I'm going to ask you, Miss Parker, did you ever use drugs with Adeline or ever see Adeline using illegal drugs?" Jack kept a glare leveled on Candy.

"You said she failed one of them tests," Candy demanded of her lawyer.

"Answer the question Ms. Parker," Judge Phillips ordered.

"Not really." She pulled her mouth back into a pout.

"And did you use illegal substances while in the presence of your daughter while she was under your care?" Jack's malevolent eyes never moved off Candy. She twisted uncomfortably in her seat.

"I don't understand the question." Her pleasure at what she must've considered a solid answer seemed to thrill her.

"Did you get high while you were supposed to be caring for Adeline?"

"I was a good mother."

Logan huffed audibly, and Jack shot him a look that said for him to shut it.

"That was not the question." He edged closer to Candy.

"I never did nothing in front of her. She never needed me. Besides, she looks fine to you, don't she?" Candy threw a scowl Adeline's way.

"You stated to the court that Adeline asked for things when she was a young child? Could you elaborate on the kinds of things Adeline requested?"

"I don't remember. That was a long time ago." Candy continued to pout.

"That's fine. I'll ask Adeline when I put her on the stand."

Candy seemed to sense that she was trapped. She rolled her eyes. "Like that time she wanted that doll. I didn't have money to buy her a doll. What's she gonna do with a doll anyway? Everybody got their panties in a wad cause she got hurt. Clearly, she's fine."

What little blood had remained in Lucas's face slithered downward quickly as his head fell into his hands in abject defeat.

"No further questions," Jack assured the judge as he returned to his seat shaking his head.

"Snyder, your witness," Phillips called as Candy took her seat.

"I'd like to call Mrs. Adeline *Haydenshire*," Snyder sneered her last name.

Lucas gave her a consoling smile as he stood and allowed Adeline to walk toward the stand. She glanced at Logan and gave him a desperate gaze that said for him to rescue her.

Nausea washed over Logan in heated waves. He couldn't rescue her, but he also still felt confident this was all going their way. She was too nervous to realize her mother had effectively indicted herself.

Adeline was sworn in. Her voice shook to such a degree that she could hardly be heard. She took the seat and Snyder dove in. "When did you marry, Mrs. Haydenshire?"

"Logan and I got married December second," she stammered, but then cleared her throat. With a quick glance at Logan, she settled.

"And how long were you engaged?" Snyder fired quickly.

"Logan asked me to marry him August 28th," she supplied with a smile.

"And did you let your mother know that you were engaged or getting married?"

Logan watched Adeline debate how to answer the question. She seemed to decide on the cold hard facts. She drew a deep breath. "No, sir."

"Don't you feel that those are events your mother would like to have at least known about?"

"A couple of days before Logan proposed, I asked him to take me to the facility where Mom was being held, and he did." She cleared her throat and proceeded. "I asked to see her, and she came out and told me that she hated me and never ever wanted to see me again. I assumed she didn't really care if I was engaged or if I was getting married." Adeline's explanation held no judgment, only the heartbreaking truth that was going to be Candy's undoing.

It serves her right. Logan recalled the night at the prison and their impending breakup.

Snyder moved on after a quick grimace. "And did you and Logan have a wedding ceremony, Adeline?"

"Yes, sir." Another smile lit her face.

"Wouldn't you agree that parents occasionally say things that they may not mean?" Snyder coaxed.

"Do not answer that, Adeline!" Jack's demand startled her as he leapt from his seat. "Objection! Leading!"

"Sustained. Move on, Snyder."

"Don't you feel your mother should have at least been given the opportunity to attend her only daughter's wedding?"

Adeline considered thoughtfully. "No, sir, not really."

Logan gave her a broad, encouraging smile.

"And why is that? It seems a bit disrespectful to me."

"She wasn't ever interested in anything I was doing. She told me she never wanted to see me again all the time. She'd hated Logan since that day he stopped her from hitting me. I only wanted people that I knew loved me to be there when I married Logan, because he's the person who helped me understand that people could love me. I do wish my dad had been there, though."

With his hand to his heart, Lucas nodded his heartfelt agreement.

Quickly deciding that he should change tactic, Snyder moved back to the table while glancing nervously at Lucas.

"You were given a random drug test on September fifteenth, and you tested positive for hydrocodone. Do you have access to that medication in your work as an obstetrician at Georgetown Hospital?"

"Yes, sir, but I was given a prescription for Vicodin because of a surgical procedure I'd had the day before."

"I have no record of you having surgery," Snyder informed her.

Jack leapt up again. "I have the hospital records right here, and the prosecution and the judge were given copies of Mrs. Haydenshire's medical records before the trial."

Judge Phillips nodded. "I do have a copy of that. Mrs. Haydenshire, then Parker, underwent an emergency operation to remove a follicular ovarian cyst." He held up the copy of the records he'd been given. "She was given hydrocodone acetaminophen after the surgery for pain, and a prescription was sent home with her. Did you not receive your copy, Mr. Snyder?" Phillips looked out over the top of the reading glasses he'd placed on the bridge of his nose.

"Oh, it's here," Snyder lamented. "Must've missed that."

"Might I suggest that you move on, Mr. Snyder?" Judge Phillips ordered.

"Yes, sir." Snyder whisked quickly back toward Adeline. "Did you let your mother know that you were in the hospital?"

"No, sir," she supplied with no additional information. Jack gave her an encouraging nod.

"Seems to me that you went out of your way to shut your mother out of your life once you began dating Logan Haydenshire."

"Objection, argumentative." Jack leveled a cold glare at Snyder. He wasn't going to get away with anything.

"Stick to allowable questions, Snyder. This is your last warning." The judge informed him.

"When you left the hospital, Adeline, who picked up the prescription for your pain medication?"

Adeline's brow knitted again. "Logan took me home, and I didn't want him to leave, so Garrett went and picked up the medicine for me."

"Garrett?"

"Haydenshire." Adeline pointed to Garrett, who held up his hand as he glared at Snyder. "Logan's brother."

Jack shook his head, and she stopped talking.

"And are you involved in some kind of relationship with Garrett Haydenshire? Has he ever supplied you with drugs before?"

Disgust chiseled Garrett's features as he gasped audibly. Vindico shook his head and gave a dramatic eye roll the jury seemed to notice.

"A relationship with Garrett?" Adeline's face screwed up in anger at the audacity of the implication. "He's my brother-in-law, and he's my friend." Garrett gave her a reassuring nod. "But that's it. And I've never been given a prescription before that one. I've never had surgery before, so no, he's never supplied me with anything like that."

"Your honor, this is irrelevant," Jack demanded hotly.

"Make your point, Snyder," Phillips demanded.

"I think I'll let these make my point for me, your honor."

Logan's heart cinched his throat and choked his vocal cords. Pictures were handed out to the jury. Pictures Logan wished and prayed would simply disappear from existence. Pictures of the stupidest thing Adeline had ever done and that he'd ever allowed.

Emily's head fell in shame. That stupid party where they'd let the moment get away from them all. That moment that had cost too damn much. They were kids, stupid kids. They knew better, but dammit, they'd just gone along.

"The point, your honor, is that my client feels the entire Haydenshire family has turned her daughter against her. I'm trying to ascertain just how deeply involved Adeline is with this family, who I personally believe have poisoned Adeline's mind against her mother.

"I believe that this is a photograph of Garrett Haydenshire up on a bar. And this is Adeline quite obviously drunk and drinking more. This is her husband, Logan, and her sister-in-law, Emily. I believe that would be Rainer Lawson, Emily's fiancé, with his tongue in her navel up on a bar. Do these look like moral, upstanding examples to you? Her lawyer can dress her up in a conservative suit and call her a saint, but these pictures tell an entirely different story."

The hope and stupid assurances that had fortified Logan moments before now served to mock him. The trial was anyone's game, and there may not be anything he could do to save his wife.

"Objection, your honor!" Jack huffed. "Adeline is of legal drinking age and was in those photos. She was at a private party. None of the people in that photo ever gave Adeline anything illegal, and they never would. Stop trying to demonize my client, Snyder!"

Tears formed quickly in Adeline's eyes. She shook her head. "No! No, the Haydenshires have done nothing but take care of me since I first started going out with Logan. They are wonderful people, all of them. Mrs. Haydenshire has fed me almost every meal for years now."

"Excuse me, your honor, but the Haydenshires are not on trial here, and though I wasn't aware that I would be teaching law today, Mr. Snyder's job is to determine whether or not Adeline Haydenshire was in possession of or using illegal drugs at the time of her mother's arrest. These are photographs from an entirely different time."

But this time, Judge Phillips shook his head at Jack. "Although that is partly true, we are being asked to determine whether or not Adeline Haydenshire might've used either illegal substances as her mother claims, or legal substances in an illegal fashion that she can acquire from her job. The pictures are admissible as witness to her character."

Logan's head sank. Fionna and Emily shared a heartbroken glance. That stupid Angels party, that had already cost so much, might've just lost Adeline her job.

"Adeline, could you please tell the court if either Senator or Mrs. Haydenshire ever gave you or encouraged you to take drugs, either prescription or illegal?"

"No, never," Adeline vowed.

"Logan or any of his siblings?"

"No!"

"Your witness, Mr. Stariff." Snyder smiled like the cat who just swallowed the canary.

"Thank you," Jack sneered. "Adeline," he greeted her with a warm smile, "have you ever taken any kind of drug, legal or illegal, that was not prescribed to you by a doctor?"

"No, sir."

"Would you care to explain the photographs the jury now has?"

"Yes, sir. It was a party after a sporting event. I didn't mean to drink too much. I've never done it again. I suppose we all make mistakes, and that was certainly one of mine."

"Were there any drugs, legal or illegal, being passed out at that party?"

"No, sir. None."

Jack gave a quick nod. Logan prayed that whatever happened next would somehow expunge those stupid pictures from the jury's collective mind.

"Adeline, can you tell the court how old you were when you began paying the household bills for your mother?"

Adeline glanced from her father to her mother. One looked disappointed and deeply concerned, the other flippant and uncaring, parts they'd both perfected.

"I was in either third or fourth grade, I think. Paying bills always made my mom angry, and it scared me. So, I would usually take some of the cash that she…" Adeline choked and then shuddered slightly before forcing out the word, "*earned,* and I would pay the bills that I could find. I got better with it as I got older. When I turned fifteen, Mom wanted me to get a job, so I started working at Francetti's Pizza Pies after school. I would use my tips and paycheck to pay the bills when Mom didn't make me give the money to her."

Logan was thoroughly convinced that his heart could not withstand much more of this trial, but Jack had done an effective job of bringing the jury's attention back to Candy's failings and away from Adeline's.

"Your mother made you give her your tips and paychecks? Do you know why?"

"Usually to pay her dealer." Adeline's pallor hued slightly.

"Her drug dealer?"

"Yes, sir," she admitted as pain broadcast from her features. Her pain not only physically affected Logan, but it visibly affected Rainer, Governor Haydenshire, Vindico, all of Logan's brothers, and most of all, Lucas.

"Can you tell us how old you were when you and Logan began dating?" was Jack's next question.

Some of her visible pain abated. "Yes, sir. I was sixteen."

"And Senator and Mrs. Haydenshire offered for you to come and live with them on their farm, did they not?"

"Yes, sir, several times," she answered readily.

"And why did you choose not to go and stay at the Haydenshires'?"

Lucas studied her closely. It seemed he wanted the answer to that question as well.

"I didn't want to be in the way or any trouble, and I always worried about what might happen to my mother if I wasn't there. I did all of the grocery shopping, and paid the bills, like you said. Sometimes she would take too much or drink too much, and I would take her to the hospital or take care of her if she was sick."

Jack glanced at the jury. Their faces were now appropriately aghast. Logan felt that stupid hope start to form again. He shut it down this time.

"Your mother was a prostitute for most of your childhood and adolescence, is that correct?"

"Yes, sir." Adeline shrank farther down in her seat. Jack offered her another kind smile.

"I'm sorry to make you go over this, but I need for you to explain to the jury what you did when you were growing up when your mother had clients at your apartment."

Adeline nodded, though each question seemed to physically exhaust her. "After Logan and I started dating, I would always ask either him or Rainer to come and get me, and I would stay at the farm until they were gone."

"And before you and Mr. Haydenshire began dating?"

Logan's stomach seized. Rainer offered him a sympathetic glance. Logan knew the answer, but it always made him physically ill to hear his wife discuss it.

"Sometimes I would go over to Ms. Bingham's. She was an older lady who lived in the same apartment building. She would make me dinner, and give me my bath, and let me stay in her guest bedroom. It was nice there," she pointed out hopefully.

Then, drawing on deep resolve, she willed herself to go on. "If Ms. Bingham wasn't home, or if her grandchildren were over, then I usually sat in the hallway of our building and read or slept until they left."

Fury lit Governor Haydenshire's rhythms as horrified silence filled the room.

"And how many times a week would you say you slept in the hallway of the apartment building you lived in, a building in which I will point out the hallways are not heated and have concrete floors."

"At least two or three nights a week, probably." Adeline focused on Jack. She seemed to will everyone else out of her line of sight.

"I would add to that." Jack moved back to the table and held up another file folder. "I have Adeline's permanent files from the elementary and middle school she attended where, though she always made excellent grades, numerous teachers throughout the years were extremely concerned about Adeline being so tired she would fall asleep in class several times a week and of her showing signs of malnutrition." Jack handed the files to the judge.

"You can sit back down, Adeline." Jack took her hand and helped her off the stand. He guided her back to her seat.

Snyder stood with defeat settled in his eyes. "I'd like to call Logan Haydenshire to the stand."

CHAPTER 9

FACT AND FICTION

Logan straightened his jacket and slid down the line of his family and friends as he progressed toward the stand. He gave Adeline an adoring gaze as he walked by her.

"I love you," he whispered as he went. Adeline smiled as she nodded her acceptance. Logan vowed to tell the truth, the whole truth, and nothing but the truth as he seated himself.

"Mr. Haydenshire, could you explain to the court a little bit more about Adeline's recent hospitalization?"

Surprised by the first question, Logan nodded. "Sure, she had an ovarian cyst, like you heard. I took her to the emergency room, and she was taken into surgery immediately. It was my understanding that both the cyst and the surgery were fairly routine."

Snyder nodded with a sneering grin. "Yes, I have several reports that you were overly demanding of the staff of Georgetown, and that at one point in the night you demanded pain medication for Adeline. Is this true?"

"Yes, that's true." Logan felt no remorse for his behavior.

Snyder seemed shocked by his ready admittance. "Care to tell us why you were demanding painkillers in the middle of the night, Mr. Haydenshire?"

Fury and irritation seared through Logan as he narrowed his eyes. "Ever been married, Mr. Snyder?"

With an arrogant chuckle, Snyder turned to the jury. "No, I'm a lawyer. I know better."

Logan didn't laugh. He didn't find the joke humorous in the least. "Okay, ever been in love then?"

"I believe I'm the one asking the questions, Mr. Haydenshire."

"Fine," Logan agreed. "Let me tell you how my world works. If my wife, who's just had surgery, wakes up in the middle of the night crying and writhing in pain, it tends to upset me. She needed medication so that she would no longer be in pain and could rest and recover. As it is my job to take care of whatever she needs, that is precisely what I went to find."

The extreme pride on his father's face as he nodded his deep approval to Logan gave him the resolve to continue.

"Has Adeline ever written a prescription for you or anyone in your family, Logan?"

"My wife is an obstetrician, Mr. Snyder. I have seven brothers." Logan rolled his eyes. "Adeline did care for my mother who was hospitalized several months ago, but to my knowledge she did not prescribe any medications at that time. Adeline is still being mentored, as this is her first year in practice. Any prescriptions she writes have to be approved by another doctor, so if she were writing prescriptions for my family, Georgetown would have already put a stop to that."

"Seems Mr. Stariff has prepared you well."

"I don't need Mr. Stariff to tell me what my wife does for a living," Logan fired back before Jack could object.

"And you are a police officer, Mr. Haydenshire, is that correct?"

"I'm with an elite special forces division of the CIA." Logan remembered what he was supposed to tell the Non-Gifted about Iodex.

"And were you involved in Ms. Parker's arrest?"

"No, I was not. My priorities that evening were Adeline's safety and making certain her wounds were taken care of."

"But your brother, Garrett, was involved in the arrest?"

"Yes, he was."

"But you don't feel that your family's involvement in almost every aspect of Candy Parker's arrest and in Adeline's life could be seen as manipulative?"

"No, I don't. Candy is and was a prostitute. She was also using drugs, and both of those things are illegal in the state of Virginia. Not to mention her abusive and neglectful ways with her daughter, my wife. She was arrested for breaking the law, not because I don't like her."

"Logan, could you please tell the court the sleeping arrangements on the nights that Adeline stayed on your family's farm?"

"Objection, irrelevant," spewed from Jack's mouth.

Snyder shook his head. "We all know, your honor, that young people can be very impressionable. I still don't believe the Haydenshires were a good influence on Adeline. We have photographic evidence of that fact. Being involved in a physical relationship with Logan could have tarnished her thinking about her mother. He's just admitted to not liking my client."

"I'll allow the question," the judge decreed.

Logan's stomach twisted uncomfortably. Every fiber of his body sought escape. His shield tensed disconcertingly. His father and Vindico shared a concerned glance.

"Uh, most of the time Adeline slept in my sister Emily's room, and I stayed in my room." He damned the obvious hole in his factual statement.

"But not every time?" Snyder pointed out pompously.

"No, not every time." Logan refused to meet anyone's eyes. How had this gotten so fucked up? He ran his hands through his hair and prayed for some kind of reprieve from the insanity.

Snyder slithered back to his table. "Your witness," he sneered to Jack.

Jack gave Snyder a polite nod. "Logan, could you briefly describe Adeline's injuries on the night of her mother's arrest, the night you graduated from Venton Academy?"

After a deep breath, Logan accepted that being done with Snyder was the only reprieve he was going to get. He forced himself to remember that horrifying night. It seemed years had gone by, not months. So much had happened. So much had changed.

"She had a badly broken wrist and several bruises and gashes on her face. She was also understandably terrified and emotional for the next several days."

"From the time you began dating Adeline, how often would you say you saw her, even for a brief period of time?"

"Most every day at school, and she stayed at the farm most weekends. If she didn't stay over, then I went to see her to make certain she was all right." The current knot in his stomach served as a vivid reminder of the terror he felt every time he drove to the apartment to make certain she was okay.

"Logan, I'm going to leave this up to you. Would you care to address the last question that Mr. Snyder asked you? I will be happy to ask you some follow-up questions," Jack offered kindly.

As he considered that, Logan met Adeline's gaze, trying to discern how she wanted him to handle this particular turn of events. Very slowly, she nodded.

"Okay." Logan braced for incoming questions about his and Adeline's physical relationship in front of not only his entire family, but her father and dozens of complete strangers. His shield sealed in his own muscles and was visible to every Gifted person in the room. Even Vindico offered him a sympathetic gaze.

"You don't have to respond. Simply tell me, and I'll withdraw the question."

The judge looked wary but allowed him to continue.

"How long had you and Adeline been dating when you began your physical relationship?" Jack did look truly sorry to be asking.

With another measured breath, he took in the extremely sympathetic gazes he was receiving. "Almost five years, and it wasn't until after we'd graduated."

Jack looked relieved. "Do you feel that your physical relationship in any way influenced Adeline's views or opinions of her mother?"

"No." His body began to ache from the solidification of his shield in his muscles. He wondered what Jack might ask next.

"Ever try to influence Adeline to do anything she wasn't certain she wanted to do?" Jack kept his back to both Mr. Nguyen and Governor Haydenshire.

"No, never," Logan pled adamantly.

"Ever try to get Adeline to stay over at your home in order to participate in your physical relationship?" was Jack's next harrowing question.

"No. I tried on a regular basis to get Adeline to move to the farm, but never for that. I was terrified for her safety. Rightfully so." He threw his hand out toward her mother.

Candy met his glare with a sneering scowl.

"Have you ever witnessed Adeline using legal or illegal drugs recreationally, Logan?"

"No, never." Logan wondered what Adeline's father was hearing in the answers to his questions. He was certain it was more than he wanted to know.

Jack smiled. "You can take your seat, Logan."

Relief lifted his body for him. He stepped off the stand. As he moved forward, Jack extended his hand. "Can I shake your hand, Logan?"

Furrowing his brow, Logan instinctively grasped Jack's hand. "I think you may be one of the finest young men I've ever had the privilege of knowing, Officer Haydenshire."

"Uh…thanks." Logan's face glowed hot once again. But as he made his way back to his seat, he saw Lucas nod adamantly, and then his father stood and slapped him on the back as did Vindico.

Rainer offered him their customary smirk, the one they'd shared for two decades. As he reseated himself, Rainer offered him his hand as well which Logan shook.

Judge Phillips seemed speculative for a moment before turning back to Snyder. "Any further witnesses?"

"No, your honor." Snyder didn't sound quite as self-assured as he had when those pictures had been presented.

"Mr. Stariff," Phillips nodded.

"I'd like to call Mr. Daniel Vindico to the stand."

Vindico stood and glided smoothly to the stand carrying a file folder of his own. He was sworn in and then seated himself. Logan glanced Fionna's direction and noted her trying to hide her pride-filled beam.

"Chief Vindico, could you tell the courts what you do for a living?"

"I'm the chief officer of the same elite special forces unit of the CIA that Logan and Garrett Haydenshire are a part of. Garrett is second in command. For any of you that have any doubt of his character, let me assure you that he is an outstanding officer and a gentleman."

"Did you arrest Miss Parker on June second of last year?"

Vindico shook his head. "I was not the arresting officer. I was called in after police arrived and apprehended Miss Parker, due to the nature of Adeline's attack and the quantity of illegal drugs found in the apartment."

"But you were involved in the chase of one of Adeline's would-be attackers?"

"I was," Vindico agreed. "We were actually after both of the men. One pulled a pistol and fired at one of my officers. We returned fire. He was killed at the scene. The other man, a Mr. Gary Elderand, was apprehended and is currently serving time." Vindico looked up the name in the folder he'd carried.

"So, the men that Miss Parker had in her and Adeline's home were armed. Would you consider them violent?"

"Absolutely. It terrifies me to think about what might've happened if Adeline had returned home earlier or hadn't been able to outrun her attackers." A shudder of very real disdain gave credence to his words.

"When you arrived back at the Haydenshires' farm, can you tell us more about Adeline's reactions to everything that had happened?"

"Objection, narrative," Snyder quarreled.

"Overruled. Continue, Chief Vindico," Phillips commanded.

Vindico glanced Logan's way. "Once I was certain that Adeline's injuries had been taken care of," he allowed instead of using the word *healed*, "and that Adeline had not sustained any form of sexual assault, Logan requested that I leave her alone. She was in a state of shocked trauma. He seemed to be the only person she wanted near her in those first few hours, which I completely understood. I returned the next morning to take her statement. She was still quite jumpy, again, understandably so."

"Thank you, Chief Vindico." Jack smiled and offered Snyder the questioning.

"Chief Vindico, did you perform a urine or blood sample drug test on Adeline when you arrived at the Haydenshires'?" Snyder demanded with a vicious grin.

"No, I did not, as that is not protocol for dealing with the victim of assault and battery. She was and is the victim, Mr. Snyder, not the criminal."

With a huff, Snyder spun back into his seat. "No further questions, your honor."

Jack straightened his jacket, pulled himself to his full height, and smiled at Adeline. "The defense calls Lucas Nguyen, Adeline's biological father, to the stand."

Logan offered Adeline a reassuring gaze, though his heart pounded in his ears. This was it. As soon as word got out that Lucas was Adeline's father, she would become an extremely appealing target for Wretchkinsides.

Another round of terror and nausea washed over Logan as he watched Lucas be sworn in. The roller coaster of emotion threatened to do him in.

"I assume you have DNA to back that up?" Snyder spat angrily.

"Naturally." Jack handed copies of the blood work performed on Adeline and her father to Judge Phillips and to Snyder. "Not that it's terribly necessary." He gestured from Lucas to Adeline.

"Mr. Nguyen, could you please tell the court when you last saw Candy Parker?" Jack began.

Lucas drew a steadying breath. "It was about twenty-two years ago. I was seventeen. My brothers and I were visiting the States that summer."

"And you are from?"

"Sydney. My family is one of the ruling parties of Australia," Lucas explained, not elaborating on which part of Australia they ruled.

Candy looked excited for a moment as she began demanding that Snyder get her money from Lucas. He waved her off.

"And the circumstances that you met Miss Parker, Mr. Nguyen?" Jack ignored Candy's heated whispers.

"She was a hooker—I believe that's what you call them here. A prostitute if you will. My brothers felt it was high time that I engage in sexual activity," Lucas grimaced over the words. "They hired her for me. I could clearly learn a great deal about being a man of character from my son-in-law." Lucas watched a broad grin spread across Adeline's face.

"So, Miss Parker was involved in prostitution before she gave birth to Adeline?"

"Yes." Lucas nodded.

"Can you tell me if Miss Parker was high or using drugs during your time with her?"

"I couldn't tell you if she was using at the time, but I can tell you that she offered me something she said would help with my nerves. I believe she called it a sex vitamin," he quipped wryly.

"Objection! This was over twenty years ago! This shouldn't be admissible," Snyder demanded.

"One doesn't usually forget one's first go," Lucas offered the judge, who nodded his agreement, though he looked slightly disgusted.

"Did Miss Parker ever attempt to contact you about her pregnancy or Adeline?" Jack continued.

"No, never, and if she had, I assure you that my daughter would not have been brought up in the cold hallway of an apartment building by an abusive mother. She would have been raised in Sydney with the very finest of everything. I would have seen to it."

Although the sentiment was meant to show that if Candy had put forth any effort into discovering Adeline's father, she wouldn't have to have dealt with the child she clearly viewed as nothing more than an annoyance, Logan's stomach always churned every time he considered Adeline being raised on the other side of the world.

Adeline's eyes met Logan's. She didn't like to think about it either. He gave her an adoring grin. His heart swelled through his pain.

She looked so frail and frightened there at the table alone, and he longed to move and sit beside her, to hold her hand. It was the way their world worked. Nothing made sense unless she was beside him.

With a deep, desperate, harrowing sense of urgency, Logan longed to pull her from the courtroom. He wanted to take her home, release her from the stiff conservative dress suit that she'd been instructed to wear and put her in one of his T-shirts and a pair of sweatpants. He wanted to lie on the couch and cradle her against his body. He needed to cover her up in the quilts that she loved as he ran his hands over her luscious body.

He wanted to hold her in his muscled embrace and whisper how much he loved her until her energy soothed and soared from his vows. He wanted to lock the world outside of his shield while he held her tenderly in its fierce protection.

She didn't deserve this. She'd done nothing wrong. He was supposed to protect her, not allow her to have to go through something like this where her character and their relationship was poked, prodded, and scrutinized by people that cared nothing about either of them.

Logan was shaken from his remorse-filled reverie by Lucas exiting the stand. Jack began calling medios and nurses from Georgetown to plead Adeline's good character, work ethic, and her talent for medicine.

He moved on to Garrett, who explained that the morning after the attack when he and his brothers had gone to Candy's apartment to remove Adeline's belongings, he'd found that she'd destroyed everything belonging to Adeline.

His parents were next, explaining all that they'd happily done for Adeline over the past several years. Jack had asked Mrs. Haydenshire how many children she had, and then asked if she remembered her first pregnancy.

When she'd assured him that she had, he asked her what the likelihood was that Candy had gone on for months not knowing she was pregnant, driving home the point that Candy had used during her pregnancy with Adeline.

But the judge reprimanded him, pointing out that Logan's mother was not an expert witness. Logan had found that genuinely humorous as his mother had rolled her eyes right on the stand.

CHAPTER 10

THICKER BLOOD

Still feeling a gnawing sense of terror riddle his body, Logan watched as Snyder stood to make his closing statements.

"This case has proven nothing when it comes to my client. Mr. Stariff, with his vast resources, has teamed up with a senator, an extremely wealthy man, and has found Adeline's father, but where was he when my client was left alone and afraid to raise a daughter on her own? Put yourself in my client's shoes. What would each of us have done in the same situation, uneducated, young, alone, raised on the streets? Is prison really where my client belongs, and if so, what exactly are her crimes?

"Adeline is a grown woman, healthy and working as a doctor. A difficult task that she clearly didn't accomplish on her own, I would like to remind everyone," he threw back toward the Haydenshires. "She abandoned her mother who, despite everything Mr. Stariff has alleged, did in fact love her daughter dearly. She married the man her mother despised in an obvious act of nothing more than calculated rebellion. I believe the photographs I presented show exactly what kind of woman Adeline Haydenshire is and what kind of family she has associated herself with."

Logan's jaw clenched as he leaned. Rainer caught him and shook his head. His father shot him a look that said to simmer down, and

Logan tried to draw steadying breaths. The infuriated look on Adeline's face did nothing to quell his temper.

"Did my client turn to prostitution in an effort to provide for her daughter? Yes. Is that a crime more than allowing her child to starve? Is it a crime with any real victims? I think we would all agree that it was not, and I urge you to consider these things, because it wasn't only Adeline who was a victim. It was also her mother."

Jack stood. "Mr. Snyder asked you to put yourself in Miss Parker's shoes. Well, I'm going to ask you to put yourself in Adeline's.

"Her mother was a prostitute long before Adeline was conceived. Her father sat right here and admitted to being one of her clients. She is not only using drugs, she is offering them to the men she services and dealing for her pimp on the side. I'm sorry, but I *do* believe she has committed numerous crimes and that she should be prosecuted thusly. Were there no other jobs available? Stable, steady, honest work that would have not necessarily provided Adeline with the finest things in life, but would have given her a solid home with heat and electricity on a regular basis? Or food and running water?

"My client took on responsibilities meant for adults at the age of ten. Her mother's chosen profession put her in constant danger until her graduation night when she was actually attacked. Then, in an act of cold, cruel, calculated rebellion," he threw back at Snyder, "she got angry that her daughter's attackers didn't pay for her services, and she threw away the very few things that Adeline owned. So, no, I do not believe that Candy Parker loved her daughter at all.

"In fact, the very night that Miss Parker was paroled, she showed up at Georgetown Hospital, causing another scene when Adeline was trying to work. So if you believe, as I do, that this country and this commonwealth stand for justice and righting wrongs, then please, let's give Adeline a little peace and time to heal and foster and nurture her new marriage to a man I don't think any of you could deny clearly loves and adores her.

"Candy Parker has yet to show any remorse for the way Adeline was raised. She's shown no sign that she won't go right back to the life she was leading before her arrest, and no signs that she will leave Logan and Adeline at peace. She needs to serve time. We do not allow drug dealers to walk the streets of Arlington, Virginia. We do not allow people who neglect and abuse children to go on without reprimand.

"Do your duty to the commonwealth. Do your duty to this country. Do your duty to Adeline. Because when each of us were tucked up warm and safe in our beds at night, that little girl sat alone in a cold hallway, wondering where her next meal was coming from and whether or not she could convince her mother to pay their bills. Being exposed to potentially dangerous men night after cold, terrifying night!" Jack Stariff pulled out all of the stops. Logan sat in awe. The jury was visibly moved.

But when Candy realized that Jack had just effectively sealed the case for Adeline, she began to come unglued. Logan's eyes goggled as she stood and glared at Jack. Her face grew red in her volatile temper.

Logan had seen her like this a few times before, and Adeline was always the target of her violence. Logan stood, heading Adeline's way, but Lucas calmly positioned himself between Adeline and her mother, daring Candy to come anywhere near his daughter.

"This is all your fault!" she screeched at Lucas. "You're one of them people, aren't you?! That's why she has all that stuff she can do! Just like all of them!" She threw her hand toward Logan and everyone seated on the witness benches for the defense.

The bailiff stepped toward Candy as did Jack.

"And he isn't a senator!" She stomped her feet furiously and threw her right hand toward Governor Haydenshire.

"He's a governor, or something like that."

The judge looked terrified. Snyder appeared bewildered as the jury stared wide-eyed with their mouths hanging open in confusion.

"Ms. Parker, take your seat or be held in contempt!"

"And that school she went to—it's for all of those weirdos," she continued to screech.

Lucas stood, blocking Adeline completely as Candy continued to stalk closer.

"Excuse me, your honor, but has she been given a drug test today?" Jack seized the opportunity unfolding before his very eyes.

But Candy wasn't going to back away. Logan could see it in her eyes. He heard several feet hit the floor beside him as he leapt over the railing and pulled Adeline behind him. Candy lunged at her daughter with her hands aimed for Adeline's neck.

Lucas grabbed her. "You will never touch her again. If I have my way, you'll never see her again," he growled furiously.

"Bailiff, please detain Ms. Parker!" Judge Phillips ordered.

Candy fought Lucas combatively, still trying to get her hands on Adeline by any means possible, but he kept her at bay.

As she was handcuffed and dragged away, Jack turned to Judge Phillips. "I think we rest."

Logan pulled Adeline into the safety of his embrace as she trembled violently in his arms.

"I can't imagine you'll need to deliberate long, but we'll take an hour for lunch. Let me know when you've reached a verdict." The judge still looked stunned by the turn of events.

Adeline hid her face against Logan's chest. His heart pounded as his panic began to abate. He noted that Rainer had leapt the railing a half a second after he had. He was followed immediately by Garrett and Vindico. Those were the feet he'd heard. His father and each and every one of his brothers had moved toward Adeline as soon as they'd understood what was about to happen.

"Are you okay, sweetheart?" Lucas looked heartbroken as he moved toward Logan and Adeline after the jury had exited the room.

She nodded against Logan but then pulled away and fell into her father's arms.

"Thank you so much," she managed.

"Keeping you safe is one of the many jobs I wasn't there to do when you were growing up, but I will keep you safe now, love, always."

Governor Haydenshire handed Lucas a handkerchief. "Good to keep on you when you have girls." He gazed adoringly at Adeline, tucked up in her father's embrace as Lucas began to dry her tears.

Several hours later, everyone was standing in the farmhouse kitchen as Mrs. Haydenshire, Emily, Fionna, the governor, and most of Logan's brothers worked on huge pots of Mrs. Haydenshire's gumbo.

Fionna was baking numerous batches of corn bread. Vindico stared at her every time she bent over to check the ovens.

Lucas and Adeline were seated on the bay window bench seat. They'd been discussing something that seemed to thrill Lucas.

"So not only guilty, but got a psych evaluation and headed to the Virginia Mental Health Institute." Rainer grinned and made certain that Adeline couldn't hear him discussing her mother's new living arrangements.

Logan chuckled. "I don't care where she goes as long as she stays the hell away from my baby."

"Amen to that," Garrett chimed in. "She's nuckin futz. Dad's not a senator. Clearly she's crazy," he teased as Vindico joined in his laughter.

"I saw you jump that railing. I thought they were going to arrest you for choking her." Vindico gave Logan an extremely proud grin.

"Yeah, trust me,"—Garrett was still laughing—"you do not mess with Adeline. He will end you violently." He slapped Logan's stomach with the back of his hand.

"Good man," Vindico vowed.

"Yes, he is," the governor joined the conversation.

CHAPTER 11

THE PRINCESS AND HER CASTLE

As everyone began inhaling bowl after steaming bowl of the gumbo, Logan settled on the couch with Adeline. Her relief was still evident in her eyes as she ate.

"I was so hungry," she admitted sheepishly.

"Well, eat, baby. There's plenty."

They ate in peaceful silence for a few long minutes, finding respite in the house full of people. Nathan and Tad were discussing plans for Rainer and Emily's wedding. Everyone in the kitchen was listening intently.

"Are you okay?" Logan wondered how she really felt about her mother being sentenced to spend time in a psych hospital.

"I don't know," she admitted. "I'm relieved I get to keep working and that it's over with, but I'm still worried about her, I guess."

Lucas joined them just then. "Mind if I sit?" He still looked mildly uncomfortable eating dinner on the couch, but there were no available seats at a table or countertop.

Adeline gave him a genuine smile. "I haven't told Logan yet. I was just about to."

Lucas grinned at her. "Whenever you want, love, but I heard you say that you were worried about your mum."

Her cheeks pinked as she nodded.

"I know that what happened today was rather odd, but I do wonder if your mother receiving psychiatric care might not be good for her. She does seem to be rather self-destructive. But, more importantly, you cannot save her. You pulled yourself up out of that situation, and she can do the same, but only if she wants to."

Adeline nodded her hesitant agreement. "I had a lot of help, though. I think everyone who's somehow able to get out of lives like mine have so much help. I hope I can help people do that the way the Haydenshires did for me."

Lucas beamed at her. "I have no doubt that you will do everything you set out to do, but I want you to know that if your mother wants help, I'll help her, because we share this amazing woman that is our daughter. But darling, you've done enough. It's time for you to relax a little. Heal. Enjoy being a newlywed. Come visit your old Dad every so often," Lucas teased her and reveled in Adeline's grin.

"You're coming back for Rainer and Emily's wedding, right?" Adeline surprised Logan with her fervor.

"Yes, but you and Logan are welcome in Sydney anytime. You call me, and I'll have a jet here as soon as possible."

"I'm going to miss you." Adeline seemed somewhat surprised by her own admittance.

Lucas gazed at her tenderly. "Not half as much as I'll miss you, but you just say the word, and I'll be back. You pick up the phone, I don't care what time it is here or in Sydney, and we'll talk about anything at all. I'll be there whenever you need me."

Adeline gave him the smile that Logan had fallen head over heels for so many years ago. "Thank you." She choked back tears as she began to really understand what she meant to her father.

She hugged him tight as he wrapped her up in his arms. She settled back down, curling up beside Logan.

"So," she bit her lip nervously as Logan studied her. "My...dad..." she allowed, and Lucas appeared to take a moment to remember to breathe as he beamed at her, "and I were talking, and I think that I might like to change my name again."

"Okay..." Logan waited on the inevitable explanation as her energy changed from nerves to elation.

"I think I'm going to officially be Adeline Nguyen Haydenshire," she stated with a tremendous amount of pride lighting her eyes.

"That sounds perfect." Logan leaned and kissed her cheek.

"I think so too."

"And if you change your mind on the coronation, it would please your grandmother so," Lucas urged, though Logan sensed he was teasing. He chuckled as Adeline cringed.

"Aww, come on, baby, you know I always sort of think of you in a tiara," Logan teased, though as he thought about it, he realized what he was saying was quite truthful.

She rolled her eyes. "No coronation. I just want to be your daughter. I don't need to be a princess."

"Well, you have always been my daughter, and that makes you a princess. But after today, I really do understand that you'd rather be Logan's princess here in your castle than in a Realm you've only been to once. I'm hoping someday you'll understand how very much you mean to me, and that I, too, will always think of you as my princess. That you'll understand how much I love you."

Adeline swallowed hard and drew strength from Logan. He held his breath. "I love you too, Lucas." She hugged her father, and Logan's heart swelled with pride.

～

A few hours later, Lucas was seated at the kitchen table drinking coffee with Governor and Mrs. Haydenshire, Logan, Adeline, Rainer, and Emily.

Everyone else had returned home except Nathan and Tad, who'd gone to The Wharf for dinner. They planned on helping Mrs. Haydenshire for the rest of the week, and Emily had several wedding items she wanted their attention on as well.

Though Emily was tucked up contentedly in Rainer's lap on the window seat, she and Adeline were whispering back and forth with Logan and Lucas eyeing them and chuckling.

Governor Haydenshire was still smarting over having walked into Emily's bedroom a half hour before to find Emily fully clothed but lying under Rainer as he kissed her heatedly and grinded against her.

Lucas noted the governor's eyes narrowing slightly as he watched Rainer rub Emily's thighs. "Now, I believe the way it was explained to me was that my baby girl,"—he gestured to Adeline—"was madly in love with and had married your son, and that their acts of amorous playfulness were a healthy part of a relationship. I believe I was informed that it shouldn't upset me. That they weren't children anymore, and that my son-in-law adored my daughter and meant no harm in what he'd done." Lucas let the governor know that he not only had his number, he'd been listening for the past few weeks.

Logan, Adeline, Rainer, Emily, and Mrs. Haydenshire all cracked up. "Oh Lucas, honey, I knew you were gonna come around and fit right in." Mrs. Haydenshire reached and squeezed Lucas's hand.

The governor nodded his acceptance of his dressing down and his own words being thrown back in his face.

"Yes, well," he sighed, "I suppose maybe I didn't give quite enough credence to the fact that she is your baby girl. Perhaps I saw it a little more from my son's perspective," he admitted as everyone continued to laugh.

With a wry grin the governor raised his eyebrow. "So Logan, keep your hands off your wife's rear end if her father is in town, all right, son?"

Logan feigned consideration while taking Adeline's hand. "Can't really promise that, but I'll consider trying," he allowed, effectively cracking everyone up again.

"Lucas, Emily and I were talking, and she and Rainer are going to stay here tonight and tomorrow night. I was sort of hoping that you'd stay with me and Logan for the rest of your trip."

"I'd be thrilled, sweetheart. Nothing would make me happier."

"And where exactly will Rainer be sleeping, baby girl?" the governor huffed as Mrs. Haydenshire rolled her eyes.

"Would you prefer she tell you the truth, honey, or that she lie and tell you that he's going to sleep in his old room when you know perfectly well he isn't?"

Blood pooled in Rainer's face, and Emily laughed hysterically.

CHAPTER 12

HARD WORK AND REWARDS

DAN VINDICO

Fionna grinned as she pulled the new seat belt across her lap. She'd hated the original harnessing that had come with Dan's 599 GTB Fiorano. He'd had Sam modify the car. He was perfectly fine with the fact that he was probably the only warm-blooded, American male who'd ever had a Ferrari downgraded. He'd do anything for her, and he didn't need a race car. She got his blood pumping like nothing ever had anyway.

Fionna grinned. "So that all went better than I ever could have imagined. Her mom really needs help, and now hopefully she'll get it."

Dan allowed himself one moment to rev the engine before he drove out the gates of Haydenshire farm headed home. "I've sat through more trials than I care to remember, Gifted and Non-Gifted, and I think that was definitely one of the most bizarre things I've ever seen." Dan still couldn't believe the turn of events from one trumped-up charge to another.

"I thought it was kind of interesting. I've never been to court, thank goodness. It was a little weird that you were all kind of lying but not lying about what you do under oath."

The CIA cover bothered her. He knew it would. Fionna valued honesty and integrity above anything else. It was yet another thing he loved about her.

"Boomslang was sixty-five when he retired, and I took over. He was chief of Iodex for thirty-odd years, and every single time he had to testify in a Non-Gifted trial, he'd cross his fingers when they asked him what he did for a living." Dan chuckled at his own memories of the man who'd taught him so much.

The determination set in his gut again. He'd started fighting Wretchkinsides and the Interfeci under Boomslang, and dammit, he was going to finish the job.

She tried to hide the concern from her features, and he tried to modulate the anger and determination that pulsed in his energy. She could read him so easily. She could read everyone around her effortlessly, but she'd never been so intimate with anyone. He'd experienced every beautiful opening of her luscious body. He'd cared for her when she was sick, dried her tears when she was sad, and had united their bodies in an endless and desperate rhythm that said one was never meant to exist without the other. He could hide nothing from her, and he never wanted to.

"I know you think I'm somehow unhappy with the way things are —not being able to tell anyone about us—but I'm not. I love you. I love us just the way we are. I don't need anything else, except maybe to see you more. You've been working so much lately."

He signaled and changed lanes to give himself a moment before he had to respond. "I told you I can do it all. Okay, baby doll? Just give me a chance. We're close. I can feel it. I'm going to end him…soon."

She held his eyes with her own for a moment before she glanced downward. He prayed she'd drop it. He'd been about to explain that he was going to leave her at home and head into the office for a few hours, but he decided against that. His laptop and office they'd set up in one of the guest bedrooms at home would do for a while.

"You know, the whole thing about what Iodex is to the Non-Gifted changes all the time. Every few years or so the governors get a new report on the new lie, and we have to go in and memorize it all over again."

"Trying to distract me, Chief Vindico?"

"Is it working?"

There it was again. That infectious laugh that made the golden flecks in her sienna eyes dance like a sparkler on the Fourth of July. The one that made her olive cheeks glow. It made her breasts jostle in a distracting tango that made him willing to do most anything to keep her giggling.

"Okay, fine, if you're in the CIA now, what will you be doing next year?"

"I've been in for twelve and a half years now, if you count my senior year at the academy. So far, I've been in the CIA, the FBI, an officer of the US Intelligence community, in the Virginia State Police Bureau, and once we were a subsidiary of the navy. I thought the specialized forces for the Department of Homeland Security would stick, but that only lasted six months. I'm pretty sure Rainer and Logan are holding out for either The Justice League or The Avengers next."

That did it. She cracked up. He beamed as the laughter took over her entire body.

She shook her head at him and regained a little of her composure. "Why do they change it all the time?"

"It depends on what they believe the Non-Gifted know to be true. The FBI does a lot of investigation work, but they leave the arresting to state police forces. Most people know that. The CIA is supposed to handle intelligence on foreign companies or individuals and not act against American citizens at all, but most people don't know that. If the case involves an arrest made by Iodex, it's easier to cover that up using the CIA. Plus, their headquarters is in Langley, so I think that's why they went with that. It gives credence to where our offices actually are. But who knows? Whatever turns them on, I guess. We just do what we're told."

"You can ask me." She was clearly willing to let her powers show today. She usually tried to keep them hidden. She never wanted to frighten people.

"Ask you what?" Nervous excitement had lilted in his rhythms. He'd tried not to think too much about buying her a ring. He wanted to ask her moments after he ended Wretchkinsides, but he knew he needed to plan out something special for her. He didn't want her picking up on anything before he was ready.

"What I felt from that Ramirez guy at the trial."

"Oh." Air exited his lungs in relief. "Yeah, well, I wasn't looking to get another lecture on working, so…" He winked at her. She stuck her tongue out at him, and he shot her a cocky half grin that he hoped was sexy.

But the playfulness bled from her features. "He felt really, really scared."

That wasn't what Dan had expected her to confirm.

"Scared, and there was a lot of regret. He's done some bad stuff, but the fear was the primary emotion. Of course, people do bad things because of fear. That's always the foundation."

Dan nodded. He knew she was going to ask him why Ramirez was scared. He didn't want to tell her.

"Is Wretchkinsides going to kill him?" The emboldened reserve ignited in her. She stared at him as he watched the road.

"Probably." He couldn't have lied. She would have known. "He didn't get out of town fast enough. As soon as Candy was arrested, he was supposed to have split. I think they had something going on. He wanted to defend her, and she was a great source of income. That's why I had officers there to take him immediately. He'll be safe in jail, hopefully."

She hugged the wool shawl closer again. Dan casted the heater in the car and drove it up several degrees, but he suspected that the chill came from the discussion not the frosty early January air.

Dan drove the heels of his hands into his eyes. He tried to rub away the fatigue and the spinning numbers. Pendergrath was opening new bank accounts. Dan had to figure out where they were located, and why money was being diverted to three old accounts in Belgium in small increments. What was Wretchkinsides planning? Why Brussels?

It was only eleven. He had a few good hours left in him. He tried to order himself back to the documents on the computer screen in front of him. The particleboard desk shifted disconcertingly as he leaned the full weight of his arms on top of it and continued rubbing his eyes and forehead, hoping to massage his brain into functioning again.

He heard the television in the living room click off. Fionna had given up on him and was heading to bed. Guilt only offered him further fatigue.

When Nic Wretchkinsides burned, then Dan could set fire to the sheets with Fionna any time he wanted. Now, he needed to figure out these bank accounts. They were the key. Money drove Nic and his thugs. That was all they ever wanted, and there would never be enough.

Choking out the incoming cash sources wasn't doing it. He had to hit them where it hurt most. He had to take what they'd already acquired to drive them out of hiding.

He heard the customary creak the hallway gave when she whisked past. His heart ached. Holding her in his arms while she slept was more pleasure than he'd known possible. Making love with her was otherworldly perfection, and he was missing both.

He let the ache drive him. Refocusing, he pulled up the emails Fitz had uncovered and began comparing the money being discussed in the messages to the amounts being transferred in and out of Belgium. Closing his eyes for a moment, he pushed his shield away and tapped into his Visium Predilection. *Think, Vindico.*

"I'm going to bed," her sweet voice beckoned. His blood quaked to its sound. Quickly deciding that he could at least indulge himself in a few good night kisses, he spun the chair to face her.

But all thoughts of work were incinerated in the searing knots of need that shot through his veins. "Damn," he growled as his eyes took in the feast before him. The real estate in his jeans became nonexistent, and his muscles throbbed.

She loved lingerie as much as he loved her in it, but this was better than anything he'd been treated to thus far.

She stood before him in a see-through, white ruffled nightie that tied between her lush tits with a long silk ribbon. They were spilling out of the insubstantial cups. He could see the sepia hue of her nipples. Saliva flooded his mouth. He needed a taste.

There were smaller versions of that same ribboning attached at her shoulders. With a few quick pulls, the ruffles and satin would be gone. He continued to track his eyes down those ruffles.

It parted over her adorable navel and skimmed her waistline. His perfect baby doll dressed the part. The panties were equally as see-through, but fabric did cover her full backside. They were puckered and ruffled with a bow in the back. She slowly shifted to the side, making the ruffles sway and showing off the cutout in the panties under the bow that revealed a tiny peek of the center of those lush cheeks.

She looked every part the delicious virgin so willing to be sacrificed. Work be damned. "You look like a walking wet dream, baby doll. Come here to me."

Her eyes flashed in intrigue as she glided toward him. She let her bottom lip slide through her teeth, playing innocent, spiking his blood as it sluiced through his veins. Her hips swayed. His cock burned thick and fierce. He sat back in the chair and spread his legs slightly.

"Come sit in my lap. Be a good girl for me and let me touch you."

The quick, hungry moan stole her breath as she spun. The lavish cheeks of her backside nestled his zipper line. He thrust against her, and her body rolled. "So fucking sexy. You feel that? You feel how hard you make me when you're a good girl and do what you're told?"

He traced his fingertips along the waistband of her panties. With his left hand, he swept her hair away and glided his fingers over her shoulders softly, patiently. When he finally finished with her tonight, there wouldn't be a single inch of her body or of that tight little pussy he hadn't touched, and coaxed, and filled. He could see the wet heat gathering in those virgin sweet panties. A low groan thundered from his chest.

His hand slipped to the silky crotch, and he teased her lightly, making her writhe and pulse. With constant strokes over the panties, he used the satin to ignite her. "So sweet, baby." He thrust again and began to tease down her slit with his middle finger. He let his index and ring finger prime those swollen lips. "That feels good, doesn't it? Look how wet you get all for me."

"Please," she panted.

He smirked. He wasn't giving in anytime soon. "You know I like you greedy, baby doll. Nice and hot and dripping wet all for me. Be patient. Let me play. I want you to beg."

Her body seemed to plead for air she couldn't provide. She wriggled against him. He continued his torturous strokes. As he slipped his hand from her opening upward, he pressed and circled around her clit, making her beg indeed.

He kept her lips spread with his thumb and middle finger. With his index finger he stroked the silk against her clitoris. It swelled and distended, so anxious for his affection.

With his other hand, he pulled the ribbon between her breasts and watched the gown fall down her arms in a jaw-dropping image of seductive carnality. The coconut perfume and musk of sex that she created naturally permeated the air he breathed.

He wrapped his left arm around her and cupped her right breast. Her nipple pebbled against his palm. He kneaded her, feeling her ample tit spill through his fingers.

Unable to wait, he slipped his hand down the front of her panties.

"Yes, please," she moaned and shook in need. So many things he wanted, and she offered them all. He slipped two fingers just between her folds, still teasing her. Not entering her yet. The wet heat, full of desperation, coursed around his fingers. She whimpered in protest.

He circled her opening and felt her muscles contract in an effort to pull him inside. "So needy, baby. My naughty girl. You sure as hell look sweet as sin. And I know you taste as sexy as you look." He pressed his fingers fully inside of her.

A moan of relief rocked through her. She ground against his hand, giving herself over to him. He gathered the sweet cream on his fingers and gave her a modicum of relief, then pulled his hand away and sucked the dew from his fingers.

She panted and moaned. Her head shook back and forth against his substantial shoulder. "Now get on your knees like a good girl."

Frantic and eager, she lowered herself to the ground on her knees in front of him and licked her lips. My God, how had he gotten so lucky? She was absolutely incredible.

He had the snap opened and the zipper down on his jeans in

record time. He leaned up, and she lowered the denim and his boxers until he could feel her hot breath tease his steel-hard strain.

"In your mouth, baby doll. I want to see my cock in your hungry mouth. Take it all like my good girl. Show me what that mouth was made for."

A long, low, luscious groan burned through him from her lips to his cock as she licked up his shaft and then drew him in, sucking and pulling until he thought he'd lose his mind.

His ridge slid along the roof of her mouth and down the back of her throat. She slipped back to his head and spun her tongue around him, cleaning the salty need leaking readily from him.

"That's a good girl. Drink it then suck it again."

She drowned him. Her throat contracted around him, and he was certain he was going to come unglued.

He backed off, letting her set the pace. As long as she kept him between her lips, he didn't give a damn how fast she went.

His Double-Predilected bands of energy sizzled. His head shook. She was too much. It just felt too damn good. He needed to be inside of her right fucking now. He cradled her face, watching her cheeks hollow as she sucked.

"Stop, baby. You're gonna make me lose it, and I'm gonna own you over and over tonight. But every time I come, it's gonna be deep inside of you. Are you casted?" He summoned the erotic energy spilling from her pores and set to move it up her body to seal her womb, Gifted birth control at its finest.

"I already did it. Just, please…" She stood and begged, with her lips swollen and glowing a deep red from her work.

He threw the gathered energy back into the air and drew her back to him. The gown still hung from her elbows. He slowly lowered the panties to her knees, rather enjoying the provocative display.

"Turn back around and sit in my lap again. Be a good girl, and take it all." This time he was fully exposed.

He grasped her waist and lowered her down his cock. He was hung so heavy he ached. She held the only antidote to his exquisite pain.

With one full, deliberate thrust, he permeated her. Slipping up that perfect column of hot liquid silk that pressed around him, encasing him in ecstasy.

"So damn tight. You feel so fucking good." He grunted, and she began to ride. Pushing and rocking against him, it took several passes for her body to seat him fully. But when she sank to his hilt, he groaned in absolute ecstasy. It was like being drowned in warm honey straight from heaven.

"I'm still hungry, baby doll. I want more of that sweet cum." He licked his fingers again and teased her clit as she rode. Stroking with more force, he gathered her liquid heat with his fingers then brought them to his mouth and sucked.

She shuddered and gasped from the sight. He pushed her over in a matter of moments. The way she came for him was automatic. He knew where to touch and what to say to make her dissolve all for him.

But he needed more. He stood, forcing her up with him. "Put your hands on the desk and hold on tight." She leaned and complied, and he began to pound into her with fierce ragged thrusts that commanded consent.

"You're gonna take it all, baby. Then we'll slow it down," he promised. Her temperature shot upwards. Her moans were loud and eager. Her back arched.

Those lush cheeks of her backside tensed against him. His name spilled from her beautiful lips. He traced his fingertips down the center of her backside, igniting the nerve endings pulsing there, all for him. He stroked the puckered opening. She groaned in elation, and the orgasm rose from her mound and rocketed through her in waves.

He let go and was immediately consumed. He filled her full with a gasping grunt of deep satisfaction.

A moment later he withdrew, turned her, and cradled her to him. Her entire body continued to quake. She buried her face against his chest. He nestled the nape of her neck with one hand and circled his other around her back, letting the climax develop completely.

"You know, you're not really teaching me not to work late," he teased as he lifted her up in his arms.

"Yum. It was worth it." Her giggle was cut off by a yawn.

"Don't go to sleep, baby doll. We're not near finished yet." With another cocky smirk, his secondary energy bands willingly gave themselves over to his desires.

He carried her to their bed and laid her gently on the pillows. He slowly slipped the panties off her legs this time and tossed them away. He removed that gown that should be illegal.

Slower this time, now satiated and wanting to connect their souls as much as their bodies, he glided his hands up her inner thighs and traced her swollen mound, wet from their mixed releases. "I want you again. I want you all night. All mine."

She shivered, still not quite accustomed to being taken so many times in repetition. He didn't do it as often as he would like. He never wanted to be pushy, and she was always so tight.

"I'll be gentle, sweetheart. But I need you again."

She spread her legs and let her eyes close as he continued to map and explore her beautiful body softly with his fingertips. He lingered in the valleys that held heaven on earth. He trailed warm, wet, open mouth kisses down her neck, over each of her nipples, suckling and pulling, then down her abdomen, soft and expectant, until he reached her mound, swollen plump and so tender she shook from all he'd already done.

Her clitoris gave a timid pulse, not yet fully retracted, so he began there. Soft laps of his tongue then gentle sucks from his lips until it bloomed again, and she was desperate and begging for more.

He reopened her with his fingers and began all over again.

An hour later, she was sound asleep in his arms. He kept her tucked in a sated cocoon of afterglow and of his all-encompassing love and fierce protection.

She'd appeased all of those demons that drove him mad. With his eyes closed, he concentrated on her slow, steady breaths as they whispered through the hair on his chest.

There were several things he hated about being a Double-Predilect. For one, he could be mind-casted with ease. *The one weakness in the extreme power,* the Gifted textbooks mocked him.

Everyone in class would turn to stare at him whenever Double-Preds were discussed.

He hated the way his friends and colleagues would occasionally stare at him in bewilderment when his bands would shift from his shield to his Visium rhythms when he needed to discern something complicated.

But being able to be with her like that twice without having to wait—well, that made up for it all. There certainly wasn't anything weak about that. His chest contracted in a huff. She shifted, and he ordered himself to remain still and keep her safe and warm through the night.

He began making plans. Valentine's Day was fast approaching. She loved love. She loved Valentines. He knew—though she'd tried to pretend it didn't matter that he couldn't take her to some swanky restaurant attached to an equally seductive hotel or have dozens of roses sent to the arena with a note of his love attached—he had to do something. He had to figure something out that was romantic and worthy of a woman like Fionna.

He needed to talk to Tad Anderson about a ring. He wanted it in his possession. Another reminder of what he could have when he finished his work.

CHAPTER 13

PLANS AND SURPRISES
RAINER LAWSON

As the freezing winds of January set in near the end of the month, Rainer smiled as Emily cuddled up on his chest.

"Hey there, baby." He let his eyes open hesitantly.

"Rainer," Emily whispered in the darkness of their bedroom.

"Emily," he matched her tone.

"We're getting married in two months!" She vibrated in her excitement.

"I'd heard something about that." Though he teased her, he began going over all of the things he needed to do before the wedding.

He'd already had Vindico check his choice for honeymoon locations, and he'd requested that Fitzroy also check it on the national Iodex register. He was taking no chances. He wanted to know everything Europe and America had on the Interfeci.

He'd made absolutely certain no one would know where they were going to be for two weeks. Rainer planned to steal her away, but he wanted to go over everything again. He had to be sure they would be safe and that Wretchkinsides had no idea where they would be.

He needed to phone Fionna about the huge surprise he'd been planning that wouldn't arrive until the day before the wedding.

Emily had informed him that most of the weekends between the beginning of February and their actual wedding they would be attending showers and parties given in their honor.

He still had to plan the rest of their Valentine's surprise. He wanted it to be special and to give Emily a break from all the work she'd been doing for the wedding.

At Emily's insistence, Rainer had finally settled on groomsmen. He'd asked Dan and Garrett to join Logan in escorting Fionna, Chloe, and Adeline in the wedding.

Dan had been pushing them all hard. Logan and Rainer had been moved up the chain when Barron and McCoy had joined the Elite force. They'd spent every available moment chasing down every single lead they could find on Wretchkinsides and the Interfeci, with Vindico sending in new teams on a regular basis to clone cell phones from members that were at The Tantra Gentlemen's Club.

They would work six or seven hours straight and then spend two to three in the gym or in training exercises. He'd eased up slightly in the last week. Everyone assumed Fionna had complained about the late hours, and he'd relented.

Mrs. Haydenshire had been put back on bed rest. Her blood pressure had spiked with well over a month left in her pregnancy. The Crown Governor was in the office less and less. He stayed home as often as he could and leveled her blood pressure with his own.

The kids were all taking turns helping out with the twins, and Rainer had worried about his request for Emily's wedding surprise. He was relieved that both Governor and Mrs. Haydenshire sounded thrilled with the idea and pointed out that it would actually be a big help.

"I don't want to get up. I'm warm under here with you," Emily fussed.

"I'll always keep you warm, baby," Rainer bragged as he let heat push out of his pores. Emily snuggled herself tighter into his embrace. "But we do have to go to work." He would love nothing more than another weekend day to lie around the house with her.

"Don't forget, we're going to look at Fionna's house tonight with her and Dan," Emily remembered suddenly.

"I know. I'm hoping that means I'll actually get to leave by five." He was irritated with his boss's dogged desire to work without end.

Emily and Fionna had gotten used to being picked up from practice by either Rainer or Dan and coming back to the office. Logan would get Adeline as soon as her shift ended as well.

Barron was doing the same with his fiancée. Portwood and Ramier's wives and kids had details assigned to them. Ericcson's steady boyfriend was also a Shield and had balked at extra protection, but Ericcson kept close watch. The ladies had taken up several empty desks and would typically help Emily out with wedding planning until Vindico let everyone go home.

"How about this," Rainer negotiated. "If I go make us some coffee, you could stay warm under the covers, and then after we drink it and cuddle a little more, we'll get ready to go."

Emily's broad grin spread against his chest. "You're the best fiancé ever."

Rainer returned a few minutes later with steaming mugs of coffee. Emily propped herself up on her pillows as Rainer handed her the mug. "Does Fionna not mind him working like this? He stays later than all of us." Rainer knew Dan was pushing the limits of the time Governor Haydenshire thought was appropriate for him to be at the office because the governor was distracted with Mrs. Haydenshire and the baby.

"Kind of, but they also can't really go out or be seen anywhere together until he takes down Wretchkinsides. I think she sees it as a means to an end, and she's waited for him for years. She's a very patient person. Plus, I think she's very content to be up there with him."

Emily didn't draw the comparison outright, but Rainer knew she didn't necessarily like being stuck at Iodex after practice and on her off days. She would vastly prefer to be home or out doing something fun with Adeline or Fionna or on her own.

When the coffee cups were empty, Emily climbed in the shower.

Rainer touched Fionna's name on his cell phone.

"Hey Rainer, everything okay?" Fionna sounded rather exhausted.

"Yeah, I just wondered if you'd help me out with a favor for the wedding. I didn't mean to wake you up." He apologized, but she had to be at practice in an hour.

"Oh, you didn't," Fionna assured him.

"Why is Lawson calling you?" He heard Dan's gruff voice in the background teasing her.

"Because he's planning on asking me out," Fionna sassed. Rainer laughed heartily.

"I will kill him, and he is aware of that," Vindico assured her, and Rainer heard the muffled sound of what he was fairly certain was a kiss on Fionna's cheek. "Make it quick, Lawson. We were busy," he chanted in the phone.

"Oh god, I'm so sorry."

"Would you stop harassing him? We were not. We were eating breakfast."

Rainer tried to regain his equilibrium and prayed he hadn't interrupted them.

"I'm happy to help. What's the favor?" Fionna's demeanor and her ever-pleasant disposition led Rainer to believe that he hadn't interrupted anything too important.

He explained his elaborate plan and what the Haydenshires and Garrett had agreed to and then what he needed her to do.

"Oh, my gosh!" Fionna was in tears by the end of the conversation. "I'm so excited. I can't even tell you how amazing this is! It's the best thing I have ever heard! I can't wait!"

If Emily reacted the same way, Rainer would be delighted. Fionna agreed to do everything Rainer needed, and he got off the phone in time to hand Emily a heated towel.

CHAPTER 14

INVITING INVITATIONS

Dan dropped Fionna off at the arena at the same time Rainer was dropping Emily off. Per their running agreement, Dan left the Ferrari in case Fionna needed to drive somewhere, and he climbed in Rainer's Porsche.

"Please tell me you were kidding this morning." Rainer couldn't shake the case of nerves that came with the knowledge that he'd interrupted them.

Dan laughed. "If she's answering the phone in the middle of that, I'm clearly doing something very, very wrong and should probably be put out of my misery. She's thrilled, by the way, with what you're doing. That's really nice of the Haydenshires with everything they have going on."

"Yeah, I think they're hoping it might help with the twins," Rainer explained as they pulled onto the interstate.

Dan had been wearing a cocky grin since he'd walked Fionna into the stadium.

"Have a nice weekend?" Rainer asked.

He shrugged. "It was okay. I flew up to New York yesterday to do a little work. Got in late last night."

Rainer wasn't certain why he was so curious, but Dan's energy strains were pulsing with eager excitement. They were almost childlike. It was an odd juxtaposition, a frustrated excitement, and it was definitely not a pattern he'd ever picked up from his boss before, unless he had his hands on Fionna.

Uncertain how to respond and having no idea why his boss had gone to New York, Rainer pulled into the parking deck noting that Vindico's broad grin never left his face.

Rainer fell into his desk across from Logan who was already looking over the texts from the phones that had been cloned over the weekend.

Garrett sauntered in a few minutes later.

"How's Mom?" he quizzed Logan.

"Dad got Medio Sawyer to agree for Adeline to stay with her for the next few days, so he'll be in to get caught up on work," Logan explained. "Adeline says she's doing better, but that Abigail needs to be bigger before they can induce."

"Dad kept her casted most of the day yesterday. He's exhausted," Garrett filled in for everyone listening and concerned about Mrs. Haydenshire and the baby.

Logan nodded. "Yeah, when I took Ad over this morning, Mom's blood pressure was stable, and she was holding it on her own. Brad was on his way over. I think they may try putting her on medicine that will control it so Dad can get a break. He's the only one that seems able to keep it steady. Adeline says it still spikes occasionally when she casts Mom."

The customary terror that had taken up residence in Rainer's stomach ever since Mrs. Haydenshire had been put back on bed rest washed over him again. He and Emily were planning on staying at the farmhouse that night to take care of the twins. He hoped they could somehow let Mrs. Haydenshire relax.

"Lucy took off work, and Patrick's only going in for a little while, so they're looking after Keaton and Henry," Logan informed his brother.

"Yeah and I still have tomorrow off, right?" Garrett reminded Dan.

"Of course. I told you, getting the newest Haydenshire here and keeping your mom safe and healthy is top priority. If you need to go help, then go," Vindico assured them.

"Keaton's been asking about Fi. You two should come by," Garrett informed Vindico wryly.

"Kid's got excellent taste," Vindico teased as everyone laughed.

Suddenly, Garrett's eyes lit and then narrowed in on Vindico. "That reminds me." He chuckled. Vindico seemed to know what was coming. "Come here." He slapped Rainer on the back and then gestured his head toward Logan before moving into Vindico's office.

They all followed. Rainer noted that his boss was still sporting a broad grin. Garrett closed the door and then spun with a goading smirk on his face.

"So,"—he raised an eyebrow to Dan, who'd moved to his desk—"talked to Uncle Tad this morning. He's planning on coming down again this weekend to help out with the twins, but he mentioned that you'd gone by to pick up something last night from the shop."

Rainer and Logan both grinned.

"I might've done that," Dan allowed, but he seemed unable to halt his own chuckle.

"Well, let's see it," Garrett demanded.

"Are you serious?" Rainer was a little shocked.

"I haven't asked her yet." The warning was implicit in his tone. He unlocked his briefcase and pulled out a black velvet box with Tad's store logo on the bottom. He handed it to Garrett.

Garrett popped the box open and gasped. "Damn," he drawled out into approximately ten syllables. "How much did you pay for this?" He turned the box around for Rainer and Logan to take in the gargantuan diamond ring.

The center stone was easily over four carats and the two others weren't much smaller. The band twisted delicately in three strands of one point diamonds.

Rainer asked, "How'd you go by there without her knowing, or did she pick it out?"

Dan laughed at them outright. "I hope she's as excited as you all are. I really just went ahead and got it as a carrot for myself, no pun intended. I'm not asking her until Wretchkinsides is done for. She can't exactly wear that without people noticing that she's taken, which was obviously my goal. But since the entire Realm thinks she's dating you, that might be a little awkward," he reminded Garrett.

Garrett looked hesitant to agree. "I don't know, man. I hate that you're hanging it up on him though. He's ruined your life for long enough."

Dan shrugged out his agreement as he reached and pulled the box from Garrett's grasp. "Not asking her until he's through. If you want me to do it sooner, let's get to work."

"Maybe ask her now, and she could just wear it around the house," Garrett negotiated.

"Yeah, because that's what women want to do. They want to be engaged and own a ring like that but not be able to show anybody."

Logan and Rainer laughed. He was absolutely correct.

"Hey, what do I know? I'm sure as hell not ever buying one," Garrett combatted.

"Did Uncle Tad make it or just ship it in for you?" Logan still seemed quite impressed with the ring itself.

"I showed him a couple of things I knew she'd like and told him I wanted every guy within a fifteen-mile radius of her to know she was mine. He crafted it, and as you all already know, he does excellent work." Vindico opened the box again and admired Tad's craftsmanship. "It's not imbued with promethium, but as soon as we take Wretchkinsides down, hopefully Emily won't need to use that portion of her ring anymore," he offered Rainer.

"That would be nice," Rainer allowed.

"Are you gonna ask her dad?" Garrett shot Dan a knowing grin.

Vindico placed the ring delicately in his desk drawer. He locked and casted it closed. "I've always been more of an ask for forgiveness not permission kind of guy, and her dad is definitely not my biggest fan. But that seems like something that would mean a lot to Fi." He studied the men standing in his office, clearly looking for opinions.

"He's coming around though. He and Gretta came by the farm the other day to bring Mom some cookies and bread to let her know they were thinking of her, and he called you by your first name instead of *that guy taking advantage of my sweet Maylea,*" Garrett laughed.

Rainer and Logan cracked up, but Vindico looked defeated. "Suppose that's something."

"Dad tried talking to him. Not sure how far he got, but he went to bat for you."

"The governor said yes when I asked," Rainer pointed out, but he was met with disdain from everyone.

"Of course Dad said yes. He raised you." Garrett rolled his eyes.

"You should have just gone ahead and proposed at our eighth birthday party." Logan chuckled.

"I was a little short on funds what with me trying to support my Hot Wheels collection."

"Oh, remember! That was the year we got those fly tracks."

"Yeah, those were cool. Remember the car wash thing?"

Dan and Garrett cracked up.

"If you two would like to rejoin us here in the big boy world,"— Dan shook his head—"I do have to figure something out about the Angels and Wretchkinsides."

"Okay, but on the asking her dad front," Garrett brought everyone back to the original conversation, "try asking her stepmom and her dad together because her mom really, really likes you."

Vindico considered that for a moment. "I'm thinking I'm gonna stick to my asking forgiveness plan, but we have a lot to do before that, anyway."

He opened a file folder and threw down a paper cutout of what appeared to be a corset. It had black ribboning laced through holes in the folded pink striped paper.

"These are going out today," he explained.

Curious, Rainer lifted the paper and pulled the ribbon. As he unfolded the corset, he realized he was holding a paper doll of sorts. It was an invitation displaying a naked woman from her chest to her thighs. There was a piece of vellum that fell in Rainer's lap. He lifted it and read the words:

We all know Em is oh so sweet
So get her something to knock Rainer off his feet
Get her some feathers, some leather, and lace

So she can shake it right in his face

Some little something to make their night complete

We all know Rainer wants a naughty treat

She'll be so lovely in her gown made of white

But we're gonna spice up their honeymoon nights

No flannel, or T-shirts, only satin and lace

Let's put Mr. Lawson hot on the chase

So ladies, only toys, accessories, and attire

meant to set Rainer Lawson's heart on fire

Go get something naughty with a great deal of sass

Make him want to spank her sweet little...

The word *ass* wasn't actually printed, but it certainly didn't leave much to the imagination.

"Oh my God." Rainer's eyes bugged. Blood pooled in his cheeks. He was quite certain his face was on fire.

Logan grimaced in horror. "Ugh, I will never get that image out of my head."

Garrett laughed and then cringed, and Vindico gave Rainer a sympathetic nod.

While adamantly refusing to meet anyone's eyes, Rainer noted that written on the actual corset-shaped invitation were Emily's bra and panty sizes, the date and time of the lingerie shower, and Rainer's preferences in color and styles, that he assumed Emily must've supplied.

He let his head fall in his hands and willed himself to wake up from what he was certain must be some kind of extremely odd nightmare.

"If you think that's bad, wait 'til you see what Fi got her." Dan shook his head.

Rainer whimpered, "Why exactly did you show me this?"

Dan refolded the invitation. He must've thought getting it out of view might help. "Like I said, these are going out today, and obviously, all of the Angels will be in attendance as it's being held at the arena. Wretchkinsides is still furious that we made a fool of Pendergrath when he attempted to buy out the Angels. He's out for blood, and it won't only be the Angels in attendance. Brooke will be there, and Adeline, all people that Wretchkinsides is extremely interested in. So while all of the ladies are consuming mass quantities of alcohol and supplying Emily with everything mentioned on that invitation, we're going to be at the arena to make certain no one without an invitation decides to come inside."

"I have to attend my little sister's lingerie shower?" Logan looked horrified.

"Not exactly." Vindico shook his head. "The party is going to be in the ballroom. We'll just hang out in the arena. We'll keep an eye on everything. So, two weeks from now, plan on sitting *outside* of your fiancée's lingerie shower. I somehow doubt any of the ladies will need to be driving after the party anyway."

"Seriously, I wish I had a picture of the look on your face when you read that." Garrett was still laughing as he punched Rainer's shoulder.

Vindico's cell rang and Fionna's name popped up on the screen. "Hey, baby doll, you feeling any better?"

Everyone politely ignored him as Garrett began chastising Rainer about exactly what kinds of things would make him want to spank Emily's sweet little ass.

"I'm sorry I wasn't there to cast you last night. I shouldn't have gone. Why don't I pick you up, and we'll go home for lunch? You can rest," Vindico urged, though Rainer noted it sounded more like a command.

However Fionna responded, it had Dan grinning broadly. "I could definitely do that," he assured her. "Love you too, baby. I'll pick you up in a little while."

"Fi okay?" Garrett's brow furrowed.

"Kind of. I've got to get the schedule of this down better. She didn't sleep much," he explained somewhat cryptically.

The very few clues that Vindico had allowed seemed to let Garrett in as to what was actually going on. He grimaced and nodded his understanding. "Sick to her stomach, writhing in pain, little bit bitchy, but will be better by tomorrow?" Garrett quizzed, and Dan hesitantly agreed. His jaw tensed and everyone got the distinct impression that he was not discussing Fionna with any of them anymore.

Both bands of his rhythms pulsed in synchronization. He seemed to forcibly shake off the desire to tell Garrett to fuck off. Rainer and Logan shifted uncomfortably. They wished they could escape the stare down Garrett and Vindico were engaged in. Dan drew an audible breath.

"All right, let's see what we can get done this morning. If I can talk Fi into not going back to practice after lunch, I'm going to stay home with her. I'll work from there."

Rainer wondered what had brought about Dan's willingness to stay home. Whatever it was, Fionna was clearly the key to Dan Vindico.

CHAPTER 15

PLAYING GAMES

Rainer picked Emily up from the arena. Dan had stayed home with Fionna, so Elite took the opportunity to actually leave on time. Dan also rescheduled Rainer and Emily seeing Fionna's house that evening.

"Are you okay?" Rainer leaned and kissed her cheek before he cranked the car. She was gnawing on her bottom lip.

"Yeah, but I overheard Fi and Chloe talking about my lingerie shower."

Rainer was still trying not to cringe over the invitations. "Yeah, I saw the invites."

Emily's eyes goggled. "I swear, I didn't know they were going to do that when they asked me about your favorite stuff. I thought they wanted to know for their own shopping. I never thought they would put it on the invitations." Her face promptly turned the color of her hair. Rainer chuckled and squeezed her hand.

"Well, the initial embarrassment factor aside, I will say I'm pretty excited to see what you come home with."

She giggled but was still showing signs of a bad case of nerves. "I need to ask you something."

"Sure, baby." Part of growing up with the girl you fell head over heels for when you were a toddler meant that Rainer and Emily had been through it all before. He was living on the farm when she'd first started her period.

She'd been almost as stunned as he had when he woke up one morning after a few weeks of his voice cracking horribly and suddenly sounded much more like a deep bass than the tenor he'd been before.

He'd physically watched her breasts develop and grow at what she considered an alarming rate. He'd been enthralled. She'd been annoyed.

"Remember when Dana was teasing me in Brazil about me only ever sleeping with you?"

Rainer clenched his jaw over his irritation and general dislike of Dana Mathers. She was Emily's teammate. He had to at least be polite.

"Yeah, I remember."

"Chloe asked Fionna if she would pick up the condoms for the party and the cucumbers for one of the games." She sounded thoroughly nonplussed. "Apparently they think it's a good game, because trying to get Gifted girls who've had a great deal of alcohol to put the condom on the cucumber is rather funny." She was still glowing the color of an overripe strawberry.

Rainer supposed that was probably true as he considered the fact that most Gifted girls would have very little experience with a condom since they could cast and close their own wombs, blocking out any and all sperm, even if they were sleeping with a Non-Gifted guy.

"Okay…" Rainer tried to determine what Emily's take on the game was going to be.

"I was just thinking that since I've never even seen a condom,"— she shuddered slightly—"Dana's just going to tease me more if I completely screw up the game."

With a slight chuckle, Rainer pulled the Porsche into the garage and kissed her forehead. "I can tell you everything I know about them, but I cannot go buy condoms. The press would go insane."

This was yet another time that the Gifted press's fascination with them drove him crazy. If he went into a drug store and purchased condoms, every paper in the Realm would scream that he was cheating.

"Yeah, didn't think about that," she lamented. "Maybe Garrett or Connor would get me some to practice with."

Rainer had to laugh at her desire to be successful at a drunken bridal shower game.

"I'll ask Garrett for you if you want, but I really think it's just supposed to be fun."

Emily seemed to realize that she might be taking everything just a little too seriously. She rolled her eyes. Heat still permeated her cheeks.

"I guess I'm just a little nervous after seeing that invitation."

"Well," Rainer soothed, "as it turns out, Dan wants several officers at the arena for the party since the Angels are one of Wretchkinsides's obsessions, so I'll be around. If it gets too bad, you just say the word, and I'll bring you home." Rainer knew perfectly well that Emily Haydenshire would never leave a party given in her honor, but he also knew it would ease her mind if she knew she always had an out. Rainer would be there if she needed him. He was always her Shield.

CHAPTER 16

POMP AND PREPARATIONS

DAN VINDICO

Dan was seated at the kitchen table eating the toast and eggs Fionna had fixed while he watched her begin her methodical work.

She pulled the numerous trays of thin, heart-shaped, sugar cookies from their refrigerator and began turning them upside down. She iced the curves on half of them to look like breasts in a low slung bra and the other half to look like curvy ass cheeks in thong underwear.

Dan shook his head as he took in her creatively made, sugared undergarments. He doubted that when her father shared all of his knowledge and skill on being a pastry chef and baker with her that this was what he had in mind.

"Oh, that would look so pretty with pearls," she commented to herself as she began placing tiny white sugar pearls along the top of several of the bras.

She gave him a sheepish grin when she realized he was watching her intently. When she'd completed the dozens of bra and thong cookies, she began working on a large tray that she'd cut to look like corsets.

A mischievous grin cast her face as she waggled her eyebrows at him while he placed his plate and coffee mug in the sink before starting to load the dishwasher for her.

"Hey, honey…" she called.

He laughed just taking in her expression.

"I need to work on the cake, and I think I need you to model for me."

Dan reveled in the warmth and contentment he only felt when he was in her presence. He grabbed her hands and pulled her to him. "I just showed you last night, baby doll," he growled in her ear, thoroughly delighting her.

"I know. I can't seem to stop smiling." She always made him feel like a king. He grasped a handful of her gorgeous ass and gave it a tight squeeze as she wiggled it for him.

"I really do not want my junk to be the model for Emily Haydenshire's cake." He grimaced from the thought as she cracked up.

"Uh, yeah, because that is all mine. Every delicious inch," she teased.

"You already getting in the mood for the party tonight, baby doll?"

This seemed to bring her back to the task at hand. Dan released her to her icing bags as he moved to the fridge, pulled out a Dr Pepper, set it on the counter, and opened it for her before getting one for himself.

"Thank you." She leaned up on her tiptoes to brush a sweet kiss on his jaw. She began going over a list written on a notepad as she refilled the white icing bag.

"I have to get the condoms." She checked the clock on the stove.

Dan laughed. "You threw away a bunch I had when we first started dating. You could've used them now. And, by the way, women are so much dirtier than guys, and we get a bad rap."

"Both of those points are completely true, but the condoms you had were way too mundane for what we need tonight. I have to get the rainbow-colored ones that glow in the dark or the jet-black ones. You know, ribbed for her pleasure." She cracked up at her own teasing.

She was completely adorable. Dan kissed the top of her head. "Of course, what was I thinking? And these are to be placed on the dozens of cucumbers in our refrigerator, right?" He recalled her explanations of all of the games she and Chloe had come up with.

"That and tons of other stuff. They'll be balloons and decorations."

A wicked thought of Governor Haydenshire walking in on this ode to debauchery given in his daughter's honor had Dan laughing again. "And would you like me to go and purchase those for you, sweetheart?"

"You would do that?"

"For you, I would do anything," he reminded her. "So, yes, I will be happy to make the pimple-faced teenager at the drugstore laugh hysterically as I buy dozens of rainbow-colored condoms. And it wouldn't be a bad idea for me to be seen buying them. If, for some reason, the press gets wind of anything, or if Wretchkinsides has someone tailing me again, then me buying condoms certainly doesn't say I'm in the most important relationship of my life with the most beautiful, exceptional woman in the Gifted Realm. It says I'm still an asshole who will take what I want and walk away." He offered a verbal effigy in hopes of atonement for his life before her.

She gave him that sweet smile that righted everything in his world. "Dan,"—she shook her head—"I love you so much."

"I love you too, baby."

She wrinkled her nose adorably and lifted one of the upside-down heart-shaped cookies decorated with a white lace thong and popped it in his mouth. Despite its decorating, it tasted delicious. She was outstanding in every possible way.

But he knew it was going to be a wild night when Fionna giggled and informed him that if he wanted to eat anything else in a thong, she had something for him.

Dan kissed her cheek as he pulled on the motorcycle jacket she'd given him for Christmas. "I'm going to the drug store."

"Hey wait," she called. He turned back, certain there was something else she needed him to pick up for her. "Thank you for doing that for me. And thank you for what you said about us. I've never been happier, but I do have a question for you."

Chuckling at her formality and her overly pink cheeks, Dan winked at her. "What's that?"

"Chloe will be over in a little while, so I have to ask you this now." She sauntered toward Dan with a sexy grin that took his breath away as he watched her, dressed in one of her favorite aprons, sucking icing off her fingers with flour on her cheek.

She placed another icing-covered finger in his mouth, and he sucked it flirtatiously. "I want you to promise me something."

"Okay." He hoped he could promise whatever it was she wanted. If she was going to start in on him working too much again, this was going to get tricky.

"I'll promise only to have a couple of drinks tonight if you promise that even if I'm tipsy, we can have fun once we get home." Her voice took on an excited thrum.

Dan raised his left eyebrow and narrowed his eyes. "When you go out and have fun with the Angels, you're usually asleep by the time I get you home."

"I know, but if I'm not asleep, I'm asking you now so you're still a gentleman because I'm completely sober when I asked."

He laughed at her outright. "All right, fine. If you're not asleep and you haven't had enough that I would feel like a complete asshole that was taking advantage of you, I'll see what I can do."

Her eyes lit as she nodded. "Deal!"

~

When Dan returned, Garrett and Chloe were in the living room with Fionna. Garrett was scowling as Fionna and Chloe began arranging party favors on the coffee table.

"This is my little sister. This is over-the-top even for me. Why do I have to be here?" Garrett demanded. Chloe laughed as she began counting out cheap, black lace thigh garters with hot pink pins declaring the wearer to be a bad girl.

Dan shuddered as Fionna began piling penis-shaped ring pops into the bags they were taking to the arena.

"Before every challenge, Rainer gives her a ring pop because she loves them, and because she can't wear her real ring when she plays. I think it's some kind of thing from when they were growing up, so we thought this would be perfect," Chloe explained to him.

Garrett scowled and shook his head. "Em used to make Rainer

play wedding with her constantly, and she would make him give her a ring pop in the ceremony."

"They are so adorable." Fionna sighed wistfully.

There were also penis-shaped candies in Angels' colors being thrown in the bags, plastic diamond-shaped drink cup rings that would hold a shot, enough boas for every attendee, and sashes distinguishing the ladies as the Bride, Bridesmaid, or the Matron of Honor. All of the others had *Bride's Bitches* written across them in silver glittered letters.

"Condoms," Fionna called to Dan as she moved down her list. He handed her the bag from the drugstore full of dozens of boxes of condoms.

"You are the best." She popped a kiss on his cheek.

Garrett rolled his eyes.

"Wait 'til you see the cake." Dan sank down on the couch beside Garrett.

"Do you have the bra and panties?" Fionna quizzed Chloe.

"Yes, and I got all of the Angels to go ahead and write on theirs so we can hang them up when we get there. But I still need Adeline, Brooke, Sarah, and Lucy to do theirs. And I went ahead and did the bra."

"Yes, that was exactly what I wanted to think about Rainer doing to my baby sister." Garrett gagged.

Dan was thoroughly confused. His brow knitted. Fionna giggled as she extracted an inexpensive white bra from one of the bags Chloe had supplied. He agreed with Garrett's assessment as he read Chloe's handwriting in black marker. She'd written *Suck Me Here* on one cup, and *Bite Me Here* on the other. He didn't have to see the panties to get the idea.

Chloe rolled her eyes as Dan and Garrett both grimaced. "What is wrong with you two? Em has a huge rack. She probably likes Rainer to suck on them."

"Oh my god, Chloe. Seriously!" Garrett shuddered in horror.

"Want to go grab some lunch?" Dan offered him a lifeline.

"Now." Garrett stood and headed to the door.

"We'll bring you back something," Dan offered.

"Okay, love you," Fionna called as she continued to go through bags, consolidating things for the party.

~

Several hours later, Dan helped Garrett load up the bags and all of the food into his Highlander. "How did we get roped into helping to decorate for my little sister's lingerie party?"

"That would be because the women planning it let us play in their lingerie," Dan informed him wryly. He finally got a chuckle out of Garrett.

"Rainer's gonna flip when he sees all of that shit." He gestured his head to the back of the Highlander.

Dan laughed outright. Rainer Lawson was both extremely protective of Emily, as any Ioses worth their salt was about the person they were in love with, but he was also a little naïve. He was going to run a steady shade of puce for most of the night, Dan had no doubt.

Fionna appeared in the driveway carrying an air pump that could be casted.

Garrett scowled. "Do I even want to know what that's for?"

"For the blow-up guy. We're gonna play stick the kiss to the guy. Oh! I need tape." She ran back toward the house.

"Oh, yeah. You and Dan played something like that in Vegas, didn't you?" Garrett harassed before promptly cracking up. Dan couldn't help but laugh as Fionna's cheeks glowed a rosy pink.

~

By six thirty, Dan and Garrett had begrudgingly hung a clothesline along the walls of the Angels ballroom. Fionna and Chloe had promptly begun hanging the bra and a dozen pairs of panties, all with lurid instructions on them, along the clothesline.

Chloe had blown up the naked male inflatable doll and had positioned him in the corner with cutout lip prints with tape on the back of them stationed nearby with a tie that Dan recognized as one of Garrett's that would serve as the blindfold.

The food tables were complete with heart-shaped sandwiches, Fionna's lingerie cookies, many varied salads, and trays of appetizers. The penis-shaped cake that was frosted with the words *Emily's Going Down* written in large letters and *The Aisle* iced in tiny letters at the bottom stood prominent in the center.

Another table contained more games. The condoms and cucumbers were lined up and ready. There was a black silk bag that Dan had been informed contained many varied sex toys. The girls were to stick their hand in and guess what they were feeling.

Bottles of Reddi-wip were on the table beside long slim balloons. Chloe was adding liberal amounts of vodka to Jell-O shots.

Dan was certain the likelihood Fionna was going to get to have tipsy sex was slim to none.

"No shots," Fionna informed him quietly. He always suspected she could read his mind.

Curiosity finally got to him. As Chloe and Garrett returned to the Highlander to bring in a missing bag, Dan caught Fionna's waist. "Hey,"—he pulled her close—"can I ask you something?"

"I'm sorry. I know this is all kind of over-the-top, but we love Em and we want to send her off right."

Dan smiled and shook his head. "No, this is all fine. I want you to have fun. I just wondered why you were so hell-bent on us having sex tonight. Not that I don't want to. I always want you, but we do that with a great deal of frequency. So what's this all about?" He tried to read her energy patterns as he held her close to his body. He wasn't a Receiver and couldn't quite navigate through the embarrassment that was dominating her strains.

She shrugged. "I don't know. I just..." she hemmed uncomfortably.

"Hey, it's me. Don't be embarrassed. Just tell me."

"It's like you said, I always fall asleep. So I've never done the tipsy sex thing, and you said that we could try stuff I wanted to try. I know I'm safe with you, and I know you would never do anything I didn't want you to because I know you really love me. I just wanted to try it. It's supposed to be fun." Her face held a mixture of deep embarrassment and extreme hopefulness. "We had fun on the plane, and we'd never done that before. I'm certainly not planning on going out drinking all the time so we can have drunken sex or anything. I just wanted to try it once…before I turn thirty," she admitted with a slight shudder.

Understanding settled on him as all of the pieces began to fall into place. Fionna was nervous about turning thirty in April. Despite his assurances that thirty really wasn't any different from twenty-nine, she was having a hard time believing that.

If she wanted to do something out of character for them both, he would happily oblige. "All right, if that's what you want, then I will gallantly offer you my services."

"Well, thank you, kind sir." She giggled. "And I will try my best to blow your mind."

Dan kissed her cheek. "You always do, baby doll. You always do."

CHAPTER 17

PERSPECTIVES

An hour later, the party was in full swing. Dan was seated in an adjoining room off the ballroom with Rainer, Logan, Garrett, Barron, McCoy, and Will, who'd driven Brooke and shown up with a cooler full of beer and Big Mickey's sub sandwiches for the guys. Portwood, Ericcson, Ramier, and Tuttle had been given the night off but were on standby should they be needed.

"This is the first time Brooke's been out to do anything fun since Lily Ana was born, and my baby girl is spending the night with the twins. Levi and Connor are at the farmhouse helping out. So I was thinking she didn't need to be driving home," Will explained to everyone.

"And you were thinking you wouldn't mind getting against that after she's had a few libations," Garrett goaded his big brother.

"Might've been thinking that as well," Will allowed.

"Yeah, I'm gonna need somebody to point out to me the Angels that are available," McCoy teased, working his deep southern accent as everyone continued to laugh.

"It was really nice of Fionna to invite Neva. She's been kind of lonely since we moved. She doesn't have any friends here yet," Barron commented to Dan.

He laughed. "If she can get a condom on a cucumber, I'm sure she'll fit right in."

The men's laughter was drowned out by the loud music and squealing laughter coming from the ballroom. Rainer seemed extremely uncomfortable. Garrett offered him another beer.

"Hey, not that I'm expecting anything to happen tonight, but I'd like him to be sober if it should," Dan scolded Garrett.

"Oh my gosh! Rainer would never ever wear that," Emily chanted loudly. Her voice carried through the door between the rooms.

"Em, you have to make him. They feel so good!"

Rainer popped the top on the beer bottle and downed it quickly as everyone cracked up again.

A few minutes later, balloons began popping. Rainer and Logan shared a confused glance.

"You don't want to know. Trust me," Dan assured them.

The guys stopped drinking beer and switched to cola after each having two. They began inhaling the huge sandwiches Will had supplied.

"Okay, some of these gift bags are vibrating," they heard Chloe call out as she announced that it was time for Emily to open a few more of her presents.

Rainer ran his hands over his face repeatedly.

"Adeline!" Emily gasped. "I cannot believe you got me this."

All eyes turned to Logan who held up his hands in surrender. "I told her I didn't want to know. I have no idea."

"How goes the house hunt?" Will offered Rainer an out.

Rainer looked relieved as he set down the sandwich he'd been picking at. "Em really likes Fionna's house."

Dan was sincerely hoping that Rainer and Emily would purchase Fionna's home. They couldn't put it on the market as that would alert everyone to the fact that Fionna Styler had moved somewhere else.

"We both liked it. I kind of want to redo the floors," he noted, "but whenever I bring it up, Emily starts to cry. She really doesn't want to leave the farm."

"I'm sure Dad would let you build in one of the back fields," Will pointed out.

"I know," Rainer allowed, but then he clammed up.

"Emily needs to live off the farm. She's gotta grow up," Garrett explained so that Rainer didn't have to.

"I never said that." He didn't deny it either.

"I know. I'm saying it," Garrett came right back.

Awkward silence drowned the room just in time for the guys to hear whistles and squeals from the partygoers amongst the pops of multiple balloons.

"Fi-oooo-nnaa," drawled loudly from several of the girls. "That's right, ladies, Miss Fionna Styler will get the Head Goddess ribbon and crown as the only girl who didn't pop a single balloon," Sasha announced excitedly as the girls broke out in fits of laughter.

"Nice," Garrett guffawed. Dan's face heated as Will slapped him on the back and laughed heartily.

McCoy and Barron choked back hysterical laughter. Dan assumed they were trying to be respectful of their new boss, but when Rainer and Logan cracked up, they did as well.

"And our lovely bride only popped one, so let's hear it for our Receivers, ladies. We knew they were good at giving and receiving," Chloe slurred slightly.

Rainer joined Dan in letting their heads fall in their hands. Will, Garrett, and Logan didn't find Emily's winning to be quite as funny as Fionna's.

"Open more presents, Emily," Sasha commanded.

"Here, open mine," Dan heard Fionna order. Where Chloe and Sasha's voices rang of their slight inebriation, Fionna's did not. Dan tried not to think about her request in light of her just being named Head Giving Queen.

A minute later, Emily gasped, "Fionna, that is just scary looking."

"Here, I'll show you how to use it," Brooke's Brazilian accent broke through the laughter.

All eyes turned to Will. He smirked. "Hey, she's not shy about what she wants. That's one of the many reasons why I married her." He took the teasing much better than either Rainer or Dan.

~

It was nearing two in the morning when the girls spilled out of the ballroom. Chloe was tripping and slurring. Her eyes were vibrating slightly as Garrett caught her to keep her from falling flat on her face.

"We need to help load Emily into the presents," she informed him as he choked back laughter.

"Uh-huh, why don't you sit here and have some Dr Pepper?" He pulled a few dollars from his wallet and slipped it into the vending machine. "And we'll load up the presents."

Fionna was chuckling at Chloe, but Dan noted that she didn't appear to have had much to drink. She and Emily were not only wearing their bride and bridesmaid sashes, but were also adorned with phallic-shaped ribbons pinned on their shirts declaring that they gave good head. Fionna was crowned with a headband covered in hot pink fuzz and feathers with two plastic penises suspended on springs over her head.

Unable to help himself, Dan guffawed.

Fionna laughed with him. "This just proves that I am extremely talented."

"Yeah, I'm gonna need you to take that off before we go home." He tried to ignore the guys' hysterical laughter.

Emily seemed to find everything hilarious. Rainer shook his head at her.

"I only popped one," she fussed just before cracking up again.

"Uh-huh, I think we need to get you home, baby."

She blinked several times in an effort to get Rainer to come into focus.

"We're gonna come back tomorrow and clean up," she assured Fionna.

"We'll be here, but you don't have to come too early. I'm not sure you'll feel up to that."

Brooke gave Will a look that said she had plans for him that evening. Will looked extremely pleased as he took her hand and guided her out to their car.

McCoy gallantly volunteered to drop off the ladies who needed rides.

Dan pulled him to the side. "Do not do anything I would fire you for," he commanded. "Nothing any of them would regret later. You got that?"

McCoy nodded. "Sir, I was joking about which ones of them were available. I swear. I'd never. I'm a Shield."

"Good man."

Dan, Rainer, Will, Logan, and several of the Angels carried Emily's presents out to the Hummer. Everyone who stayed to help agreed to be back in the morning to clean up.

"Okay, Chief Vindico, I only had two glasses of wine, one shot, and lots and lots to eat," Fionna declared as Dan opened the passenger door on the Ferrari for her.

"Is that so?" Dan studied her as he settled into the driver's seat. She didn't seem to be anything more than buzzed. Her rhythms were slightly more relaxed than they normally ran. They were pulsing with more heat, but that was the only noticeable difference. "And what do you want, baby doll?" He watched her eyes flash in excitement.

She gave him a ravenous, lust-filled grin as she grabbed his crotch. She massaged it heatedly. He moaned as he guided her mouth toward his.

"Tell me, honey. Tell me what you want." He let his other hand trace under the short skirt she was wearing. He turned his head and mated their mouths again.

She'd lost just a little bit of her inhibition. He realized she was no longer timid or afraid to tell him what she wanted or how she wanted it. His mind spun and his rhythms leapt in the excitement of what he could learn.

"Tell me all the dirty things you want to do to me and then feel how wet you make me," she commanded.

To illustrate her desire, she edged her skirt up high and revealed the fact that she was wearing nothing underneath. Dan growled. His heart slammed against his rib cage as he slid his hand to her inner thigh, barely touching her slit with his fingertips. She writhed in his car in the parking deck with no one else around.

"I might just pull you over here, spread your legs over my lap, and make you take it hard and rough. Make you ride me while those gorgeous tits bounce in my face, baby doll." His cock throbbed eagerly for her. She cried out as he slipped his fingers inside of her forcefully.

"Yes." Her eyes flashed in heated desire. She spread her legs farther and gave him a look that set him on fire.

"More," she demanded.

"So wet. Always such a good girl for me." He pushed deeper, desperate to feel her walls closing in on him. Greed filled his mind. What she was offering and what he planned on taking cinched his muscles.

Dan's entire body was hot-wired and thrumming to feel her wild and free, telling him and showing him exactly what she wanted.

"Take me home," she ordered.

Dan pulled his hand away.

"Taste it," she commanded. Her eyes were full of fire and a storm of rebellious passion.

"Oh baby, I planned to. Sweetest damn thing I've ever had in my mouth." Dan placed his fingers in his mouth and sucked the creamy nectar from them. Her breaths sped.

He cranked the car and harnessed the engines. He could have her home in mere minutes.

His mind was full of her and what he planned on learning while she was so freely giving away the delicious hidden secrets of her sexuality. The garden she allowed him to harvest from but was reluctant to discuss. The fantasies and deep desires she kept tucked away safely, even from herself.

Suddenly, Fionna reached and popped the snap on Dan's jeans. She lowered the zipper.

His mind scrambled. He feebly tried to remember why he should stop her.

"I want to suck you," she cooed. He shuddered from need acute to the point of pain.

She leaned across the center console, pushed his jeans down enough to get what she wanted, and then she dragged her tongue up his stiff, throbbing length.

While forcing himself to keep the car on the road, Dan groaned as she engulfed him in the wet, fiery heat of her mouth. Her tongue licked his ridge and his entire body tensed in need.

He managed to steer the car into the garage before turning it off as she lifted her head. A thundering groan echoed from him as he began stripping her in their garage.

"Yes," she kept up her orders, "I want you to lose control. I want you to take me hard. Bite me, suck me, mark me, make me beg. Punish me. Then bury your cock so deep inside of me I can feel it every time I move tomorrow. Dominate me, and tell me how good it feels. Make me know that I'm all yours."

Gasping for breath, Dan's eyes goggled as he tried not to lose it all before he'd even begun to follow her commands.

"Go get in my bed right now. You keep your legs spread and your ass and that wet pussy up and open for me. I'm gonna watch you touch yourself. You're gonna show me like my good girl. You're gonna bring yourself all for me. You lie there and start with your clit and then work your way back. You're gonna show me every single way you can come. Then I'm gonna own you. Flip you over, open you wide, and fuck you so hard you can't walk and don't remember how to say anything but yes, sir."

Loud, longing moans mewled from her as she flung open the car door and moved up the stairs. Her clothes hung off her in an erotic show all for him.

Dan was hot on her trail. His single-minded focus consumed him as his entire body reverberated with white-hot devotion. He melted down in the ecstasy of her desires.

CHAPTER 18

KEEP IT DOWN

RAINER LAWSON

"I'm really not that drunk," Emily insisted for the third time in five minutes.

"Uh-huh, how many times have you told me that?" Rainer chuckled.

Emily was walking on her own and talking coherently. She grabbed a Dr Pepper on her way by the fridge. "My mouth tastes like liquor and rubber balloons." She grimaced as Rainer followed her into their bedroom.

"You know, I could have told everyone how skilled you are with your tongue. You didn't have to suck balloons."

"Will you take a shower with me?"

"I'd never turn that down, baby." He followed her into their bathroom.

She gave him his favorite mischievous grin as she stripped for him, showing off the leopard print bra and G-string that was his favorite.

Emily moved to him, wrapping her arms around his shoulders. "And will you let me show off my skills?"

His jeans tightened as he slipped his hands under the tiny elastic strings holding her panties to her backside. "That depends on how much you had." He was not taking advantage of her. If they did anything at all, he had to know she was going to remember it in the morning.

She rolled her eyes. "Rainer, I'm fine. I learned my lesson. I didn't have that much. Please, I've been thinking about you all night."

She knew him well enough to know his objections, so she added, "Plus, how could you possibly take advantage of me? We've been together since I was four, and you're marrying me in a few weeks. And you're a Shield."

Her ability to reason reassured Rainer much more than her points. The war in his mind waged on, and he decided that he needed more data. "Let's see how you feel after our shower." He gauged her reaction.

She gave him an extremely sexy pout. "But I want to do it in the shower."

To coax the ardent temptation she offered so deliciously, Emily ran her hands down his chest and then spun her fingers over his burgeoning erection.

Rainer gave in. She was too much, too beautiful. He wanted her too badly. He simply wasn't strong enough to fight her desires.

He placed his hand over hers and forced her to grab him as he reached and popped the clasp of her bra. He watched her breasts spill forward.

"Yes," she moaned. He lifted their weight and leaned in. He spun his tongue around her left nipple and listened to her moans grow desperate. Her head fell back as she hoisted them in his face.

Knowing what she wanted, Rainer pulsed in her hands as he slowly teased her areolas with his tongue until they darkened against her alabaster skin. Then he sucked her fervently.

"You're sure you're all right?" he forced himself to ask again.

"I'm fine. Just take me."

He'd been tense and curious most of the night. Standing at half-mast long enough to ache. His mind had done nothing but wonder what she was receiving and what could be done with it.

His body began to vibrate in his need. Rainer pulled away from her. "Do you need me to cast you, sweetheart? Because I'm about to put you in that shower and take you hard." He listened to her sweet, breathy moans.

"I did it before I left. I want you," she whimpered in her desperate desire.

Rainer hoisted the panties off her and pulled off everything he was wearing as he guided her into the bathroom. He turned on the water and heated it with his hand.

After spinning her into the pouring water, Rainer stepped in behind her. He watched the water spill over her luscious curves with a hungry groan. It separated at her peaked nipples and flowed down over her crotch in a dizzying stream that his hands longed to follow. His cock jerked in anticipation.

"You are gorgeous." He watched her pleading eyes darken in her yearning desire. "Turn around for me, baby."

A shiver quaked through her body. She spun, placed her hands on the tiled wall, and looked back at him as she pushed her backside out and swept her hips side to side, brushing his strain with each pass.

A deep thundering moan echoed around the tiled bathroom as Rainer lathered his hands. He washed away the remnants of the party and anything that wasn't a part of the two of them together. They needed to exist as one without any intrusions.

He coaxed her legs apart with his knee and then tenderly dipped his fingers between her pulsing folds. She was swollen, slick, and fevered. She had been thinking about him. She trembled and writhed between Rainer and the wall.

"Does that feel good, baby?" he drawled in her ear as she cried out for him.

The drinks she'd consumed had her relaxed, and it seemed the party had all of her thoughts on what she wanted from him. It didn't take much for him to push her over the edge.

Her energy spun in tantric twists, but they weren't as tight as he'd become accustomed to them being as she unfurled around him. She was relaxed and longing to be cared for.

"You ready, baby?" He was desperate to feel her clench tightly around him, for her to nurse away the hungry ache he'd carried all night.

"Yes." She arched her back and pushed what she wanted filled against him. She rubbed herself over his slick cock.

Rainer grasped her waist and penetrated her. She gasped and moaned her ardent approval.

"Is that what you wanted, sweetheart? Is that what you've been thinking about?" he demanded as he listened to her moans of ecstasy.

"Yes," she panted, "it feels so good. Harder, more," she begged as he groaned in elation.

He gently eased her shoulders farther forward and filled her. He drove her harder, pounding against her, burying himself deeper with each pass.

She swelled suddenly as her breath stuttered. Her entire body tensed and rolled.

"I'm gonna…" she warned, but the climax stole her breath entirely.

"I know, baby. I feel it," he assured her. "You need to come with me," he commanded as she broke hard, and with a final, ragged, driving thrust he buried himself to his hilt and exploded inside of her.

She writhed around him, gasping for breath. Rainer eased out of her and cradled her tenderly.

"Geez! Would you two keep it down!" Logan banged on the bathroom wall, which was the same wall as his and Adeline's bedroom.

Emily cringed into Rainer's chest.

"Em, baby, we have to move." He assumed afterglow wasn't necessarily the ideal time to discuss this, but it seemed necessary after what had just happened.

"I know," she agreed as he began washing away all that he'd done.

A little while later, Emily dried her hair and crawled into bed, curling up on Rainer's chest.

"I really do love Fionna's house, and that was an amazing price they offered us."

"Yeah, well, they want to get rid of it, and they can't put it on the market because then people will know she's moved."

"Do you think it's too small?"

"It's a lot bigger than this house."

"I know, but you have all of this money, and I feel like if it weren't for me you'd build something you wanted with ten garages or something."

Rainer chuckled and brushed a kiss against her soft, warm hair.

"Baby, I don't need ten garages. All I need is you. If you're there, I'm good. And you loved all the upgrades she'd done in the kitchen. It has two extra bedrooms if the twins or the new baby want to come over and spend the night."

"I've never lived anywhere but here on the farm," she whispered in the darkness.

"I know, sweetheart, but I kind of think we need a place for us to start our lives together, maybe just a little bit away from your family."

"It is really close to the arena, and you could use that room off the living room for an office. And maybe in a few years, when we decide to start a family, we could build a bigger house with garages for all of your cars."

"We can do whatever you want, but I think we need to find something soon because in just a few weeks you're going to be Mrs. Lawson." His energy soared as he considered that fact.

She felt it too. She was now full of his energy, potent from his release.

"I can't wait. I'm just a little nervous about moving."

His heart ached for her. Rainer cradled her tenderly. His sweet baby was scared and that killed him. He had to prove to her that he would take care of her, that he would be what her father had always been for her mother and all of his kids.

They needed to move away for the two of them, for their relationship. They needed to make it on their own, and he was desperate to prove himself.

CHAPTER 19
UNAWARE

Emily had a slight headache the next morning. After supplying her with pain medication, Rainer fixed eggs and sausage links. She felt much better after she'd eaten.

Adeline had to work and apologized for not being able to help clean up at the arena. Rainer and Emily assured her that it was fine. They would get everything done.

When they entered the long corridor leading to the ballroom, Fionna was standing with Dan. They were leaned up against a wall waiting on Chloe to arrive with the interior keys.

Fionna was cradled in Dan's arms with her face pressed against his neck. He was whispering something to her, and his hands continually roved over her back.

It was odd. Rainer and Emily slowed their progress toward them. Dan was always so cautious with her. He never allowed anyone to see them together, but that morning he seemed unaware that anything existed outside of the two of them.

He tenderly rubbed his right hand up to the nape of her neck and nestled the back of her head in his massive hand. With his left, he kept her tucked against his body. She nodded her head slightly, and he continued whispering.

His shield was pulsing hungrily under his hands but hadn't

surrounded her. Rainer assumed they were simply cuddling, but Vindico's shield seemed desperate to protect her though nothing appeared to be wrong. It pulled toward her constantly. Everything about his boss nurtured Fionna. The softer side of Dan Vindico was quite a change.

An uncomfortable half smile creased Emily's features. She didn't seem to know if she should speak. It was very unlike Fionna to ignore them. She was always so kind and polite, but today she seemed unwilling to lift her head or acknowledge their arrival at all. Everything about her was homed in on Dan alone.

A few minutes later, Chloe arrived. She looked rather bedraggled. Most of the Angels trooped into the ballroom. Rainer's eyes goggled as he took in the disastrous display.

"You were aware that women are much dirtier than we typically are, right?" Dan laughed, but he kept his hands on Fionna. He moved with her almost symbiotically.

All Rainer could manage was a nod as his eyes roved over numerous pairs of white panties strung on a clothesline, all with instructions written on them from all of Emily's party guests.

Harder was written on several pairs, along with *Lick me here,* and one pair had *Spank me* written on the back.

"Wow." Rainer tried to steady his breath. He noted cucumbers lying all over the room, most of them encased in broken condoms. Whipped cream was stuck to the tables and floor. An inflatable doll with stickers of lips all over it was slumped over in one corner.

"You don't have to stay. We can clean up." Emily's face blended in perfectly with her long auburn hair.

"No, it's fine. I'll help," Rainer assured her.

A black bag was slung near one of the punch bowls with vibrantly colored vibrators spilling out of it.

"Hey, Em, we have a few of the ring pops left over. Do you want them?" Chloe called as she began boxing up leftover party favors.

Emily laughed. "Uh, I'm going to go with no on that."

Rainer discovered that the ring pops Emily's friends had gotten for the party were penis-shaped.

"Aww, Phil went soft," Sasha teased. The girls began giggling as she finished deflating the blow up doll.

Dan and Rainer shook their heads and shared a slight shudder.

With a discreet eye roll, Dan popped the clotheslines down and wound them up, complete with the bra and panties. "Did you want your instructions, or do you think you have it down?" he joked as he threw the wad in one of the trash cans.

"I've got it." Rainer tried to relax and find something to do. As most of the items from the party ended up in the trash, a couple of hours later, the ballroom was restored to its previous pristine state.

Rainer and Emily had decided the night before to accept the price Dan and Fionna had offered on her bungalow in Alexandria.

Eager to discuss the closing on the house while Emily was excited about it, Rainer asked Dan if they'd like to go get some lunch.

"We could go to Lesco's, and Fionna and I could sit together. Sort of like we went out and friends of ours tagged along," Emily strategized.

Fionna's eyes sought Dan's. Concern plagued her features.

"Absolutely not." His terse growl at Emily's plan had Rainer's back up, but he knew better than engaging in a verbal sparring match with his boss. "If we want to discuss this now, we can go to Fi's old house, our house, the office, the farm, but no one will see us together in public."

Fionna nodded, but she tried to soften the blow. "Yeah, it's not a good idea. Why don't we just go by my old house? It's just five minutes from here." With that she returned to her earlier position, lying on Dan's shoulder with his arms wrapped around her. His shield pulsed much more vehemently this time as he drew her into his body.

Rainer couldn't quite figure out what was going on with either of them. Previously, Fionna seemed to find his obsessive insistence that they never be seen in public together a little over-the-top. Now, she was completely on board.

"You should really buy it under an alias," Dan explained as Fionna unlocked the door to what would become the Lawson's first house.

"Yeah, that's what I thought too," Rainer agreed. Emily shivered. The house was freezing. Rainer guided her to his chest and pushed heat out through his shield. Dan performed the same move with Fionna while reaching to turn up the heat. "And we're planning on paying cash so there shouldn't be a paper trail," Rainer continued the conversation.

"That should give you some relief from the press hopefully," Vindico offered.

As the cozy house warmed, they discussed all of the logistics. Fionna and Emily discussed decorating options and whether or not Rainer and Emily wanted to purchase any of the furniture Fionna hadn't taken when she'd moved to Dan's house.

Eventually, talk of the house bled into Valentine's Day plans. Dan was apparently taking Fionna off somewhere, but it was a surprise. Emily offered a few guesses, but he gave nothing away.

Glancing at his watch, Rainer grimaced. "We better go, baby. We're supposed to watch the twins this afternoon."

"Oh, you should come by just for a few minutes. It would mean so much to Mom…and to Keaton," Emily extended the invitation with a chuckle.

Fionna raised her eyebrows hopefully as she and Dan had a silent conversation.

"If you want to." He didn't seem too thrilled with the plan, but he obviously wasn't going to tell Fionna no.

They pulled into the barn behind Rainer and Emily. The governor and Connor had the twins bundled up outside on the swing set.

As soon as Keaton spied Fionna, he began kicking his legs wildly until Connor relieved the swing of his weight.

"Ni-on-na!" He sprinted toward her. Fionna lifted him up into her arms, and Keaton hugged her fiercely.

"Hey, little man."

"Hi." Keaton batted his long eyelashes at her.

Everyone laughed as she brushed a sweet kiss on his cheek.

He slapped his hand over his cheek with exuberance in effort to protect the kiss.

"Is that what Daniel does when you kiss him too, sweet girl?" the governor teased as he made his way to the new arrivals.

"Nah, I do something a little different." Dan laughed.

Upon seeing the Hummer pull in, Nana called from the side porch, "Emily, I just finished taking in the waistline on your gown. I was hoping you'd stop by. Would Fionna mind helping you try it on again, and I've got her gown finished as well."

Emily looked thrilled as Fionna nodded her agreement. "I'm going to go help Emily okay?" Fionna explained to Keaton. "You play with Dan and Rainer, and we'll be back in a few minutes."

"No!" Keaton shook his head back and forth.

"Come here, son." The governor lifted his little boy out of Fionna's arms. "Dan might not mind you getting a few kisses, but I think we better let the girls dress on their own."

"No," Keaton shouted defiantly. The governor seemed weary, but gave Keaton a look that had him quieting down.

Keaton turned and extended his hands to Dan. "I help," he requested in a much sweeter tone.

Dan chuckled as he took Keaton from the governor. "How's Mrs. Haydenshire?"

Connor released Henry from his swing and walked with him toward Rainer and Dan.

Henry bounded into Rainer's arms. "Hey buddy." He grinned as he scooped him up.

"Mommy is a-sleeping."

Rainer nodded. "That's good. She needs to rest."

The governor forced a smile. "She's a little better. The medicine seems to be helping, but it makes her tired. I think she feels better when either I'm home or Adeline is with her. I'm not sure how we're going to go on for another five weeks like this, though."

"If Fi and I can do anything to help…" Vindico offered as visible pain hardened the governor's face.

"Thanks. I appreciate it. We may have to take you up on that."

"Just say the word."

"I'd invite you inside, but I was trying to wear them out for their naps." He gestured to the twins.

"We could probably help with that," Rainer volunteered. "Henry, do you and Keaton want to play football?"

Keaton's eyes lit as he nodded and wiggled down from Dan's grasp.

The twins sprinted into the barn and returned, each carrying a football awkwardly.

Dan laughed. "Okay, so how does this work?"

"Come on, Dad. You need to blow off a little steam," Connor urged his father. Connor, Rainer, and Henry squared off against Governor Haydenshire, Dan, and Keaton for a loosely interpreted game of football.

After a half hour of the guys running them up and down the backyard, Keaton stopped with the ball midfield to yawn deeply.

Dan scooped him off the ground and ran Keaton and the ball in for a touchdown. The guys all laughed. Emily and Fionna joined in. They'd come out on the back deck to watch.

"I think it's time for your nap," the governor instructed the twins after he caught his breath.

"I want to take a nap with Ni-on-na," Keaton fussed pitifully.

"Ah, they start so young," Connor teased.

Dan scrubbed Keaton's hair. "Not a bad move though. You know, we're just gonna take a nap. Work the pity aspect."

As soon as they reached the deck, Keaton held his arms up to Fionna insistently.

"Here, let's go get you cleaned up for your nap," she eased as Keaton tucked his head on her shoulder. Emily took Henry and the ladies headed back inside.

"Thanks, girls," the governor called as he went into the kitchen and returned with a cold beer for everyone.

CHAPTER 20

TIMES PAST

"Do I want to know anything at all about my baby girl's shower last night?" the governor seemed pained to ask.

"Probably not, sir." Rainer shook his head.

"I had a feeling." The governor drew a long sip of his beer. "And do we have Valentine's figured out, gentlemen?"

Rainer smiled. "Actually, I'm still working on it. I just got a new idea an hour ago."

Dan smiled and studied the area around him. He seemed to deeply appreciate the peace and security the vast acreage and the high gates of the farm provided.

"Yeah, I rented a really nice chalet up near Deep Creek Lake. It's supposed to be very secluded, no one around for miles. Has a gourmet kitchen, a waterfall in the suite, the works."

Governor Haydenshire and Rainer both noted the excited thrum his voice took on.

"See, sometimes hiding your relationship from the world isn't such a bad thing," the governor pointed out.

"I just hope she likes it."

The governor smiled wryly. "The first Valentine's Day after we married, Will was just a few weeks old, but Lillian's parents told me they'd watch the baby so I could take her camping." He shook his head as he recalled the story. "She didn't want to go, but she would never have said that to me. I couldn't afford to do much else. I took her out to a campsite in Great Falls." He laughed and his face colored slightly. "Now, mind you, it was February in Virginia. It was freezing, and she'd just had a baby six weeks before." He shook his head at his own stupidity.

"I had an ancient red canvas tent. She'd made a big pot of vegetable stew, and I packed embarrassingly cheap wine along with hot chocolate. We were all right for a little while. Let love keep us warm, so to speak. But in the middle of the night, while I tried desperately to keep Lillian from freezing to death, and she tried desperately not to scream at me to take her home, though I definitely deserved it," he sighed, "it started to downpour."

Dan and Rainer both cringed as they envisioned themselves in the same situation.

"When the sun finally came up the next morning, we discovered that the red canvas tent bled all over everything. Our sleeping bags, our clothes, our blankets, and even our skin was red for days. The campsite and my truck looked like a mud pit." He laughed with Dan and Rainer. "But," he drawled with a wry grin, "that November Garrett was born, and that is still one of Lillian's favorite stories to retell. So, I guess it all depends on how you look at things."

"And does Garrett know the story of his conception?" Dan continued to chuckle.

"Are you kidding me? He's our favorite person to tell, especially after all the hell he put us through when he was growing up."

Fionna and Emily returned to the deck. They were both beaming. "That is the most beautiful gown I've ever seen!"

"Thank you." Emily moved to Rainer and he wrapped his arms around her. "I can't believe I get to actually wear it for real soon."

Sudden emotion reddened the governor's eyes. He swallowed harshly as he gazed at Emily. Rainer felt fear and sadness wash over her as she took in her father's emotions.

She pulled away from Rainer and wrapped her arms around her father's neck. "I love you, Daddy."

Governor Haydenshire's eyes closed as he hugged her tight. "I love you too, baby girl, more than you'll ever know."

Fionna blinked back tears as well. She could feel the emotion swirl around her. Dan wrapped her up in his arms and elicited a smile.

Rainer decided they would tell the governor later that they were moving off the farm. He smiled at them both.

Emily pulled away as the governor kissed her forehead. "You're sure you like your dress?" she asked Fionna.

"Are you kidding me? This will be the first time I've been a bridesmaid that I'm actually excited to wear the dress."

"Good! I want my girls to look hot." Everyone laughed as she effectively broke through the sentimental sadness that had set upon the group. "Adeline voted for the bouquets with the ribbon, so you're sure that's the one you like as well?"

"Yes, they're beautiful," Fionna assured her again.

Emily turned to question her father. "But you don't think we should give the twins the actual rings?"

He laughed heartily. "Not unless your goal is to never see them again. Giving your little brothers the wedding bands and turning them loose in our fields would be a recipe for disaster."

"Oh, are they going to carry one of those little pillows with fake ones?" Fionna leapt back in the conversation.

Emily giggled. "Nana and I tried that, but they just kept hitting each other with the pillows. So I think I came up with something better. I'll tell you later."

Fionna grinned broadly as she nodded.

Rainer could feel the excited energy roll off both of the ladies.

"Aww, I want to get married," Fionna admitted wistfully, but then suddenly seemed to realize what she'd just said.

The original version of the Haydenshire smirk lit the governor's face. He stared Vindico down.

Fionna immediately backpedaled. "I mean…not anytime soon or anything. Just at some point…in the future. You know… like a long,

long time from now." She stammered over her words. Terror broadcast from her features.

Rainer stared steadfastly at the ground. He didn't want to give anything away. But Dan chuckled over Fionna's heartfelt declaration and her ensuing panic.

"Hmm." He pulled her back to him and let her hide her face against his chest. "We'll have to see what we can do about that."

Everyone watched stunned disbelief wash over Fionna.

Exhaustion clouded Rainer's mind as he fell into his desk chair.

Logan was on his cell. "Yeah, I was just checking the room for Thursday night. Uh-huh," Logan agreed with whatever the clerk was telling him.

Rainer knew that Logan planned on taking Adeline to the Georgetown Inn for Valentine's. It was probably the most romantic hotel in DC, and Valentine's reservations were nearly impossible to come by.

Logan had worked his Crown Governor's son angle and managed to get one of the nicest suites.

"Nope, that sounds perfect. I really appreciate you accommodating us." The grin on Logan's face let most of the office know his plans for Valentine's Day had less to do with the actual suite and more to do with what he planned to do once they'd arrived.

A minute later, Logan ended the call and dialed another number. "I just wanted to check our reservations for Thursday night," Logan explained again. "By the windows over the water. Great, thanks." Logan ended that call as the governor strode through the Iodex wing toward his office.

"How's Mom?" Logan asked as he set his cell on the desk. A grin formed on the governor's face. "Much better." He sounded thrilled. "Whatever medication and casting schedule Adeline figured out seems to be the key. She was able to get up last night, even have a cup of tea without her blood pressure spiking, and little Abigail's monitoring stayed stable. I'm hoping she'll just continue to improve."

"Good." Logan was genuinely relieved, but then teased, "Because I slept with Keaton's foot in my face most of the night."

The twins had stayed over with Logan, Adeline, Rainer, and Emily the night before in hopes that if they were out of the house Mrs. Haydenshire might calm even more.

Emily had fixed them a pallet on the floor, but the boys decided they would prefer to sleep with Rainer and Logan. Henry had wiggled between Rainer and Emily, shoving Emily off Rainer's chest forcefully and then taking her spot.

Keaton had demanded to sleep with Logan and Adeline by jumping on the mattress and refusing to leave the bed.

The governor laughed heartily. "Just think about that feeling for a good long time before you and Adeline decide to make me a grandpa again."

"Yeah, sleeping through the night sounds really good to me."

"Sleeping through the night," the governor drawled with a goading grin. "Don't think I've done that in the last thirty years or so."

"Sorry," Rainer and Logan offered quickly.

Governor Haydenshire laughed. "I suppose you were worth it."

Rainer hadn't heard the Crown Governor joke so lightheartedly in weeks. He hadn't realized how much he'd missed it.

~DAN VINDICO~

A knock sounded on Dan's door at three Tuesday afternoon. Annoyed with the constant interruptions that day, Dan huffed, "What?"

"Sorry, but we gotta talk." Ryan Tuttle slid into the office and closed the door behind him.

Dan tossed down the pen he'd been abusing for the past ten minutes as he'd watched money be moved from one Interfeci account to another. He'd been planning on shutting one down, but his gut told him to wait. Something else was coming.

"Okay, talk."

Tuttle was an outstanding officer and a hell of a detective. He could find evidence where ten other officers swore none existed. His undercover work was stellar, but he got on Dan's last nerve with his risky stunts and wild lifestyle.

"It's Bridgette. She's acting weird, and Nic is way too comfortable with her. Keeps tipping her higher and higher for dances, walks her to her car, shit like that. I think she's two-timing us. No," Tuttle shook his head, "I know she is. That's how she got the Audi."

"Nic's been at the club?" Momentary panic spiked his blood before he remembered the precautions he'd set up expecting this.

Bridgette knew very little about Iodex. He'd lied to her with ease and been vague every chance he'd gotten. Governor Haydenshire's warning that she'd made up the story of being a Felsink guard's daughter had set him on edge for months though. As long as she kept Iodex supplied with as many facts as she could, he'd keep paying her for spying. Most of what she'd told them had panned out, so he'd kept the paychecks coming. But Nic wasn't supposed to be back in the States for another week. The emails confirmed he'd been spending time in Minsk.

"Yeah, he was there today. I followed him to the O'Ryans'. He checked in on Marlisa then headed back out on his jet. He's probably in Minsk now. But he flew Malicai in with him, and he didn't go back. But, Dan, I'm telling you he's paying her vastly better than we are. She just moved out to Columbia Heights."

Dan drummed his fingers on his desk. "I don't give a shit. Bridgette doesn't really know anything. I should never have gotten her into this anyway."

"You mean you should never have slept with her to get her to spy for us," Tuttle corrected him with a smirk.

Dan shuddered and all but gagged over the truth. "If we can break ties with her, I'm all for it. She doesn't know about Fi. That's all that matters."

Tuttle nodded his understanding. "Do you still want me to keep tabs over there and with her?"

"For a little while. As long as she's safe, that's all we owe her. If she wants to become one of Nic's pets, I can't stop her. He's certainly got enough money to keep her happy as long as she doesn't mind his pesky habit of fucking dozens of women and killing them off when they get on his nerves."

Tuttle stared at him for a long drawn moment. "I don't think I'd wish that on anyone. What the hell is wrong with you?"

If Ryan Tuttle was questioning his morals, maybe he had gone several steps too far. "I'm sorry. I'm just sick to death of this. I could arrest Nic for forging Governor Lawson's custody docs, but I need Pravus and Pendergrath first. I constantly feel like I'm beating my head against a brick wall."

"Maybe lay off a little. That brick wall is fucking you up."

CHAPTER 21

LONG DAY

RAINER LAWSON

By 3:30 Thursday afternoon, everyone sat at their desks logging everything they'd found in another safe house that Mitchell O'Ryan had informed Vindico about. His father was out of prison now, thanks to Mitchell, and he was helping as well. They'd made it appear that he'd been released for good behavior and because his health was declining.

Marlisa, Wretchkinsides's daughter, was still staying with the O'Ryans, so their help was truly at the cost of their own necks.

Rainer yawned. He rubbed his eyes. Vindico had planned the raid with precision. Elite Iodex busted through the front and back doors at three that morning under the cover of darkness.

They'd arrested four relatively low-level members of Interfeci, and then had gone through the house with a fine-tooth comb.

Firearms, vials of altered methamphetamines, about a dozen laptops, and two file cabinets that Vindico had loaded up into the evidence truck had been brought back to Iodex.

Everyone but Dan was lagging. They'd been up since midnight. Vindico looked as if he was being physically rent in two as he watched the clock tick closer and closer to five.

Since it was Valentine's Day, he was well aware that all of his officers would demand to leave on time for the many varied reservations and activities they were participating in with their dates.

That, coupled with the fact that Fionna texted every few minutes, had him on edge. His jaw worked rhythmically as he stood over the men trying to hack into the laptops with Ramier.

Dan had personally shattered the locks on the filing cabinets and was going through every file he found.

Garrett stepped in. "Dan, all of this will be here Monday, and you know we'll tear it up. Fi's over the moon about wherever you're going. Don't do this. Don't decide to leave in the morning instead, or not to go because you could work more and might be a half step closer to bringing him down. If you take down Wretchkinsides but you lose her, it won't matter."

Dan narrowed his eyes in a menacing glare. "We're going tonight. I'll leave in a few fucking minutes. Lay the hell off."

Garrett held up his hands in surrender. "I know you better than you think," he reminded before going back to the filing cabinets.

Rainer glanced at the clock again. He'd requested to leave at four to set up his surprise for Emily and then pick her up from the farmhouse, but he was hesitant to remind Vindico that he needed to go. His temper was already visibly escalating.

Rainer decided that if he completed the task he'd been assigned, maybe his leaving early wouldn't irritate his boss quite so much, so he turned back to the laptop he'd been working on.

Ramier had already broken through the passcode screens, but the information on the laptop appeared to be encrypted. Ramier had written some software to try to break the encryption, but it was slow going.

After rubbing his eyes and blinking several times, Rainer tried to will more energy into the task.

Ten minutes later, the letters and numbers on the screen were swimming.

An annoyed sigh echoed from Vindico. "All right, I want everything we took in gone over slowly and carefully with fresh eyes Monday morning. It's been a long day. Go on. Enjoy your night. I'll lock up and head out as well," he directed to the entire force, though he was still glaring at Garrett.

"Thank you." Logan had his jacket on in record time.

"Yeah, I really appreciate it," Rainer echoed.

"No problem. Enjoy your evenings and your weekends. Do not be late Monday morning."

Everyone assured him that they'd be in bright and early Monday as they began gathering their things.

"Hey, how's your mom doing?" Dan quizzed Garrett suddenly.

He seemed to be pleased with the mood reversal. "Great, actually. Nana and Paps have the twins. Dad's home making her dinner. Her color is much better. Her blood pressure hasn't spiked in nearly a week. The baby's scans look good."

Logan nodded. "Thank goodness. I've barely seen my wife in the past week, not that I don't appreciate what she's doing."

"I'm certain you'll make up for it tonight, little bro."

"That is definitely my plan."

"I've gotta get out of here." Rainer glanced at his watch. "Have fun tonight," he called to everyone as he raced out to the Porsche.

The wind had picked up, and the sky was darkening. It wasn't quite cold enough to snow, and Rainer sincerely hoped a storm wasn't rolling in. Emily hated storms, and he needed tonight to be perfect.

He pulled onto the street with a no outlet sign and pressed the pedal a little harder. He flew into the driveway of their new home. They hadn't signed the papers yet, but when he'd asked Fionna if they could use the house Valentine's night, she'd quickly agreed and had given Rainer all of the keys.

He unlocked the front door and stepped inside. A broad grin spread across his face. He could see it. He could see Emily there curled up on the couch or standing in the kitchen. She would make it home.

After setting the meal he'd picked up on the way on the remaining kitchen table and moving to raise the thermostat, he lit the fireplace and began arranging dozens of candles around the living room.

He spread out the quilts and blankets he'd snuck out of the house the day before. After pouring two glasses of wine and heat casting the fire and candles so that they would remain lit without burning down, Rainer rushed back to the car.

Valentine's being their first night in their first home together seemed perfect. He hoped it would help Emily understand that he wanted to build a home with her and for her and make it a sanctuary for the two of them just like the farm had always been.

~

Dan Vindico

"Are you taking Chloe out tonight?" Dan quizzed Garrett as they walked to the parking deck together. He was still furious with him, but was trying to be pleasant by reminding himself of all that Garrett had done for both him and Fionna.

"Yeah, but she's getting too attached. After tonight, I need a little space."

Dan rolled his eyes as he unlocked the door to the Expedition he'd signed out for his and Fionna's trip. "Do you ever wonder why she's the one you keep going back to? For the last fifteen years or more, you've fucked any woman that would lie still for you and then gone back to her."

"Oh, hell no! Do not go there, man. I don't need to hear it from you too. You sound like the governor and Lillian. Don't forget I'm the one who makes you and Fi possible. Just because Fionna Styler has some kind of nutcrackin' man catcher in that sweet snatch between her legs that you've gotten yourself all tangled up in does not mean that I'm walking that road. You worry about getting yourself married. I am happy as a clam," Garrett spewed derisively.

Dan's jaw clenched tight. He glared at Garrett. "Could you not make up names for any part of the woman I plan on marrying at the first available opportunity, or shall I go ahead and pound you into the ground now?" he growled.

Garrett laughed in his face. "Good luck with that plan, Danny. You and Fi have fun. Tell her I love her, and that I said to make you work for it." He revved his Harley to life and sped away.

Dan climbed into the SUV and tried to will away his irritation. He didn't need relationship advice in front of the whole damn team from Garrett Haydenshire. And he hadn't been caught in some trap Fionna had laid. He was madly in love with her, and not being able to get down on one knee and prove to the world that he was capable of taking care of her for a lifetime was what made him want to pull the endless hours.

As he drove toward home, he began to consider that though there was a dramatic difference in working for revenge and working for love, the differences in his behavior might not be that apparent to people who didn't have access to his head, his heart, or his energy.

CHAPTER 22

THE BEST-LAID PLANS

Dan grinned as he pulled in the driveway. He was genuinely excited to leave work and to take Fionna off for the weekend. If this place was even half as nice as it appeared online, they were going to have one hell of a good time.

He grabbed the folder with the reservation information, the fake ID with the alias he'd used to book the chalet, and his warmest coat. He opened the front door and stepped inside. It looked like snow was heading their way, and he hoped Fionna would find that romantic.

She had numerous duffle and toiletry bags piled on the couch.

"Hey, I'm up here. I'm almost ready," she called from their bedroom.

Dan added the file folder to the pile of bags and took the stairs two at a time.

"You do know we're only going for three days, right?" he teased her as he located her inside of the closet shoving more clothing into an additional bag.

He hooked his finger through the back belt loop of the tight black velvet jeans she was wearing and dragged her to him. "By the way, hey, baby doll, I'm home." He leaned his head around to kiss her heatedly.

She gave him a moan as he released her from the kiss. Her eyes danced and darkened slightly. Her now kiss-swollen mouth formed a sexy grin.

"I do know that we are only going for three days, but since my boyfriend won't tell me where he is taking me, I have to pack for contingencies."

"I told you everything you needed to know, Miss Styler." He patted her bottom and deeply appreciated the way the velvet formed around its sculpted curve.

"I plan on you being naked all weekend and using a tremendous amount of body heat to keep you nice and warm. You don't have to pack anything except maybe a toothbrush."

Fionna shook her head at him. She walked out of the closet, letting her hips sway as she moved. He followed hypnotically.

"And what would you do with me if I were naked for three days straight?"

She spun back and wrapped her arms around his neck.

After giving her the shuddering growl she was after, Dan feathered tender kisses over her cheek and then nipped her earlobe. "First, I'd lay you out and run my hands all over this luscious body." He let his hands return to her backside and squeezed it tight.

Her eyes flashed. She gave him a look that had fire igniting in his groin.

"And then what?" Her heated breath caressed his jaw.

"By then I'd be so turned on I'd just spin you around and fuck you hard from behind. Slap that sweet ass, baby doll, make you take it all. But, after that, I'd slow it down. Worship that body. Give you a bath, let my tongue and my fingers touch whatever the hell I want until you were begging me for more. Then I'd spread those gorgeous thighs and fuck you nice and slow, and then we could start all over again until you just can't take it anymore."

She was panting from his promises. Her dark eyes locked on his. "Fine, I'm not packing anything but a toothbrush." She waggled her eyebrows.

Dan swatted her backside with much more force this time as she moved away.

She shook it for him and then shot him another mischievous grin.

"Does that mean I shouldn't bring the crotchless panties I packed?"

His already burgeoning erection began to throb. Dan's eyes lit. "Throw those in a bag with our toothbrushes, and let's get out of here. I have so many plans for you tonight."

They stopped by Zach and Kara's house on the way to Maryland. He thanked his sister profusely for her help. Dan had paid for everything, but Kara had agreed to grocery shop and prepare all of the food for their trip since there weren't any restaurants or stores near the chalet.

She and Zach were dressed up and heading to Citronelle, the restaurant where Zach had proposed on Valentine's Day several years before.

Dan and Fionna wished them a Happy Valentine's and thanked Kara again for her work before loading the food in the back of the Expedition and continuing on their journey.

Logan Haydenshire

"You're sure you'll be all right?" Adeline asked Logan's mother for the tenth time.

Logan ground his teeth. "She's so much better. Look at her. You're a miracle worker. Now, let's go, or we're going to miss our reservation."

"I really do feel much better, sweetheart. You and Logan go enjoy your first Valentine's Day as a married couple. I promise we will call if we need anything," Mrs. Haydenshire assured her.

"I'll take care of her. Don't worry," the governor added.

Logan noted that his father seemed to want Logan and Adeline to leave as badly as he wanted to get out of there.

His parents certainly couldn't have sex given the extreme complications of the pregnancy, but they seemed eager to spend Valentine's alone together.

"All right, but call me if anything changes," Adeline ordered.

"I promise." Governor Haydenshire held the door open for them. He all but tapped his foot impatiently.

Logan guided her toward the truck, waved to his parents, and secured her inside of it, lest she decide she needed to run one more test before they left.

"I really am excited about tonight. I'm just worried about her," Adeline apologized as soon as Logan was inside the truck cab.

"I know, baby, but she looks so much better. The baby's scans have been good all week. So tonight, I just want it to be you and me. No Iodex, no baby, no Mom, no Lucas—nothing but us, please."

Adeline nodded. "What are we going to do after dinner?"

Logan chuckled at her adorable attempt at engaging him in a little bit of dirty flirting. "That depends on what you want to do." He reached and squeezed her thigh before sliding his hand higher up the skirt of her dress.

"Mmm, that." She gestured her head to his hand.

She was definitely the cutest thing he'd ever seen. "You want me to rub your leg all night, baby?" He couldn't help but enjoy the slight embarrassment that bloomed across her cheeks.

"I want you to rub other things too," she informed him with just a little bit of sass that drove Logan wild.

"Good," he groaned. "Because we have a lot of time to make up for, and I plan on rubbing a whole lot more than your legs."

Her breaths quickened, and she let her bottom lip slip through her teeth. Her onyx eyes danced. He considered skipping the restaurant altogether and taking her on to the hotel. There were numerous things he wanted to lick and suck and taste, but none of them were on a menu at a restaurant.

~

Rainer Lawson

"What are we doing here?" Emily quizzed, but she didn't sound annoyed. She sounded thrilled.

"You'll see." He opened the passenger side door for her and led her up the walkway. He unlocked the front door and moved to let her enter ahead of him.

She gasped. Her hands flew to her mouth.

"Happy Valentine's Day, baby, and welcome home." He watched her eyes dance in the candlelight.

"Oh my gosh! This is perfect." She hugged him fiercely.

"I'm glad you like it because I really wanted our only Valentine's Day as an engaged couple to be perfect. And I wanted tonight to be our first night in our new house." He guided her farther inside, handed her one of the glasses of wine, and gestured for her to sit down on the quilts with him.

"We're staying all night?" The fire danced in her eyes. Its warm glow was not only coming from the hearth but from deep within her.

"That's up to you. We can have dinner here, hang out for a while, then go home, or we can sleep here." She beamed at him and settled on the blankets beside him. Rainer opened the boxes of food he'd had prepared for their picnic.

"I really want to stay, but I really don't want to do it in Fionna's bed. She and Dan probably got it on there a million times." She wrinkled her nose.

Rainer laughed. "Yeah, me either. That's why I packed those." He pointed to the stacks of sleeping bags and the air mattress he'd borrowed from the Haydenshires' barn.

"We're going to camp out in front of the fire?" Emily's reactions to his plans couldn't have been more perfect. He loved that it was always the little things, the smallest gestures that brought her the most happiness. He could've rented her the penthouse at the Four Seasons, but it wouldn't have delighted her as much as this.

"Whatever makes you keep smiling at me like that."

"You are amazing."

Rainer shook his head. "Eat, baby, because I've been thinking about you since I busted down a door at three this morning. For hours, all I've wanted was you all alone here. I'm starting to lose it."

Her eyes flashed in desire.

CHAPTER 23

NAVIGATIONS

DAN VINDICO

Dan took the 95 split and settled in to continue their trek out into the forests of Maryland. Fionna watched as the city lights and sounds began to fade away. They were replaced by trees and homes scattered along their route.

"Please tell me we're not going camping," she panicked suddenly.

Dan laughed and shook his head. "I think I know you better than that."

"Not that camping with you would be a bad thing." She cringed.

"I spent enough nights of my childhood and adolescence sleeping on the cold, hard ground on the Haydenshires' farm to cure me of any desire to freeze my ass off ever again. And my goal is to get you to take your clothes off, not to make you bundle up while you sit outside thinking that I'm the worst boyfriend ever."

Fionna grinned. Relief eased her rhythms. "I would never think that. I'm just more of a heating, air conditioning, hair dryer, indoor plumbing kind of girl."

Dan lifted her hand and brushed a kiss across one of the dips between her knuckles. "I'm well aware, honey. Believe me, I'm all about running water, a roof over my head, and you curled up nice and hot in my bed."

Fionna beamed and seemed to settle into their trip. Her phone chirped, and she pulled it from her purse. She laughed and shook her head. "Garrett says for me to make you work for it. That I've been giving it up too easily."

Dan rolled his eyes. "Tell him to go play with Chloe, and that I said to go to hell."

"No, I know how to take care of Garrett."

She texted back her reply with a heavy smirk as she sent it away.

"What'd you say?" Dan watched for the signs for the gorge.

"That guys who are hung like a horse and can go all night don't have to work as hard for it. Then I told him how sorry I was that he didn't understand."

Dan laughed. "That wasn't nice, Miss Styler."

"He knows I'm teasing."

Garrett texted back a moment later and informed Fionna that if she'd like to see what she was missing out on he'd take her for a long ride, and Dan decided that her reply probably wasn't mean enough.

He turned off the highway and began the twisting two-lane roads that led farther away from city life. Fionna checked the map on his phone for him as he navigated the narrowing roads. They watched light, fluffy snow gather on the pine trees and melt on the blacktop.

After turning around once, Dan pulled beside a small, brown, shack-like building that was the check-in for the chalets. He leaned and pulled the fake license he'd created from the file folder.

He placed it in his wallet. "I'm gonna cast the car, so don't get out, okay?"

Fionna nodded. She was studying the area through the dark.

"I'll be right back." He leaned and kissed her cheek before sliding out of the Expedition into the freezing night air. He immediately casted the car in his shield and added heat to keep her warm.

She blew him a kiss and then summoned to light one of the interior lights. She began flipping through a magazine she'd brought along. Dan jogged inside, pulled open the clapboard door, and brushed the snow off his coat before smiling at the elderly couple seated near the fire.

"You must be Mr. Mueller?" the woman inside soothed as she moved behind a small desk. Her sweet smile smoothed a few of the wrinkles on her kind face.

"Yes, ma'am." Dan always felt guilty for giving an alias to anyone who wasn't either a criminal or involved in law enforcement in any way. He pulled his wallet from his pocket, slipped the fake ID out, and handed it to her. He'd already paid via his credit card over the phone which made hiding his identity much easier.

"That's fine, dear." She patted his hand, not really looking at the license. "Now where's your lovely bride?" She began gathering brochures and placing them in a small basket.

"Oh." Dan knew he'd made the reservations for two, but he hadn't referred to Fionna as his wife. "She's in the car. I didn't want her to get cold." He decided not to correct the woman.

Dan glanced at the man seated in a rocking chair near the small fireplace. He appeared to be dozing.

The woman sighed. "When we were your age, we used to stay out late dancing the night away. Now, he's asleep as soon as he sits down after his supper."

Dan chuckled politely. "He must just be content."

She gave Dan another warm smile and handed him the basket that contained the keys and map to the chalet he'd rented, along with brochures for things to do all the way back down the mountain.

She'd added a bottle of wine and a baguette. "Well, there is something to be said for contentment, but try to enjoy every moment you have. They go away so quickly. We never know when the people we love won't be with us anymore."

Dan's jaw clenched. Dammit, not tonight. He wasn't going there. Amelia was long gone. He'd somehow been given a second chance at love and at life. He just had to keep her safe.

"Have a lovely Valentine's. Make good memories. Let her know how much you appreciate her. She'll carry those with her when you're asleep by the fire in your rocking chair on Valentine's night a few years from now." She laughed.

"Thank you, I will." Dan offered her a wave and sincerely hoped that at some point in the next few hours her husband would wake up and celebrate Valentine's Day with his wife.

After releasing the cast on the car, Dan crawled in and began studying the map to the chalet. Each cabin was situated off the main road along a different lane. The cabins were spaced several miles apart to offer the renters complete privacy.

Snow continued to fall, but it remained off the cement lanes. It created a picturesque scene on the moonlit trees.

Fionna leaned and nuzzled her head near his neck. She inhaled deeply.

Dan kissed her cheek. "Are you okay, baby doll?"

"You smell like a fire and your cologne, all masculine and yummy. It makes me want you really bad," she teased with a twinkle in her eye.

Dan reached and squeezed her thigh. "Believe me, the feeling is mutual. I'll see if I can't take care of all of those wants when we find our chalet."

With one more glance at the map, Dan took the last turn and drove up a long one-lane road.

"Here it is." He parked the Expedition next to a two-story chalet.

Fionna smirked. "Well, it's certainly secluded, Mr. Alexander Mueller," she sassed before cracking herself up.

She was adorable. Dan joined in her laughter as they exited the Expedition. "Saw that, did you?"

"Yes." She nodded. "Now is that the name I should call out when you drive me wild, or is Dan still all right?"

He opened the back of the SUV and gathered up the many varied bags she'd packed. "The lady who took the reservation apparently believes that you are Mrs. Mueller, so does that mean I get to call you my old lady?"

Fionna grabbed some of the food and headed up the walkway toward the front door. He saw her bend over as he leaned to gather the rest as well.

Suddenly, a loosely formed snowball slapped his backside with a thwack. It soaked his jeans. Fionna cracked up as she shot him a look that dared him to retaliate.

"Careful there, baby doll. Don't get in over your head."

With a knowing laugh, Fionna waited on him to unlock the door. "You won't throw a snowball at me."

"Oh, really?"

"Yes, really, because I'm your girl and you're a perfect gentleman," she informed him smugly. "Until I get you between the sheets."

Dan turned the key in the lock and chuckled at her assessment. He stepped back and let Fionna enter ahead of him. As she went by, he swatted her backside much harder than he normally would have. "Behave, Ms. Styler. You never know what I might do."

"Yum, do it again," she sassed as he followed her in the house.

Dan set the boxes and bags in the entryway and gave her a longing growl before he returned to the car for the last few items.

After setting them down, he gave Fionna a hungry grin. "Come here to me."

She narrowed her eyes. She'd figured out that he was up to something, so she moved to him cautiously. He grabbed her waist and jerked her the rest of the way. He slipped his hands up the wool sweater she was wearing, and pressed his massive, freezing-cold hands against her back. He'd run them through the snow on his way back inside.

She shrieked and tried to wiggle away, while laughing. He tickled her as she continued to try and escape. He kept her trapped with ease.

"Your hands are freezing!" She stamped her feet making him laugh.

"I know."

"Let go of me!"

"Never!" He didn't let go of her, but he did summon heat from the room and soothe what he'd done.

She giggled and settled down to let him warm her back up. He scooped her up and carried her to the large sectional sofa in the middle of the cozy living room. The chalet did have rustic décor, but the amenities were quite nice.

"Can I ask you something?" She folded her body up against his and nuzzled her face between his shoulder and neck again.

"In just a minute, you can ask me anything you want. Right after I do this." He tracked one hand out from under her sweater and used it to cradle her face. He leaned and guided her mouth to his.

He kissed her slowly, hesitantly, with a sinful pressure that spoke volumes as to his plans for their evening. He licked the perfect curve of her cupid's bow and then devoured her luscious lips. He threaded the hand that was on her cheek through her hair and leaned her back. He let his other hand cup her backside.

He pulled her closer as he began slowly consuming her. He dipped his tongue between her lips as she let them fall open for him.

With a great deal of that sexy grace she had, she leaned up and straddled her legs on either side of his so she could grind against him.

A hungry groan, low and rumbling, echoed from his lungs. His right hand reached down the back of those jeans that made him ache every time he caught a glimpse of her ass. He grasped her backside firmly and began guiding her hips in a rhythmic dance around his rapidly hardening length.

She sucked his tongue and let her hand trail down his open jacket, then she traced her fingers up his zipper line. But something else had distracted Dan.

He felt the delicate lace on the panties, but there were metal clasps running along the center of her lush cheeks. His mind spun as he continued to explore. He pushed his hands lower and found a silky crotch. The clasps extended all the way to her opening. His cock threatened to unzip his jeans itself. A man could only take so much tempting, and she was sliding her crotch up and down over him.

He moved his hands back to the top of the panties and confirmed his theory. Hook and eye closures, similar to what might be on a bra, joined the panties together.

She pulled away with a sexy grin that said she was eager for him to release her in every possible way.

"Have I mentioned how much I love your lingerie?" His voice was strained. He was on a ragged edge, and she knew it.

"Happy Valentine's Day." She leaned in for another slow, sensuous kiss. Her eyes were at half-mast, hungry and dark. But, after another taste of his lips, she pulled away and laid her head on his shoulder.

His heart thundered in his rib cage, and he forced himself to slow.

He cradled her to him, feeling her warmth and her tender healing spread through him as he held her. Contentment soothed her soul as she let him wrap her body up in his.

"What did you want to ask me, baby doll?" he gently reminded her.

She smiled against him and giggled. "I don't remember."

CHAPTER 24

CONVERSATIONS

Dan was delighted. He squeezed her tight, still trying to imagine what her delectable ass would look like in the panties he'd just run his hands all over.

"Okay, do you wanna look around and see if you remember?"

"Yeah, let's explore." She climbed out of his lap.

"Oh, honey, believe me, I plan to explore those panties in depth." He took her hand, summoned, and lit the lamps around the chalet.

"I was certainly hoping you would. That's why I bought them."

They walked hand in hand into the kitchen. "I'm not sure what you paid for them, but I promise, I'll put them to very good use."

She gave him a broad grin as they traveled back through the cozy living room. Dan lit the gargantuan fireplace with his hand. The room took on a soothing glow.

"Is there water running somewhere?" Fionna's brow furrowed.

"Ah." Dan smiled as he led her to the one bedroom in the chalet. He lit the fireplace in the bedroom, which was much smaller than the one in the living room, and pulled back curtains that ran the length of one entire wall to reveal glass doors.

Fionna's mouth fell open as her eyes lit excitedly. Dan slid one of the doors open, and they stepped out into an enclosed sunroom that contained a small, heated, stone swimming pool. One side of the pool consisted of a small waterfall. There was a cozy nook behind the falls constructed of stone as well.

"Wow," she gasped, furthering his delight. "This is amazing!"

"I think you're pretty amazing."

She wound her arms around his neck. "Did you know I have a waterfall fantasy, Chief Vindico?"

Certain his jeans were never going to become comfortable again, Dan panted. "Is that so?" He braced her backside in his hand again, making certain she felt what she was causing. "If you'll tell me your fantasies, I'll do my best to make them all come true." His voice was low. His entire body ached.

"Just feeling how much you love me when we're together is better than any fantasy I could ever have dreamed up."

"Yeah, well, I still want to hear the fantasies. So would you like to play in the waterfall, or would you like to have dinner? Or you could open your present?"

"I thought this was the present." She gestured to the chalet.

Scoffing, Dan shook his head. "This is the house where I get to hold you hostage all alone with me for the next forty-eight hours. This is not the present."

"It sounds like a present to me."

After deciding they were hungry, Dan helped Fionna heat a few of the things Kara had packed. He poured two glasses of red wine and set them on the small glass table in the dining area of the living room.

"I remembered what I was going to ask." She sank her teeth into her bottom lip just the way she did when he was about to send her over.

"What, baby?" he managed to answer without taking his eyes off her lips. "That looks absolutely delicious, by the way."

She smiled. "Your sister made it, not me."

"I wasn't talking about the food." He watched heat creep seductively up her slender neck and settle in her cheeks. "Now what did you want to know?"

"How do you choose your aliases? Do you just pick a name and go with it?"

He grinned at her. "Sometimes you do just have to pick a name if you're having to do it on the fly, but that can be dangerous because you have to remember to answer to that name whenever someone says it, just like you would your real name. So, if I get a chance to create a name, I try to pick something that interests me. That way when I hear it, I'll instantly perk up. Like I did with Mueller. Alexander Mueller is the physicist who figured out how to give the Non-Gifted Realm superconductivity. He gave them the computer chip, and his work has always fascinated me. If I'm going into a situation where it's very unlikely there will be any trouble, I use his name because when I hear it, I immediately pay attention."

∽

Logan Haydenshire

"I'm so sorry, sir. I apologize again for the delay. We're just swamped this evening. You understand," the maître d' pled to Logan for the third time.

Adeline smiled at her kindly as Logan clenched his jaw.

"It's fine," Adeline pledged.

"As soon as the party at your requested table leaves, we'll seat you immediately, and your appetizers will be on the house tonight."

Adeline elbowed him, and Logan forced a half nod. "Thank you. We understand."

As the woman departed, Adeline turned the full force of her pleading eyes on him. "Don't be mad, please."

"I'm certainly not mad at you," Logan assured her.

"I know, but I don't want you to be mad at anyone. It's fine. The food will taste that much better when we get it."

"This is not at all how I saw this night going." It was nearing eight o'clock, and they'd had a seven o'clock reservation.

"But we're here together, and the view is amazing, and your arm is around me, so I think it's perfect."

Logan forced a smile as he kissed her cheek. The fact that his wife was extremely easy to please because she seemed to be perfectly happy with nothing at all didn't help soothe his irritation.

179

He'd wanted this night to be perfect. He wanted to feed her an outstanding meal and take her to a swanky hotel. The past few months had been rough. They'd found her father, faced her mother in court, and then found out that her mother was going through psychological testing and imprisonment. Then Adeline had devoted her life to keeping his mother and the baby as safe and healthy as she could. He'd wanted a night away from it all where he could spoil her rotten, and if he were being perfectly honest he wanted to spend hours locked up in their suite equipped with a vast Jacuzzi tub, a steam shower, and a king-size bed.

He wanted to spend hours making her forget that anything else existed except for the two of them. He'd planned to tediously tend to her every desire and then he wanted to own her.

"What are you thinking about?" She laid her head on his shoulder.

"What I want to do to you when I get you to the hotel."

She trembled against him. Her breath stuttered. It made him ache and did nothing to quell his rapidly building fury at the time they were having to wait.

~

Rainer Lawson

"Do you think it's okay if we look around?"

Rainer watched intently as the tines of the fork left Emily's beautiful lips. They'd been finishing the pieces of pie Rainer had ordered from the deli that had fixed their picnic.

It took him a full minute to remember how to speak. His mind was full of provocative fantasies of him in her mouth being slipped in and out. He drew a ragged breath.

"Sure, baby. We're buying it, and she's moved most everything out she's not planning on selling."

Her grin only proved to seize the breath in his lungs. Rainer helped her up and followed her into the kitchen. He reminded himself that his main goal for the evening was to make her comfortable in their new home, so he tried to push away the thoughts that had been swirling in his mind for most of the day.

His libido had been in overdrive since he'd sat down at his desk with the laptops from the raid that morning. The banality of the work had left his mind free to fantasize. The knowledge that they were going to actually have an entire home, their home, all to themselves had several ideas flowing rapidly through his veins. They pulsed endlessly between his groin, his shield, and his brain.

Emily bit her lip as she took in the kitchen. She switched on one of the burners on the large stove. She reached for a cabinet and turned back to Rainer. "You're sure this is okay? I feel like I'm going through Fionna's house."

"It's our house, baby. Fionna even said if we wanted to start moving stuff in that it was fine. We're supposed to sign the papers next week."

"I know you can't feel it, but this house has really good emotional energy. It feels good here."

"Good." Rainer was even more encouraged. "I'm sure that's part of why she bought it."

Emily pulled open the cabinets and studied them intently, as if the answers to every question plaguing her mind might be hidden in the spice cabinet.

Heat fevered her face as she slowly moved around the kitchen and then into the empty dining room.

"I sort of feel like I'm having this weird dream where I'm twenty, but we're in the loft because I made you play house with me."

He laughed. "I didn't construct this house for you out of toy bins and your play kitchen. And I'm pretty sure none of your brothers will show up and try to destroy it with pinecones and kickballs." She gave him another one of those dazzling, heart-stopping smiles. "It cost a little more than our playhouses did too."

Emily slid to him and laid her head on his shoulder and buried her face in his neck.

He cradled her and tried to push soothing energy into her as he kissed her forehead and eased his hand under the sweater she was wearing. Somehow, his shield knew what his brain had yet to acknowledge. It spilled out of his pores and surrounded her without him summoning.

"I'm scared," she finally admitted in a pained whisper.

"I know, but I'm right here."

She lifted her head. Tears leaked from her eyes, effectively breaking his heart. "I don't know how to do this, and I thought I did. I was so sure. I don't know how to be a wife or how to have a house of my own. What if I do everything wrong? What if I'm a horrible wife, and you don't like being married to me?" She seemed unable to halt the terror as it took word and poured out of her heart.

Rainer soothed, "Hey, listen to me."

She began to sob in earnest as he swayed her back and forth. "Baby, just listen for a minute, please." She shuddered against him. "No one knows how to do this when they first start." He willed her to believe him. "And we're going to mess things up. And there are going to be times that things don't go the way we want them to go. And we're going to get mad at each other and argue. There will be days when everything seems to go wrong just like there are now.

"But I will be here, and I will never leave you or decide that I don't want to fight for us anymore, because you're everything to me. At the end of the day, if I get to crawl into bed with you and hold you close, that's all I'll ever need. I swear to you, as long as you're in this with me, we'll figure it out, and we'll make it work no matter what."

Rainer let her cry, not certain what else to say to shatter through her terror and her grief.

"Come here, sweetheart." He led her to the couch in the living room. Leaning back against one of the corners, he pulled her onto his chest. "You know, there are a lot of things we didn't know what the hell we were doing when we did them, and we eventually got pretty good at them."

A small smile broke through her anguish. "We were terrible at French kissing."

Rainer nodded. "Yeah, we really were, but we're pretty good at it now."

She studied him. Tears glassed her beautiful emerald eyes. "I'm just so scared I'll disappoint you or that someday you're going to realize

I'm the only girl you've ever kissed or you've ever been with, and you'll decide you want to try out someone else for a change," she choked.

Before Rainer could assure her that nothing like that would ever happen, she continued. "And you…you've already done all of this. Only you were only fourteen years old when you had to go and live with"—she shook against him—"with him. And then you had to come and live with us. I keep thinking about that and how scared you felt. Your dad had just died. I'm so sorry. I'm being such a baby."

Rainer shook his head and tried to soothe her so he could get through to her. "I was scared. I mean, I was relieved when your mom and dad took me home from the Senate that night after they'd forced the trial." He wondered if they'd ever really discussed those harrowing hours late in the night.

Rainer had come to school with his right eye swollen shut. A gruesome black and purple bruise marred his entire face. He'd spent the previous night sleeping on the sidewalk outside his uncle's apartment. At that time, Stan had lived out in Braddock, which wasn't too far from the home where Rainer had grown up in Falls Church.

The guidance counselor had immediately pulled Rainer out of class. Logan had demanded to go with him and had stood solidly by Rainer as he managed to explain to the counselor what had happened.

Governor Haydenshire had been called, and both of the Haydenshires had flown to the school. The boys had been taken to Nana and Paps's house for the rest of the school day.

Governor Haydenshire didn't want Stan to know where he'd sent Rainer. He needed to know Rainer was safe while he forced the governing board to meet secretly that night, after the Senate closed.

Exhaustion and terrorizing fear had made Rainer unable to reason, and he hadn't understood at the time why Will and Garrett had come immediately from work and stayed at the Andersons' home with Logan and Rainer.

Nana would try every few hours to heal Rainer's eye, but his shield had just fully developed. He had little to no control over it, and he blocked her out. He was too exhausted and too emotional to attempt to pull it back.

Will and Garrett tried as well, but neither succeeded, and no one had been willing to force Rainer to do anything he didn't want to do.

Already thoroughly embarrassed from showing up to school with a black eye, Rainer had waited until he thought Will, Garrett, and Logan were out of earshot to approach Nana Anderson. "Do you think Emily will come over here after school?" He could still hear his terror-filled, trembling voice as he'd asked.

Tears had pricked her eyes as she'd wrapped him up in a tender embrace. She'd guided him to her kitchen table and plied him with more milk and cookies.

"They're going to get you all fixed up, sweet boy, and we're going to see if we can't just move you right onto the farm so you don't have to be without Emily ever again, okay? Cal picked Emily up from school, and they've taken her and the other boys out to the Vindicos' home. They don't want any of you kids on the farm just yet. Let Stephen get this worked out, and you'll be safe and sound in your bed in your and Logan's room tonight."

Rainer nodded his understanding, but all he recalled feeling was hopeless defeat. Emily wasn't coming, and in that moment of endless confusion she was all he'd wanted.

It was a testament to the gravity of the situation that though Garrett and Logan had overheard Rainer's plea for Emily, neither of them had even entertained the thought of teasing him.

He gazed into Emily's emerald eyes. "I was a mess," he allowed. "They took me to your grandparents' house, and I asked for you." Another round of tears took her over. "Because any time in my entire life that I've been afraid, or felt like life was just too much for me to handle, it's you I want. You make everything in my life better. You're it for me, baby, and I kind of thought that's how you felt about me too."

Emily smiled through her tears once again and wrapped her arms around him. "I do," she vowed.

"You could never ever disappoint me. I'm happy just getting to come home from work to be with you. To know that you're Mrs. Lawson, nothing will ever make me prouder than that. So please, please don't be afraid that you're going to upset me, because if I have you then I don't need anything else."

She drew a shuddered breath. "I'll try to not be so stubborn, and demanding, and pouty if I don't get my way."

Unable to help himself, Rainer cracked up. "Em, baby,"—he shook his head, trying to think of the best way to phrase his response—"you aren't demanding, and I kind of think you're cute when you pout. I fell in love with you, and I want you to be *you*. My sweet, spiteful, sassy, stubborn, red-headed, and my beautiful, caring, brilliant baby. You're all I've ever wanted, and you are all I will ever want. I don't want you to ever change one single thing about you.

"Even with all of that stuff that happened to me, you *are* the only girl I've ever kissed. The only girl I've ever felt up. And my God, the only girl I've ever made love with, and that makes me the luckiest guy on this planet or any other. How did I ever get so lucky to get the girl who's perfect for me on my very first kiss?"

CHAPTER 25

HEAT

LOGAN HAYDENSHIRE

"Thank you." Logan sighed as their main courses were finally set in front of him and Adeline at eight forty-five.

"I'm starving," Adeline confessed as she began twirling her pasta around her fork. He was at least thankful that now, after living with him for the last eight months and being married for almost three, she would admit when she was hungry and let him try to do something about it.

Still infuriated the restaurant had overbooked the tables on Valentine's Day, Logan cut into his steak and stabbed a piece vengefully with his fork.

"I love you," Adeline whispered from across the candlelit table. She effectively rescued Logan from his engulfing irritation. He smiled and drew a deep breath. He reminded himself of all that he had seated across from him.

"I love you too, Mrs. Haydenshire. So much."

"How's your steak?" She studied him as she took another bite of her linguine covered in seafood and cream sauce.

He debated. He didn't want to embarrass her, but his mind wasn't focused on his food. "Not nearly as good as you're gonna taste," he went on with the first thing that popped into his mind when she'd asked about his dinner.

Her eyes flashed and she blushed, but she looked delighted with his assessment.

Logan chuckled and winked at her. A broad grin spread across her face. She looked extremely pleased as she sipped her wine.

They were seated in one of the small round booths that overlooked the Potomac. Still blushing, Adeline glanced around and then she scooted her plate and then her body beside Logan instead of across from him. She looked momentarily afraid she was going to be scolded.

Logan draped his left arm over her shoulders as he continued to eat with his right. "Is the pasta good?"

She nodded, but then hesitantly leaned and brushed a kiss across his cheek before sinking back and picking up her fork. She seemed to be willing resolve and courage from the air around them as she ate.

While wondering what was on her mind, Logan copied her move. He leaned and kissed the side of her head. Her breath caught momentarily. She grinned up at him.

Her eyes caught the light of the candle in the darkened restaurant. The fire reflected in their onyx depths. Her cheeks were flushed the color of a dark pink rose. She took his breath away.

"I am the luckiest guy in this entire restaurant to have you sitting right there beside me. To be married to you," he continued, "and I'm sorry. I don't want to rush you, baby, but my God, I want you. I want to hold you with nothing between us. I want you naked in my arms all night long."

Her energy spiked as she let her eyes close for a long moment. "Let's just go," she finally begged. "Please. You're all I can think about."

Logan signaled the waiter.

~

Dan Vindico

"Let's hear this waterfall fantasy, Ms. Styler." Dan gazed at Fionna as she took another delicate bite of the mousse his sister had prepared for their dessert.

She giggled as she swallowed it down. Her cheeks flushed as she lifted her wine glass gracefully and drew a small sip. "I can't tell you that."

"Please." He'd beg if he had to. She rolled her eyes as her blush grew more pronounced. "Come on," he urged. "Is this a Tarzan and Jane style fantasy, or more of the waterfall in some huge resort where you might get caught because there are other people everywhere? Voyeurism, being dominated, or taken advantage of? Any of the other top ten?" He stated a few of the fantasies he was fairly certain were quite common among most women, two of which he already knew she had.

"Do you just think you have women all figured out?"

"Oh, honey, I would never even pretend to think *that* in a million years."

She wrinkled her nose. "It really isn't all that elaborate. It's more like you and me behind a waterfall, maybe with a little of that being caught thing and a whole lot of that being taken advantage of thing," she admitted sheepishly.

Now we're getting somewhere. Excitement and fervor surged through him. Part of what made him so good at what he did was his dogged drive to find things out, to search and hunt down the tiniest detail that often made a dramatic impact.

Finding out things about Fionna had quickly become his obsession. He smiled at her and hoped if he kept quiet she'd keep talking.

The requests she'd made and her responses to him after the lingerie party had only served to make him all the more avid in discovering her every sexual desire.

"It did start with one waterfall in particular," she offered next.

He nodded and scooped up another bite of the mousse on his plate. He offered her the spoon. "You keep telling me, and I'll feed you for all of the good details I get."

She grinned at the idea of his game. "There's this tiny waterfall near my grandparents' house on Kauai." She licked the spoon seductively. His cock jerked to attention. "It's perfect, secluded and in this tiny spring, but it's deep enough to swim in. The water would probably come up to your chest. Every time I go visit them I always think how romantic it would be to skinny dip. And, you know, maybe hang out for a little while behind the falls."

"I hope you'll take me to see it sometime."

Her eyes lit as she nodded. "I would love for you to come with me to Kauai. It's my favorite place on earth, except maybe anywhere that I'm in your arms."

Dan grinned. "Then I'll make both happen. I'll keep you safe in my arms in Kauai."

Immediately thinking that Hawaii sounded like an excellent honeymoon destination, Dan stood to refill their wine glasses. Fionna's cell rang.

"Who could that be? Everyone knows I'm off with you."

She took the phone from her purse and studied the number quizzically. "It's a DC number." She shrugged and then answered.

Dan returned to the table with the refilled glasses and waited on her before he finished his dessert.

He could barely make out the hesitant greeting and explanation of who was calling as he watched all of the color that had settled in Fionna's cheeks fade away.

"Jared!" She cringed. "Uh…how are you?"

Dan clenched his jaw, not certain what to feel in that moment. Equal parts possessive fury and concern over Fionna's obvious panic rocketed up his spine. She trembled as she sank down on the couch. Her rhythms tensed constantly. "I told you when we broke up I never wanted to see you again. I'm seeing someone. It's quite serious."

Bile shot violently to his throat. Dan's entire body clenched. His muscles prepped for a fight that wasn't coming.

"No, not even just to talk. I've moved on," she insisted.

Jared's voice went on for a long drawn minute with Fionna growing more and more uncomfortable. "No, I moved. I don't live there anymore."

Dan stood. His mind conjured images of Jared's pathetic body being crushed by his fists, and Fionna nursing away the inevitable hard-on fighting always left him with.

Irritation plagued her features, "Yes, I moved in with him. I told you it was serious. It's Valentine's Day. I'm hanging up. Never call me again."

Dan debated taking the phone from her and letting Jared know what he thought of him giving Fionna a booty call on Valentine's Day, but he forced himself only to pace closer.

This wasn't some prick who had taken what he'd wanted and left or treated her badly. This was a guy she'd been with for almost two years, and though she'd never told him that she loved him, Dan knew Jared had been in love with Fionna.

"Jared," Fionna huffed with a defeated sigh. "No!"

Jared continued to talk rapidly.

"Yes, if he asks," spilled from her mouth in a defiant declaration. "No, it isn't Garrett. This conversation is pointless."

In one quick step, Dan was beside her and held his hand out for the phone. Instead of giving him the phone, she took his hand and drew from him.

As their energy connected, he heard Jared make his final plea. "Fionna, baby, I love you, and I want to be with you. I don't know who this guy is, but he doesn't love you like I do. He can't."

Incensed fury quaked and reverberated in every cell of Dan's body. His shield flared. He grabbed the phone and seated himself beside her. Fionna looked momentarily panicked.

"Jared." Dan forced his voice to remain moderately calm but appropriately lethal. "This is Fionna's boyfriend."

Fionna's head fell into her hands with frustrated defeat.

"No, I'm not going to put her back on the phone. I think you two have talked quite enough. So if you're really stupid enough to want to talk to someone, you can talk to me," he snarled.

Fionna raised her head, and Dan saw relief broadcast from her features. "Thank you," she mouthed as she curled up and laid her head in Dan's lap.

He kept his hand sliding up and down Fionna's back both to soothe her and to keep his own energy somewhat calm. Dan listened to Jared tell him that Fionna needed him and that they'd been perfect together.

His shield sizzled with furious red heat that frightened her. She sat up. His jaw clenched as he ordered himself to calm down.

"Listen to me, you narcissistic asshole. I'm trying to be patient, but if you keep this up, I will not be kind. Do not call her again. She is mine. There are a lot of things that really piss me the fuck off. One of them would be when other guys call her baby. She is *my* baby. If I ever hear that again, I can assure you that you won't just hear my voice, you'll see my face, and you'll feel my fists. You don't want to fuck with me. It will not end well for you. When I'm finished with your pathetic little ass, your own mother won't recognize you."

Silence was the reply to Dan's threat. Quickly ending the call, he tried to force his shield to calm. The throb of incensed blood pulsing was the only sound he was capable of hearing for a long moment. He tried to breathe deeply. He would never lose his temper with her, but dammit he wanted to hunt Jared down and destroy him.

"I'm so sorry." Fionna covered her face with her hands and whimpered.

"It's okay. I'm sorry I reacted like that." He wasn't certain that was true, but he had to get it together.

"He does this every six months or so. Whenever he breaks up with whoever he's been dating, he calls me. I have no desire to ever talk to him or see him again. I wish he didn't exist. Thank you for telling him never to call me again." She fell forward into his arms. He caught her with ease.

"We dated for a long time, but he just never made me feel much of anything. I kept thinking if I hung in there long enough I would feel something. I knew I wanted to break up with him eight months before I did because I knew he would take it really hard. I didn't want to have to feel his devastation. I was a coward."

Dan shook his head. "You were nothing of the sort."

"I used to beg Chloe, and Garrett, and Sasha and whoever I could find to come over or to go out and do something with me so I didn't have to hang out with him. I was miserable. He was happy." She rolled her eyes.

"I made Chloe come over and stay in the room with me when I told him it was over because I couldn't stand to be alone with him. I didn't want a goodbye kiss. I didn't want him to touch me, and I knew he'd try. I should have broken up with him long before I did. It got completely toxic, and now the sound of his voice still makes me want to puke."

Dan tried to let that further his slowly gathering composure. "Did you ever meet up with him when he called after you broke up?"

"Ugh, NO!" She all but convulsed. "Like I said, he does this when he breaks up with whoever he's been dating."

"And when he's lonely on Valentine's," Dan fumed.

"All right, fine." Her jaw clenched tightly for a brief moment. "The last possible thing I want to talk about while I'm in the most romantic chalet I've ever seen with the guy I'm crazy in love with on Valentine's Day is my old boyfriends, but since Jared called, here goes."

Dan shook his head to stop her, but she was determined.

"Jared was never in love with me."

It was very clear that whatever she was going to say she needed to get off her chest, so he listened. He ordered himself to be there for her. They both had pasts. She'd accepted Amelia with no qualm and no question. He owed her the very same.

"He was cute, and nice, and safe—very, very safe." She scowled. "So he fell in love with the girl I pretended to be for the first six weeks of our relationship. He didn't hate that I challenge for the Angels, but he hated that I made so much more money than he did. And he hated most of my friends. If I wanted to go out and have a few drinks with Chloe, or Sasha, or any of my teammates, he complained endlessly about how much the drinks cost. We could buy a bottle of wine and stay home. I got a Brazilian every month. He said he would rather I put that money in the bank."

Dan smirked. The guy was not only an asshole, he was an idiot.

"If I offered to pay for anything at all, he got his feelings hurt. I said I wanted to spice things up in the bedroom. He said it was high time I settled down. Told me that we were in a serious, mature relationship, and that the kinds of things I was talking about were inappropriate and not something that girls of good moral fiber wanted.

"He wanted to get married. I wanted to run away. He talked constantly about me quitting the Angels and settling down and starting a family. I said I didn't want to quit even after I got married, and he said that I would change my mind once I got used to staying home." She gagged involuntarily.

"He informed me one night when I emerged from my bathroom wearing a black lace nightie that lingerie seemed like such an unnecessary expense. I refused to sleep with him for the last ten months we were together. I wouldn't even be alone with him. He saw that as my trying to reawaken my virginity for our wedding night."

Fionna was shrieking in her pent-up aggression toward Jared.

Dan was trying very hard not to laugh over her last statement. "Reawakening your virginity?"

She finally began laughing. "Yes, I guess at some point when I was nineteen, it just fell asleep!"

They laughed together for a long moment before she continued. "The last year was awful." Her voice lowered slightly. "He found my vibe drawer and threw them out. He said that was like cheating on him. I used to hide my Starbucks cups before he saw my car because I always got this huge lecture on how my coffee drinking was really getting out of hand. He calculated how many cups of coffee I could perk at home versus how much a cup out cost." She halted abruptly as she shook her head. The recollections seemed to exhaust her.

With a renewed breath, she continued, "I never ever told him about my mom. Never told him what my tats mean. He didn't like them anyway. I never told him anything about Kauai. I never even told him that I can surf or how much hula means to me. I never even told him I'm Hawaiian. He was too self-absorbed to notice.

"I mentioned once that Malani was entering the Mavericks surfing competition out in California, and that I wanted to fly out and cheer her on. He told me that surfing was a ridiculous sport and that it was not only extremely dangerous, but it was also overly branded."

Dan knew that Malani and Fionna had been best friends since they were toddlers. They'd grown up together on Kauai. Malani and her husband worked for Fionna's grandparents on their farm.

They still talked frequently and saw each other whenever they could. Dan was eager to meet Malani. Every time she phoned,

Fionna's energy soothed and swirled in peaceful happiness. She brought Fionna so much joy.

Fionna's enraged voice brought Dan back to the present. "He picked me up from the arena one day, and I had on a miniskirt. He told me it wasn't really appropriate at my age. I never told him I loved him. I never loved him," she corrected instantly.

"I never let him stay over. Never stayed at his house. He never knew that I prefer to sleep naked. He never knew me," she sighed. "And that was my fault because I spent the first few months of our relationship pretending to be everything he said he wanted. I didn't go out with my friends. I sat and listened to him tell me all about his stupid, boring job, and I met his parents wearing a maxi skirt and a turtleneck. I lied about my past, and that's what he wanted. There for a while, I think I thought he was right. He said all the things my dad always told me. I was wild and that was bad. I was Maylea. The things I wanted were bad, and I was a bad person for wanting them. But when I just couldn't pretend to be someone else any longer, he didn't know what to do."

They sat in silence for the length of one heartbeat.

"Look at me." Dan gently lifted her chin so she was staring into his eyes. All traces of possessive fury had bled from him in light of her terror over who she was. "Jared is and was a motherfucking moron because the real Fionna Styler, Maylea…" he urged.

Her beaming grin undid him. It was the first time he'd ever used her nickname.

"She is the most amazing woman I've ever had the privilege of holding in my arms. I love each and every thing about you, sweetheart. And I will take care of Jared if he ever calls again. But I want you to hear what I'm telling you. There is not one single thing about you that I don't love. There is nothing you want, whether in our bedroom, or in a waterfall, or anywhere at all that makes you a bad person. You are perfect. I don't deserve you. You not only have a beautiful face and a gorgeous body, honey, you have the most beautiful heart and beautiful soul and a brilliant mind. I cannot ever tell you what it means to me that you let me see those.

"And every single thing I discover as we travel down this road at a breakneck pace only makes me fall more and more in love with you. So please don't let Jared's imbecilic prejudices make you think there is something wrong with you. You are absolutely amazing, and I love you so much."

"You have no idea how badly I need to hear that sometimes." Her body trembled against his as he folded her up in his arms.

Dan's heart fissured and seized.

She lifted her head again. "But I wish you would stop saying you don't deserve me. I love you so much. There isn't any part of you I don't love or care about, even the parts that you can't quite give me yet. I'll wait forever if I have to for you to let me have all of you. For you to be done with him."

He had no intention of making her wait forever. He brushed a loose strand of hair behind her right ear tenderly and then guided her beautiful lips to his own. "I love you so much," he whispered just before he plundered her mouth.

His tongue sought hers. His body needed to show her what she meant to him. He sucked and dragged his teeth over her bottom lip in a heated claim of ownership. They sought redemption in each other.

She moaned in his mouth. Her eyes closed as she gave in to the pressure and persuasion of his lips. His hands slipped back up that sweater. He needed to feel her soft, silky skin. Pulling the sweater up over her head took no time at all. Her breasts beckoned his hands with magnetizing force. He squeezed her nipples between his thumb and the side of his index finger, making her shiver in need as the lace of her bra abraded her. Impatient greed thrummed through him.

"So damn beautiful always, baby doll. But when you're hungry for me, my God, you're exquisite."

She panted as he trailed his kisses lower down her neck to the cleft of her collarbone. He spun his tongue there and popped the clasp of the bra, a saucy crimson lace number that drove him wild. Her back arched as he tugged the bra down her arms and tossed it away.

She panted. "You make me so wet. If you'd touched me when you were telling him that I was yours, I would have come," she confessed in a heated testimony as her body glowed from his care.

A low, voracious growl shook from his lungs. "Stand up for me."

He used his height to his advantage, sitting up on the edge of the couch. He watched as she unsnapped the black velvet jeans. His mouth watered, and he helped her slip them down her long legs. She lifted her feet one at a time so he could dispense with the socks she was wearing.

Unable to take his eyes off the crimson lace panties, he traced over them with his fingertips. The hooks ended between her legs, and he couldn't access them from the front.

In his vast experience, any idiot who thought a woman like Fionna was too wild was clearly intimidated by her desires. He couldn't satisfy her, and he knew it. So he told her she shouldn't want what he had no hopes of providing.

With another smirk, he ran his index finger over her mound in a straight line down her slit. She trembled, all for him. He had everything she needed and more, and he deeply appreciated her naughtier side.

"Turn around for me, baby doll. Let's see these panties."

She spun, and he slid forward. He held her hips in his hands. He performed the same move with his finger, this time tracing down the row of hooked closures.

He groaned from the intoxicating sight. "You are a naughty, naughty girl, baby. Just like I want you to be."

He released the first clasp, leaned in, and spun his tongue at the very base of her spine. She shook.

"Oh god, yes," she gasped as she realized where his hands and his tongue would ultimately lead him.

The next clasp loosed, and she swayed as he continued his feast. His tongue and his fingers slipped lower and deeper. With every clasp he unfastened, she came undone.

He leaned her forward. She braced her hands on the coffee table in front of them so he could spin his tongue over her perineum and then forward over her opening. He groaned against her. She was indeed soaking wet.

"So sweet, baby. You taste like heaven." He lowered the panties, and as she stepped out of them he spun her back to face him.

With his index finger, he tenderly sussed out that liquid heat.

Bridgette, Jared, Wretchkinsides, work—it could all go to hell. He needed to stake his claim. He'd been on a ragged edge for too damn long.

He gathered that sweet spun sugar that was flowing more copiously than he was accustomed. He added another finger, working just at her opening, letting her drip all for him. With his other hand he eased back the hood of her clitoris until his fingers were covered with her juices. Sinful, sexy sounds mewled from her.

She watched him intently. Her eyes were dark and ravenous, as he pulled his fingers away and painted her nipples with the nectar of her.

Her entire body trembled. He steadied her and leaned to bathe the swollen throbbing tips with his tongue. He engulfed each one in the flames of his mouth. His tongue scorched her as he sucked her clean.

"Oh, my god," she gasped as he worked.

"When I'm finished, baby, you're gonna have cum all over that gorgeous body. I'm gonna cover you in it. You're all mine."

She groaned in elation as he unbuckled his belt.

CHAPTER 26

INTERRUPTIONS

LOGAN HAYDENSHIRE

Logan spun Adeline into their suite and kicked the door closed. They never broke from their impassioned kiss. She pulled away, gasping for breath, and he slid his hands up her waist and lifted her breasts. He kissed down her neck and groped her without reprieve. "I've missed you, baby. I need you now," he begged. She trembled against him. It drove him wild.

Her phone gave the shrill ring meaning the hospital was calling. He all but whimpered.

"No, it's okay. Someone just forgot I'm not on call tonight." She tried to keep him calm as she lifted the phone from her purse.

"This is Medio Haydenshire," she answered confidently.

Logan took several measured breaths and smiled. He loved watching her in action at the hospital. She was a phenomenal medio, already outstanding in her field, and her demeanor reflected her knowledge and her hard work. The accolades she'd received since she'd begun at Georgetown didn't hurt either.

Assuming that one of her patients had gone into labor, Logan ordered himself to be patient. She would alert the medio who was on call for the night and then he could get back to unzipping that dress.

Before his eyes, all of the heated color that he'd brought to her face drained quickly. Terror etched her delicate features. "No, I'm on my way. I'm only a few blocks from the hospital. Prep me an operating room."

~

Rainer Lawson

Emily moaned into Rainer's mouth as he groped her breasts.

"You are so beautiful. I can't wait anymore, baby." He reclined her on the couch where they'd been talking a few minutes before.

After convincing her that when he held her in his hands he had everything he would ever need, she'd leaned in, and he'd needed no more encouragement than that.

A full minute later he'd pulled her turtleneck over her head and had popped the clasp of the pink bra, complete with red lace, that encased her alabaster cleavage to perfection. Her breasts pled for his attention. Her nipples were swollen pink and throbbing. She looked like a candy confection made only for him. He wanted to feast.

He trailed fiery kisses down her neck. Her breath panted and her body writhed under his caress.

"I want to suck you, baby. So beautiful. Damn, I need them in my mouth."

"Yes!"

He lapped at her right nipple before drowning it. He licked and sucked alternately with fervor as she shuddered and moaned.

He heard her cell phone ring from her purse, and he pulled away. She gasped. Her body rolled from the sensations he'd brought her.

"Don't stop." She popped the clasp on the tight jeans she was wearing to reveal open-crotch panties, constructed of nothing more than a few white pieces of elastic and an open red heart over her lips. There was another red satin heart that sat at the top of her backside. Clearly she'd decided to break out a few of her gifts from the lingerie shower before their honeymoon.

He was unable to even hear the phone continue to ring once he'd seen the panties. A thundering growl echoed from Rainer's lungs as he jerked the jeans off her and began lapping his tongue over the open satin heart.

Another minute passed and then both of their cells were ringing repeatedly. "Dammit!" Rainer jerked the phone out of his pocket. "What?!" he demanded of Logan.

~

Dan Vindico

"You ready, baby?" he panted as he lay out over her on the couch. He'd waited long enough. He prodded her with his head until she could feel him throb, and her soaking wet pussy slicked him. She was swollen and primed. She was so ready for him it made him dizzy with need. His body shook with desire.

Suddenly, Dan's phone blared the signal that meant there was a broad range security call.

Fionna's body shuddered. She gasped for breath as a long trail of expletives spewed from his mouth. He got up, completely naked, and grabbed the damn phone.

"That's the noise your phone made the night I was dancing with you when Cascavel took Governor Peterson's daughter."

Shocked that she'd remembered that, Dan nodded and answered, "This is Vindico."

"Dan, I'm patching you through to Haydenshire," Sorenson, the Non-Gifted police chief, explained.

"Dan?" Garrett sounded panicked.

"Yeah, it's me. What's going on?" He reached for Fionna. "It's Garrett," he mouthed as she moved into his embrace. She looked terrified.

"I'm sorry, man. I need you here. Mom's gone into labor. Her blood pressure bottomed out, and they lost the baby's heartbeat. Dad called an ambulance, and the ambulance driver called the press. Georgetown is swimming with reporters. The medios can't get through. I can't get through. And Dan, Adrian Malicai is here in this disaster. That's why he flew in with Nic.

"Wretchkinsides had him here waiting. He knows the baby will be here tonight if they can save her. I can't do this by myself. Malicai brought friends. Logan's here, and Rainer's on his way. I tried everybody's cell. Dad didn't want it going out over the Gifted alert because that would mean more press, so I just had them use it to call you. Please, I need some help."

Dan had never heard Garrett Haydenshire sound so overwhelmed, defeated, and completely terrified.

"I'm on my way," Dan assured him. "I'll be there as soon as I can, and I'll take care of getting you some help now. We'll be there. Deep breath. It's going to be okay. I'm on my way."

"Thanks," Garrett choked, and Dan's heart ached for Garrett and for the governor.

"Get dressed for me, baby." He tried to whisper, but Garrett heard his request.

"I'm really sorry," he apologized again.

"It's fine. We'll be out of here in ten minutes. Go take care of your mom."

~

Logan Haydenshire

"Get the hell out of her way," Logan shouted at the dozens of cameramen blocking Adeline's access to the maternity ward.

"Get me scrubbed now," Adeline demanded. Logan had never heard his wife demand anything with such strength.

Suddenly orderlies appeared, putting a mask over Adeline's face and pulling her hair up in what looked like a shower cap.

"She only wants Medio Haydenshire," one of the nurses stated as she ran by. "Adeline," she halted abruptly.

"Mrs. Haydenshire's blood pressure just shot to 160/85 then crashed again. Her mucus plug is out. We broke her water. There's protein in her urine. The baby is in distress. We can't keep a heartbeat."

Logan's heart seized. He didn't understand any of that, but clearly something was wrong.

"Prep her for surgery. I'm on my way," Adeline commanded.

Rainer and Emily made their way through the onslaught. Emily was crying. Rainer was shouting at the press to get the hell away from her.

Suddenly, every Iodex officer available raced off the elevators.

Garrett spun. His eyes flashed in shock as they heard Portwood bellow, "If you have a camera or a microphone and you're on this floor, you will be arrested by order of the Chief of Iodex for breach of security and privacy. If any of the Haydenshires request that you leave and you refuse, you will also be arrested for the same crimes."

Adeline moved to the sinks, and after she was scrubbed and gloved she flew past Logan and into an operating room, followed by Brad, Medio Sawyer, and a team of medios and nurses that Logan didn't know.

Rainer and Logan shared a relieved sigh as reporters began fleeing.

"Vindico?" Logan guessed. Portwood nodded.

A half smile finally eased Garrett's face. "Yeah, he's a hell of a guy when you need him."

"Mom," Emily gasped. Her terrorized plea shattered Logan's heart as he spun to watch two nurses run with his mother on a gurney. They were headed into the operating room.

She wasn't conscious, but she was clinging to the governor's hand. Logan had never seen his father look so terrified and helpless.

They all edged toward their parents. Their legs seemed to move of their own accord, but the metal door was closed in their faces.

"We need every available neonatal intensive care unit to report to operating room AEGB. We need every available neonatal intensive care unit to report to operating room AEGB." The harrowing request projected over the speakers in the wall and reverberated through every one of the Haydenshire children.

They watched people dressed in surgical scrubs race into the room Mrs. Haydenshire was occupying.

Dan and Fionna flew out of the elevator. They both pretended they hadn't arrived together. They joined the waiting family members.

Fionna immediately moved to Garrett. "It's going to be okay," she whispered. He nodded and then fell heavy into her embrace as he blinked back tears. She held him tight. Logan saw her cast work through him.

Logan's grandparents had brought the twins to the hospital. They both looked just as terrified as Logan felt.

Barron and McCoy sprinted off the elevator next. Vindico immediately took over.

"I want a team outside Mrs. Haydenshire's room the entire time she is in this hospital. No one, not a medio, not a nurse, not one of her children, not the Crown Governor himself gets in to see her or the baby without you making certain that they are who they say they are!"

"Yes, sir." Barron and McCoy immediately leapt into action. They took up guard outside of the operating room.

"If the baby has to go somewhere without Mrs. Haydenshire, they will each have a separate team with them at all times." He continued his shouted commands as Non-Elite chanted out yes, sir.

Tuttle and Ramier made it to the hospital last, but immediately announced that they'd arrested Paul Gensen, a known kidnapper for the Interfeci, trying to sneak up the back stairs.

"Good work." Vindico sounded beyond furious. Both of the twins broke down in terrified tears. Rainer took Henry, trying to soothe both him and Emily.

Logan took Keaton and set his shield around him.

CHAPTER 27

AN ENDLESS MOMENT

RAINER LAWSON

The waiting was endless. Each minute seemed to last ten. Rainer rubbed Emily's back and tried to assure her that everything would be fine, but she knew he had no way of knowing that.

Henry slept periodically but would awaken often and plead for Mrs. Haydenshire.

No one had come in or out of the operating room in over an hour. Rainer couldn't breathe. He couldn't fathom what would happen if Mrs. Haydenshire wasn't all right. How could life go on without her? It was an impossibility. The air hung thick with tension and the unknown.

"What is Adeline doing in there? Can't they tell us something?" Patrick demanded of Logan.

"Back off," Logan growled.

Will stepped in and pulled Patrick back. "She's trying to save Mom and save Abigail. So, let's let her work, okay?"

Scowling, Patrick shook Will's hands off his shoulders and continued his relentless pacing beside several of his brothers all on the same path to nowhere.

Just as the clock moved past eleven, the door opened.

Every single person in the waiting area braced with fear clouding their minds but hope permeating their hearts.

Rainer's body eased as the governor stepped out pushing an enclosed incubator that contained a tiny, red-headed baby girl.

"Daddy!" Emily raced toward them. "Is Mom...?" she choked. She couldn't force the words out of her mouth. She broke down, and Rainer handed Henry to Fionna and wrapped Emily up in his arms.

"She's all right. They're going to be working on her for a while. The placenta ruptured. We almost lost your mother and your little sister, but Adeline managed to save them both." The governor strangled on the words. He'd been sobbing, and the tears returned in cascading waves.

All of his sons stepped in to embrace him. "Hey, she's all right, Dad. Listen. She's asking for you," Will soothed. As everyone quieted, they could hear Adeline assuring Mrs. Haydenshire that the governor was coming right back.

After scrubbing his face with his hands, he returned to the delivery room.

Rainer studied the baby. There was something different about her.

Two nurses had followed Governor Haydenshire and Abigail out of the operating room. "We need to take her to the NICU. You can come with her if you'd like," they offered Emily.

"And I was already informed by the Crown Governor that Abigail Hope Haydenshire has her own security team," the nurse assured Vindico who stepped in with a vicious scowl.

"Is she okay?" Emily asked as they all walked behind the nurses, heading toward the neonatal nursery with a broad range security detail surrounding the entire crowd.

"Her Apgar scores were not good. I don't know how Medio Haydenshire managed to save them both. I really don't, but she came around. She does appear to have Down syndrome, but her Gifted energies did read in the last scan we took. We'll have to see how that works, but for now she's all right. We're going to keep her in an oxygen tent for a while. As soon as they get your mother healed, which I expect will take several hours, we'll get her back in the room with her. That always makes them better."

Emily was scrubbed and then escorted into a windowed room full of incubators. She slipped under a clear, plastic sheeting as the nurse arranged the oxygen tent near the windows where everyone was watching them.

Abigail's tiny hand took tight hold of Emily's finger. Rainer grinned. The nurse gestured to a rocking chair, and Emily sat down and began to rock her back and forth. The baby was wrapped in some kind of casted blanket that lit rhythmically.

Everyone was enamored watching the two of them.

"Her hair looks exactly like Emily's when she was born," Nana Anderson recalled.

Rainer was overwhelmed watching her. She blinked back tears as she stared down into Abigail's tiny, beautiful face.

Emily had surrounded her with her soothing energies. The entire family could see the fierce magenta glow.

Vindico barked to Portwood and Ericcson, "I can't fathom why Emily and Abigail Haydenshire are in a room in this hospital that you aren't standing in front of."

"Yes, sir." They both recalled their orders. After being given clearance, they were masked and gloved, and took post outside the tiny neonatal room where Abigail had been assigned.

Though Garrett's arm was still slung over Fionna's shoulder and he was clinging to her, she reached nonchalantly and let the back of her hand touch the back of Vindico's. He turned to her. She gave him a smile, and he seemed to calm.

Everyone watched Emily cradle Abigail tenderly. She eased the casted blanket back enough to place her hand on the baby's chest and stomach. Rainer saw the faint heat glow from Emily's hand.

She closed her eyes in concentration. Fionna gave a hopeful gasp as her hand went to her mouth.

"What's she doing?" Vindico and Garrett demanded simultaneously.

Tears began leaking down Fionna's face as she watched. "She's reading her." Everyone turned to stare in desperate hope.

Emily's eyes flew open, and she moved to the window. She waved Fionna into the room.

"Is that okay?" she mouthed. Emily nodded and moved to the door. The nurse assigned to Abigail looked uncertain about Emily's request, but she seemed to decide that turning down both of the Crown Governor's daughters might not be a wise career decision, so she allowed Fionna into the nursery.

They watched intently as Fionna scrubbed her hands vigorously and donned a mask and gown.

Emily delicately laid Abigail in Fionna's arms after she'd seated herself in the rocking chair. Fionna rocked her slowly for a few minutes. All eyes were on her.

"Is Fionna gonna read her too?" Logan whispered.

Vindico nodded. He glanced around, pleased that there appeared to be no one in the hallways of the NICU that wasn't in some way related to the Haydenshires.

"Yeah, she's relaxing and getting the baby used to her energy," he explained, still watching Fionna. "She's the strongest Receiver of our generation. If anyone can pick up on the baby's energy, she can."

Everyone watched Fionna heat her hand and lay it tenderly on Abigail's bare chest. Her eyes closed just as Emily's had. But they flashed back open in a split second. She shared a stunned expression with Emily.

A delighted smile lit Fionna's face. Her mask fell away slightly as she turned, catching Vindico's eyes with tears in her own.

Abigail's little eyes opened and then her entire face contorted in a soundless sob. Fionna's face fell. She suddenly looked devastated. Rainer didn't understand why he hadn't heard the baby cry. Emily took her back, and the nurse handed Emily a bottle of enhanced formula.

It was often given to Gifted newborns. Henry had taken it for several weeks after his birth, because his birth weight was so much lower than Keaton's.

CHAPTER 28

A FAMILY

A few minutes later, Fionna rejoined everyone in the hallway. She was still blinking back tears. Dan walked toward her but seemed to remember that he shouldn't embrace her.

"She's amazing. She's a Receiver." She stared into Dan's eyes. She seemed unable to move her gaze. Everyone nodded. "But that isn't the amazing part. She's really powerful, and her internal shield has already developed. Most Receivers develop it over time. I think that must be why they couldn't get readings from her before she was born.

"She was afraid and shielding. She picks up on people's energies really quickly. Mrs. Haydenshire told me that Abigail would kick and move and Mrs. Haydenshire could feel her elated energies when the governor had his hands on her belly. She kept telling the medios that Abigail was Gifted, but only Adeline believed her. The baby not only recognized the governor's voice and his rhythms, but she understood she was safe when he was there. That's how strong she is. She knew to be scared and to block her own energies. I bet she saved herself from that poison."

"Wow." Garrett seemed to try to comprehend his newest little sister as he gazed at her in Emily's arms inhaling a bottle.

Fionna continued, "I think that's also why she was better sometimes when Mrs. Haydenshire was off bed rest. She knew if her mom was up using her own energies that everything was okay. But as soon as Mrs. Haydenshire went to the medio, her own worries would trigger Abigail's internal shield."

Rainer watched Abigail drain the tiny bottle. The nurse smiled and had to offer Emily no instructions as she turned Abigail, laid her tenderly on her shoulder, and patted her back to get her to burp.

Fionna returned to the window. She stood between Dan and Garrett. "I wish you could hold her. She's amazing," she stated, though no one knew if it was Garrett or Dan she was talking to.

"I don't think any of us would feel her like you and Emily can, sweetheart," Dan whispered quietly.

❧

Logan Haydenshire

Still pacing outside of the operating room that his mother and his wife were both locked in, exhaustion waged war with Logan's nerves. They'd called in a Gifted surgical response team an hour before.

No one knew what had happened to Mrs. Haydenshire. They all took turns watching Emily with Abigail and waited anxiously on word.

McCoy and Barron were still stationed outside of his mother's room. They kept giving Logan sorrowful glances. He wished they'd cut it out. It was unnerving.

Vindico had been on his cell phone constantly. He'd been arranging Elite security teams to be at the hospital in twelve-hour shifts with both Mrs. Haydenshire and Abigail until they were allowed to go back to the farm.

Finally, just before midnight, the door opened, and all eyes turned to see who would appear. Brad issued out, followed by Medio Sawyer and Medio Dawson. They all looked exhausted.

Logan swallowed down emotion and prayed. A moment later, Adeline appeared, covered in blood. Her eyes were bloodshot and swollen, but she was smiling at Logan.

"Hey." He paced to her. He didn't care what might be on her. She held up her hand halting his progress.

"Hey, uh, wow." She shook her head. "Did you see Abigail?"

"Yeah, Em's in there with her. How's Mom?" He forced himself to ask the question.

"She's all right, finally. It was really scary there for a little while."

"But she's okay? I mean you… she's… going to be fine? You…you saved her?" He just needed her to say the words.

"She'll be fine in a few days. They're keeping her casted. They're trying to heal everything. Your dad's doing it now. She's terrified for him to leave," she whispered. This seemed to fascinate and concern Adeline.

"Yeah, Mom's tough, but he's definitely a big supplier of her strength," Logan tried to explain.

"I know." She smiled. "Just let me go get cleaned up, and then we can take Abigail back down to meet her."

Logan nodded and watched Adeline disappear into another small room.

He hadn't made two lengths of the corridor when she appeared in clean scrubs, free of blood and bodily fluids that he assumed belonged either to his mother or his little sister. He shut that thought down as it made him queasy.

Adeline looked worried as she moved back to him. She took his hands. "Will you come talk to me for a minute?"

"Of course." He followed her down a hallway and into a closet. "What's wrong?"

"Your mom is fine, or she will be in a few days. But I was and am her primary medio. I had to call in for help because it got really scary there for a few minutes. But that means that her treatments are up to me."

"Okay." Logan was confused by her apprehension. "That's good. You're amazing. You're gonna run this hospital one day."

She shook her head in ardent disagreement. "I'm not supposed to tell you this."

"What's wrong?" Logan didn't give a damn about hospital policy for the moment. "Dad said the placenta ruptured or something."

Adeline nodded. "Yes, it was bad. Honestly, it could have killed both of them." Logan's entire body trembled. "So, I had to act quickly. I had to get Abigail out and keep your mom's heart beating. But the bleeding in her uterus was extreme, so I asked your dad in a split second if I could remove it. He screeched, 'Yes, now!' But I don't know if he really realizes what that means exactly."

"In terms of what?"

"In terms that her recovery will be much longer than they're used to with all of her other pregnancies. And she won't be able to have more children. I just performed a partial hysterectomy."

Logan drew a deep breath and then a genuine chuckle escaped him. "Baby, my mom is over fifty. She's given birth to eleven children, and she's helped raise God only knows how many others. And even my dad's split-second decisions are good ones. They'll be fine. If Mom's going to be all right and Abigail is healthy, that's all they'll care about."

"Abigail has Down syndrome." Adeline teared up as she confirmed what Logan already knew. "But she is Gifted. I don't know how that's going to work."

"Hey." Logan wrapped his arms around Adeline. "No one knows what it will mean, but we'll be right there on the farm to help out with whatever she might need. And she'll have Keaton and Henry keeping up with her, so trust me, no one will mess with her."

Adeline smiled as she nodded. "I also have to tell your mom and dad some embarrassing stuff."

"Just pretend it's just a patient you don't really know."

She gave him a quizzical look that said that would be impossible, but she sighed and seemed to come to terms with what had to be done. "Will you come with me? Your parents will understand, and we can take the baby to them."

"Sure." He watched as Adeline put on another mask and waved her hospital badge over the door to the NICU. Her credentials were checked by Portwood. She didn't seem to mind at all. Emily beamed, but she looked exhausted. She nodded and handed Abigail to Adeline.

After hooking up an oxygen tube and stringing it into Abigail's tiny nostrils, she laid her back in an incubator, fixed the casted glowing blanket around her, and rolled the cradle out of the nursery.

"Baby sisa," Keaton squealed, and he raced toward Emily and Adeline.

Fionna smiled and lifted Keaton up to see Abigail. "Isn't she beautiful?"

"No." Keaton shook his head making everyone laugh. "She's red. I touch her?"

After having a momentary unspoken conversation with Adeline, Fionna nodded. "You have to be very, very soft."

Adeline released the top of the enclosed cradle.

Fionna guided Keaton's hand to Abigail's blankets.

"Hi, baby." Keaton softly patted the blanket. "I'm name is Kea-ton," he whispered, leaning down near her ear.

Everyone swooned over his tender care.

"You have to take good care of Abigail, okay, little man?" Logan demanded of Keaton.

Keaton lifted his eyes to Logan's. He seemed to understand. "I will," he vowed.

Everyone turned their gaze to Adeline as she closed the incubator. They wanted information and instructions. She gave a weary smile. "We're going to take her to meet your mom and dad, but they aren't really ready for visitors yet."

Everyone nodded their understanding. Logan tried to brace himself before he entered the room and took in his mother.

She was pale and weak. Her eyes were almost black in their depths. He understood why she had to be constantly casted. His father kept his cast flowing constantly over her, but he didn't appear to have any energy to spare.

"Medio Kemper can take over for you whenever you're ready." Adeline gestured to one of the waiting medios in the room.

The governor gave a defeated nod. He released his cast and moved so the medio could begin a healing cast over Mrs. Haydenshire.

Mrs. Haydenshire offered Logan and Adeline a weak smile. "Can I finally see her?" Adeline raised the bed slightly so that Mrs. Haydenshire could hold the baby.

Logan moved back to the door. "Hey, Dad needs food and lots of it," he called out to his family and friends in the waiting room.

Ten minutes later, the governor was devouring food from the hospital cafeteria and five different nearby fast food joints. His energy immediately soothed, and he looked like a new man.

Logan wasn't certain if getting to hold Abigail and seeing that she was really all right had his mother looking so much better, or if it was being constantly casted by an actual medio with Gifted energy to spare.

Adeline drew a deep breath and glanced between Governor and Mrs. Haydenshire. "Okay, so did you tell her anything that happened when we sedated her?" Adeline asked Governor Haydenshire hesitantly.

"Oh, sweetheart, are you the one that has to have this talk with us?" was his concerned reply.

Adeline nodded, and the governor chuckled. It was a sound that Logan found oddly soothing. Mrs. Haydenshire smiled from hearing her husband's laughter.

"Here, let me help." The governor stepped back to Mrs. Haydenshire's bed. He settled beside her legs. "I don't know what the medical part of this talk will be,"—he glanced at Adeline sorrowfully before starting again—"but, baby, you went out and I didn't think you were gonna…" He went pale suddenly, and Adeline stepped in to save the Crown Governor.

"Mrs. Haydenshire, I'm so sorry, but when I delivered Abigail, with everything that happened, we ended up taking your uterus. It was badly damaged when the placenta ruptured. You were bleeding out. I couldn't keep your heart beating, and save Abigail, and save that. I'm so sorry."

Logan grasped her hand.

Mrs. Haydenshire took her husband's hand and tried with her limited energies to soothe him.

"Stephen, honey, I'm okay."

He managed a nod, but tears flowed down his face once again.

She turned to Adeline instead. "Sweetheart, I really think that after eleven children, my uterus has performed admirably. I was certainly planning on my sweet little Abigail being my last. And even if I hadn't decided that, I'm very certain Mother Nature would have decided that for me. Please don't worry about your decision. Thank you for saving my life and hers." She patted Abigail, who was quite content being held by her mother.

Adeline looked relieved as she forced herself to continue. "You'll have to stay here for a while, both for you and Abigail. And, uh…" Adeline stammered.

Governor Haydenshire laughed through his tears. "Now we're getting to the part I thought she was going to open with."

With another deep breath, Adeline let her eyes close for a moment. "You'll be casted constantly for the next twenty-four hours minimum. It might be longer. By the time we release you to go home, everything should be healed for the most part, but, you know…you'll probably be…"—she blushed violently—"tender."

Logan grimaced but remained steadfast by his wife.

"And, you're going to need to take several weeks off before you resume sexual activity, at least four weeks. Five would be better. But that's less time than Non-Gifted women should wait." She spoke the ending quickly as if she was offering a consolation prize. "And you'll need to be cleared by a medio first." She stared at the floor and refused to look at either Logan or his parents. "I'm sorry."

Mrs. Haydenshire cringed slightly as she laughed.

"I'm also supposed to say that you need to keep all sexual activity relatively mild and low key until everything feels back to normal."

The governor cracked up. The laughter dried his tears. "I'm sorry," he offered Adeline. "I swear, I'm not laughing at you. I'm laughing at the look on Logan's face." He pointed to his son, eliciting laughter from everyone in the room.

Mrs. Haydenshire joined in. "That's fine, and you did a remarkable job for having to have said all of that to your in-laws."

Relief broadcast from Adeline's features. She was clearly overjoyed that the informative lecture part of her job was over.

"The Gifted pediatricians from Children's National will be by at eight so they can tell you more about Abigail." Adeline smiled tenderly as she moved to the bed and gently caressed Abigail's head.

The laughter had disturbed her slumber, and she was debating another muted scream.

Concern tensed in Adeline's rhythms again. "Um, they tested her hearing and it was normal, but she does appear to be mute. That could change in the future though."

Governor Haydenshire stepped in. "Come here, baby girl." He scooped the baby out of Mrs. Haydenshire's arms.

"Watch the oxygen line," Adeline warned.

He sat on the edge of the bed and cradled the baby in his arms. Logan knew as he watched Abigail soothe instantly that Fionna had been correct. She felt safe when she felt her father's rhythms.

"The more you sleep the faster you'll heal," Adeline reminded Mrs. Haydenshire.

"I know." Mrs. Haydenshire gazed at Abigail in her husband's arms.

A nurse entered the room with another tiny bottle for the baby. The governor settled down in the chair to feed her.

Logan and Adeline returned to the waiting room.

"What was so funny?" Rainer quizzed with a wry smile. Everyone edged closer to hear.

"Well." Logan assumed everyone could use a good laugh after the night they'd had even if it was at his expense. "Apparently, when my wife is informing my parents that they have to wait several weeks before they resume rough sex, I tend to look horrified, which Dad found hysterical."

Raucous laughter broke out from all of Logan's siblings, their spouses, and friends.

"Poor Dad," Garrett teased, bringing on more laughter.

"Yeah, the Crown's probably going to be in a bad mood for a few weeks." Vindico laughed heartily.

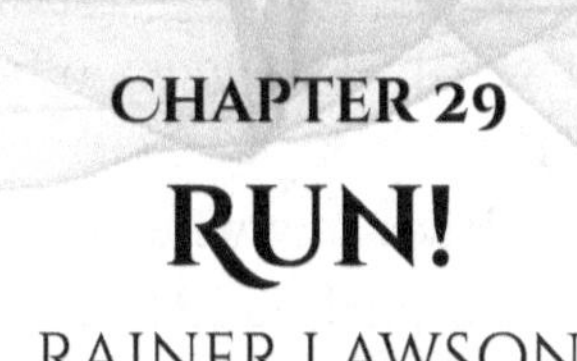

CHAPTER 29

RUN!

RAINER LAWSON

The following Saturday, all of Iodex was back at Georgetown to ensure that Abigail Hope Haydenshire, whose birth had been heralded by every Gifted paper, news station, social media site, and magazine across the Realm, got into the governor's Suburban and back on the farm without being photographed or chased.

Rainer and Logan were providing Mrs. Haydenshire and the baby security from their room that morning. They'd been there since midnight. Vindico was on hand to oversee everything.

The press was being held at bay by Iodex. Most of the Haydenshires were on hand to help with security as well.

Emily, Brooke, Lucy, and Fionna had stayed at the farmhouse to make sure everything was ready for Abigail's arrival home.

Mrs. Haydenshire still looked rather worn despite the healing casts she'd undergone throughout the week.

Dan had offered raises to several members of Non-Elite who wanted to join the Haydenshires' typical security task force. Pictures of the newest Haydenshire were sure to bring astronomical prices, and the Crown Governor was adamant that Abigail not be photographed for many years.

"Let's do this," Vindico commanded. He was standing at the door to Mrs. Haydenshire's room. He was carrying Abigail out himself.

Governor Haydenshire looked vicious as he glared out the window of the room and down onto the throngs of press. "This is insane," he huffed.

"Sir, I'd feel better if you'd let an Iodex officer drive them home. You're going to be chased."

"I know that. But I've driven my wife and each and every one of my babies home from this hospital, and Abigail will be no different."

Dan nodded his defeat.

Abigail had gone through batteries of tests and had been seen by most every Gifted pediatrician in the area. They'd explained several things to the Haydenshires which they'd promised to share once they were back on the farm.

On Wednesday afternoon of their week-long stay, the governor had halted all testing on his newest baby girl. The tests not only made Abigail fussy and irritable, but they seemed to make Mrs. Haydenshire sob every time another medio came to take the baby from the room.

As tears had welled in his wife's eyes again, the governor had stood, informed the medios that his baby girl was not a lab experiment, and he'd promptly removed his daughter from the nurse's arms. He'd informed them that they had all the information they needed, and that unless Mrs. Haydenshire had something specific she wanted tested they were to stay the hell away from his wife and his daughter. That had been that.

Since that moment, which Rainer and Logan had witnessed personally, Mrs. Haydenshire had gazed adoringly at her husband, who'd not left her side since Abigail's birth. They'd cradled Abigail tenderly between them for the rest of their stay.

"Governor Haydenshire, they've got the car waiting. You're first," Vindico ordered.

"All right." He leaned down in front of Mrs. Haydenshire who was in a wheelchair to be wheeled out after the governor made a quick speech to the waiting crowds. "Are you okay, sweetheart?"

Dan, Logan, Garrett, and Rainer all turned away. They tried not to eavesdrop, but they were unable to move farther away. Mrs.

Haydenshire gave him the grin that Rainer had watched her give her husband since he was a little boy. As he thought back, he couldn't recall her ever smiling that way at anyone else, including all of her children.

"I'm fine, Stephen. I just want to get her home. I just want to be with you and my children."

Emotion cinched Rainer's throat.

Governor Haydenshire leaned and brushed a tender kiss across her forehead. "Then I will make that happen. I promise you."

She nodded and smiled, but worry and fear plagued her features. Her fear seemed to drive the governor. His fury gained ferocity.

"Let's just do this quickly. I want her home," he barked at Vindico. "This has been ridiculous."

Rainer knew he was referring to the relentless testing they'd attempted to perform on Abigail, not to mention the fact that just that morning a visiting student medio from Venton had adamantly insisted that Mrs. Haydenshire attend the How to Care for Your Newborn class that the hospital offered. According to him, newborn care had become much more advanced due to the fact that the up-and-coming generation was more intelligent and had so much knowledge to offer the Realm when it came to caring for a baby. He was certain newborns today were not the same as they'd been when Mrs. Haydenshire had first begun having children.

The governor had promptly informed the student exactly what he thought of his ideas, where he could go when he left Mrs. Haydenshire's room, and how quickly he could go there.

"We're ready, sir," Ramier called. He, Tuttle, McCoy, and Barron were waiting in the corridor. They were ready to shield the Crown Governor and rush him to the waiting car. No one was taking this particular assignment lightly.

"Go now," Vindico called. Governor Haydenshire moved to the center of the Elite team. They casted and walked quickly to the elevator.

Vindico moved to the windows and watched closely. Governor Haydenshire offered the crowds half-hearted waves. He halted at the Suburban. "Thank you all for your congratulations and your support," he called as his photograph was taken thousands of times over. "I'm certain you understand that my wife and our newest little one need some time to rest and recuperate. I cannot tell you what it would mean to me if you would please give my family a little space and time to get settled."

Rainer could hear the press chanting the governor's name and screaming out questions about what was wrong with Abigail and if she was Gifted.

The Crown Governor moved to the driver's seat as officers opened the passenger side door for Mrs. Haydenshire's arrival. They moved back into place as other officers held the lines to keep the press away from the vehicle.

"You're sure you've got her, Daniel?" Mrs. Haydenshire was on the brink of tears again.

"I've got her, Mrs. Haydenshire. You know I would never let anything happen to her." He used the tone Rainer recalled him using to soothe Fionna when she'd called because Eric Kent was at the arena.

Mrs. Haydenshire nodded. She seemed to draw fortitude and resolve from the air around her.

"Okay." Her eyes sought solace from Rainer and Logan. Logan moved to push his mother's wheelchair. He set his shield over her. Rainer added his as Portwood, Ericcson, and Garrett casted and surrounded her and moved to the elevators. They raced out of the hospital with what seemed like millions of flash bulbs going off constantly.

The press thought she was carrying Abigail. Garrett moved and helped his mother up into the vehicle. He closed the door firmly. Non-Elite blocked her, and the rest of Elite raced back into the hospital.

"Let's do this." Vindico exited the elevator wearing Abigail, who was sleeping soundly in a chest harness carrier. He'd fitted his bulletproof vest around her. The press wasn't getting pictures of Abigail on his watch, that was certain.

He checked the baby carefully and cupped his arm under her

diaper to prevent her from being jostled. He wrapped his other arm over her tiny body and shouted, "Let's go."

Vindico ducked and sprinted. His bright luminescent green shield surrounded himself and the baby. It pulsed constantly. All of Elite Iodex ran in casted formation around him. The press broke through the lines and began racing toward Vindico.

"Shit," he spat as Elite held them back. He flew into the Suburban and slammed the door behind him. Rainer and Logan leapt in the other side. They all blocked the windows. Dan unstrapped Abigail and placed her lovingly into her car seat.

Garrett, Rainer, and Logan fell into the farmhouse kitchen completely exhausted.

"Thank you." Mrs. Haydenshire fussed over them. She kissed the tops of each of their heads. Rainer was astonished at how much happier and calm she seemed now that she was back at home.

She was moving around the kitchen with ease, though the governor continually asked her to sit and let him do whatever needed to be done.

"Stephen, honey, I've been sitting in a bed for a week. I want to move. Now get out of my way."

"I know, sweetheart, but you also had a baby not to mention major surgery," he reminded her.

"All right, give me a minute," she demanded.

The governor backed off.

Abigail slept soundly in a casted bassinet that had a sensor that would alert them if she cried since she didn't make sound.

"Well, shall we tell them about their little sister?" Governor Haydenshire urged as soon as Mrs. Haydenshire had prepared herself a sandwich and a glass of iced tea which seemed to delight her.

"Oh, we'll just go." Fionna looked terrified that she and Dan were intruding.

"You will do nothing of the sort. You will sit down. It makes me smile to see you two together in my kitchen," Mrs. Haydenshire ordered with a wry grin.

Dan chuckled as he seated himself at the table and pulled Fionna into his lap.

Mrs. Haydenshire smiled and nodded for her husband to begin. Governor Haydenshire, who also seemed thrilled to be back on the farm, winked at his wife and then took in the vast number of eyes all gazing at him.

"Abigail does have Down syndrome, as I'm certain you can tell." He choked slightly, but Mrs. Haydenshire squeezed his hand, which seemed to bring him fortitude. "However, she is extraordinarily Gifted." Fionna and Emily shared an excited smile. "She is a Receiver." He nodded to Emily, who was beaming. "From what they've deduced, the poison changed Abigail's DNA, but then Abigail's shield developed instantly to protect her from the poison." He shook his head over all that had happened to his little girl.

"Her shield is exceptional. She could feel Lillian's nervousness whenever we were at the hospital for a test, and she would set her own shield even though she was no more than a fetus. She kept us from really being able to tell anything about her before her birth."

"I told you," Fionna whispered excitedly.

"It will take her a little longer to develop. She is mute and may not ever be able to speak. But the specialists are fairly certain she'll be able to communicate via her energies, so she may want to touch you when she needs something rather than speak to you."

"Will she be able to go to the academy?" Will asked hesitantly.

The governor gave his oldest son a weary smile and shrugged. "That's a long way off. For the next few years, at least, we'll be taking Miss Abigail one day at a time. If nothing changes from what we've learned over the past few days, and she works very diligently, then yes, she should be able to attend Venton with Keaton and Henry. However..." The governor drew a deep breath. He reached for Mrs. Haydenshire's hand. She supplied it readily. The motion alone seemed to bring her peace. "Given my job and the press's insanity over her, we think it would probably be best if most of Abby Hope's education happened right here on the farm, so unlike all of you and the twins, she won't be attending preschool. So, we'll be asking for all of your help in teaching your little sister."

With that, the bassinet gave a slight jostle, and the monitor gave a soothing pulse.

"She's hungry," Mrs. Haydenshire stated knowingly.

The governor stood and retrieved a bottle that had come home from the hospital from the refrigerator. He summoned and heated it then lifted his little girl into his arms. Her silent wails stopped before he'd even gotten the bottle into her mouth.

CHAPTER 30
BABY ABIGAIL
DAN VINDICO

"She's just amazing." Fionna sighed tenderly. She held Dan's hand as he drove off Haydenshire farm. "She's so much stronger than I am. I've never ever met a stronger Receiver." She was thoroughly enrapt with Abigail. Fionna blushed suddenly. "I mean, I wasn't bragging or anything."

Dan squeezed her hand. "I know, honey. I did feel her when I raced her out of the hospital this morning. I've held Keaton and Henry, Fitz's kids, and Oliver and Olivia, and I've never felt much more than burgeoning energy from them, so she is definitely incredible."

A deep yawn overtook Fionna. It was barely three in the afternoon, and Dan had kept her tucked tenderly beside him in their bed until well after nine that morning.

"You tired, baby doll?" He wondered what she'd been doing while he was helping the Haydenshires escape from the hospital.

"A little. I don't know why. I played with the twins and helped Emily clean up, but I'm completely exhausted."

Certain that playing with the twins alone would be enough to have worn her out, Dan picked up her hand and brushed a kiss on her knuckles. "Maybe you're still tired from last night."

She gave him that sexy grin that made him weak. "Mmm, that was delicious."

"I'm glad you enjoyed that." As Dan let their long lovemaking session that had begun on the couch while watching a movie and had culminated on the floor of the living room replay slowly in his mind, his trousers strained, but then he recalled something he'd wanted to ask her.

"Hey baby, everything felt okay last night, right?"

"It felt so much better than okay."

Dan had to agree. It had been an incredible evening. Their bodies seemed to have linked in every available capacity. He'd never felt so close to her. It seemed as if he was already a part of her before he'd ever entered her.

"Why?"

Dan shrugged. "It just felt a little different when you let me cast you. I wanted to make sure there wasn't anything wrong." He didn't want to frighten her.

To his relief, Fionna nodded. "Yeah, it does that sometimes if the twenty-four hours is almost up, but not quite and you cast it again."

Certain that was probably it, Dan's chest and shoulders relaxed.

"Although..." She frowned.

"What?" His panic made a rapid return.

"I noticed a couple of times that it would feel different when those cysts were developing. I hope I'm not getting another one. It could also just be a yeast infection."

"Do you want me to go with you to see Adeline? Or...do you want me to take you to a drug store?"

"No." She shook her head. "If it's a cyst, I'll know soon enough," she sighed. "I haven't had one in over a year. I was sort of hoping I'd outgrown them. If I get itchy, then that's relatively easy to heal."

"I would feel better if we got everything checked out."

But she shook her head again. "No, I just went to the medio right before we started dating for my checkup. She said everything was perfect."

Dan let his mind move in reverse for a few seconds. They'd really only been together for three months, though to him it felt like a lifetime. He knew that his life had ended when he'd stood beside Amelia's grave and dropped a rose on the lowering coffin, and that it hadn't begun again until he'd escorted Fionna out of Anglington's on that fate-filled night.

He supposed that seeing a medio three months before and having been given a clean bill of health probably meant Fionna was fine.

"Besides, if I needed to go back to the medio, wouldn't Garrett have to take me?"

That effectively sealed the deal. Dan nodded his begrudged agreement. He certainly couldn't accompany her to a gynecological medio and it not alert the Realm to their relationship.

"Okay, but if you need to go, or you need me to back off, or ease up, or you need to take a break for a while, promise me you'll tell me."

She gave him his smile. The one that flooded peace and happiness through his veins. The one that gave him life.

"It's not like that. If I have another cyst, it'll either come out on its own, usually when I have a horrible period, or they'll cast me and take it out at some point, but it doesn't have anything to do with you or with sex."

"You're sure?" He wasn't willing to let her sweep this under the rug.

She laced her fingers back through his. "I promise I'm fine."

CHAPTER 31
WHEN THE SKIES COME TUMBLING DOWN

"Where is she?" Panic seized in Dan's shield as he tried Fionna's cell for the fourth time. His heart pounded in his throat. Memories of an empty house, marred with images of Amelia's capture, sliced through his every thought. He casted his phone and located hers.

She was at home, but his shield continued to pulse. He raced out the door. Amelia had been at home as well.

In less than three minutes, he flew into the garage. There were no other cars nearby other than in his neighbors' driveways.

He flung open the door. "Fi..." he started to shout but halted abruptly. His hand flew to his chest. He was afraid his thundering heart would awaken her. There she was. His precious baby was sound asleep on the couch.

"Thank God," he breathed as he slipped into the house and locked out the damp air. He shrugged off his jacket and his boots. He moved soundlessly, grabbed a quilt off the chair, and tenderly spread it over her sleeping form. She didn't move.

He smiled down at her and wondered how long she'd been out. They'd practiced until noon, and the last text he'd received was around five. Concerned that she might be sick, he gently touched her forehead. She didn't seem to have a fever, but she was a little pale.

He wondered if she'd eaten. He headed into the kitchen. Two coffee mugs were in the sink. She always got a clean mug when she made another cup, meaning she'd had two cups of coffee since noon and had still fallen asleep, but there was no sign that she'd eaten anything.

She'd texted that she was going out to lunch with Emily, but she had to be hungry now. He debated. After deciding to let her sleep until eight, he headed upstairs to his office to see if he could get a little more done before he made them dinner.

Wednesday afternoon, he just couldn't shake the gnawing fear that something was horribly wrong. The Angels were practicing half days for the next few weeks. Dan lifted his cell and called her. He was determined to fix whatever it was.

"Hey," she answered.

He squeezed his eyes shut and willed her to sound happy to hear him again. Anything would be better than the fear that haunted the few disbanded words she spoke around him now.

"I miss you," he tried.

"Oh…uh, I'm leaving practice in a few minutes."

Nothing. Nothing but dejected sadness and harrowing fear. What the hell had gone so wrong?

"Do you want me to come get you? I could pick you up. I could get whatever you want to eat on the way. I'll take the afternoon off." He prayed that he could somehow repair whatever it was he'd broken.

He'd stop working so much. He would do anything to have her back. But all she offered was the hollowed shell of the woman he'd fallen madly in love with.

"No, I'm just going to go home or something. You work. Bye."

A week and a half later, Dan lay in the bed in a state of all-consuming terror. What he'd done couldn't be fixed. My God, how could he have let this happen? He prayed that somehow he wasn't seeing and feeling what he knew he felt.

He'd just lifted her head up out of the toilet. She managed to tell him again that it was the flu. The lies were somewhat easier for her the more despondent she became.

She'd fallen back into a depressive sleep almost instantly. Her breasts were huge, swollen and fevered against his bare chest. He closed his eyes again and begged the ether for mercy. How the hell were they going to do this? She wouldn't even tell him. She'd hardly spoken to him in over a week.

Unable to remain there any longer, he eased out of the bed and went into work.

Garrett appeared at his office door just after eight. "They're waiting on you at Lindley's hearing. Did you forget?"

"No." Dan drove his fingertips into his eyes and tried to hide the emotion he'd given in to. He stared at the computer screen. He saw nothing before him but a hellish abyss without any available acceptable future.

"Don't you need to go testify? Don't you want her to get some help? She needs to go to rehab. You said that yourself." Garrett moved into the office and closed the door behind him.

"I don't give a shit about Lindley right now, okay? Just leave."

"What the hell is wrong with you?"

Dan lifted his infuriated eyes and stared Garrett down. "Get the hell out of my office now."

Unaffected by Dan's order, Garrett studied him as if the answers were written on his face. Finally, he shrugged and made his exit. Dan lifted his office phone.

"Kara," he choked out his sister's name.

"Dan? What's wrong? Aren't you at Lindley's hearing?"

"No, I can't go. Uh…" He swallowed down another round of assaulting emotion. "Would you mind if I came over for a little while? I need to talk to you."

"Of course. Are you coming now? Are you really going to leave work?"

"Yeah, is that okay?"

"Sure, do you want me to meet you there? We could go out to lunch. Just…please tell me what's wrong. How can I help?"

"No, Mom and Dad are up here for the trial, and I can't risk anyone overhearing us. Can I just come there?"

"Of course."

The infuriated slam of his office door got everyone's attention. "I'm leaving. I'll be back later. Please, for the love of God, figure some-fucking-thing out today!"

Uncomfortable glances traveled around the room. They crawled over his skin. He knew he was being impossible. He just didn't care.

A half hour later, he paced in his sister's living room and tried to figure out where to begin. She'd offered him some tea, but he couldn't seem to locate the ability to function outside of his abject panic.

He ran his hands through his hair. "Uh okay, how long after you figured out you were pregnant did you start to look pregnant?"

Kara's kind brown eyes goggled. He watched realization form on her features. "Well, let me think." Protectively, she ran her hands over her slightly protruded stomach. "You don't show as quickly with your first. That's what Meredith said."

Dan tried to let that information calm him.

"I think I was probably at least ten weeks along before I even had a little bump. And, uh, it depends on your frame."

He turned to stare at her and tried to determine what she was telling him.

She attempted a broken smile. "I mean, I'm kind of little." She gestured to her chest. "If someone like Fionna were pregnant, she'd be able to hide it a little longer because she's a lot curvier than I am normally."

Dan didn't respond, so Kara filled the silence. "Her boobs are way bigger than mine." She glanced up uncomfortably. She was gnawing the inside of her mouth just like she did when she was a kid and was about to be punished for something.

"How do you figure out the weeks thing? How do you know how far along you are? Is it from when you conceived, or when you figured out you were pregnant?"

"From the time of your last period, but a lot of women don't know they're pregnant right at first."

He mentally added a week and a half to the date of the lingerie shower, Dan's body gave a convulsive shudder. Six weeks. If she was going to start showing at ten weeks, he had just over a month to take down an entire criminal organization and to convince her that he could take care of her and their child.

"Dan, please say something."

"What the fuck do you want me to say?"

Tears sprang to her eyes. Dammit, now he was taking this out on his little sister.

"Tell me what you're thinking." She swallowed down raw emotion.

"I…" He shook his head and collapsed on her sofa. "I don't know what to do." He finally gave in and let the terror consume him. "She's a disaster. She's either crying and hiding it from me or sleeping. What the hell am I supposed to do? Let Garrett Haydenshire pretend that the baby is his as well? Wretchkinsides will kill her, just like he killed Amelia. He'll kill her and the baby as soon as he finds out it's mine. And she can't challenge under that aegis if she's pregnant. She's going to lose her job, and there's not a damn thing I can do to stop it."

"She could have an abortion," Kara whispered.

Dan nodded. "She hardly speaks to me, but if she'd wanted that I'm betting it would already be done. She's always wanted kids. She wanted to have kids with me." He shook his head in abject disgust that he'd let this happen. It was entirely his fault.

"Is she scared of Wretchkinsides or of you?" Kara's voice turned soft and soothing.

"I'm sure she's scared of both of us right now. I haven't been much fun to live with the last few weeks. She's terrified of how Mom will react and about the Realm finding out. And I can't help her with any of it."

~

Rainer rolled his eyes in disdain and listened to Logan chuckle as they pulled into the Iodex parking deck.

"I swear, I'm surprised they don't show up in our freaking shower," Rainer spat furiously.

There was another gaggle of press awaiting him in the parking deck.

"Hey, do you still want Ad and me to come over and help you paint tonight?" Logan asked quickly before they exited the Porsche.

"If you don't mind. We'd like to get all of the work done before the wedding so we can move in when we get back from our honeymoon. I'm scared if we hire painters, they'd tell the press where we moved. I already had to get Garrett to arrange the people who refinished the floors."

Rainer braced himself, stared out through the gap of the concrete structure where he'd parked, and took in the cherry buds just beginning to break through on the trees.

Spring was well on its way, and in a few short weeks, Emily Anne Haydenshire would become Emily Haydenshire Lawson.

After deciding that whatever annoyance the press was causing was more than worth it, he exited the car.

"Rainer, Rainer, Rainer." He never knew the sound of his own name could be so annoying. "Are you looking forward to the gala this weekend in your honor, Rainer?" A reporter hoisted a microphone in his face, running along beside him.

"Have you and Emily purchased a home off Haydenshire property?" a woman Rainer recognized from the *Realm Times* called.

"How is Emily handling the pressure, Rainer?" called another woman, this one from *Realm Bride* magazine.

Rainer considered screeching at the woman. The only reason Emily was under so much pressure and scrutiny was because of the press. They'd snapped photos of Rainer and Emily eating at a deli near their new home. Emily had been biting into a ham sandwich on pumpernickel when they'd taken the first shot. The headline the next day had questioned Emily's ability to fit into her gown if she kept eating like that.

Rainer had been furious and so had the Crown Governor. Emily, however, had stopped eating out altogether and had lost several pounds, much to Rainer's chagrin.

He was extremely concerned about her. She wasn't handling the pressure all that well if the truth were told. He and Logan sprinted inside the Senate and slammed the steel doors in the face of the press.

"Is your fan club still out there?" Vindico somehow sounded even angrier than he had when Rainer had left at ten o'clock the night before. He'd been in a terrible mood for the past few weeks.

"Yeah, sorry."

Vindico shrugged. "I assume if you could've gotten rid of them, you would've by now."

Rainer gave a weary nod. He wondered how much longer Vindico was going to force them to work until well into the night.

"As soon as McCoy decides to get his ass to work, we'll get on with the meeting," Dan snarled to the elite team.

Governor Haydenshire moved through a moment later.

"Hey, Dad. How's Abby?" Logan asked after sharing a withering glare with Rainer over Vindico's mood.

"Your mother is astounding, as you know. I'm tempted to call up Venton and alert the Valeduto Predilects that, though they apparently feel newborn care has changed since we first started having children, my baby girl slept through the night last night at only four weeks old."

Everyone chuckled and offered the Crown Governor their congratulations. He'd been looking rather worn as of late, between caring for Mrs. Haydenshire, Abigail, the twins, and with all of the events leading up to Emily and Rainer's wedding.

McCoy showed just a few minutes late. He looked morose. Everyone had been walking around Vindico on eggshells.

He ordered everyone to his office and slammed the door behind them. "I just got off the phone with Fitzroy. He's got some intelligence for us. We're going to make a show out at the O'Ryans' today. Then we're going to see if we can't get some real work done. I've got things that need to be taken care of, and I need Wretchkinsides ended now!"

Rainer had heard this speech on a daily basis for the last two weeks.

"Apparently Fitz's guy who's imbedded in the French Interfeci found out that our pal Dominic is coming to the States. He's due in this afternoon, but I don't know why. We're going out to the O'Ryans' mansion to fake a search. I have to make it appear to Marlisa that I'm looking to put Mitch back in prison. I can't have Nic coming in and discovering that O'Ryan's been helping us.

"In other news, Fitz's guy also found out that Clarence Pendergrath is looking to be instated in the Interfeci ranks officially. He wants to follow in his old man's footsteps. The rules for entry are a hundred thousand dollar take or you help with a hit," he reminded everyone. "Kid's barely seventeen years old, and I'd like to save him from himself if we can. Unfortunately, he hasn't done anything I can arrest him for and just knowing he's planning something isn't going to cut it. Is there anything anyone needs to tell me before we head out to the O'Ryans' and kick the door in?"

"Yeah, I need the afternoon off. I've got a few things I need to take care of." Garrett's voice was distant and tunneled. Rainer turned to stare at him. He sounded sick.

The entire team grimaced. Asking for time off, in light of Vindico's recent mood, seemed like an incredibly stupid thing to do.

Vindico's eyes narrowed as he glared at Garrett hatefully. A heated staring match ensued across the desk between the two men. But to Rainer's shock, Dan nodded. Bitter realization seemed to warp his chiseled features.

"Yeah sure, whatever you need to do." His tone bordered on kind.

"Thanks." Garrett gave him a single nod.

The entire Elite team knew something was going on that only Garrett and Dan were aware of, but no one had any idea what it might be.

Fionna crossed Rainer's mind. Garrett was Fionna's best friend, and the Angels had the afternoon off.

"All right, we're leaving in five minutes for the O'Ryans'. Make it look good. We're conducting a search and seizure." Vindico never dropped Garrett's gaze. "Let's go." He opened the door to his office. Everyone moved out quickly.

CHAPTER 32

TESTS

GARRETT HAYDENSHIRE

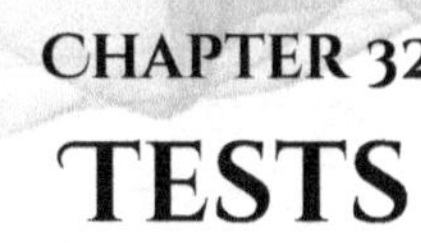

Dan stopped Garrett at the door. "Hey, this is no big deal. Why don't you go on and pick her up? Just take the day." Absolute defeat perforated his tone.

Garrett stared at Dan and wondered how much he'd already figured out.

"Yeah, thanks." He moved toward his desk, but Dan caught his arm. "I love her," he choked out in a desperate plea. "I love her so fucking much."

Fuck, fuck, fuck. How the hell did you let this happen? He wanted to scream at him, but he managed a slight nod. "I know, Dan." He grabbed his car keys and left. He refused to meet any of the curious stares he was receiving.

"Man, who is this for?" Will's tone held no judgment, only deep concern as he handed Garrett the drug store bag.

"You can't say anything to anyone, not even Brooke." Garrett wasn't accustomed to keeping things from Will. He wasn't certain he even knew how. He'd shared a room with his big brother for most of his life. They were less than a year apart and had been inseparable since birth.

Quickly glancing around the parking lot they were standing in, Garrett drew a steadying breath. "It's for Fi," he choked, "so it's certainly not mine if it's positive."

"Oh fuck, does Dan know?"

"He knows something's up. Not sure if he thinks it's this, but he may." Garrett held up the bag.

"Hey, tell her if she needs anything…" Will offered instantly.

"I will. You know I'll take care of her."

"Yeah, I know you will, but you're not the guy she needs if that's positive." He gestured back to the pregnancy test he'd purchased for his brother.

"She's my best friend. She called me sobbing. She's a fucking disaster. He's torn up because she won't talk to him. I'm not gonna let her shut him out and have nobody. If she needs me, then I'm there. No questions asked."

Will nodded his understanding. "He gave you the day off?"

"I told you he knew I was going to get her. He knows something's up."

"Do you want me to come with you?"

"No." Garrett shook his head. The last thing Fionna needed was someone else knowing that she was in an inescapable disaster.

"I'm gonna head to Alexandria, take her back to my place, give her a little while. Maybe it'll be negative."

"How late is she?" Will asked.

"She told me she wasn't quite sure, but then also said at least three weeks. I'm betting it's way more than that, and she's lying to herself. She does that sometimes. Like I said, she's a disaster."

Will's eyes closed in defeat. He shook his head.

"I'll call you later." Garrett climbed back in the Highlander and headed to the arena.

Regret washed through him. He hated having to ask Will to buy the test for him. Fionna Styler certainly couldn't walk into a drug store and purchase a pregnancy test as that would effectively end her career.

The entire Realm was under the impression she was dating Garrett, so he had to play by the same rules.

240

He parked around the back of the arena. He didn't want Emily or Chloe to see that he was there or who he was picking up.

Fionna appeared beside his Highlander. Her eyes were weak and heavy. Garrett was certain it was from the sheer number of tears she'd sobbed in the past few weeks whenever Dan wasn't home with her.

She'd tried to play it off when he was there. At least that's what she'd told him the night before on the phone.

Garrett hadn't reminded her that Dan wasn't only an Ioses Predilect, he was also a Visium Predilect, and that he knew perfectly well she was keeping something from him.

"Hey, baby." He pulled Fionna into his chest and wrapped her up in his arms. She began sobbing again. Garrett felt the same bitter ache in his chest anytime he held Fionna and let her cry.

"Come on. Let's go find out what we're dealing with, okay? I'm right here."

An hour later, Garrett paced outside of the master bathroom in his apartment waiting on Fionna to emerge. *Will's right. I'm not the guy who should be here for this.*

She slowly walked out of the bathroom. Garrett could see the test on the counter as he watched her crawl into his bed and curl up in her customary ball. He checked his watch and walked into the bathroom. But he didn't have to wait the recommended two minutes as the instructions had suggested. The plus sign was glowing bright blue.

His heart sank into his stomach as he tried to think of what to say to her. He crawled into bed beside her.

"Hey," he soothed, "come here." He unfolded her and laid her on his chest.

Her tears fell in convulsive sheets as she sobbed against him. He let her cry, rubbed her back, and kissed her forehead. He let her hide away from the world for just a little while. He set his shield firmly around her.

"It's all right. I promise you," he continually assured her.

"It's not all right. He's going to go insane. And the whole freaking

Realm thinks I'm dating you! I'm gonna lose my job! I have nothing. Dan doesn't want kids right now. He's never even home. All he cares about is ending the Interfeci."

Garrett nodded. He debated telling her that Dan's renewed obsession had everything to do with her being pregnant. Dan knew. Garrett should have already figured that out. "Are you gonna keep it?"

"I don't know." She shivered in his arms. "I shouldn't, but I want it."

Garrett wiped away another round of tears. "Fi, baby, you need to tell him."

"No…not yet."

"All right, but if you decide you don't want it, please tell him first. Don't do that on your own."

"If I decide to not have it, will you go with me?" Her voice trembled in her tender plea.

"Baby, I will be wherever you need me to be at any moment that you need me to be there. You know that, but," Garrett choked, "I don't think it's an either or proposition. I know this isn't how you and Dan planned it, but he's not going to blame you for this. He's a good guy. You know that. You fell in love with him. You don't have to decide between having him or having this baby. You can have both." Garrett knew perfectly well that having Dan Vindico's kids was in Fionna's future, even if it came to pass just a little faster than they would have liked.

"His dad's a governor, and his mom will freak," she reminded Garrett in a terror-ridden sob. "So I've pretty much ruined his life."

Anger timed in his rhythms. "Hey,"—he raised her chin with his hand so she was looking into his eyes—"you didn't do this by yourself. And you haven't ruined anything. You saved him from the hell he's been living for the last ten years. Give Dan a little credit. He loves you, and he won't give a damn what his parents think. You are all that matters to him. Do you hear what I'm saying to you?" His voice rose in accordance with his fervor.

"And what about Wretchkinsides? I thought if he knew I was with Dan, he'd kill me just like he killed Amelia." She wrapped her arms around her midsection like she was physically protecting the fetus from harm.

Tension clenched his jaw and terror clawed his shield. He had no answer for that. Dan was right. Wretchkinsides would hunt her to the ends of the earth. He'd kill her and the baby just to punish Dan. And this was effectively a disaster.

"Just hold me, please." Her chin trembled as another round of tears cascaded down her beautiful face.

"I will lie here and hold you for as long as you want. You mean the world to me. You're my best friend. You will always be my best friend, but I'm not the guy who should be here right now. You have to tell him." Garrett wrapped her back up in his arms and cradled her tenderly until she cried herself to sleep.

~

Dan Vindico

It was almost nine, and Fionna still wasn't home. She was with Garrett. She was safe, but her pulling away from him hurt far worse than the terror of her being pregnant with his child. He prayed she still loved him and that she was just afraid to tell him.

He moved around their home, desperate for something, anything that might give him some semblance of hope. His hands gently touched the perfume bottles on the dresser. He opened the drawer and let the silky undergarments slip through his fingers.

Without thought, he rushed to the bathroom but left the room darkened. He could see by the moon alone. He lifted the brown glass bottle of kukui and coconut oil, sent to her by her grandmother recently. Pulling the stopper, he inhaled deeply of the scent of her, but that wasn't quite right.

Not stopping long enough to consider the fact that he was effectively losing his mind from terror and lack of sleep, he carried the bottle to the hamper, lifted the panties she'd worn the day before, and inhaled the perfumes together.

The scent clawed at his throat. The need to hold her, to tell her that he'd figure something out, that he would make this right, ate at him.

He returned the bottle and the panties and moved to the bedside table. He pulled the Browning .22 from the drawer and affixed the silencer. He slid into his jacket and pulled a baseball cap low over his eyes before he climbed back in the Ferrari.

~

He stood against a massive oak keeping the gun down. The lights were on at the O'Ryans'. Wretchkinsides's Vanquish, the same one Pendergrath had driven when he was in the States, was parked in the driveway. Dan waited. He'd texted Garrett and informed him that he was working all night. He knew Fionna would stay there. She didn't want to see him anyway. He had all night to hunt.

The front door opened at ten. Dan's heart timed itself to his breaths. One by one. He could do this. He slid to the side and watched while keeping himself hidden in the shadows.

Marlisa stood on the front porch with her father. "I miss you. Why can't I go with you?"

"Marlisa," Nic tsked as if his daughter missing him was ridiculous. "I have work to do. This is quite an undertaking. Stay here. I'll get you when we've taken care of everything."

She shrugged and returned to the house. This was his chance. Dan raised the gun, but Fionna's beautiful face swam in the tears in his eyes. *Dan, don't. Not like this.*

~

Rainer Lawson

Emily moved beside him, and Rainer grinned. "Hey there, baby," he yawned and pulled her back onto his chest.

"Ugh, this is going to be such a pain."

Rainer hated to agree. The Saturday the Haydenshires were hosting a huge gala for Rainer and Emily had finally arrived.

"The Angels will be there," he offered hopefully.

"Yeah, but so will the owners and the entire freaking Senate, so we all have to behave."

Rainer laughed and kissed her forehead. "I like it better when you misbehave."

Emily grinned and nuzzled her head against him. "I can't believe in just a few weeks I get to be Mrs. Rainer Lawson. It's what I've wanted since I was four years old."

Rainer's heart skipped a beat as he thought about the wedding and then about the wedding night. "I can't wait." He let his hands travel down her chest and across her stomach.

"Once you marry me, then I get to boss you around for real."

Rainer cracked up. "Oh, so the last sixteen years have just been for practice?"

"Yes," she assured him through her hysterical giggles.

In a quick move, Rainer turned and pulled Emily underneath him. He moved up her body until his erection was braced against her mound.

She stopped laughing as a broad grin formed on her face.

"You know, if you ever want to boss me around in bed, I would really enjoy that." His voice turned low and thrumming.

"Is that so?"

"Oh yeah, baby."

"You know, when we were little and I made Logan marry us and made you give me a ring pop, we never played pretend honeymoon."

"I'm pretty sure if we had, your dad would've put a stop to all of the play weddings."

"I know. So I was thinking we should play honeymoon now."

Rainer moaned. He pulsed against her. "Do you think so?"

Emily gave him a heavy nod, and his pulse raced.

"We can play, but it'll have to be quick because we're supposed to be at your parents' in an hour. But our wedding night is gonna be nice and slow. I plan to see just how many times and how many ways I can make you come undone for me before I lay you down and make you my wife."

Emily panted. Her pulse raced as she trembled beneath him. "I don't want to go today. I just want to be your wife. I don't want to wait anymore."

After swallowing down his own deep desires, he nodded his understanding. They'd been attending shower after endless shower given in their honor. It seemed each wedding gift was attached to advice that had been heaped on them in heavy doses.

The press was relentless. They couldn't seem to escape. They'd given up on even going to see their new home because they were constantly followed.

News vans had shown up at the tux shop when Rainer and all of his groomsmen were there for the final fittings. They'd gotten shots of the tuxes. Emily had been devastated.

Rainer and Emily had both seriously considered just going to one of the other Realm governors like Patrick and Lucy had. They could sneak out one night. All Rainer wanted was to be married to her, but every time he thought of all of the planning Emily had done and of her dreaming about their wedding since she was a little girl, he'd talked her out of going.

"I tell you what. Let's get ready to go, but tonight, I'll bring you back here, tuck you up in our bed, and make you forget every hug, and piece of advice, and pleasantry we've had to endure all day."

Peaceful calm washed through Emily's energy. "That sounds perfect. And after the wedding, you're taking me away for two whole weeks where no one knows where we are, right?"

"Oh yeah, baby. I'm taking you away from everything and everyone. Two whole weeks just you and me."

"I can't wait!"

"Me either," he assured her.

Thinking about hiding Emily away in the lap of luxury deep in the Florida Keys for two entire weeks all alone had been how Rainer had gotten through the press's relentless quest to find out everything they could about the wedding, and how he'd gotten through Vindico's horrendous moods that only seemed to worsen with each passing day.

CHAPTER 33
CAPTURE TIME

After Rainer had assisted Emily's brothers in hoisting numerous canopies up in the Haydenshires' back fields and had watched the teams of caterers set up for the shower, he was being slapped on the back by Gentry Livingston.

He'd been an acquaintance of Rainer's grandfather. He still considered himself to be a major player in the Senate though he'd retired from Iodex long before Rainer's father had become Crown Governor and the constitution had been rewritten.

With a quick adjustment of his collar and tie, Rainer tried not to roll his eyes.

"You're making a huge mistake there, Richard." Gentry wheezed and coughed all over Rainer's plate of finger sandwiches and fruit salad.

Quickly deciding not to correct Mr. Livingston on his name for the third time, Rainer glanced around for Emily. She was giggling with her mother and Adeline as they watched him.

"Oughta play the field before you settle down there, boy. Only way a marriage works is if you go deaf before you walk down the aisle so you don't have to listen to 'em harping."

Rainer offered the required polite chuckle and then shot Logan an SOS glare.

Connor and Logan stepped in. "Hey Rainer, Em needs your help with…something."

"See, already ordering you around. Run while you still can, boy! Run, run!" Mr. Livingston urged vehemently. His tone echoed out to everyone standing nearby.

Governor Haydenshire approached and handed Henry to Rainer. "Mr. Livingston, it's so nice of you to join us." The governor effectively saved Rainer.

Henry was busily consuming a butter cookie with his right hand. He had two others in his left hand for later snacking.

"Lillian, I was hoping we'd get to see little Miss Abigail. I brought something for her," Marian Vindico urged.

Rainer noted Dan rolling his eyes. He kept his jaw clenched tightly. His gaze continually travelled to Fionna and Garrett talking in the corner. They'd been locked in a tight-lipped conversation since the gala had begun.

"The baby is inside with my mom, Marion. She's asleep, but it was so sweet of you to bring a gift. You didn't have to do that." Mrs. Haydenshire looked rather weary of being asked if Abigail would be making a debut at the shower.

"Perhaps I could just sneak in for a peek."

Dan stepped in to rescue Mrs. Haydenshire. "Mom, the baby is inside for a good reason. It's to keep her safe. You don't need the Haydenshires to risk Abigail's safety so that you can tell your Bridge Club you saw her."

Mrs. Haydenshire looked panicked as she glanced between Mrs. Vindico and her son.

"Why are you not with Fionna, Daniel? Are you two fighting?" Mrs. Vindico quipped.

Rainer's ears perked up. He'd been wondering the very same thing for the last several weeks.

"No, Mother, we're not. You know perfectly well why we aren't together. Could you please keep your voice down? If you run your trap about us being together to the hundreds of people here, there's really no point in us making ourselves miserable by being apart, now is there?"

"Emily," Mrs. Haydenshire called frantically. "Why don't you and Rainer open your gifts, honey?"

"Oh, uh, okay." She and Rainer were whisked into white folding chairs in the center of the tents while everyone situated chairs around them.

Rainer hated this portion of all of the showers he'd attended over the last few weeks. He never felt like he expressed his appreciation appropriately, and some of the gifts they'd received were rather odd.

While keeping an eye on Dan, a sense of relief washed over Rainer as Fionna discreetly moved until she was standing right beside him.

He smiled at her adoringly and moved until the backs of their hands were touching.

Garrett remained by her side. He kept up appearances that they were together, but Fionna's weary eyes sought Dan. Rainer wondered if she'd been crying. He'd never seen her look so depressed.

The first gift Emily opened was a place setting of the dishware that she'd selected and registered.

She'd shown Rainer picture after picture of different dishes, trying to get his opinion. He'd finally admitted that he didn't really care what the dish looked like as long as it had food on it, so she'd finished their registry herself.

"This is from the Carringtons," Lucy supplied as she handed Emily a package from Regis and Serena.

Emily insisted that Rainer open it. He pulled the paper off the package and offered the Carringtons an appreciative smile as he pulled a long, silver, cylindrical tube out of the box.

Emily smiled. "Uh, thank you," she offered quizzically. Rainer tried to determine what they'd been given before he offered his thanks as well.

Governor Carrington chuckled. "It's a time capsule, you two. Serena and I took the liberty of placing one of your wedding invitations in there, and we were hoping that you would add a few things to it. Perhaps you could bury it wherever you two decide to set down roots that will be all your own."

Rainer was deeply touched that Governor Carrington understood that he was looking forward to having somewhere that was really his own, just him and Emily.

"Thank you, Governor," Rainer urged sincerely, "that really means a lot." He stood to shake Governor Carrington's hand, but as he moved toward him, Rainer's cell gave its shrill ring.

His eyes goggled as he listened to Dan's, Logan's, and Garrett's phones make the same noise. The deafening sound echoed around him as every Iodex officer's phone began blaring.

Fionna and Adeline shared a terrified glance as Logan and Vindico answered simultaneously.

~

Dan Vindico

"This is Vindico," Dan demanded.

"Dan, it's Cahill," the Gifted police officer who was running the switchboards confirmed. "Wretchkinsides somehow managed to get several of his guys back in the country. Fitzroy just called. Nic just bought dozens of AKs and Mac 10s. They're headed to DC. Pravus is with the dealer. We got him on an interstate cam on 64. I can't think where he might be heading if it's not to the Haydenshires', Everyone knows the big shindig is there today."

His heart seized and his blood ran cold. Dan was momentarily unable to speak. *This is quite an undertaking, dear.* Wretchkinsides's malignant voice echoed in his memories. But realization finally jolted through his shield. He was going to end them. This was his chance. No more lies. No more hiding. He'd tell the world tonight that Fionna was his and that she was carrying his child.

"He's not coming here. He's not getting that far," Dan spat furiously when he regained the ability to speak.

Every Iodex officer that heard the conversation on their phones wore the same stunned, terror-filled expression. Governor Haydenshire had casted Logan's phone and pulled the signal into his own. He'd heard everything Cahill had to say.

"Let us know what you want us to do," Cahill urged.

"Will do." Dan ended the call. His heartbeat rang in his ears. With a deep breath, he set to work. "So sorry folks, but the party is unfortunately over. Please move quickly to your cars and head home."

"Stephen, what's going on?" Mrs. Haydenshire demanded.

"Governor Haydenshire, I need you to get Abigail and the twins and go with them to Will's. Stay there until you hear from me. I'm sending a team with you."

"We'll get her." Lucy and Patrick raced toward the farmhouse.

"Please take Fionna and Emily with you and Adeline as well. Keep them there," Dan heard his own voice fracture.

Governor Haydenshire nodded his understanding. "Lillian, go pack bags for the boys and get enough bottles for Abigail for several days," the governor ordered.

Mrs. Haydenshire took both of the twins and followed Lucy and Patrick into the house.

"What are we gonna do?" Logan stepped in.

"We're gonna end Wretchkinsides, once and for all. I'm done. This is it," Dan vowed.

Determination rose like bile in the pit of his throat. Today was the day. It was all going to end. He was going to end the hatred, end the violence, end the threats. He was going to have a life with Fionna, a real life. They were going to have a child, his child. He wasn't walking away this time until Dominic Wretchkinsides was dead.

He pulled Fionna into him forcefully. "I love you so much. And this is it. I'm done. I'm not playing his games anymore. By tonight, I'm going to tell the world you're mine." He discreetly rubbed his right hand over her midsection. "I love you."

"Dan, stop. You're scaring me." Fionna trembled. She stared down at his hand on her slightly swollen waistline.

"It's okay, baby. I promise you. I'll take care of everything." He kissed her passionately, no longer caring who saw him, and gave another loving caress of his child's current residence. "I'll come to Will's and get you when it's all over."

"Daniel, just what are you planning, son?" Governor Vindico demanded.

"This is my show, Dad. Stay the hell out of my way. Okay, each partnered team should have a vehicle. Everyone meet me at the Senate building," he ordered the Elite teams and then pointed to Rainer and Logan. "You two, come with me. We're making a quick stop first."

He'd come up with this plan as he'd paced the halls of his house. This had to work. It was their only chance.

CHAPTER 34

MOVE THE MOUNTAIN

RAINER LAWSON

"What's he doing?" Logan mouthed as Vindico steered the Expedition into the O'Ryans' circular driveway.

Rainer shrugged. He had no idea.

"Let's go," Vindico ordered.

Rainer and Logan slid out of the car and sprinted behind him as he raced up the brick front stairs and busted the front door open violently.

While ignoring the stunned disbelief on the members of Mitchell's family's faces, Dan marched inside. He had cuffs on Marlisa and her casted and drained in a matter of moments.

"You're under arrest." He dragged her out the front door and threw her in the back of the Expedition. "Keep a pistol on her," he demanded of Rainer.

Rainer pulled his gun and stared bewildered at Logan who shrugged his shock.

Several minutes later, Vindico jerked the Expedition into park. He hoisted Marlisa out of the back seat.

"You can't do this. I didn't do anything wrong!" She'd regained enough energy to be belligerent.

"Shut up," Vindico growled. All of Elite Iodex watched in stunned disbelief as Vindico threw her into one of the holding cells in the Senate. He spun and raced back to his office.

Dogged determination cast Garrett's face. "All right, listen up," he called to the team in Vindico's absence. "Dan is not going to lure Wretchkinsides in and then get himself killed. We're going with him, right beside him, and we're ending this with him. This is it, gentlemen. This is what we've been training and working for all this time. So let's get this done for all the people that he's tortured and killed. Let's do this for my brother, for Amelia, for Samantha Peterson, for Governor Lawson, and please, please let's do this for Dan. He deserves to be able to bury the dead and go on with his life."

His speech visibly moved the entire team. They stood ready to fight beside their leader, to fight for good, to end evil, and to take the opportunity to make their world a safer place.

"I'm so proud of you, Rainer. Always keep Emily safe," Rainer heard the words of his father echo in his mind as he stood in the hallowed halls his father had established.

Vindico returned with the most recently cloned phones from the Interfeci. Two Non-Elite officers had cloned Pendergrath's phone Friday at The Tantra.

He photographed Marlisa in the cell and then texted it to every contact in the list.

"You want her back, you come and get her -V," was the message.

As they awaited a reply, Vindico turned to the waiting teams. "This is Pravus, for those of you who might not know." He held up a mugshot photograph of Pravus for everyone to see. "As you heard, he is currently traveling with a great deal of weaponry. So keep your shields up constantly. We are shooting to kill until you get to Wretchkinsides. He's all mine," Vindico sneered hatefully.

Rainer's stomach knotted. He wasn't going to let Dan end his own life just to be the one that took out Wretchkinsides.

Marlisa would mouth off occasionally, but the enhanced cell kept her energies low.

Time ticked by slowly. Rainer tried not to look at Marlisa. He tried to forget that she was being used as bait in an extremely dangerous game.

Suddenly the phone made a foreboding chirp, and everyone moved in to see.

A horrified gasp came from Vindico as, "Oh my god," fell from his lips in utter shock.

"What?" Rainer turned to see the screen. His eyes goggled as he took in the picture that was Wretchkinsides's response.

Bridgette was bound and gagged in front of a brick wall. She looked terrified.

"If you want her back, come get her, and bring Marlisa, or she'll suffer the same fate as dear Amelia. You have fifteen minutes before the games begin," followed the gut-wrenching picture.

"How did he find out she was spying for us?" Garrett demanded.

Vindico shook his head. "She told him." Suddenly breath hissed between Vindico's teeth. "I know where he is. That's the basement of The Tantra!"

"Are we taking her?" Garrett threw his arm out to Marlisa.

"No." Vindico shook his head. "Listen up! They have a relatively innocent woman they've taken hostage. Make certain you don't hit her if you fire. Take them down with energy, cuff them, fire if you're fired upon, but be absolutely certain you know who you're hitting."

Everyone strapped on bulletproof vests, energy synced jackets, and loaded ammo into the cars.

"Let's go," Vindico demanded as the SUVs flew from the parking decks headed to The Tantra Gentlemen's Club in a flood of blue lights.

～

Crown Governor Stephen Haydenshire

"Hey Fi, are you okay?" Will offered Fionna a cup of tea that Brooke had prepared for her. She'd been crying since they'd all arrived at Will's home a few minutes before.

Stephen had been keeping a close eye on her. Emily had stuck by her and tried to calm her frantic energy streams, but she seemed too distraught.

Stephen soothed. "Sweetheart, Dan is an outstanding officer. He'll be all right." He considered anything else that might be causing her tears. "And Garrett as well."

Fionna nodded but continued to cry.

"Hey Em, could you go help Brooke with something in the kitchen, please," Will commanded his little sister.

"Oh, uh, sure," Emily stammered confusedly.

Mrs. Haydenshire moved to sit beside Fionna. She clearly hoped that she could mother her into feeling better. "You've been through so much with all of this and having to pretend to date Garrett, and not be seen with Daniel. That can't have been easy." She offered Fionna a place to begin in an effort to get her to talk.

Fionna did lay her head on Lillian's shoulder and allowed herself to be embraced tenderly.

"Here." Stephen handed her a handkerchief.

Will seemed to be debating something when Emily's cell phone rang.

"Oh my gosh!" she gasped after a few minutes of silence. "Okay, please be careful!" her voice choked. "I love you too," she fussed as tears welled in her eyes.

"What did he say?" Brooke hugged Emily to her as she trembled.

"Wretchkinsides took Bridgette hostage, and Iodex is going to try and get her back from The Tantra, but Dan thinks all of Interfeci is there waiting on them."

"Oh my god." Fionna sounded horrified. Stephen had no idea how to reassure everyone at once.

Something made Will decide to act. "Hey, Fionna, I hope you don't mind, but Garrett told me what's going on. He needed my help. I really think you better tell them." He gestured to his parents.

Emily and Adeline moved back into the living room. Fionna looked woefully lost for a long drawn minute.

"Do you want me to tell them?" Will offered kindly.

Fionna shook her head as she gazed into Lillian's eyes. "What's wrong, sweetheart? What's going on? Let us try to help."

Fionna's face fell into her hands. "I'm pregnant," she managed to get out between gasping sobs.

Stephen's heart seized as he shared a terrified glance with his wife.

"Okay, it's okay. Does Dan know?" Lillian kept her tone calm and pacifying. She kept Fionna cradled close.

"I think he suspects," she admitted in another choked plea.

"I'm sure he does." Stephen recalled the telltale signs that Lillian had tried to hide when she was pregnant with Will and hadn't worked up the courage to tell him yet.

"I have to tell him. He can't just go in there and get himself killed." Fionna stood in fitful determination.

"Wait, I'll go with you," Emily declared.

"Me too," Adeline agreed as the girls all grabbed their things.

"Excuse me, but none of you are going anywhere," Stephen commanded.

"I'm sorry, Governor Haydenshire, but I'm not your little girl. You can't stop me," Fionna informed him defiantly. She grimaced. "You don't understand. Before, he couldn't be broken because he already *was* so broken. Now, he's not anymore."

Stephen let the wisdom and truth of that wash over him. She'd saved Daniel when no one else ever could've. "Then I'm going with you. Will, stay here with your mother and the kids," he ordered his oldest son.

"You sure you don't need me to come?"

"No, but she's right. Dan needs to know. A man who's a father makes entirely different decisions than a man who isn't."

～

Dan Vindico

"I want every available Gifted officer on the grounds. Our priority is to remove Bridgette Meyers safely from the basement, then I want every man there processed and either in Coriolis or in the ground by nightfall!" Vindico ordered Cahill over the phone as he drove with the sirens blaring and lights flashing down the interstate.

After hanging up, Dan threw his cell onto the console and concentrated on the task at hand. Garrett was beside him. His jaw worked rhythmically. Dan was certain it was in an effort not to reveal Fionna's secret.

Dan was painfully aware that he knew, that Fionna had called him, that Garrett was who she'd turned to when she was terrified. The bitter regret ate him alive.

"I'm giving her the ring as soon as he draws his last breath."

He and Garrett had a silent conversation. Dan used his eyes to plead with Garrett to confirm what he already knew.

"Good." Garrett nodded. "She needs that."

"I know." He slammed the Expedition into park on the gravel lot of The Tantra Gentlemen's Club. "I know everything," he urged. Garrett gave another heavy nod.

Iodex cars and jet-black Expeditions pulled in all around him. As his boots crunched in the gravel, determination burned hot in his gut.

"I need eyes on the top level. Make absolutely certain that all of the dancers and waitstaff are out of the club, along with any patrons stupid enough to show up here today," Dan demanded.

The Virginia Gifted Police force raced inside. Two minutes later, Dan watched a few middle-aged men exit. They looked extremely sheepish. The club owner and bartender were next.

"I sent the girls home. What's going on in there?" the owner demanded.

"Cuff them both, and put them in a car. I want them for questioning," Dan ordered an officer standing nearby.

"We're moving in on my count. I want an Elite team in each battalion. I will lead one, and Officer Haydenshire will lead the other." He pointed to Garrett.

"My battalion will enter the basement from the rear entrance." Dan pointed toward the back of the club beside the dumpsters to a concrete staircase that led to the basement. When they'd been dating, that was where he'd pick Bridgette up to make certain no one ever saw him.

"The other battalion will enter from the top. Our focus is to overwhelm them with power. Go in with guns drawn and shields up. Do not lower your shield, ever, for any reason."

"Sir," rang from every officer standing beside him.

"Make me proud," Dan commanded.

CHAPTER 35

THE END

RAINER LAWSON

Rainer fell into line beside Logan and behind Vindico. They were backing Portwood and Ericcson up.

Terror surged through Rainer's veins, though he tried to will it away. He set his mind on the goal. If Wretchkinsides went to Coriolis tonight in cells beside all of his men, the Realm his father had fought and died to create would be safer. Good would have won out over evil once again. Emily would be safe.

Vindico gave a single nod to the officers traveling as the point men. The enhanced two-way radios in all of their ears chimed.

"We're in position. Just say when," Garrett said.

Dan touched the mic in his ear. "On my count," he ordered quietly.

The countdown began, and Rainer's heart pounded in his ears in cadence with the numbers. On one, the officers at the front of the line kicked down the door, and hell rained down on them as they flooded into the room in a sea of green protective shield casts.

Round tables were folded against the walls, stacks of chairs were all over the floor, dancers' costumes were in boxes in the corner, and a dozen metal poles were leaned against the concrete brick walls.

Thinking quickly, Rainer threw a bullet headed his way back toward the shooter, and then shot his own magnetic cast at the poles.

He used the force to pull them onto the concrete floor in a deafening heap, bringing two Interfeci members down with a lethal groan.

The Interfeci members in the front room who hadn't seen his cast were distracted long enough for four of them to be casted and taken out.

Gifted police had them cuffed and out the door.

Logan and Portwood had two others down on their knees in the hallway with their hands behind their heads just beyond the doorway. Rainer drained one while Ericcson pulled the energy from his partner. They moved away, letting Non-Elite take over as they made their way deeper into the basement of The Tantra.

~

Garrett Haydenshire

Garrett used all of his massive leg strength to kick the door leading to the basement from the backstage room of The Tantra open. With one brutal kick, he drove the metal hooks on the back of the door deep into Adrian Malicai, who was supposed to be standing guard.

Adrian crumpled to the floor, bleeding badly from the mouth, throat, chest, and groin. His head hit the concrete block wall and then he slithered to the ground.

"Get him in a car," Garrett ordered the police officer standing beside him. He was certain he was dead, but he wasn't taking any chances.

Dan cannot get himself killed. The thought pulsed with every frantic pound of his heart.

He's gonna be a dad, and Fi won't make it without him. Garrett thundered down the steps, gun drawn and shield up followed by thirty of the best damn officers in the Realm.

"Entry room cleared. Moving down the hall," Garrett heard Dan call over the two-way radio.

"Took out Malicai on the stairs. Meet you in the middle," Garrett answered. A bullet flew by Garrett's face. He caught it in his shield and threw it back to the shooter, hitting him in the gut.

"Gunman down in the hallway to right of stairs," he shouted into the radio, ordering half of his team to move to the left and the other half to follow him.

Suddenly Garrett's heart refused him the next beat. The blood that had been coursing through his body froze as Dan's voice shouted, "I've got an Elite officer down, repeat, Elite officer down! Bullet wound left shoulder. Medios move in immediately!"

Terror flooded Garrett's entire being. He raced to another corridor and wrapped his arms around Menendez, whose back was to him. He threw him to the ground, but Menendez managed to chamber his pistol and take aim.

"Not in the mood today, asshole. This is for my brother." Garrett unloaded two bullets, one in his head and one in his chest before he moved on.

Spinning, he brought his boot down on Ferratus's chest. Several ribs cracked under the weight. He drained him and cuffed him instantly.

Logan and Rainer's faces pulsed constantly in his mind. They were only kids. How could they be down here in all of the hell surrounding him? Garrett couldn't make sense of it. He couldn't bury another brother. He couldn't survive that.

"Officer Ericcson is headed to Georgetown. It's a surface shoulder wound, Dan. His shield shattered the bullet. It's just the shrapnel. He'll be fine," an emergency medio tapped into the line.

Breath returned to his lungs as Garrett continued his trek through hell.

~

Dan Vindico

Where the fuck do they have her? Dan methodically scanned the dimly lit spaces through a haze of gunsmoke and reflective casts. He let his focus drift to Fionna. The knowledge that if he got everyone out of this alive she wouldn't have to be afraid anymore drove him. He'd marry her tomorrow if she'd agree. He'd be a daddy. The thought made him reel. He turned the next corner, gun drawn high.

"Vin-di-co, you lost, man?" Shane Zacharian had a deranged look in his eye. His voice was haggard and guttural. "Nic's waiting on you." He was clutching his side, still trying to be tough as he slowly approached death. Blood seeped under his fingers and pooled on the cool concrete beneath him.

"I'll find Nic. Don't worry." Dan kept his pistol aimed at Zacharian's chest. He could put him out of his misery.

The flash in Zacharian's eyes was Dan's only warning. A massive force came around his back, squeezing his chest, trying to shut off his air supply.

"Fuck." Dan spun and slammed the idiot on his back hard against the concrete wall. He spun and landed his fist in Foster's face. He heard Zacharian's pistol chamber.

Without need of more provocation, Dan fired once toward the man on the ground and another time at the man he'd thrown against the wall. He was walking away today, and anyone that tried to stop him would be meeting their maker in short order.

❧

Logan Haydenshire

Bullet smoke and resonating casts filled the air. Logan tried not to breathe too deeply as he backed along the wall to move into the next hallway. He nodded to Rainer as they spun and met with two pistols in their face. Derisive laughter haunted the air.

Through the darkened haze, Logan could see Varenina and Xavier. Rainer had Xavier down, but Varenina pulled the trigger.

"No!" Logan shouted. Panic rocketed upwards from his soul. His heart stalled. He leapt in front of Rainer, adding his shield to his best friend's. They watched as the bullet reflected and hit Varenina's face, shattering his eye socket. They turned away. It was gruesome.

A Gifted policewoman moved in to cuff Xavier. "Nice work, Haydenshire," she complimented.

Logan nodded, but bile blazed his lungs and throat. Tears stung his eyes.

"Thank you," Rainer managed. His voice was harrowed and frightened.

"You're not leaving my baby sister at the altar." Logan's words gave strength to his decision.

"Where could Bridgette be? That's four rooms," Rainer shouted over the whirring sound of bullets and the cold, atrocious groans of death. They coughed against the choking puffs of concrete being hit with cast after cast.

A fist appeared from the dark, and Logan ducked without thinking. Rainer threw a cast and then leapt over Clarence Pendergrath.

"What the fuck, man?" Rainer screeched. "You wanted to be in this, well here you go. You can play with Daddy and all the big boys out at Coriolis." He cuffed Pendergrath and shoved him out into the hallway.

Rainer and Logan took another guilt-ridden glance at Clarence's terrified face as he was dragged off by another officer.

"Wait! Where's my dad?" He sounded distinctly like a frightened child.

"Follow me." Vindico raced by Logan and Rainer, headed toward the northwest corner of the club, down another darkened corridor.

"Logan, are you okay?" Garrett spun out from a hallway on Logan's right, startling him, but he was quite certain he'd never been so thankful to see his big brother in all of his relatively short life. Garrett hugged him forcefully, and Logan allowed it.

"Rainer, look at me." Garrett grabbed Rainer by the scruff of his neck. He pulled him into the hug as well. Logan tried to really see Garrett's face through the smoky mist. He acknowledged what he'd known his entire life. If Garrett was there, everything would be okay.

"Are you all right?" He tried to sound soothing. Rainer nodded his lie. "No, you're not, but it's almost over. Just stay with me. I'll keep you safe."

Rainer and Logan joined McCoy, Portwood, and Tuttle in a sprint to what Logan assumed was the end.

"Where's Barron?" Rainer asked McCoy.

"Took a ricochet to the shin. Looked bad. He's out in the ambulances."

McCoy looked lost without his partner.

~

Crown Governor Stephen Haydenshire

"Fionna, sweetheart, I cannot let you go in there," Stephen demanded as Fionna flew from his Suburban out into the parking lot of The Tantra Gentlemen's Club. One thing was for certain, the girl might've been pregnant, but she was in outstanding shape. Stephen suspected she could outsprint Daniel.

"Dan!" Fionna screeched as she took in the dozens of Gifted ambulances healing up the wounded, and Iodex officers loading man after man into squad cars until they were full and then leaving for Coriolis.

Vomit swirled ominously in Stephen's stomach as he searched the harrowing scene, not certain who or what he might find. Three of his sons were either in an ambulance or were still in that club.

"Dan," Fionna screamed again.

"Fionna." One of the new officers, Barron, reached from a gurney and caught Fionna's hand. A medio held a cast on his shin and was trying to rebuild the bone.

"Shattered it. Took a ricochet off a shield," Barron explained to Stephen. "Fionna, he's all right. He's in there. He led a team in. He's with McCoy. Your kids are in there with him, sir," Barron assured Stephen.

"I have to talk to him right now," Fionna demanded of Barron.

"Hey, okay." He shared a concerned glance with Stephen. "It quieted down a minute ago. I think they'll be out soon. You can't go in there." He cringed and blinked back tears as the medio intensified the cast on his leg.

Fionna jerked her wrist away from Barron's hand and sprinted toward the club. Emily took off with her. Adeline seemed to debate, but then she stepped into the ambulance. "Let me help keep it from hurting him so badly," she urged the medio. He nodded for her to help.

"Girls!" Stephen shouted, but they were much faster than he was. He watched in horror as Fionna threw open the front door and raced inside. He followed them and demanded that they stop, but no one listened.

~

Rainer Lawson

As the sounds of bullets and casts began to dissipate in the air, Rainer heard muffled pleas for help and someone thrashing around several feet ahead of them.

"That's Bridgette," Vindico huffed. He halted the advancing team before they turned the last corner. Suddenly a deep, menacing drawl echoed around them.

"That's Wretchkinsides." Vindico scowled. His eyes hardened with visible malice.

They listened. "Bridgette darling, maybe you've been lying to me. It doesn't appear that Vindico feels about you the way he felt about dear Amelia."

Since Wretchkinsides himself had taped Bridgette's mouth shut, he knew she couldn't respond. He was playing with her before he killed her. Disgust and fury swirled in the pit of Rainer's stomach.

"Vindico thinks he can outplay me. I had more spies than just you at the Crown Governor's inaugural ball despite all of the Receivers in the Realm that were there. I won't be stopped. I have a hand in every single thing that happens, never forget that," Wretchkinsides sneered. "I no longer require your ineffective help. I will not be played or pitted against him for your affections."

A harrowing slap echoed in the air, followed by a muffled scream. Vindico gasped, as frenzied revulsion filled his features.

~

"Let her go!" Dan demanded as he spun suddenly, shocking all of his officers that had followed him to the end. Pendergrath and Pravus were standing before Dan with Wretchkinsides holding a gun in Bridgette's face.

"I'm who you wanted. I'm right here. Let's end this. Let her go." Dan kept his eyes fixed on the cold malevolent glare of Dominic Wretchkinsides.

Malevolence fueled every beat of his heart. Spite darkened his soul.

Dan hadn't let such utter revulsion consume him since Fionna had so thoroughly healed him. She was the antidote, but that seemed like a distant memory in light of standing face to face with the man who'd ended Amelia's life.

Pravus narrowed his beady black eyes. They twitched from Garrett to Logan in a derisive glare. "Come to avenge dear Cal, gentlemen?" He paced between Garrett and Logan.

Using the distraction Pravus was causing, Dan edged closer and closer to Bridgette. He kept his gun aimed at Wretchkinsides. But Nic was too close. He was hovering over Bridgette. Dan couldn't get a shot off without hitting her.

"He was a coward, Calvin," Pravus quipped with a hate-filled chuckle.

Dan saw Logan flinch like he'd been hit.

"Shut up," Logan demanded. Delighted that he'd gotten to him, Pravus filled the hall with contemptuous laughter.

Dan took another step toward Bridgette.

~

Rainer Lawson

Burning gall welled in Rainer's eyes as he swallowed down the hate that choked his lungs. Cal Haydenshire was not a coward, not by a long shot. The injustice and fury ate him as he watched Pravus spew out insulting lies.

McCoy elbowed him. Rainer turned slightly and saw what Portwood was about to do.

~

Logan Haydenshire

"He sobbed as I killed the girl he was out with that night. Kept telling me they'd only been out once, as if I cared," Pravus chanted.

Garrett's eyes goggled. Logan swallowed down vomit. "What a bitter disappointment to the new Crown Governor, that three of his many, many sons will not only be dead, but will have died cowards."

Fury seared through Logan's veins. His heart hesitated to beat. His breath caught painfully in his lungs. Confusion clouded his mind. He couldn't fully understand what was happening. His mind and soul were somehow separated for a long moment. He existed only in his shield. Cal's face swam in his eyes.

The roar of completed justice was the only sound he was capable of understanding. He felt the trigger of his gun pull, and he watched Alexi Pravus crumple to the ground.

~

Rainer Lawson

Too many things had happened at once. Rainer couldn't make sense of it all. He felt the reverb off Logan's pistol. He saw Pravus crumble to the ground with blood pouring from his gut.

Rainer leapt and drained Pendergrath on Portwood's call, but there'd been another gunshot. And he heard an echoing scream of Dan's name.

Moving on instinct, Rainer kept his boot on Pendergrath's chest as Portwood cuffed and cast him.

"Rainer," the sound echoed off the concrete walls. *Emily?* Rainer realized instantly whose voice he'd heard.

She couldn't be there. It made no sense. As the broken fragments of present time began to seep through Rainer's consciousness, he understood the second gunshot.

Wretchkinsides had killed Bridgette at point-blank range. Her blood and body were splattered against the concrete wall.

Vindico's guttural shout seemed to echo through the protective shield Rainer's mind attempted to erect.

"Dan." Rainer heard the desperate cry again. He spun to see Fionna and Emily as they raced toward them.

Panic filled Rainer's body. "What are you doing here?" he demanded furiously. Suddenly, some lackey for the Interfeci leapt in front of Emily.

"No," Rainer screamed.

"Get out of my way!" Emily summoned with the ring and threw the idiot hard against the concrete brick wall. She knocked him out cold. His body lay limp at her feet. She stepped over him with an eye roll.

Governor Haydenshire raced toward them, gasping for breath. Rainer turned back. McCoy screamed, "Vindico! No!"

~

Garrett Haydenshire

"Fi, what the hell," Garrett demanded.

"Dan!" Fionna screeched in a horrified peal. She shuddered violently from the dark energy surrounding her. Her face went ghost white and she swayed.

Garrett spun back to watch Dan, dazed and confused, as he lowered his gun.

"Dan! No! Stop!" Garrett pled.

A formidable orb of pulsing pink and grey energy spun in Wretchkinsides's hand. He'd mind-casted Vindico.

"Nic, she's right there. Kill them and take the ring," Pendergrath demanded of Wretchkinsides.

Before Garrett's eyes, Rainer's boot landed in Pendergrath's face, bouncing his head against the cold ground. He was already cuffed. The bones of his face crushed under the weight of Rainer's acrimony.

"Dan, please, please, it's me. Listen to me." Fionna inched closer.

"Fionna, get away from him," Garrett demanded. Dan's head jerked spastically toward her voice.

~

Rainer Lawson

"Fionna, keep talking." Rainer kept his pistol aimed at Pendergrath's head.

"Dan, it's me. Please," she broke down. "I love you. I've always loved you, and..." She convulsed slightly. Vindico's head shook. He blinked repeatedly trying to see her.

"Dan, I'm pregnant," finally fell from her trembling lips.

And as the broad, hate-filled, evil grin spread across Wretchkinsides's face, Rainer knew his fate was sealed. Every unbearable demand Vindico had made the last few weeks suddenly made perfect sense.

Wretchkinsides would never give Dan peace, and Dan wouldn't allow his wife and child to live like that.

Fionna's plea had been in an effort to shatter the mindcast, but she'd just hammered the nails in Wretchkinsides's coffin.

Suddenly, Rainer reeled around. He saw Pravus move. He thought he was dead. It didn't seem possible. Blood gushed steadily from his gut where Logan had buried a slug. He still had his gun.

Pravus took weak aim at Fionna's abdomen and pulled the trigger using his last energy, his last motion, his last breath, to take another life.

"Fionna!" Vindico shattered through the mindcast as soon as the gun fired.

Wretchkinsides kicked Vindico's pistol away. They watched Fionna crumple forward on the ground.

In a horrifying split second, a deep inky black orb formed in Vindico's hand, and he pulled the very life force out of Dominic Wretchkinsides. He killed him instantly.

He threw the black energy against the concrete walls, trying to keep his body from taking it on, and flew to Fionna.

"Oh, God please, Fi, please baby, say something!" he sobbed.

"Dan, the ambulances are right outside," Adeline rushed in.

"Here!" Emily pulled the promethium filled engagement ring from her own finger and shoved it on Fionna's. "Just please work," she begged the ether in a terrified whisper.

Rainer watched the blinding green energy surround Vindico and Fionna as they raced out of the basement of The Tantra under Adeline's healing cast.

CHAPTER 36
TRAUMA

Rainer held Emily in his lap in the cold waiting room chair of the trauma unit of Georgetown Hospital. They'd been there for hours. Emily had sobbed steadily for most of them.

Governor Haydenshire paced outside of the room Dan and Fionna had been inside of since the ambulance had flown to the hospital. Adeline was in there as well.

Will offered Garrett coffee. No one let on that they knew Garrett Haydenshire had sobbed as he'd been driven to the hospital.

Mrs. Haydenshire tried to soothe Emily and Garrett as best she could though her own tears welled up constantly.

Will sat steadfast in the waiting room beside Garrett. He wouldn't let anyone else near him. He seemed to understand that Garrett couldn't even speak, and he would allow no one to make demands of him. He was there for his brother and there for Dan, though no one knew what was happening on the other side of the concrete walls.

All of the Angels sat in the waiting room with tears spilling down their faces as they tried to comfort one another. The Stylers had been called and sat with morose expressions quietly in the corner.

No one was willing to tell them that Fionna was pregnant or what had happened.

Governor and Mrs. Vindico were situated near Mrs. Haydenshire, although no one had informed them of Fionna's pregnancy either.

Kara and her husband, Zach, were sipping coffee quietly as they stood watching the door to the operating room.

Garrett's cell phone rang. The sound startled everyone awaiting news of any kind. After clearing his throat in a feeble attempt to sound like he hadn't been crying, Garrett answered. "Hey, man, are you here?" He nodded. "Yeah, we're on the third floor, Trauma Unit. We're all out here in the waiting area." He paused. "No, he hasn't been out, and no one's been allowed in." Garrett blinked back another round of tears. "I guess just tell them you have no comment. See you in a few." Garrett ended the call. "Fitzroy's cab just pulled up. The press is swarming out there. He's on his way up."

Governor Vindico edged closer to Governor Haydenshire as he took the seat beside his wife. "I know there's more to this than what I've been told."

Governor Haydenshire gave a defeated nod. "Yes, but you're going to have to wait to talk to Daniel. I'm sorry."

"I just don't understand what she was thinking. Why did she go out there?" Mrs. Vindico demanded.

Fury washed over Mrs. Haydenshire's features. "She went out there because she loves him, Marion, and she was terrified for him. Now, why don't we all take a deep breath and wait to hear what we can all do to help Fionna and Daniel recover."

Mrs. Vindico crossed her arms over her chest in a pout.

Fitzroy appeared off the elevator. "Still no word?" He dragged a chair over to Will and Garrett.

Governor Vindico offered Fitzroy his hand.

Fitz smiled consolingly as he shook it.

Rainer cradled Emily tenderly, but he kept a close constant watch on Logan. He hadn't spoken since he'd killed Pravus, but Rainer knew the harrowing reality of what he'd done was still settling on him.

Garrett shook his head as Fitzroy studied him.

"Wanna take a walk down to the Coke machine? I talked to Dan yesterday," he elaborated, and Rainer understood Vindico must've told Fitz that Fionna was pregnant.

Rainer wasn't certain if Fitzroy wanted Garrett to confirm the suspicion or if Fitz was just as worried about Garrett as everyone else and thought he might could help. He assumed both.

~

Dan Vindico

His hands were still shaking. He couldn't make them stop. Her beautiful body was laid out open before him. Gloved hands moved in and out of her. Dan couldn't make sense of it. He couldn't see. His eyes burned with some kind of liquid fire that he didn't understand.

He tried to remember. He needed to feel the horrifying pain. He deserved it. It was the only thing that grounded him to what was happening. Maybe he was losing his mind. Maybe that would be better than this.

"I'm losing her pulse again! The oxygen isn't working. Her body is rejecting something. We're losing her!"

A dry, convulsive sob broke from Dan's lungs. He jerked his body back away from Fionna. *My God, I'm killing her.* He'd summoned black. He remembered now. He could feel some remnant of the dark energy in his own.

If they managed to save her, he could never be around her. He had to leave. He didn't deserve her anyway. That's what her body was rejecting—him. How could he have been so stupid?

"Dan! No!" Adeline's screech shook through him. "Don't do that! You have to keep casting her! Look!"

CHAPTER 37

TENSION AND EXPLANATIONS

GARRETT HAYDENSHIRE

"Hey, I'm not trying to intrude, but Dan told me he thought she was pregnant and keeping it from him," Fitz whispered as soon as they were out of earshot of the waiting crowd.

Garrett nodded his confirmation and prayed Fionna wouldn't mind. The need to talk flooded his body. He let his eyes close in defeat.

"I doubt if she is now actually."

Fitzroy's hand reached and steadied Garrett. He hadn't understood why the hospital had started to spin.

"Whoa." He held him solidly. "I've got you. You'll be all right. Deep breaths." After a solid minute, Garrett managed to stand upright. Fitz put several dollars in the vending machine and plied him with a Dr Pepper. The sugar and the extra energy did help. "I'm not sure if I'm more stunned Dan finally took him down or because of all the evil they caused on their way out."

Suddenly remembering how Pravus had died, Garrett panicked. He needed to talk to Logan. He needed to make certain his little brother was going to be okay. Watching a guy bleed out from a trigger you pulled changed a man. Garrett needed Logan to know he understood.

Fitz and Garrett walked slowly back into the waiting area. The elevator opened, and Garrett's mouth dropped open. "Jared, what the hell are you doing here? This is not a good time."

"It's all over the news. I just wanted to make sure she was all right," Jared pled.

Garrett summoned and switched on the TV mounted in the corner of the waiting room. He pushed the channels upward until he reached a Gifted news network.

There it was, blaring across the screen. Dozens upon dozens of news vans were in the shot taken from the front of Georgetown Hospital.

Fionna Styler, lead Receiver for the Arlington Angels listed in critical condition was scrolling along the bottom of the screen constantly.

A female reporter stepped in front of a camera. She adjusted her casted lapel mic and offered a fake air of concern as she began her newscast.

Garrett's muscles clenched of their own accord. His shield flared as he braced to learn what the press knew.

"This is Sharon Palaver of *Realm News* reporting. We're bringing you up to date with what we know to the minute, so keep your sets summoned here. We have confirmed that Iodex was responsible for a hostile takedown at the Non-Gifted gentlemen's club called The Tantra today. Involved in that takedown was Dominic Wretchkinsides and numerous members of the Interfeci Criminal Organization. Iodex precincts from Arlington, Alexandria, and DC have confirmed that Wretchkinsides did not survive the takedown, nor did Alexi Pravus, known gun and drug runner for the Interfeci. We can also confirm that over forty members of the Interfeci organization were taken to Coriolis Prison late this afternoon.

"Now, we get to the confusing part, folks." She feigned regret. "We are stationed outside of Georgetown Hospital where numerous Iodex officers are being treated for injuries they sustained in the takedown today. We have also learned that two officers from the Arlington precinct have been confirmed dead, but Iodex will not release the names until their families have been contacted."

Garrett's heart sank as he thought of the men they'd lost.

"However, Ms. Fionna Styler, famed Receiver for the Arlington Angels, did arrive by ambulance coming from The Tantra, though we still haven't gotten confirmation on why she was there. And this story has more questions than answers at this point unfortunately, Jim, but when Ms. Styler arrived, she was carried in by Chief of Iodex, Officer Daniel Vindico. He informed the awaiting surgical team that he was her boyfriend and that he wasn't leaving her side. He was taken into the operating room with Ms. Styler. This was news to us all as Fionna Styler has been linked with the Crown Governor's son, Garrett Haydenshire, for the past several months.

"This is unconfirmed as well, but upon interviewing one of the ambulance drivers, it appears that Miss Styler is being treated for a gunshot wound to the abdomen. I can also tell you that when Miss Styler arrived at Georgetown there was a Gifted Obstetric Emergency Surgical unit waiting to assist hospital chief of staff, Medio Harrison Sawyer. We can confirm that Miss Styler was listed as pregnant when she was taken in. Whether the baby is former boyfriend Garrett Haydenshire's or current boyfriend Daniel Vindico's I can't tell you. But we will stay here until we can provide the Realm with the information they deserve." Palaver signed off.

Garrett's head fell as everyone stared at the television in stunned disbelief. He hadn't really considered the fact that the majority of the people awaiting news of Fi hadn't known she was pregnant.

"Arthur." Mrs. Vindico came completely unglued before everyone's eyes. "Make them stop saying that. It isn't true! What will people say?"

To Garrett's shock, fury lit through Kara like he'd never seen before. Zach tried to halt her march toward her mother, but she jerked away from his grasp.

"Just shut up, Mother!" she shrieked. "Just shut up! It doesn't matter what people say! It matters that Dan is in there completely devastated and that Fionna might not survive. And the baby! I can't imagine how it would have survived a gunshot, but the very last thing that matters is what other people think!" Her body trembled in her anger.

She spun into Zach's chest and began sobbing convulsively.

"You knew she was *expecting*," Mrs. Vindico whispered the word as if it were diseased.

Kara clung to Zach's shirt as she turned back and glared at her mother. "Dan came by the house a few weeks ago. He was a disaster. He was so worried about her. She was terrified to tell him," Kara shrieked at her mother. "And she was scared to tell him because of you!"

Governor Haydenshire stepped in. "Zachary, son, why don't you take Kara for a nice slow walk. Everything is going to be okay, sweetheart," the governor promised Kara.

Zach nodded as he slowly turned Kara and guided her down the hallway sobbing.

"Maybe everyone will assume the baby is yours." Mrs. Vindico gestured her head to Garrett.

Garrett rolled his eyes. He didn't give a damn who the Realm thought the baby belonged to. He just needed Fionna to be okay.

But Mrs. Haydenshire seemed to have had enough. She marched to Mrs. Vindico. "You know, Marion, I've kept my mouth shut for many, many years now on Daniel's account when it came to you, but I think it's high time I spoke up." Every eye in the room was on her.

Governor Haydenshire seemed to know better than to try and stop her, so he stood steadfast by her side. "Your son is one of the finest young men I've ever known, not that you ever gave him credit for anything that wasn't your idea. He has been through hell at the hands of Dominic Wretchkinsides, for no other reason than the fact that he is a good person who wanted to do what was right. But you chose to sweep all of his efforts and all of his horrendous pain under the rug, because it wasn't how you'd envisioned his life working out. Well, guess what, this isn't how Daniel envisioned his life either!

"But right now, he is in that room clinging to the love of his life, willing her to live, and praying desperately for the child they created together out of their love. And you're sitting out here worrying about what the Realm will think when they find out that his girlfriend is pregnant!"

Her tone turned derisive as she continued. "I'm certain everyone in the entire Realm will be thoroughly shocked. Daniel Vindico is thirty-two years old and involved in a loving relationship with a women he adores more than life itself. And she loves him so much she couldn't bear to think about what might be happening to him so she flew to his side today because she didn't want him to face the demons she knew he would face today all alone," Mrs. Haydenshire choked.

With another deep breath she went on. "So, I'm sure that the Realm will be thoroughly shocked to learn that Daniel and Fionna have sex!"

Broad grins spread across most of the faces in the room as they continued to watch the first lady's diatribe. "Please, for the sake of your son, for the sake of the woman he wants to spend the rest of his life with, please stop worrying about what the Realm will think and start worrying about Daniel!" Mrs. Haydenshire roared her conclusion.

Stunned outrage etched Mrs. Vindico's face. "I feel certain you would feel differently if one of your boys had gotten a girl into *trouble*."

"Fionna is not *in* trouble," she raged in Mrs. Vindico's face. "She's in love. And if I were upset, I would be just about the biggest hypocrite in the Realm!" Mrs. Haydenshire threw her hand out to Will.

Eyes goggled around the room. "Thanks, Mom." Will rolled his eyes, and Garrett couldn't help but chuckle.

"I've never been spoken to so rudely. We're leaving, Arthur," Mrs. Vindico demanded righteously.

All eyes turned to Governor Vindico. "You can leave if you'd like, but I'm not leaving. I'm not going to leave Dan here to deal with all of this alone. I won't allow him to face any more pain all by himself. He's my son, and it's high time we stood by him. And I will be here to assure Fionna that we couldn't have loved her more if she'd been ours, and that nothing would make me happier than for her and Dan to work through their pain together and for her to become his wife. And if by some miracle they save the baby, then I will assure both of them how proud and overjoyed we are to have another grandchild."

CHAPTER 38

ANSWERS

Before Mrs. Vindico could reply, the door to Fionna's room opened.

Medio Sawyer exited, followed by Adeline and teams of other medios and nurses.

Everyone stood in the endless moment of desperation. Adeline flew to Logan. Garrett watched his little brother, who'd been lost and despondent since they'd arrived at the hospital, appear to come back to life at Adeline's touch.

"Daddy," Chloe pled as renewed tears poured from her eyes.

"It will be touch and go for the next twenty-four hours, but I believe Fionna will make a full recovery, sweetheart. As long as she stays with Chief Vindico, that is. When he let her go, we lost her momentarily." Medio Sawyer said the words that carried blood back to Garrett's heart and air back to his lungs. "We were unable to save the fetus," he concluded morosely.

Emily sobbed in Rainer's arms. Mrs. Haydenshire's chin trembled as the governor pulled her into his chest and let her cry.

"I didn't know. She didn't tell me," Chloe managed before she began to sob in earnest.

"She was still in her first trimester. I'm sure she was frightened," Medio Sawyer soothed before he turned to the waiting crowd. "Dan and Fionna will be seeing a very few visitors at this point, and Dan will be determining who sees her and how long they stay." Sawyer explained what Garrett was certain had been Dan's orders.

"Fionna would like to see Emily for a few minutes, and Dan has requested Garrett and Rainer come in. I can assure everyone that Chief Vindico is in a rather vicious mood, so I wouldn't try to get in without his permission."

"Good for him," Governor Haydenshire complimented.

❧

Rainer and Emily stood while Garrett knocked hesitantly on the door. A full minute later, Dan opened it and stepped back.

Garrett gasped as he took him in. He'd pulled a pistol out of Dan's mouth twice, and even with that, he'd never seen Dan Vindico truly broken. His eyes were bloodshot and swollen almost shut. His shirt and BDU pants were covered in blood from many sources, but most of it was Fionna's. There were finger-shaped bruises on his biceps.

At some point in the past few hours, Fionna had clung to him hard enough to leave bruises. Garrett knew it had been out of pain.

He swallowed down raw terror and eased into the room. He tried to brace himself to see Fionna laid up in a hospital bed.

Rainer and Emily followed solemnly behind him.

"Hey there, baby." Garrett was mildly impressed with how he was able to normalize his voice as he took her in.

Her eyes were just as swollen as Dan's. Her body was pale and drawn. There was blood in her hair, and her abdomen was swollen and heavily bandaged. It made her proportions oddly out of shape under the sheets.

Several bags were hung from the pole connected to her IV.

"I am so sorry, man," Rainer choked on his humble whisper.

Dan nodded and offered him a slight smile.

"Hey," Fionna finally managed, though tears continued to flow down her face.

Garrett eased his arms around her as best as he was able. "Are you okay?"

"Not really."

Dan moved back to her and took her hand. He brushed her hair away from her face.

"Oh, here." Fionna seemed to remember suddenly as she pulled her hand from Dan's and removed Emily's ring.

Emily smiled at her adoringly as silent tears flowed down her face.

"It saved my life, so thank you." Fionna reached for Dan again.

"Of course."

"Would you do one other thing for me? Then I think I'd kind of just like to be alone with Dan." Fionna looked terrified to make the simple request.

"Anything," Emily vowed.

Offering a weak smile, she seemed relieved that no one was offended by her plea. "Would you hug Dan for me?"

Emily's brow furrowed as did Rainer's and Garrett's.

"I believe you, Fi. I swear." Dan was the only person in the room who understood the request.

"He doesn't. Not really. But if you hug him, then he'll see."

Dan shook his head. "I summoned black to kill him, and I was afraid I was making her sick. She keeps insisting that I'm not."

"Oh." Emily looked relieved. She smiled at Dan. "That's not how it works."

"That's what Fi said."

"You threw it off you. He's not in you," Garrett reminded Dan, but he shook his head in feeble argument.

"Here." Emily wrapped her arms around Dan's broad chest. "See, I'm fine. Nothing." Emily stepped back. She looked the picture of health. "And it wouldn't have mattered if you hadn't thrown it, because energy is darkened by the intent, not by action."

Fionna nodded adamantly.

"You did it to save her, so it wasn't dark at all. And she won't feel anything like that from you. I bet she's worse when you aren't with her actually."

Dan's brow furrowed.

Fionna managed a broken smile. "He tried to let go of my hand while they were doing surgery. He thought he might be making me worse, and I flat-lined."

Emily patted Fionna's leg tenderly. "When I was in the wreck and they were working on me, they noticed that my rhythms calmed when Rainer held my hand. My energy needed to be protected because a Receiver's shield is so easily damaged. So I used his protective energies as my shield until I was well enough that my own could be reestablished. She needs you to stay with her until she's healed."

"I sincerely hope I'm not going anywhere," Dan sighed. Keeping one hand on Fionna's, he turned to Garrett and Rainer. "Could you two do me a favor?"

"Anything," Rainer agreed.

"Uh,"—he used his left hand to fish keys out of his pocket—"this is the key to my desk. I'm certain I won't need it anymore, but could you get the thing that's in there and bring it back to me."

"You got it." Rainer smiled as Garrett nodded his agreement.

"We'll go and let you rest," Emily soothed. "I'll be right out there if you need me again."

"Thanks." Fionna held her arms out to Emily for a hug. They embraced gently, and Rainer and Garrett headed toward the door.

"I want only you to be in here for a while," Fionna begged in a terror-filled, trembling plea to Dan.

"I'll be right here, baby, only me." He seated himself hesitantly on the bed beside her. "You heard that," Dan called to Garrett.

"Hey, nothing would make me happier than pissing off a waiting room full of people in your place," Garrett teased.

"I can't think of a better man for the job." Dan's voice bordered on normal, though pain continued to perforate everything about both of them. "Fitz is here, just so you know." He wasn't certain Dan was aware he'd been called.

Dan looked truly touched. "I'll come out there later."

"I'll tell them."

CHAPTER 39

LEAD FROM THE FRONT

GOVERNOR STEPHEN HAYDENSHIRE

While watching Garrett exit Fionna's room, Stephen studied him and then Rainer and Emily. Hopeful faces met Garrett's. Everyone expected to be asked in to see Dan and Fionna next, but Garrett shook his head. "Dan says no one else for a while. He'll be out in a little while to see everyone."

Everyone nodded their sympathetic understanding.

"Can we do anything for them?" Kara begged.

"Yeah, actually, why don't you and Emily run over to Dan and Fi's house? Get them both some clean clothes, toothbrushes, shampoo, stuff like that. He's not gonna leave her even to do that." Garrett's thoughtful request impressed Stephen.

Maybe his kids had listened to him occasionally growing up. They'd all certainly turned out to be phenomenal adults. But Stephen knew that several of his children needed him right then. He was going to have to take them one at a time, however.

"Rainer and I are gonna run a quick errand for Dan. We'll be back in just a few."

Or maybe two at a time, Stephen amended his original plan.

Emily and Kara looked thrilled to be of service, and Zach immediately offered to drive them.

"I think I'm going to come along, son. We can talk," Stephen informed Garrett.

Garrett nodded. His worried glance at Logan confirmed what Stephen already suspected.

"Garrett, dear, did you tell Daniel that his father and I are waiting to see him?" Marion Vindico asked with an air of martyrdom.

Garrett chuckled, and Stephen knew he found it humorous that moments before she'd wanted to blame the pregnancy on Garrett, and now she was calling him dear.

"He knows you're here, Mrs. Vindico, but right now Fionna is his only concern."

She turned to Arthur with a huff. "Well, why doesn't he want us to come in and show our support?"

Stephen rolled his eyes. Marion Vindico had once again managed to not only miss the mark but the entire field. "Sometimes when you're going through hell, it's nice to just be with the person who's going through it all with you. Now, I'm certain that once our little ones are all settled in for the night, I won't be able to pry Lillian out of here with a crow bar. So why don't we just all get comfortable and let Dan and Fionna know that we're out here if they need us."

With that, he followed Rainer and Garrett to the elevators.

"Do you think I should go ahead and clear up the whole thing with Fi and me?" Garrett asked his father and Rainer.

Stephen was certain there would be many more questions from all of his boys, but he was happy someone was finally talking.

"I think Daniel and Fionna need a fresh start without any involvement from you. It might soothe Dan's frazzled nerves for the Realm to know whom she belongs to. Since I'm assuming we're going to pick up the engagement ring Dan purchased from your uncle, it would probably make everything much less complicated for the two of them."

"Yeah, that's what I thought you were gonna say." Understandably, Garrett did not look forward to facing the press.

For what must have been the thousandth time since Will had been born, Stephen wished he could step in and make life easier for his kids. But he couldn't, and Garrett had to do this. So he slapped his son on the back and offered him a sympathetic smile as they exited the hospital into throngs of press.

"Just get it over with. I'll be right behind you. I'm not going anywhere," he assured his son.

"Is it? Yes, folks, Garrett Haydenshire is exiting Georgetown Hospital with his father and soon-to-be brother-in-law, Rainer Lawson. Let's see if we can get a word." Reporters swarmed around them.

Garrett ran his hands through his hair the way he'd done since he was a little boy and had to do something he didn't want to. He nodded his agreement to answering a few questions.

"Have you seen Ms. Styler since she was brought in this afternoon?" a reporter Stephen despised from *The Sun* chanted.

"I just left Fionna's room," Garrett explained.

"We were informed that her condition has just been upgraded to stable. Can you tell us more about her injuries?" another reporter called.

"No," Garrett quipped. Stephen and Rainer chuckled.

"Can you clear up the confusion about her being Chief Officer Dan Vindico's girlfriend?" a reporter from the *Realm Times* called.

Garrett drew a deep breath. "Fionna and I have been best friends since we went to the academy together, but she was never my girlfriend. She and Chief Vindico have been dating for quite some time."

The broad grin that finally formed on his son's features brought hope back to Stephen. He saw the moment realization came over Garrett and Rainer both. Wretchkinsides was done for. Emily and Fionna were safe being with the men they loved for the time being, anyway.

"Is the baby Chief Vindico's?" demanded several reporters.

"No more questions," Garrett commanded forcefully. He raced away from the press. Rainer and Stephen joined him in his sprint. They ignored questions being shouted at them.

Stephen's hand shot out as an enhanced boom mic came dangerously close to Garrett's shoulder. "My son said no more questions! Move on."

As the press had the parking decks blocked, they decided to take the Metro to the Senate.

A few minutes later, Stephen followed Rainer and Garrett into Dan's office. Nausea washed over him in waves. He couldn't pretend that he hadn't watched Daniel kill Dominic Wretchkinsides. Nor could he pretend he hadn't done it by summoning the energy out of him.

Cal's kind face swam before Stephen. He swallowed down raw pain. His son was gone, and as much as he would like to rejoice that they'd managed to take down the Interfeci, Dan had to be held accountable for what he'd done.

Garrett unlocked the top drawer and then sent the required magnetic pulses to release Dan's cast. He lifted the ring box from Tad's store and locked the drawer again.

"I have a feeling after the conversation we're all about to have in my office, I'll be needing those," Stephen lamented.

Garrett nodded as he slipped the keys to everything in Iodex off the key ring and handed them to his father.

❧

Rainer Lawson

While settling into one of the leather chairs in the Crown Governor's office, Rainer's stomach churned uncomfortably.

"All right, boys, let's establish one thing before we begin this conversation," the governor commanded. "I want you both to understand that I am now and will always be your father long before I am the Crown Governor or any other role that I serve. I'm not trying to take anything away from Joseph, Rainer."

"I know, sir." Rainer wasn't offended. Governor Haydenshire had been his father alone for the past eight years, and he'd certainly helped raise him for the past twenty-one.

"Let's just pretend we're sitting at the kitchen table at the house instead of in this office. But as I am also the Crown Governor, I do need to know everything that happened today from beginning to end, so that I can best decide how we can all move forward."

Garrett and Rainer shared a quick uncomfortable glance.

"Let's start with how Daniel got Wretchkinsides and all of the Interfeci together and in the basement of that club."

Garrett nodded. He seemed to realize that the faster they came clean, the faster they could get the ring back to Dan. "They were all already together. They were planning to attack the farm, remember? But, uh….Dan took Marlisa from the O'Ryans' house and locked her up here."

The governor's eyes closed for the length of one heartbeat. He rubbed his temples. "Please tell me she's not still here."

"Portwood let her out and drove her back to the O'Ryans'. I have no idea what he said to her though."

"How did they end up in The Tantra?"

Rainer stepped in. Garrett didn't have to do this on his own. "Dan sent a picture of Marlisa to the Interfeci, then Wretchkinsides kidnapped Bridgette Meyers from The Tantra. I think he thought she and Vindico were still dating. I don't know. It was weird. Tuttle said she'd been getting real chummy with him. I'm pretty sure she either was spying for Nic or was trying to get him to let her spy for him. But anyway, Wretchkinsides said he had spies at your inaugural ball, so he saw them there together, I guess." Rainer still couldn't quite make sense of everything.

Garrett shook his head. "No, he said her help was ineffective and that he had spies *besides* her at the ball. She was supposed to be one of the spies, but she got drunk. Remember? Dan thought she was safe after he ended it with her, because, to our knowledge, no one ever knew about the two of them. He did try to keep her safe. He's had Tuttle and a few Gifted police officers keeping tabs on her constantly. That's how we knew she was extending her hours with Nic," Garrett elaborated. "Fi and Dan ran into her one night when they stopped in for takeout. Fi freaked. Tears, door slamming, everything. You know how women are."

The governor chuckled, neither agreeing nor disagreeing.

"Anyway, Dan didn't want to upset her, so he never saw Bridgette again until today. She really hadn't had much information for us lately. Every time we had officers in the club, she was all over Nic."

"Is there anything I need to know about from the time you all entered The Tantra to the time you made your way back to Wretchkinsides?" The governor studied Rainer intently.

"It was horrible," spilled from Rainer's mouth without him really meaning to confess that. He shuddered as the memories seeped back into his conscience against his will.

"It definitely was," Garrett confirmed, and Rainer knew it was to make him feel like he wasn't a coward. He and the governor were having an unspoken conversation with their eyes. Rainer wanted Emily.

"Well, you usually want to talk things over with Emily Anne, and then Logan, and then me, but I'm here right now if you want to skip a few steps. If not, I'll be around to talk whenever you need me." Governor Haydenshire gave Rainer a loving gaze, the one he used for all of his children.

Rainer nodded. He was immensely thankful for the knowledge that Governor and Mrs. Haydenshire would always be there for him, but that wasn't who he wanted to talk to about the hell he'd been through that day.

"I think I'll stick with my usual pattern, sir." Rainer earned a nod and chuckle from the man who had raised him.

"All right, now, how about one of you tell me what happened with Logan?" The governor struck upon the one question he obviously didn't want to ask, and Garrett and Rainer didn't want to answer.

The silence was deafening. "How about I take a guess? You got back there, saw Bridgette tied up, and Pravus started running his repugnant mouth about Cal." It seemed he knew perfectly well what had happened. "He said a few things Logan couldn't let go. He deeply admires all of his big brothers,"—the governor nodded to Garrett—"but all three of my Shields were particularly close."

Garrett and Rainer nodded. They were both thankful that they weren't the ones who had to tell the story.

"I'm assuming it was your brother's gun that ended Pravus's life?"

Garrett and Rainer nodded again.

"Truthfully, in light of everything that happened, I think my take on it would have to be that I'm sorry he didn't aim for his head instead of his gut," the governor quipped. Rainer was momentarily shocked. "Am I to also assume that if this story ever left this office, your brother would no longer have an Iodex badge?"

"McCoy and Portwood were there too. And I don't know what Pendergrath might've seen." Garrett sounded terrified for Logan. "But Pravus was in it with all the rest of them. He was in the room with the woman they kidnapped. It'd be up to the Senteon to decide, I guess. But Pravus hadn't raised his gun when Logan fired."

This time the governor offered Garrett his soothing smile. "I'll take care of Candor Pendergrath. He'll be looking to cover his own hide. He always is. I can't recall a time in the past twenty-one years that Rainer hasn't covered for Logan and vice versa, and Garrett, you constantly shield everyone you love. You always have. I doubt this time will be any different."

"No, sir," Rainer vowed.

"Pravus took aim," Garrett supplied instantly.

"He was going to shoot," Rainer leapt in.

The governor drew a deep breath, "I had a feeling that was the case." He shook his head over all that had happened. "This morning I was annoyed that half of the Senate was going to be on my farm. It's been a long day." He sighed. "Is Fionna having any trouble being around Dan after what he did?"

Garrett shook his head. "No, Emily said it's intent that makes dark energy dark, and that Dan had the best of intentions. He knew Wretchkinsides would never leave Fi or the baby alone. He was protecting his family, so it wasn't even really black energy or whatever."

The governor hemmed, "That is true to a certain extent, but I think the fact that Fionna adores Daniel more than life itself probably has a great deal to do with why she doesn't feel anything dark from him. But whatever the reason, let's get that ring back and see if maybe we can end this day with a smile on Dan and Fionna's faces. I think they deserve that much."

CHAPTER 40

TOGETHER

Rainer and Garrett followed the governor back into the waiting room. Several of the Angels had gone home, but they'd left cards, flowers, and balloons with well-wishes for Fionna.

Logan's hand was laced through Adeline's, but fear and exhaustion still plagued his features.

"Logan." Governor Haydenshire moved to him. "How about I take you and your wife out for a little something to eat. We can come right back and maybe see Dan and Fionna for a little while before she goes to sleep," he suggested, though Rainer noted that it was more of an order.

Logan looked like he was being thrown a lifeline just as the tidal waters threatened to engulf him. He nodded. Adeline looked relieved as well as they stood and followed the governor out of the hospital.

Emily gave Rainer her sweet smile. "Fionna's parents sat with her for a little while, but she asked for Dan again. We gave him their clothes and stuff when the nurses went in to change her bandages, so he's giving her a bath and helping her change."

Rainer wondered how long he needed to wait to let Vindico know they were back with the ring.

Garrett, who seemed much quicker that evening, texted Dan with the information that they'd returned and for him to let them know when he wanted the ring.

"Mrs. Vindico got all mad again when Kara came out and told her that Dan was giving Fionna a bath." Emily rolled her eyes. Garrett and Rainer both laughed harder than the story called for, but it felt good to laugh.

"Mom went home to get Abigail and the twins to bed. She's coming right back. Nana's staying with them."

Garrett's phone chirped, and a broad grin spread across his face. He moved back to Fionna's door and knocked. Dan opened the door. He looked much better now that he was wearing a clean polo and jeans. Garrett offered him his hand, and in a handshake he discreetly slipped him the ring.

~

Garrett Haydenshire

"Actually, would you, Rainer, and Logan mind coming in for this?" Dan asked hesitantly.

"Dad took Logan out to talk. How about me and Rainer and Em?"

"That'll do, I hope."

Garrett wondered why Dan wanted an audience for this. Rainer and Emily made a return trip to Fionna's room.

Relief washed through him again as Garrett grinned at Fionna. She looked so much better than the last time he'd stood by her bed.

Dan had washed her hair and done a decent job of drying it, but she'd pulled it up in a long ponytail. Some of the color had returned to her cheeks. She looked much more like herself.

Someone had healed the bruises from Dan's arms.

Emily grinned at Fionna. "You look like you're feeling a little better."

"Yeah, well, he kind of has that effect." Fionna reached for Dan's hand again. He did his best to hide his deep regret, but Fionna either saw through his efforts or she felt it.

"Come here, baby." Rainer guided Emily into his arms. Garrett joined them against the far wall to let Dan work.

Dan gazed at Fionna adoringly. She studied him. She seemed to have discerned that he was up to something.

"Fi, baby, I love you so much." Dan blinked back another round of tears.

She nodded. Her tears returned as well. "I love you too." She sounded frightened. Dan leaned and kissed her forehead.

"And I know this is kind of a hell of a place to do this," he lamented. He stood up from the bed and considered the logistics for a moment.

It took Garrett a moment to figure out that Dan was trying to calculate if Fionna would be able to see him if he got down on one knee since it had to hurt for her to sit up or lean to her left side. He shook his head. "Just do that part later, man."

Dan drew a deep breath and seated himself again. "Fi, honey, I know I can't ever make up for all of the pain I've put you through, and I honestly don't know why you still want me around." The emotion settled thickly in his throat. Garrett squeezed his eyes shut and prayed that somehow, something better was on their horizon.

"Dan..." Fionna shook her head.

"Sweetheart, I want to be with you forever, for as long as you want me." He was unable to halt the tears this time. "So, I was wondering if you'd do me the extraordinary honor of marrying me, Fionna?" He popped open the ring box.

Fionna's eyes goggled as she took in the ring. "No, you don't have to do this." She began to sob. Garrett understood immediately why he and Rainer were there. "You don't have to propose just because of the baby." She cringed inward as she tried to argue.

"No, baby, just listen to me." Garrett moved in. Dan urged him on. "He's been planning this for a while. He bought the ring way back when he went to New York."

"Months ago," Rainer added.

"He actually had Uncle Tad design it way before that," Emily leapt on the bandwagon.

Fionna looked stunned as Dan nodded his adamant agreement through his own tears.

"What if this isn't all okay? What if I can't have more kids? I don't want you to give up anything for me." Fionna continued to sob.

"Fi, honey, you're here. We're here. By some miracle, I didn't lose you too. I could never, ever ask for more than that. I'm not the one giving up anything, you are. Adeline told you she healed you herself and that you're probably going to be fine. But even if that wasn't true, I don't care. I want to be with you. That's all that matters to me. If you want kids, we'll adopt. As long as I have you, that's all I'll ever need."

A smile finally broke through Fionna's anguish. She nodded. "Okay, yes," she agreed. Her smile turned to a broad, delighted beam. It lit the entire room. "Yes, yes, yes," she announced as she tried to draw deep breaths when Dan slipped the ring on her finger.

"We should go." Garrett gestured Rainer and Emily to the door.

"No," Fionna fussed, "come tell me how pretty it is."

Everyone laughed as they moved back to admire the ring.

"Just remember that I'm most definitely out of a job, and I may be headed to prison," Dan huffed, only partially kidding.

Garrett had put forth a concerted effort not to think about the way Dan had killed Nic Wretchkinsides.

"I don't care. I'll be married to you in jail!"

Dan shook his head. He still seemed unable to believe just how much Fionna Styler loved and adored him.

$\sim$

Dan Vindico

"Okay, now go away, so I can kiss him." Fionna was clearly feeling more herself much to Dan's delight.

Rainer chuckled as he guided Emily out the door.

Garrett shook his head. "Geez, he puts a ring on your finger, and you think you can just order everybody around." He kissed Fionna's forehead tenderly.

"Yes." She giggled, but she shifted uncomfortably, and Dan knew why she wanted everyone to leave. Garrett waved on his way out.

Dan moved to her side and gently eased her body upright using all of his strength so she had to use none of her own.

"This is so embarrassing." The tears started to fall again.

"Baby doll, you just said that I get to be your husband, so this is my job. It really doesn't bother me. Please let me take care of you," Dan pled for the third time in the last few hours.

She couldn't wear underwear or pants as her abdomen was still heavily bandaged. Taking her to the bathroom wasn't difficult other than getting her there. He managed to guide her and roll the IV pole along as well. They hadn't want to catheterize her if she could manage without that. They were worried about infection, but they were also flooding her body with fluids so she had to go often.

He eased her along and watched over her as she made tiny fragile steps.

He helped her sit and then closed the door behind him as he made his exit.

"Okay," she called a few minutes later.

Dan reopened the door, and she was standing at the sink.

"Fionna," he scolded. She wasn't supposed to stand on her own. She looked sheepish, but he couldn't continue to get on to her. She'd been through enough.

He lifted her back into bed and tucked her back in. He sealed heat in the blankets just like he did at home.

"I still don't want to see anybody, but I kind of do want everyone to know we're engaged."

Dan nodded his agreement. "How about if I go out in a little while and see everyone. I'll tell them you've just made me the luckiest guy in the entire Realm and then I'll come back in here and we'll see if we can't get some sleep."

She nodded but then began crying again. Dan couldn't stand to watch her cry. Every tear was entirely his fault.

"I'm so sorry I didn't tell you sooner," she choked.

Dan cradled her as tenderly as he could. "It's my fault you didn't think you could tell me. And it's Pravus's fault that this happened. None of this was your doing."

"I was so scared," she confessed, effectively shattering his heart.

"I know." Dan let his tears fall in her hair. "But you don't have to be scared anymore, and I will be here the entire time. We will get through this together, all of it."

Fionna nodded against him. "I hated not telling you. I don't ever want to keep anything from you again. It was horrible. I was so lost, and I knew no one would ever be able to find me."

"I will always search until I find you. Always. I just had to figure out how to get you back. And I don't ever want you to keep anything from me again either."

"Are you going to be okay? You had kind of the worst day ever, except for maybe…" She halted abruptly before she brought up Amelia's death.

"It will be a long process for both of us." Dan knew that the next few weeks would be particularly difficult. "But please don't ever think that I'm not aware that my child was killed today. That it wasn't real for me, because it was. I'm sick over it. A complete disaster, until I look into your eyes. So together, we'll get through this."

He wondered momentarily if there was somewhere he could take her where they could both do a little healing.

His revelation seemed to restore her. She shuddered against him, and he held her close until she leaned back on the pillows and managed a timid smile up at him. It soothed his weary soul. When she smiled at him, everything that had happened, and that stupid fragment of malignant energy he'd taken on, disappeared completely.

"Okay." She let her eyes close as he continued brushing tender kisses on her forehead. "Will you go tell everyone that you put a ring on it?" She giggled, but then grimaced. It hurt to laugh.

Dan placed his hand tenderly over the bandages. He pushed soothing energy through the loose weave, and she relaxed.

"I'll be right back."

"Not for too long, please." She seemed to rethink her request.

"I won't go at all if you don't want me to, but if you do, I'll come right back. Here." He reached and pulled her cell phone from her purse and placed it on the rolling tray beside the bed.

"If you get lonely, just text me, and I'll come right back."

"Will you send Mama and Emily in to stay with me? Their energy always feels good."

"Of course."

CHAPTER 41
WEARY HOPE

He stared at all of the faces offering him tender remorse and hope, all of the people who loved him and Fionna.

"Ms. Styler, Fionna wants you and Emily. Would you go sit with her for a few minutes?"

Mrs. Styler patted Dan's arm as she followed Emily into the room. Dan sank down in the chair between his father and Will.

"I'm so sorry, son." Tears pricked his old man's eyes. Dan could count on one hand the number of times he'd seen his father cry. The emotion choked him again.

"Me too, man, so sorry," Will echoed.

"I don't know whether to congratulate you or tell you how sorry I am first." Fitzroy chuckled.

This brought a genuine grin from Dan. He stood to hug his best friend. "You didn't have to come out here."

Fitz hugged him fiercely. "Nowhere else I'd be."

Governor Haydenshire and Logan rejoined everyone in the waiting room. Adeline knocked and stepped into Fionna's room. Dan assumed it was to check her bandages and blood pressure again.

"Are you okay?" Dan quizzed Logan. He'd had a hell of a day himself.

"Pretty sure I will be eventually," Logan allowed.

"If you need me, you know where to find me," Dan pledged.

Logan looked genuinely touched as he nodded his appreciation.

Dan turned back to the crowd and forced a smile. "Well, after everything, I did convince her to marry me."

Cheers lit from most everyone around him as Dan's hand was shaken and his back slapped by numerous loved ones. His eyes fell on the two people seated nearby. They both looked morose in the midst of all of the congratulations. One of them was Fionna's father, so he wasn't terribly surprised.

His brow furrowed as everyone returned to their seats. "Who the hell are you?" he demanded of the other guy seated nearby. He was not in the mood to deal with interlopers after all they'd been through.

Garrett shook his head. "This is Jared. I've told him about a dozen times to leave, but he insists that he's not going until he sees Fi with his own eyes to make certain she's all right."

"Mrs. Haydenshire." Adeline peeked her head out of Fionna's room. "Fionna was wondering if you'd come in and see her."

"Of course, sweetheart." Mrs. Haydenshire slipped quickly into Fionna's room and closed the door behind her.

Dan's mother stood. "I'm certain she would like to see me as well."

"Mother," Dan bellowed. "If Fionna wants to see you, she'll ask for you. Sit down." He turned to Jared and glared at him hatefully. "And you are not going to see Fionna!"

"I think that should be up to her," Jared quipped. "Once she knows I'm here, she'll want to see me."

Dan narrowed his eyes. Fury swam through his waning energy. "You know what, fine. I've beaten the shit out of an endless number of assholes today. Loaded bullets up in the rest, but what the hell." He moved back into Fionna's room. "Sweetheart, Jared is here and thinks that you'd like to see him," he challenged indignantly. All of the women in the room had stopped talking abruptly when Dan had entered.

"What?" Fionna gasped and then clutched her abdomen. "You mean Jared, Jared?"

"Yes, that Jared."

"Why is he here? I do not want to see him! I don't want to see anyone except the people in this room right now!"

"And she only wants us for a few minutes because then she just needs you, Daniel," Mrs. Haydenshire stated knowingly. Fionna's mother nodded her adamant agreement.

"Nowhere else I'd ever be," he assured the women staring up at him. "Baby, I'll be back whenever you want me, and I'll take care of Jared."

Fionna gave him his smile. The first one he'd seen in several weeks. His heart thundered and then finally, after days and weeks, it managed to find its steadying beat. He blew her a kiss and closed the door.

"Yeah, Jared," Dan snarled, "I'm gonna go ahead and tell you that my *baby* doesn't ever want to see you again. And if you try to go in that room, I'll fix it so they're admitting you next. I believe I informed you of this on the phone."

"And we'll help him," Garrett assured Jared, with Will and Fitz nodding adamantly. Fitzroy flexed his arms back. He showed off his impressive musculature. Will and Garrett wore the very same pompous smirk they'd always worn when they were challenged together. No one took on the Haydenshire boys and walked away unscathed.

"She said she didn't want to see me?" Jared was somehow shocked.

Dan fought the urge to choke Jared. He was now wary of his temper. He was concerned that somehow the energy he'd taken on might be the cause. "Yes, my fiancée asked that I make certain that you leave before I go back in there, take care of anything at all that she might need, and then put her to bed." Dan spelled out the relationship slowly for Jared. He listened to his friends snicker behind him.

"Why would you do all of that? Isn't that what the staff here is for? I'm sure a trauma room must cost your insurance a great deal of money. You should make the medios take care of her," Jared scoffed.

Garrett rolled his eyes. "As if we needed more evidence, suddenly everyone understands why it's his ring she's wearing and not yours."

"We're walking you out, Jared," Will informed him.

"I think I'm going to go ahead and insist on that." Governor Haydenshire shook his head.

"Tell Fionna when she feels better, I'd like to see her again," Jared pled.

"Dude." Garrett shook his head. "Fi-on-na," he drawled like he was talking to a very young child. He moved around Jared, grasped his head from behind, and forced him to look at Dan. "Is marrying him," he drawled slowly. "Big guy, big muscles. He curls men twice your size on a light day, and he gets real, real angry when people upset Fionna. Veins pop out in his head. He yells a lot. It isn't pretty. He's killed enough people today. He's tired. You need to go away and stay away for your own health."

Dan listened to Jared argue as Will and Garrett dragged him toward the elevator.

He fell back into a chair beside Fitzroy in utter shock.

Fitz cracked up. "Only you, man."

"Son, I'm going to take your mother home. She's had quite a day." Governor Vindico chuckled. "We'll be back in the morning, and if you need something tonight, just call. I'll come right back."

"Thanks. I think we'll be okay tonight."

"I know you'll take care of her." The governor slapped Dan on the back.

A few minutes later, the ladies poured out of Fionna's room. Dan handed the keys to his and Fionna's house to Fitzroy and thanked him again for coming.

After assuring everyone that he'd take care of Fionna and being told repeatedly that everyone would be back early the next morning, Dan finally edged toward Fionna's room. He was worried about how long he'd been gone.

"Dan." Mrs. Styler stopped him. "Just a quick second, sweetheart." He nodded as Mrs. Styler offered him an idea that he thought was phenomenal if he could make it work.

The endless day tugged at his shield. Dan finally made it back to

Fionna. As long as he focused solely on her and made certain she had everything she needed, he could continue to force away the haunting imagery of everything that had happened at The Tantra.

Governor Haydenshire had informed Dan that they would talk in the morning, which had done nothing to calm him.

Adeline had explained, while Fionna was under anesthesia, that though they'd healed her internal organs fully, she would be in a great deal of pain for the next several days and that she would bleed from the miscarriage for the same length of time.

She'd also explained that Fionna would be understandably emotional from all that had happened and from the hormone fluctuations from being pregnant and losing the baby suddenly. There was also remnant scar tissue in her uterus that might affect her ability to conceive and carry another child.

He let all of that replay in his mind as he gazed at her adoringly. He would be there for every tear, for every mood swing, to cast her if she hurt, for each and every thing she needed for the rest of their lives, if she'd allow it.

"I was just about to text you." She looked completely exhausted.

"I'm sorry, sweetheart. I was talking to your mom."

She nodded as a deep yawn overtook her. "I don't want to sleep by myself." Tears welled in her eyes again. They came with no provocation.

"I'll be right here, baby." He wiped them away.

"No, I want you to hold me in the bed like at home."

Unable to deny her anything at all, Dan tried to determine how he could fit in the hospital bed beside her. "I don't want you to be uncomfortable."

"I won't." She tried so hard to be brave. It was brutal to watch. "But I have this pad thing under me, and they put this diaper thing on me."

Dan had been right beside her as the pad taped in the bed had been changed numerous times throughout the afternoon and evening. Other than being terrified by the sheer amount of blood and fluid coming out of her, it certainly didn't bother him. He'd make it work.

Adeline returned with a pain pill and a glass of water. "This will help you sleep and keep any contractions from being too intense."

Dan watched Fionna swallow down the pill.

He helped her back to the bathroom and watched over her obsessively while she brushed her teeth. She let him run a cool washcloth over her face.

But when her abdomen began hurting to the point she was cringing and could no longer stand, Dan lifted her as tenderly as he was able. He carried her back to bed.

He moved with precise gentleness and helped her roll to her side and lie on his chest.

She yawned as the medicine began to make her eyes spin.

"Go to sleep, baby. I'm right here. I'm not going anywhere ever."

As he pulled the light from the fluorescent bulbs, he kissed her forehead and lay awake. He had to make certain she slept comfortably.

He refused to think about the day's events. He shut down the images, the sorrow, all that had been lost, and the things he had gained. He pulled his phone off the table beside them.

He searched for the things he would need to give Fionna the time to heal that he knew she desperately needed, that *they* desperately needed.

When his mind finally crushed his stubborn shield, he swallowed back the tears that burned his eyes.

He'd never consciously wanted children until he'd known the one he'd created with Fionna had been taken from them. Until he'd raced out of that very hospital carrying Abigail Haydenshire, he'd never even held a newborn. Now he wanted desperately to hold his own.

He brushed another tender kiss on Fionna's forehead and watched her sleep beside him. He could see what might have been. A relatively quick wedding. Allowing himself a moment of spiteful indignation, Dan pictured his mother's outrage over his shotgun wedding.

As he gazed back at Fionna, his tears obscured her face. He could see through his mind's eye. Her, swollen, ripe, and full of his baby. His hands on her protruding stomach. His lips on the swell. His heart ached physically as he thought of the emptiness he knew she must feel.

"I believe she's going to make a full recovery. You can try again when she's ready, but the scar tissue could make it more difficult."

He'd heard Adeline's soothing assurances as he'd sobbed and tried desperately to listen to everything he needed to know while Fionna had been unconscious.

The hair on the back of his neck stood, and his stomach churned as the memories of Fionna's fingers wrapped forcefully around his biceps as they'd drained her energy and began removing the bullet before she was fully out assaulted his consciousness.

She'd pled for her mother as she vacillated between life and death. It had simply been more than Dan could endure. He'd broken down completely.

He threw himself into the task at hand. He refused not to go ahead with his plan. He eased himself upright while keeping Fionna's skin in contact with his own as he set to work. He had to make her better. He had to fix what he'd done.

~

Captain Jean Paul Fitzroy, French Iodex

"Tu me manques," Jean Paul informed his wife when she answered. He'd never been very good at not getting to the point, and he missed Maddie terribly.

"How is Fionna, Jean Paul? Tell me she is fine."

"I haven't seen her yet, but I think she's getting there. Dan's a disaster though."

"That has been the case for some time."

Fitz chuckled. He certainly couldn't argue with his wife. She was absolutely correct. "Yeah, but he's worse."

"Are you there with them a la hopital?" Her English was near perfect. He'd been teaching her for years, but when she was tired she flowed in and out of French.

"No, I'm at Dan's house. I was just calling to check on you before I hit the sack. I'm gonna go out to Governor Haydenshire's farm early in the morning to plead Danny's case. I can't believe that's how he killed him, but I'll be damned if I let him go down for it."

Maddie was silent, always contemplating and wondering. He

wished he could see her beautiful brown eyes that night. He wished she'd come with him. He didn't know what to say to Fionna. Maddie was so much better at that kind of thing.

He knew she was sitting in their bedroom, sipping tea, wearing that peach-colored, silk robe he'd bought her just because he knew she would be stunning in it. The black lace always made him ache, and it showed off her shapely legs. God, he missed her so much.

"The boys are missing you. They wouldn't sleep. They kept telling me they saw a man in the garden." She scoffed, but Fitz's heart leapt to his throat. He forced himself to breathe.

"I'll get Oliver or Rutherford to come check. Just let me call them."

"We are fine. They're just eager for you to return."

"Maddie, I'm calling one of my elite teams. If you hear anything, it's them. And I don't care what time it is, if you need me, call me."

When he ended that call, he phoned the precinct. "I'm hoping you made an endless number of arrests after we got the call."

"Oui, oui," Rutherford had answered.

"I'm in America, and I'm exhausted. Speak English." Fitz had grown up here. It was easier for him.

"Bastion arrested the five he was with. We took in everyone in the safe houses we knew of. Quite a day. Lucinda was arrested by a Polish border guard. It will be remembered, what Vindico did."

"Yeah, that's sure as hell true. Listen, get Oliver and go by my house. The boys got spooked. Stay in the driveway tonight. I don't like Maddie being there alone. There are too many people far too angry that Nic will no longer be signing paychecks."

~

Rainer Lawson

Emily kept Rainer folded in her soothing cast as they lay in their bed that night. Rainer remembered he'd promised to make love to her that morning. It felt like that morning had been weeks before. He tried to sort through their endless day.

"Do you want to talk about it?" she whispered in the darkness. Rainer shook his head. He just wanted to hold her.

"Is Fionna okay?" He didn't want to think about The Tantra, or Logan, or anything that he'd seen that day.

"Kind of." Emily brushed a kiss across his collarbone. "Mom told her about her miscarriages."

Rainer had assumed Mrs. Haydenshire would share that. He hadn't been alive when the Haydenshires had lost a baby between Levi and Cal. He'd only been a toddler when she'd lost the ones after Emily, so he had no recollection of the events.

"She thinks she got pregnant after the lingerie shower," Emily lamented.

"That wasn't your fault." Rainer's voice was still haggard and weak.

"I know. I just feel bad. Dan thought she'd set the cast before they left, and Fi was a little tipsy that night."

Rainer's heart ached as he considered everything Dan and Fionna had been through.

"I love you." Emily squeezed him tighter.

"I love you too."

"Whenever you want to talk, I want to listen."

Forcing himself to prick the surface of the emotions he'd kept tightly guarded in his shield for their endless day, Rainer finally began to speak.

He wasn't certain he was making any sense, but he allowed the words to flow from his mouth and felt the healing she afforded him as she listened.

She held him close in her cast and heard every word that fell heavy from his lips. She wiped away his tears and said the things he so needed to hear.

She healed him thoroughly, just like she always had, just like she always would.

CHAPTER 42

DEAL WITH THE DEVIL

CROWN GOVERNOR STEPHEN HAYDENSHIRE

After kissing Lillian on the cheek as she fixed batches of her famous chicken soup, Stephen promised to be back soon. She stood at the stove of her kitchen, one of her favorite places in the world to be.

Though it was nearing midnight and exhaustion plagued him after the endless day, he knew he wouldn't sleep until he'd taken care of this one last thing.

"Sweetheart, why don't you go on to bed." He knew perfectly well she wouldn't. Lillian offered him a weary smile. The twins were sound asleep, as was Abigail, all safely upstairs in the serenity of the farmhouse. He knew their babies, healthy and safe, drove her.

"They're going to take that sweet girl off those fluids tomorrow, and she's going to have to eat. She needs something that will restore her and heal her. Something she can keep down, and the broth they make at that hospital is enough to make her sick again." Lillian began chopping celery, carrots, garlic, and onions and adding them to the stockpots on the stove.

Will and Garrett eased in the kitchen door. Stephen wondered momentarily, after the events of the day, if they should keep the doors locked.

As he gazed at his sons, solid and strong, he decided the amount of good they would be locking out far outweighed the potential bad they might be keeping at bay.

Peace and solace washed over him as he allowed himself a moment to listen to the rhythmic tap of Lillian's favorite kitchen knife against the butcher-block cutting board and of his sons chuckling over something as they opened the refrigerator to grab cold Dr Peppers for their journey.

"Please be careful," Lillian pled.

"We'll be fine, sweetheart."

"I made up your old beds in case you're too tired to go back home when you're finished," she informed Will and Garrett. "Brooke was worried about you driving after this, Will."

"I'm sure we'll be taking you up on that." Garrett downed a long sip of Dr Pepper.

Stephen suspected that a night in his childhood bed, surrounded by the home that had raised him, with his big brother in the bed beside his, might do Garrett a world of good. He'd love nothing more than to have all of their kids, the ones they'd birthed and the ones they'd raised, right there safe and sound in the farmhouse that night.

Stephen tried to push away the distinct feeling that he was making a deal with the devil. He pulled his wife close and kissed her fiercely. He needed to cling to his own personal angel before he stepped in front of one of Satan's demons.

"I love you." His voice shook.

She gave him that smile, the one that always made everything feel like it would really be all right, as she assured him that she loved him as well.

An hour later, Stephen eased the Suburban over the gravel drive that led to Coriolis prison.

Garrett strapped on a holster. "You're sure he's gonna go for this?"

They stepped out of the car and forced themselves to move toward the underground prison. Will shuddered and drew measured breaths.

Garrett was more accustomed to the trip, but the color drained readily from his features.

They reached the first checkpoint, and Stephen's knees weakened. The energy drain set in with crushing weight. He couldn't go on. He felt his age more than he ever had before, and there was still so much more to be done before he could sleep.

Garrett flashed his badge, though the guards knew instantly who was there.

"What are you doing out here, Crown Governor?" Lombard asked concernedly.

"Get me Pendergrath," Stephen ordered. "Senior. Keep him drained, shackled, and cuffed."

"Yes, sir, of course."

"Come on, Dad." Garrett drew a deep breath as he led Will and Stephen back to the gravel top decks where the drain was less intense.

Several minutes later, three guards escorted Candor Pendergrath at gunpoint toward them.

The imprint of Rainer's boot was bloodied and bruised on Pendergrath's face. His perfectly capped teeth were chipped and ragged from the force of Rainer's fury. His nose had been healed but would always remain at an odd angle.

He scowled, but couldn't yet manage any of his standard biting remarks. He was a broken man.

"Candor," Stephen huffed.

"Governor," Pendergrath spat.

"I assume you know why I'm here."

His energy began to steady slightly, and he became more himself.

"I assume you'd like to work a deal. That you'd like me to forget that your son killed my friend in cold blood." He managed a half-hearted laugh, but it drained him quickly. "You let me walk, I'll see what I can forget."

"No." Stephen shook his head. That wasn't what Pendergrath had expected to hear. His shock was displayed in his shattered features. "Whether Logan ever works as an officer again or not, you will spend the rest of your life here." That was not up for negotiation.

"Then it seems to me I'll have many stories to tell when they put me on the stand." Pendergrath slithered in his own mock triumph.

"Fine," Stephen allowed. "But just remember this when you're back in that cell tonight." He let the memories of Coriolis prison settle firmly in Pendergrath's mind. "It's up to me, and me alone, to determine just how long your son stays here with you." He made his offer.

"Take him back. Let's go home, boys." Stephen turned and headed back to the Suburban between his sons.

He'd made it ten paces when he heard the word he'd come to hear.

"Fine," echoed from Candor Pendergrath's vile mouth.

CHAPTER 43

REVELATIONS AND RECEIPTS

DAN VINDICO

At five o'clock, there was a timid knock on Fionna's door. Dan let his eyes open hesitantly. Panic shot through him. When had he fallen asleep? He made certain Fionna was still sleeping peacefully on his chest.

Adeline slipped in the door dressed in fresh scrubs, but she didn't look like she'd slept any better than Dan.

She smiled at them formed together in the relatively small bed. "I can't sleep without Logan either."

Fionna was still out, so Dan debated how to sit up so Adeline could do whatever needed to be done.

"I'm just going to cast her and see if we can't sort of speed up the process of everything," Adeline whispered. She didn't seem to want to elaborate on the fact that she was going to try to force Fionna's body to move on with the miscarriage. "I came in early. It will work faster if she's asleep while I do it. Then she won't have to think about it."

"Thank you." Dan was immensely appreciative of all the thoughtfulness and care that Adeline put into her work. He agreed with Logan's assessment that his wife was a phenomenal medio and a phenomenal human being.

Adeline offered another smile as Dan eased out from underneath Fionna and moved to a chair beside the bed. He kept her hand in his.

"The pill I gave her last night will have her out for another few hours."

Dan watched as a faint blue orb pulsed rhythmically out of Adeline's hands and onto Fionna's abdomen. It spun from her lower stomach to the top of her thighs.

He braced, worried Fionna would awaken, but she didn't even move.

"Governor Vindico signed the orders this morning, so I'm going to be assigned to her only today. If you need anything, I'll be here." Adeline was still shy around Dan, but she seemed to feel that she should talk to him while she was there.

"That will make Fi really happy," he assured her, and he needed to thank his old man.

"Since she did so well during the night and it seems everything is relatively healed up from the gunshot wound, other than the pain of her body being injured and then trying to heal, they wanted to move her to the obstetrics floor since the miscarriage is what's keeping her from going home.

"But I think it's a terrible idea to put women who are having miscarriages up on that floor. There are babies everywhere. It just seems so cruel, so Medio Sawyer and I agreed that she should stay here. I'm working on changing that hospital policy as quickly as I can." She talked more freely as she discussed her work.

"Do you know when I might be able to take her home?" he whispered as he rubbed Fionna's arm tenderly.

"That depends on how she is today. I'm going to have to do an internal exam, which won't be comfortable, but I'll try to be quick. If some of the swelling has gone down, then we're headed the right direction. Mrs. Haydenshire is bringing her some of her chicken soup. If she can keep that down most of the day and the swelling has improved by tonight, I might be able to release her tomorrow. If food makes her sick throughout the day, it will be another day or two."

Dan calculated that into his plans. "She'll be all right for Rainer and Emily's wedding, right?"

"I think so, but she'll still need to take it easy. She'll be up and around here soon. She'll probably still be tender and have to sit more than she stands, but she'll make it down the aisle with no problems by then."

"And she's going to be all right? I mean once we leave here, she'll be fine?" He just needed to hear Adeline tell him again that Fionna would recover.

Adeline gave him a calm, reassuring smile as she nodded. "She'll be fine, Chief Vindico. She'll be understandably emotional, and the first time or two that you have intercourse once she stops bleeding she might be tender. It might even be painful, but she'll be back to full health very soon."

He hadn't allowed himself to even consider their sex life yet. She'd been a disaster for several weeks. The first week, when she'd hoped against hope that her period was just late, she'd done a better job of feigning normality. But in the last few weeks as she'd slowly come from together to apart, she hadn't offered, and he hadn't asked.

"You don't have to call me Chief Vindico." Dan drew a deep breath. "I'm sure in a few hours Governor Haydenshire will show up with Governor Willow to inform me that I no longer have a job anyway, and I certainly consider you and Logan close friends, so just call me Dan. The governors might be telling me I'm going to jail."

Adeline continued to cast and heal Fionna. "I don't think they'll do that, but I know you're worried. Captain Fitzroy was pulling onto the farm when I left."

Dan had no doubt that Fitz would plead his case, but he had no idea if Governor Haydenshire would listen.

"Is Logan okay?" His nerves were eating at him. He needed a subject change.

Adeline considered for a moment. "Kind of." A rosy heat took over her pale cheeks.

Dan chuckled. The sound shocked him. "He's better with you but worse when you leave."

"Yeah." She seemed to appreciate his knowledge of how officers typically reacted after pulling the trigger.

Adeline kept Fionna casted until eight when she began to stir. Adeline dropped the cast and quickly changed the pad and bandages. Dan was shocked by how much healing had taken place.

"Hey, baby doll," he soothed as Fionna fought to awaken.

Adeline picked up the iPad she'd carried in and made several markings. She studied Fionna as Dan raised the bed for her. "Any pain?"

Fionna shook her head, but she reached for Dan. "Not really. It feels much better than it did last night."

Adeline smiled and nodded as she continued to write on the chart. "Did you still want us to keep everyone out of the room unless they've been given permission to enter?" She noted the demands that Dan had in place from the day before.

"Yes! Jared might turn up again." She held Dan's hand with both of her own.

Adeline and Fionna shared a knowing grin. The sight soothed Dan's soul.

"I guess I wouldn't mind him seeing my big, huge, sparkly ring." She gave a small laugh as Adeline and Dan chuckled. "But I'd prefer to not be lying in a hospital bed with no pants on if I'm going to see one of my exes."

Adeline nodded her understanding. "Since you're such good friends with the Chief of Staff's daughter, and you're engaged to one of the governor's sons, that means that you get special treatment. I get to take care of you all day, and if you're ready, I'll take out your IV. Mrs. Haydenshire is bringing you her yummy chicken soup, so you don't even have to eat hospital food."

"Aww, thank you. I feel bad. You don't have to do that." Fionna blushed. Dan was mesmerized. She'd been so pale the day before. With the glow of her cheeks, she suddenly looked almost back to normal.

Mrs. Haydenshire arrived with a cooler that contained numerous mason jars of chicken noodle soup.

"Start with just the broth," Adeline instructed, "and don't be surprised if it makes you sick. That's normal. It's just the anesthesia you had yesterday. It doesn't mean anything else is wrong."

Mrs. Haydenshire pulled one of the many Styrofoam bowls she packed and poured broth from one of the jars. She heated the bowl with her hand and placed it on the tray for Fionna.

"Want me to feed you, baby?" Dan took over.

She gave him another one of his smiles, and he became aware of his heartbeat, of the breath permeating his lungs, and the warmth of her beside him. He became aware, once again, that maybe life was worth living.

"I think I can do that," she scoffed. But as it turned out, curving her abdomen in enough to feed herself made her uncomfortable.

"Sit back, and let him take care of you, sweetheart. It will make me feel better and him feel better," Mrs. Haydenshire ordered as she tidied up the room.

Fionna leaned against the pillows Dan stacked behind her back. "Okay, fine, but very soon I want to eat and pee on my own."

Everyone laughed, and Adeline promised that she would indeed do those things on her own again.

As he finished feeding Fionna the soup, a knock sounded on the door. Dan's hand shook with the spoon. He was certain he knew who was calling.

Like a knife straight through him, the fear returned to Fionna's beautiful eyes.

"It'll be okay." He hoped against hope he was telling her the truth. He covered her bare legs with the blankets once again and made certain that she was as okay as she could be in that moment before he moved to open the door.

"Wow…the big guns." His eyes methodically moved down the line. Governor Haydenshire, Governor Willow, former Crown Governor Carrington, Governor Sapman, Governor Eleanor who'd taken Governor Haydenshire's old seat, Governor Vanzlant who'd earned herself Peterson's seat, and his father.

Governor Haydenshire chuckled, "We just need to talk for a few minutes, Daniel. Why don't we go get you some breakfast?"

Dan was aware that it wasn't an invitation he was allowed to refuse.

"Fionna, Garrett said to tell you he'll be here as soon as he goes home to change. He stayed with us last night. I had an errand I needed him to run with me." The Crown Governor moved into the room and gazed adoringly down at Fionna.

"Yes, sir," she choked. The tears returned. The first of the day, but Dan was certain there would be more.

Dan shook his head. "Look, just say whatever the hell you came to say. I'm not leaving her."

"No, it's okay, I'll be all right…I think," she choked.

"He will be right back. Does that make you feel better?" The governor effectively closed the argument.

Fionna managed a slight nod. Dan's entire body slumped in relief. He had no idea what was coming, but apparently he wasn't going to Coriolis.

"Are you sure you're all right, baby? If you want me to stay, just say the word." Dan kept his voice low but knew that Governor Haydenshire could hear his vow.

"No," she whispered. Her chin trembled. "But I know you need to know. It's making you nervous, so just go. But please not too long."

Dan brushed a tender kiss on her forehead and rubbed her cheek tenderly with his thumb. He wiped away the escaping tears. "Do you want me to wait until Garrett gets here?"

She cast her pitiful gaze on Governor Haydenshire with a pleading nod. He gave her a wink. "All right," he agreed.

Garrett slipped into Fionna's room, and she visibly relaxed. "I'll be right back," Dan promised.

Dan pulled on his sunglasses and lowered his head as he walked within the circle of governors out of the hospital. The press went wild.

"Chief Vindico, what can you tell us about Miss Styler?" they chanted.

"How do you feel about the miscarriage?" one drawled. Fury seared through Dan's veins.

"Why was Fionna Styler at The Tantra yesterday?"

"When did you begin dating?"

"Are you still dating?"

"Will you and Fionna be starting a family even though that will force her out of Summation?" a female reporter chanted tastelessly.

"Step away from Chief Vindico. He will not be answering any questions," Governor Haydenshire demanded.

Dan flung himself into a seat at a diner beside the hospital. His jaw worked until his molars ached. He wished the governors would just get on with it. He needed to be with Fionna, not in a diner listening to them tell him how sorry they were.

The board ordered, and Dan followed suit. He requested that his be brought out as soon as it was finished and not with the other meals.

Governor Haydenshire chuckled. "I guess we see where we stand."

Dan didn't join in the customary laughter the Crown Governor's comment elicited.

"Well now, you didn't really expect him to change, did you?" Governor Carrington offered Dan a wry grin.

"No, I didn't." Governor Haydenshire gave Dan a nod. "And I'd have to say I would've been disappointed if he had."

The waitress returned with piping hot mugs of coffee that Dan had to admit he did find restorative.

"Your orders will be up in just a minute," she assured the waiting table.

"Since Daniel clearly has more important things to attend to, why don't we just talk, and after he eats, we'll let him get back to his beautiful fiancée." Governor Haydenshire commanded the attention of the table. "I asked Regis to come with us this morning. Occasionally, even the Crown Governor needs a little advice."

Dan had no available patience left. "Look, you don't have to fire me. I resign." He was certain that was the hesitation and the visible strain in the governors' eyes.

"Daniel, simmer down," Governor Vindico ordered his son.

Finally seeming to get that Dan wasn't going to sit there and drink coffee chatting the morning away, Governor Haydenshire nodded. "All right, fine, let's do this. Governor Willow and I will accept your resignation." The Crown Governor's tone turned regretful.

"I will get you a job anywhere in the Realm you would like, but not in law enforcement. It isn't good for you, and you have someone who's wearing your ring and lying in a hospital bed eager for you to return. She is good for you. So before you decide on your next career, I'd like to ask that you take a little time to heal. Really heal. Not only from losing everything you lost yesterday but from the past ten years.

"I've spoken with my sons, my future son-in-law, Landon Portwood, Trent McCoy, and I got an early call from Captain Fitzroy this morning. We discussed everything that happened yesterday. None of us seem to recall anything happening that shouldn't have, so I can't fathom there being any legal repercussions."

The knot in Dan's chest eased. His stomach finally unclenched. "Thank you, sir." He turned appreciative quickly.

"The way we all figure it, you worked approximately ten years straight without taking a paid vacation. As you have effectively been forced to resign, we've taken the liberty of cashing out all of your amassed vacation days. I've decided in addition to that, the Senate will be paying your current salary through the end of the year."

Dan's mouth hung open in shock. "Sir, it's only March."

"Yes, I do have a calendar on my desk, son. But I like a nice round number, so this morning I had my oldest son place five hundred and fifty thousand dollars in your bank account." He chuckled at Dan's utter shock.

"That should allow you and Ms. Styler a few options and a little time to really heal before you go back to work. I'm not certain what you and Fionna will decide, but if she might like to end her career with the Angels, perhaps do something a little different, then I want the two of you to have that option."

Stunned disbelief washed over Dan as he tried to thank the governors and thank the waitress for placing the plate of eggs, bacon, and biscuits in front of him.

"I can't thank you enough. I don't deserve that."

Governor Haydenshire shook his head. "You gave your very life for twelve long years serving this Realm, trying desperately to end

Wretchkinsides's evil and rid the Realm of all of the horror that he held in his hands. Now, I may not always have liked the way you went about that, but you fought long and hard. Yesterday, you paid your debt to Amelia.

"I know he took things from you that no amount of money will ever bring back, but you deserve a real life. God saw fit to give you a woman who clearly makes your days so good you don't want to go to sleep at night, so hold on to her tight with both hands and never let her go. Heal together. Create a real life with her and for her. Sew the pieces back together. It's going to take a long time. But if you'll spend your life cherishing her and being her rock, none of this will have to have been in vain. If Lillian and I or any of the people at this table can help you do that, please ask, because we love you and we care about you."

Dan swallowed down raw emotion that had him in a chokehold and managed to thank them again.

"One more thing," Governor Haydenshire sighed. He pulled something from a file folder. "Officer Tuttle went through Bridgette Meyers's car this morning. He found these along with dozens upon dozens more. Quite a few of my family and your parents. An endless number of the Senate. I'm showing you these to try to alleviate a little bit of your guilt, but also to make you see that you have got to make better decisions. Let your love of Fionna drive you instead of vengeance, please."

Dan took the photographs. His heart stalled as he stared at pictures printed on computer paper that had to have come from Bridgette's phone. Pictures of Fionna getting out of his Ferrari and the Expeditions at the arena. Pictures of Dan kissing her goodbye before practice.

"I'm not sure how she got those, but based on the confessions coming in from everyone Iodex took in yesterday, Bridgette began working for Nic Wretchkinsides before she was working for Iodex. He arranged the story for her that her father was a Felsink guard.

"After she offered to become a spy for you, she convinced Nic that she was deeply involved with you. I assume she couldn't show him those photos because that would discredit her own story, so I can only assume she planned to use them to blackmail you. Don't sell your soul again, please. You should never have involved yourself in her life. You should never have taken her to the arena or brought her to the Senate at all. I'm betting this is why she asked to go."

Abject panic seized Dan's shield as he forced himself to recall his relationship with Bridgette. "The Angels' locker room," he choked.

"What?" Governor Haydenshire looked concerned Dan had finally lost his mind.

"You have to have someone go scan the Angels' locker room. Now. I think she planted something in there. When she demanded to go out there, she also wanted to use the locker room alone."

The governor's eyes closed. "All right. I'll have Portwood do that in just a moment. Even if there is something in there, you dismantled anyone they might've helped. I'm sure she knew that the Interfeci could afford to pay her a great deal more than the Senate ever could, but playing you both against each other made her a very wealthy woman."

Dan apologized profusely for his own stupidity.

CHAPTER 44

TO START AGAIN

Dan raced back into Fionna's room an hour later.

"I got sick," she fussed pitifully.

"Baby." Another round of guilt washed over him. He felt terrible he hadn't been there when she needed him.

"But you can try to eat again in an hour. It's completely normal," Adeline reminded her as she plied Fionna with a water bottle.

"And, sweetheart, I keep telling you, I've had eleven children. I have cleaned up more vomit than I care to think about. I've even cleaned up after your future husband when he and my oldest sons decided to see what might happen if they consumed more alcohol than is contained in an actual distillery." Mrs. Haydenshire gave Dan a wry smile.

"Sorry about that." He reveled in Fionna's weak laughter.

"I think Garrett and I will go and let you two rest."

Adeline changed Fionna's pad and bandages again and made her exit as well.

At the agreed upon time, Dan fixed Fionna another bowl of broth and fed her slowly.

She managed to keep it down, and the healing effect was dramatic. They talked, and Dan told her everything the governors had decided. It shocked her as well.

Fionna fell asleep a little while later, and Adeline moved to cast her once again. Dan slipped from the room to visit with Rainer, Garrett, and Fitzroy who'd come back to check on Fionna.

"Hey, Maddie really wants you and Fionna to come to Paris, let her take care of you for a while," Fitz urged.

"Maybe," Dan allowed. "We have this big wedding thing we're supposed to be in here in a couple of weeks, but maybe after that."

Garrett and Rainer chuckled.

"You know, it might be good to get her away from here soon, though," Garrett stated thoughtfully. "The press is chomping at the bit to talk to either of you, and all the owners are fending off demands for interviews until they talk to her. It's gonna be a lot to deal with, and she's not okay."

Repulsion and deep concern fought for dominance in Dan's shield as he thought about Fionna being asked just a few of the questions that had been shouted at him as he'd left the hospital with the governors. "I'm working on that. I'm going to get her out of here. I promise."

When Fionna awoke, Adeline suggested that she try some more of the soup. Each time she ate, her color improved dramatically, and each time Adeline casted her, Fionna's pain seemed to ebb.

Dan supplied her with the soup, adding small bites of chicken, vegetables, and noodles in with the broth this time.

Two hours after she'd eaten, Adeline gave her permission to have an actual shower. Dan broached the topic of the two of them getting away for a while as he dried her off.

She'd cried over his suggestion, but they seemed to be tears of joy this time instead of tears of utter heartbreak which she'd shed without stop for weeks.

"That would mean so much to me." She hugged him with all of the strength she could manage which wasn't much.

He kissed her gently and told her how much he loved her and how much he'd missed her over the past few weeks. It only served to make her cry harder.

"Let's give it a couple of days and see if I can take you home soon. Whenever you're ready to go, we'll head out."

They sat on the bed discussing their trip and purposefully not talking about anything that had happened the day before. There would be time for that later. They both needed an hour or two to pretend that life was normal and that nothing had gone so very, very, wrong.

❧

Adeline knocked again a little before five. "I know you want to go home tomorrow, so I'd like to set a specialized cast for you for a few hours tonight."

"What kind of specialized cast?" Fionna's energy was already waning. "Maybe Dan could do it."

He smiled and brushed her hair away from her face. They'd been enjoying the time alone. She'd reveled in the moments where they were them again. Another cast only served to bring back the pain and terror that their life had been for far too long.

Fionna instinctively placed her hand over her abdomen. Dan wondered what she was feeling. Pain certainly, but he suspected after all those weeks, she felt empty.

"Dan will definitely need to cast you when we're finished, but that will be more for you emotionally than physically. Because you're in such good health otherwise, you're a prime candidate for what we call an intense cast. Three medios will cast you at once. It's fairly common, and the healing will be dramatic. Your energy is stable enough now to withstand it. But the intense casting will make you very tired. And in your situation, it can be uncomfortable, so I want you to think about it and really discuss it.

"Dan's parents would like to see both of you. Maybe they could come visit with you for a little while, and then you're going to need to try and eat something a little more substantial than soup. I believe country fried steak is on the menu tonight." Adeline shuddered as Fionna's face contorted in a disgusted scowl. "I don't really see that staying down, so if you could think of anything from a restaurant around here, maybe a little less greasy, that someone could go get for you, there are several people in the waiting room who would be happy to pick up whatever you'd like.

"Maybe visit with Dan's parents, have something to eat, then maybe Dan could go get himself a meal. I know Rainer and Logan are both out there hoping to see you," she offered Dan with a sweet smile that said they would understand if he didn't make an appearance.

"If you're going to cast her after we finish the intense treatment, it would soothe her to sleep and probably complete the process, but you're going to need to eat something with a great deal of protein. If you decide you do want to do this, we'll start while Dan is gone and then he'll be back about the time we're finishing up."

Dan shook his head. "I'm not leaving her in here alone for that."

"I'll be okay. You can go," Fionna insisted.

"No," he informed both of them in a tone that said arguing would be futile. Being casted by three medios and forcing her body to complete the miscarriage in a few hours would be more than uncomfortable. It would be excruciating.

"Actually, you need to eat, and we need to make certain that solid proteins will stay down before we do the intense casting. We can still do everything I said. We'll just start the intense process when Dan gets back."

"I'll just get Fitz to bring me something here, and you do not have to see my parents if you don't want to."

"I'm going to have to see them sometime." With a shaky breath she reached for his hand. "Let's just do whatever will make me better. I want to go home. I need some space to process this." She drew heavily from Dan. It was a sensation he hadn't felt in so many weeks he'd nearly forgotten how incredible it was to have her pull his energy into her.

But his energy drained quickly, and he knew Adeline was right. He was going to have to eat a great deal if he was going to keep Fionna casted and work her through the pain of the last of the miscarriage.

He just didn't want to leave her there again. They'd been apart far too long. He wanted to be with her constantly. He needed to hold her. He needed to prove to her that he would be everything she needed. He would construct her a healing sanctuary in his arms, in his shield.

The loss was a deep, raw, horrifying pain, and he wanted her to know that he felt it as well. It wasn't a loss she had to suffer alone.

"Dan, really, I think you should go eat with all of your guys. It would mean a lot to you and to them. You'll be back in time. I'll be okay. I promise."

"You're certain?"

She gave him an adamant nod. He knew she was desperate to get out of the hospital. The constant casting, and people, and well-wishes, kind though they were, were exhausting her. She was having to feel everyone's sorrow and worry over her. She couldn't process her own grief through all of their feelings. If going home was what she wanted, he'd make it happen.

Able to think logistically somewhat better than Fionna, who was still weak from exhaustion and constant pain, he kissed her cheek tenderly.

"How about one of those grilled chicken sandwiches you like from Frye's, sweetheart?"

A broad grin spread across Fionna's face. "On ciabatta."

"Of course, and you're sure about my parents?" He studied her closely.

"I'm gonna marry you so isn't the saying that I'm marrying them too?"

"Yes, but try not to think about that too much, at least until I get you down the actual aisle." He reveled in her laughter.

"You know, Mrs. Haydenshire and Kara kind of went off on your mom yesterday. Emily told me about it." Fionna seemed to have just remembered the story.

"I'm sorry I missed that." He tried to envision his little sister telling off their mother.

Adeline smiled. "Get Garrett to tell you about it. He tells it best."

"I'll do that," Dan assured her, but he was unable to glance Adeline's way.

Fionna was gazing at him, and Dan saw something in her eyes he hadn't seen in weeks.

"Will you tell my parents I'll come get them in a minute?" Dan requested as Adeline made her exit.

He slid onto the bed beside Fionna. Her eyes were heavy, and her color was stronger than Dan had seen it thus far. He cradled her hands tenderly in his own.

She bit her lip and studied him closely. "You haven't really kissed me in so long." Her chin gave another tender tremble. She pulled toward him. The magnetism and chemistry between them could no longer be denied.

The acknowledgment of the fissure between them settled harshly in his throat. "I didn't think you wanted me to. I didn't want to make you more uncomfortable. I seemed to make you so miserable." The heartbreak he'd felt every single day as he'd watched her grow more and more depressed threatened to drag him back under.

"You didn't make me miserable. I just didn't know what to do, and then I did everything wrong," she stammered with tears falling from her eyes again.

"No, baby, that isn't true. Please stop saying that."

She turned the full power of her pleading sienna eyes on him. "Will you kiss me now? You know, like a real kiss, not like I'm in the hospital and all of this horrible stuff happened. Please. I just...I need us to feel normal again."

His heart stuttered and then began to fly. Dan edged his body closer to hers. He cradled her face in his hand and gazed at her. His entire being filled with love for her.

She eased herself up until she was sitting and smiled. There didn't seem to be any pain.

"I love you so much," he whispered the words across her lips.

"I love you too." Her eyes begged him, and her breaths came quicker.

He tried to quell the desire he'd not felt in many endless weeks. Its powerful resurgence coursed through his weary veins.

He leaned and brushed his lips tenderly across hers. He felt it instantly—the spark, the need, the essence of her.

She panted, and a low groan escaped his lungs. It had been so long. He moved his head to the other side and reveled in the swell of her lips against his own. He traced them with his tongue, memorizing the way they felt once again.

"God, I missed you." He pulled her closer and tried desperately to be gentle with her as he devoured her mouth.

She threaded her fingers through his hair as he wrapped her up in his muscled embrace. He pulled away as she gasped for breath, but he needed more.

He began kissing his way down her neck and praying that he wouldn't hurt her or frustrate her in any way, then he hesitantly let his hands slide from her neck down the sides of her breasts.

She moaned heatedly. She'd missed his caress, missed his kiss, and missed his touch as much as he'd missed her.

"I want you," she whispered in a heated plea. He felt the shame and confusion that washed through her rhythms.

A shuddering groan thundered from his chest. He would remember the confusion. They would talk about it later, but right then he needed to taste more.

He moved his lips back to hers. "You have no idea how badly I've missed you telling me that." He dipped his tongue inside her mouth. She slowly gave in to the emotions she'd kept locked away. She began to draw from him again. The sensation was heavenly.

She was still tentative and afraid of her own feelings and desires. Her rhythms faltered. Dan pulled away slightly.

"Fi, just for a minute, baby, don't think." He leaned in and kissed her again as she panted. He continued, "Just feel. Just let it all go for me, everything but you and me. Right here, right now, just feel."

She gave in. Her body relaxed. She pulled him back for more. He held her to him, sucking her tongue softly as she moaned in his mouth. Her weary energy permeated his.

Her hand traced down his chest, and he felt her brain shut out the restless worries of her heart as she slid her hand up his zipper line. He groaned from the exquisite sensation of her hands on him once again.

She began to massage him, unable to help herself, and he fought with everything he was not to lay her down and crawl over her.

Using her left hand, she grasped his right and brought it back to her breast. His entire being flooded with a heady cocktail of need and elation.

He forced himself to start slowly. He massaged her breasts, still swollen larger than he'd ever seen them, and so tender she shook from the slightest touch. Her nipples strained against the hospital gown she was wearing.

"More," she begged.

He didn't have to be asked twice. He grasped them firmly, groping and massaging her. He listened to her sweet, impassioned moans. They sang directly to his heart and to his groin.

They stayed lip-locked for several long minutes until they pulled away. They couldn't move anything further, not yet, and certainly not in a hospital bed. The temptation was simply too strong for either of them.

Fionna fell back against her pillows with a replete sigh and a smile that Dan could have sat and stared at for a lifetime. "I'm gonna need you to do that a lot for the next couple of days."

Dan chuckled and tried to catch his breath. "You just say the word."

Worry etched her beautiful face. "Do you think it's okay I want to do that?"

Pain fractured his still mending heart. "Honey, I know we've pretty much been through hell." He saw no other way to phrase it. "And I don't think we should use that to cover the pain or to keep us from talking about everything that happened. But that is an important part of our relationship, and it's going to be an important part of healing this relationship, because the past few weeks it hasn't been so good."

"I'm so sorry," she choked as renewed tears took her over.

"Me too, baby." He brushed another kiss on her forehead. "But if you've taught me anything, it's that we're worth fighting for. My life isn't worth anything at all without you. So if you want to be kissed, or held, or anything at all, then that's what I'm going to do. And," he caressed her face again, "in a few days, when you're feeling better, maybe on our trip, then I want to be with you, baby. I'll be so gentle. I swear to you. And I'll wait as long as you need until you're sure you're ready, but I want you to feel how much I love you. I want to put this back together stronger than it was before." Dan wrapped her back up in his arms and let her cry on his shoulder.

"I want that too."

He felt the full force of her healing power overwhelm him.

"Well,"—he smiled at her—"I'm currently unemployed." She giggled through her tears. "And Medio Haydenshire informed me yesterday that you will not be challenging or even practicing for at least six weeks, so how about we spend a little time, just the two of us, working through everything, and hopefully someday putting it behind us."

"That sounds perfect."

"Then let's see if they can't get you all healed up."

She smiled through the last of her tears. He stood and headed toward the door, but then he spun back. "You're sure about my parents?" he quizzed again.

She laughed. "It's fine. Just don't leave me in here with them."

"I would never ever do that, baby. I'm your Shield."

CHAPTER 45

HEALING

Dan pulled his wallet from his back pocket as he met Garrett, Logan, Rainer, and Fitzroy in the corridor. All of the men's eyes went to his wet shirt. They offered him sympathetic gazes, but no one commented.

"Hey, would you mind getting the lady a grilled chicken sandwich on ciabatta and a plain baked potato from Frye's?" Dan offered Garrett two twenties.

"Sure thing, and I've got it. I heard you were on the dole."

Dan laughed. "Yeah, well, I'll definitely be wanting my change."

"Daniel, that isn't something to joke about," Mrs. Vindico huffed.

Dan rolled his eyes and didn't comment.

After glancing at Mrs. Vindico and then back to Dan, Logan smirked. "So we heard you needed to eat your weight in meat. How about after he gets back with her sandwich, we all go to Big Mickey's?" His customary smirk and the invitation eased some of the worry in Rainer's and Garrett's eyes.

"That sounds good," Dan agreed. "Just let me get her fed and settled, and then we'll go."

"I'll be back quick." Garrett left Dan holding the money and jogged to the elevators.

After slipping the cash back in his wallet, Dan turned to his parents. "Would you like to come see Fi for a little while?"

Kara tried to hide her giggle probably at Dan's begrudging tone. She was the first one to stand up.

"Well, it's about time," Mrs. Vindico spat.

"Marion," Governor Vindico sighed, "they've been through enough. Let's go tell Fionna how thrilled we are that she's agreed to marry our son and see if we can do anything to help her heal, okay?"

Dan drew a deep breath and guided his parents, Kara, and Meredith, who'd come by to bring flowers, to Fionna's room.

He willed patience by reminding himself that his mother's carefully orchestrated world had come crashing down around her in the last few weeks.

News had broken right after New Year's that Lindley had been arrested. At the trial that Dan had purposefully missed, Governor Vindico had forced Lindley into a sixteen-week stint at an inpatient drug rehab facility run by the Auxiliary Department. She was to undergo two years of mandatory weekly counseling after she was released. After that, it was to be left up to her Auxiliary counselors if she would continue with therapy.

Now, the entire Realm knew that her son had not only gotten his extremely famous girlfriend pregnant, but he had also resigned as Chief of Iodex, a prestigious job unto itself, under relatively sketchy circumstances.

Dan knew, just as his mother knew, people would always assume the worst. He opened the door, allowed his parents and sisters to enter, and immediately went to sit on Fionna's bed. He held her right hand in both of his as he kissed the side of her head.

"Are you feeling any better?" Kara asked sweetly.

Fionna nodded, but she tried very hard not to look at Mrs. Vindico.

Shame fevered her face and flooded her rhythms. Fionna's embarrassment infuriated Dan. She had nothing to be ashamed of, and he couldn't stand that his mother made her feel like she'd done something wrong.

"I'm really a lot better. If I keep dinner down and the casting tonight goes well, I can go home tomorrow."

"I'm just so sorry. If Tim and I can do anything at all, you just say the word." Meredith was blinking back tears as she placed the cheerful bouquet of Gerbera daisies on one of the counters in the room.

"We're all so sorry, sweetheart." Governor Vindico seated himself in one of the chairs in the room as he gazed at Fionna as if she were already one of his own. "But Marion and I are so thrilled that Daniel somehow convinced you to marry him." He winked at her and made her beam.

"I didn't make him beg or anything." She giggled.

"I would have," Dan assured her.

"Daniel, that ring is lovely." Mrs. Vindico smiled at Fionna and shocked everyone in the room.

"Thank you," Fionna offered hesitantly.

"It's ginormous," Kara gushed.

"I told Tad Anderson I wanted every guy within a fifteen-mile radius of her to know she was mine, so..." He watched as her eyes regained just a little of their sparkle.

"Arthur, maybe we should go over to Dan's to get the house ready for her to go home tomorrow. I could cook a few things, tidy everything up, organize, so they don't have to worry about food," Mrs. Vindico planned.

Fionna and Kara shared a horrified expression as Dan grimaced. He spun on the bed to face his mother.

"Actually, Mom, we're heading out of town for a few days. We need to get away from the press, from everything really."

"Are you sure she's up to traveling, son?" the governor asked.

"Adeline said it would be fine."

"Well, if you're feeling up to it, I recommend it, sweetheart. You should hear the things I've been asked coming and going in and out of here. It's insane." The governor shook his head. "I know you've lost your jet privileges, son, but I do still have mine. If you'd like to use one of the Senate jets, I don't think anyone would begrudge you that."

"I will definitely take you up on that, Dad. Thanks." Dan grinned. The motion was restorative.

"You should have insisted that Daniel not lose his job, Arthur."
Mrs. Vindico couldn't hide her ire any longer it seemed.

"And here we go again," Meredith sighed.

"Mom, I quit. I don't want to be Chief of Iodex anymore. Governor
Haydenshire was right. It wasn't good for me. And, quite honestly, I
wasn't good for it."

"Well, what are you going to do, Daniel? Just be unemployed?"
Mrs. Vindico shuddered in horror.

"I don't know yet, but for the next few weeks, and maybe the next
few months, I'm going to take care of my fiancée and nothing else."

A broad beam lit Fionna's beautiful face as she squeezed Dan's
hand.

Always seeming to know when she needed to be rescued, Garrett
knocked on the door.

"Hey baby," he greeted Fionna warmly, then offered smiles to
Dan's family as he handed Dan Fionna's dinner.

Very pleased with Garrett's arrival, Fionna scooted to the center of
the bed so Garrett could sit with her as well.

Dan stood. He would no longer begrudge Garrett and Fionna's
close relationship. She loved Garrett, and he'd been there for her
when no one else could have been. And for that, Dan could never
thank him enough. And right then, in the midst of his family, he knew
she needed both of her Shields.

"Cameramen attacked me when I got back to the doors. They
wanted to know if they could photograph your dinner." Garrett shook
his head in disbelief.

The governor rolled his eyes. "I'm not surprised."

Dan and Garrett both watched over Fionna as she ate. She grew
visibly stronger with each bite she managed.

Fionna's parents came in so Dan could go eat and prepare to cast
Fionna for most of the night.

"Are you ready?" Rainer quizzed as Dan grabbed his sunglasses—
though it was evening—and his jacket.

Fitzroy grinned. "I found a few other guys who wanted to tag
along if you don't mind."

Logan, Rainer, and Fitzroy were standing amongst Tuttle, Ramier, Portwood, Ericcson, McCoy, and Barron.

"We had to have one last Big Mickey's sub together." Portwood grinned.

Already emotional again, Dan took in the men who'd stood beside him and served faithfully. The men who'd followed him into hell and had come out the other side.

"Are you two okay?" he asked Ericsson and Barron. He felt badly he hadn't gone to check on them while they'd been patients at the hospital.

"We're getting there." Barron shifted on his crutches. His shinbone had been rebuilt, but he was still having it casted every few hours and wasn't allowed to be without the air brace that kept it from moving. "How about you?"

"Getting there." Dan hoped that was true.

They exited the hospital and shifted until Dan was in the center of the men he was leaving with.

"Chief Vindico," echoed from every direction.

"Guess they haven't heard that I'm out." Dan batted an enhanced boom mic out of his face.

"Chief Vindico, how is Miss Styler feeling?"

"Will she be able to challenge?"

"Is she quitting the Angels?"

"Are you forcing her out of Summation to start a family?"

"She can't challenge pregnant—what will she do?" chanted from reporters who ran along beside Elite Iodex.

"Can you tell us if you and Miss Styler are saddened by the loss or would you say you're relieved?" called a young man dressed in a cheap suit.

Dan whipped his sunglasses off furiously and glared at the reporter.

"Okay." Garrett stepped in and shoved Dan forward. Portwood ordered the press away.

They exited the Metro and stalked several blocks to the sub shop that Iodex ate at on a regular basis. Their sandwiches were not only delicious they were gigantic. Dan ordered their largest sirloin steak and cheese.

"How the hell am I supposed to get Fi out of the hospital tomorrow without them attacking her and asking shit like that?" He threw the plastic chair back from the table and threw himself into the seat. Ever mindful of his temper now, he ordered himself to rein it in.

The men seated around him, digging into their subs, grew thoughtful.

Rainer smiled at Dan. "Let me take care of it. Just tell me when you want her out, and I can pretty much guarantee you that the press will never even see you two leave."

All Dan could do was hope Rainer could come through. He relaxed and enjoyed hearing tales of the Elite squad's heroics under his direction for the last ten years.

No one spoke of Wretchkinsides or the takedown. They all reveled in the camaraderie of being the only people to really understand the horrors they'd lived through and the images that would fade slightly over time, but that had become indelible imprints on their souls.

As the blossoming cherry trees faded with the sunlight, Dan sat quietly by Fionna's bed. He held her hand and tried to soothe her. Adeline came in and prepared the bed underneath Fionna.

"This is Medio Brad Metzger and Medio Carol Dawson. Brad was in the unit that performed your surgery, Fionna." Adeline made the introductions.

Brad shook Dan's hand. "We met at Iodex one day. I think you threatened to end me if I made a play for Medio Haydenshire," he quipped wryly.

"Sounds about right." Dan saw no need to make an apology. Fionna shook her head at him.

"Okay, Fionna, this should be the end of you having to be casted, so Dan can take you home in the morning as long as all of your readings are good throughout the night," Adeline explained. "You might feel some discomfort. It will be kind of like having bad menstrual cramps. If it gets to be more than you can handle, tell me. As soon as we're finished, you can take something for the pain. Dan can cast you, and you can go to sleep."

Fionna swallowed harshly and nodded. Dan could feel her terror. His heart ached as his dinner swirled ominously in his stomach. "I'm right here, sweetheart."

He wished for the hundredth time since he'd carried her off the ambulance the day before that he was the one in the bed.

"You can hold her hand if you feel you must, Chief Vindico, but don't draw from her. We want our efforts to go to healing her," Medio Dawson sneered.

Adeline rolled her eyes, and Dan narrowed his. "Obviously," he quipped.

Adeline and Brad shared a knowing grin as they moved beside Fionna's bed and lowered the lights in the room. Adeline pulled the bed linens down and the T-shirt Fionna was wearing up, revealing everything from the top of stomach down.

Dan clenched his jaw and stared into Fionna's eyes to keep from ordering Brad out of the room.

"Maybe just talk to her while we get started," Adeline urged in a patient whisper.

Dan kissed Fionna's forehead as tears began to roll down her cheeks. Her body tensed. She fought not to writhe in pain.

"I am so sorry, baby," Dan pled. Ignoring anyone else in the room, he focused solely on her. He whispered constantly how much he loved her and all that she meant to him while trying desperately to let his voice soothe her.

Two hours later, Dan panted for breath as he finally released Fionna's hands to wipe away his own tears. Adeline changed all of the padding again and covered Fionna back up.

"You can go ahead and cast her. She running a touch of a fever, but a little heat will be okay. Use that and soothing. She's pretty worn out after all of that, but I think that was the last of it." Adeline slipped quickly from the room.

Dan eased into the bed beside Fionna. She was too exhausted to speak, but she was still crying. He cradled her tenderly to him and pushed his shield out over her. He filled it with calming, soothing energies as he continued to whisper how sorry he was and how much he loved her.

They lay together inside of his powerful shield and cried as they felt the last of the extra energy that she'd been carrying for weeks leave her body.

Dan wiped away her tears and kissed her tenderly as she finally drifted off to sleep in his arms.

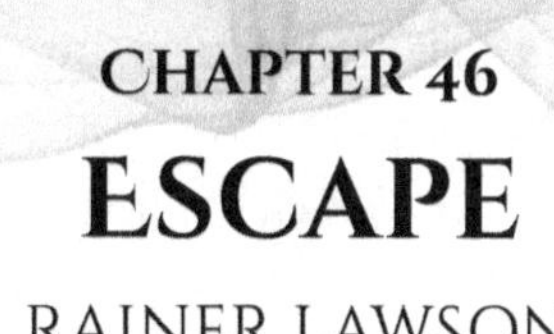

CHAPTER 46
ESCAPE
RAINER LAWSON

"Are you ready, baby?" Rainer and Emily both wore mischievous grins as they waited in the hospital that morning. Dan quickly loaded Fionna's bags and flowers into one of the Senate Expeditions and then made a fast return.

Garrett had checked the Expedition out and was driving them home. He'd parked it discreetly near the rear exit of Georgetown.

Emily was delighted with Rainer's plan.

Adeline pushed Fionna in a wheelchair just outside her room. Rainer was astonished at how much better she appeared. She clung to Dan's hand but looked elated to be leaving.

"Thank you for doing this," she offered them yet again.

"Hey, we love sticking it to the press." Rainer grinned.

He and Emily made their way to the elevators and then, holding hands, they moved slowly out into the throngs of press outside the hospital.

"Rainer! Emily!" chanted the reporters rushing toward them. "Can you tell us if Ms. Styler will still be one of your bridesmaids, Emily?"

"Can we get a few words on the wedding?"

"Are you here visiting Fionna?"

"What are your thoughts on everything that happened?" The

questions were endless, and the press stationed all around the hospital raced toward them.

Rainer smiled as Emily nodded. "We'll answer a few questions about the wedding," she announced to the crowd.

Two questions in, while Emily was explaining that she'd chosen to use real flowers, Rainer's cell vibrated in his pocket. He read Dan's text. *We're out. Thanks! I owe you several.*

He squeezed Emily's hand, and she halted midsentence.

"Okay, well, that's it," she called, thoroughly frustrating the reporters who hadn't gotten in a question.

They laughed as they raced to the Porsche and drove back to the farm.

❧

Dan Vindico

"Oh, this cannot be good," Dan lamented as he held Fionna's hand. Garrett eased the Expedition into the driveway. He was trying not to jostle Fionna. Her brow furrowed until she saw the Vindicos' Range Rover parked in the driveway.

"Man, your mom hates me," Garrett announced with a chuckle that said he wasn't particularly upset by that fact.

"Not as much as she hates me," Fionna chimed in. Her voice took on a defeated tone.

"Baby, she doesn't hate you," Dan immediately vowed.

"Notice he doesn't give a damn if she hates me," Garrett teased, making Fionna giggle.

Dan knew Fionna was thrilled to be home, and they'd even had moments in the early morning that felt just like they had before their world had been torn apart.

Dan and Garrett both rushed around the car to help her out. Before she realized what he was doing, Dan hoisted her into his arms.

"Dan," she sighed, "I *can* walk."

"And I *can* carry you."

She rolled her eyes as he carried her up the walkway. But to further his delight that she was home and safely in his arms, she gave him one of his grins. "Okay, but I'm really hormonal, so if there are curtains on our windows, I may rip them down and tie her up in them. Fair warning."

Dan cracked up. "And I will hold her down for you, sweetheart. No worries."

Garrett opened the door and stood back to allow Dan to carry Fionna in ahead of him.

Kara rushed to meet them. "I'm so sorry. I came over as soon as I figured out they were here."

Dan laid Fionna gently on the sofa. He covered her in her favorite quilt before turning to discern why his parents were in his home uninvited. He deeply regretted sharing the security codes with his family.

Fionna's eyes goggled in horror as she noted Mrs. Vindico standing at the dining room table folding laundry.

"I did all of your laundry. This is the last load to be folded," she announced as she laid out one of Fionna's particularly skimpy leopard print G-strings with two tiny hot pink bows on the sides. With a slight shudder, she added it to a pile of other lingerie that she'd washed and folded.

Dan marched into the dining room and snatched a bright teal thong from his mother's hands. "Mom." He drew a deep breath and tried to remain calm. Fionna reacted to his every emotion. "I'm perfectly capable of doing laundry."

"Apparently you aren't because both of your hampers were overflowing," she harped.

"It's been a rough few weeks, Mother."

Garrett brought in the last of the flowers and then chuckled at the thong still clutched in Dan's fist. "She'll be better soon, man."

Dan rolled his eyes in defeat and added the thong to the pile of panties on their dining room table.

"I'm heading to the Senate for a little while. Fitz rented a car. He's staying at the Marriott. He said to tell you he'd be by here this evening," Garrett reminded Dan.

"Thanks for your help with everything."

"You just take care of her, and call me if she needs me," Garrett ordered as he planted a kiss on Fionna's forehead. She hugged him tight before he rushed out the front door.

Dan's plan for their day had been to cuddle Fionna up on the couch, wrap his body around hers, and to watch movies with her to her heart's content. He hadn't accounted for the fact that his parents would have invaded their home.

"You really don't have to do all of this," Fionna pled sweetly.

Mrs. Vindico tsked, "No, now Lillian was right. I haven't always shown Daniel the support and caring that I should have, so I'm going to make up for it all right now."

"Dear God." Dan sank down on the couch at Fionna's feet and let his head fall into his hands.

"I changed your sheets, and I've scrubbed your bathroom and the guest bathroom upstairs. I also reorganized your linen closet."

She stalked into the living room carrying the laundry basket. "When you're feeling better, dear, we'll go over the proper way to fold a fitted sheet and how to organize them by size and then color. I took the liberty of putting your winter blankets in big plastic bags to keep them from getting any dust on them." She patted Fionna on the head.

"Oh, good," Fionna whimpered.

"She's been cooking as well." Kara brought Fionna some water.

"*What* has she been cooking?" Dan demanded dejectedly.

"I baked you a ham and put it in the refrigerator for sandwiches. I remembered that Fionna liked the ham I made when you first brought her by the house," Mrs. Vindico announced proudly. "And I made you a Jell-O mold that will go with the ham sandwiches."

While clenching his jaw in an effort not to scream, Dan glared at his mother. "Dad!" he shouted, startling his sister and Fionna.

"What?" Governor Vindico raced down the stairs. "I was fixing the fan in your guest bathroom. Fitz said it had a bad rattle." The governor was holding one of his many screwdrivers in his hand with his tool belt slung around his waist.

"Oh, thank you. I kept meaning to ask you about that, Dan," Fionna commented thoughtfully. Not certain if she'd just given up and decided to go with it, or if she was experiencing wild mood swings,

Dan studied her closely. She shrugged and wrinkled her nose, letting him know that she saw no other option than to let his parents loose in their home.

"Thanks, Dad. I really appreciate all of this." Dan tried to calm his voice. "But Fi really needs to rest, so maybe you could come by when we get back from our trip."

"Your mother feels badly, son. What Lillian said the other day got to her. Let her try to make it up to you."

Dan bit back the furious remark he so desperately wanted to make. He longed to inform his father that Fionna felt badly because she'd been shot and had suffered a miscarriage of their child and that he didn't give a damn if his mother felt guilty. He needed to take care of his fiancée.

Mrs. Vindico came back into the living room already talking. "I read an article this week in *Women of the Realm* that said there's an epidemic of bed bugs, so I vacuumed your mattresses. I think I might put all of your extra linens and all of these quilts you just leave lying around in plastic bags."

Fionna instinctively clung to the quilt Dan had swathed her in. She looked horrified.

"In hotel rooms, Mother. There were a few cases of bed bugs in cheap hotel rooms on the coast. Not here in our home," Dan shouted.

"Arthur, you and Daniel just slide that couch and love seat to the center of the room so I can vacuum. Fionna, just sit tight," Mrs. Vindico ordered.

Fionna shot Dan a glare as she considered the couch being moved with her lying on it.

"Oh my God. You are not moving the furniture to vacuum underneath it. You're not vacuuming at all. Fionna is supposed to be resting. She's kind of been through hell, in case you missed that story. I'm surprised it isn't typed up yet in Women of the freaking Realm!"

"Daniel, you're being very difficult for me to support right now."

Fionna and Kara began giggling uncontrollably.

Governor Vindico shook his head but then seemed to decide to ignore his wife. "Son, Stephen and I, along with Fitz and Garrett, took the liberty of cleaning up your office a little."

Dan's gut clenched. He tried to brace for the unexpected assault on his world. "Uh, okay…" He wondered what had been done in his absence. "Be right back, baby," he assured Fionna.

Her laughter faded into concern.

He took the stairs three at a time and raced to the room at the end of the hall across from their bedroom, the room that Dan had turned into an office so that Fionna could have a proper dining room when she'd moved in.

Three days ago, it had contained dozens of evidence boxes all pertaining to Wretchkinsides and the Interfeci, along with a cheap particleboard desk, but now the room was completely empty.

"It's time to move on, son," Governor Vindico stated firmly.

Dan nodded what he supposed was an agreement. He did want to move on. He wanted desperately to leave that part of his life behind, but it had been all that mattered for so long. He wasn't certain he knew how to go on without it.

Dan shut away the empty room and returned to Fionna. She was the only thing that really mattered. She was the only way for him to truly move on.

The painful, haunting memories that the empty room had brought on were quickly abated when Dan entered the living room and found his mother perched on the love seat beside Fionna's head. She was reading to her from *Women of the Realm*.

There was apparently an article written on natural remedies for hormonal mood swings after a miscarriage, and Mrs. Vindico had taken it upon herself to read it to Fionna.

Dan entered the room in time to hear that, according to *Women of the Realm*, eating over-boiled broccoli every day and applying a cup of castor oil to the abdomen and female genitalia would make the patient feel happy as a lark.

With her jaw clenched tightly, Fionna shot Dan a look that said if he didn't shut his mother up he was going to be on the receiving end of a violent mood swing.

"Mom!" Dan jerked the magazine from her hands. "I think it's all still a little fresh for us to be discussing it so freely. Now, I'm about to pull off my shirt, put on some ratty sweats, and probably help Fionna change into nothing more than one of my T-shirts. Then I'm going to lie down with her on the couch and cuddle her up under our quilts, that we will never be putting in plastic bags," he added just for spite. "I'm going to turn on some movies and cast her. If you all feel the need to stay here for that, then by all means make yourselves at home since you certainly already have. If not, could you just go? We'll call you when we get back from our trip." Dan sincerely hoped that his bluntness wouldn't upset Fionna, but sometimes you had to be brutally curt with his mother for her to listen to you at all.

To his relief, Fionna looked thrilled that he'd laid it all out for his mother. She bit her lips together to keep from laughing.

"Daniel." Mrs. Vindico was highly perturbed.

"Yes, Mother?"

"That was unnecessary!"

"Oh, I think it had reached a point of dire necessity."

"Well, dear, if you need anything at all you just call Arthur, and we'll be right back over. I have several more of my chicken casseroles at home in the freezer. You could just add some corn flakes on top and have your evening meal already complete if you're not feeling up to cooking. I put two in Daniel's refrigerator for when the ham runs out."

Dan shuddered visibly as Fionna nodded and gave the best smile she was able to force under the circumstances. "Thank you so much, Mrs. Vindico."

"That's what I'm here for, dear," Dan's mother assured her with an awkward pat to her shoulder.

Dan held the front door open impatiently as his parents and sister finally made their exit.

"I am so sorry." He slammed the front door shut and locked it firmly.

Fionna was laughing. "I started to point out to her that I really thought it had more to do with the someone rubbing their hands and fingers on your abdomen and va-jay-jay that made the patient happy as a lark and that I doubted the castor oil had anything to do with it, but I decided against that." She cracked herself up again. "I also didn't tell her that I hate mushy broccoli."

Dan chuckled. "If you want me to rub anything at all on your abdomen and va-jay-jay, you just say the word, and I already knew you hated broccoli."

She turned speculative a moment later. Her rhythms were indeed running far more erratically than they used to. "Will you really do all that stuff you just announced to your mother you were gonna do?"

"That was my plan all along," Dan assured her. He joined her on the sofa. "Is that okay?"

The chasm that had come between them seemed much more apparent back in their home than it had in the hospital. Fionna nodded and sat up. She laid her head tenderly on his shoulder as he wrapped his arms around her.

"I'm sorry. I know I was a mess, and I know I shut you out. But please, please believe me, not talking to you, not telling you what was going on was harder than anything I've ever done in my whole life, even after my mom died," she choked.

"Fi." He cradled her closer. He wondered if the ache in his chest would ever improve. "I know, baby. But this was my fault. I should have tried harder to get you to talk to me. I let you shut me out, and I did what I'd always done. I threw myself back into my work, determined that if I ended him you'd feel safe, and you would tell me. I should have made you feel safe enough to tell me, whether I'd ended Wretchkinsides or not." Dan confessed the pain that had haunted him since he'd heard Pravus's gunshot.

Fionna shook her head. "No, this is not your fault. Please don't say that. It only makes me feel so much worse."

Though he would always feel that everything that had happened was his fault, he would certainly try not to say it out loud, and he would have to modulate his emotions. Her strength and her abilities were making a return.

"Hey." He kissed her forehead. "How about if I go put on some sweats, and I help you change. Then I'll turn on some movies, and we'll lie here under your quilt. Let's just make the rest of the world wait outside for a little while."

Relief flooded through her rhythms, and her eyes lit. He saw it there in the glimmer of her beautiful eyes. Happiness doing its best to make a return.

She smiled his smile, though the sadness still tortured her. "I know we have to keep talking about everything. I want to build our relationship back even stronger than before, like you said, but right now that sounds really perfect."

"It's going to be a lot to work through, but I swear to you, honey, I love you and we will do whatever it takes to make this work."

"I know, and that makes me happier than anything in the entire world." She squeezed him but then grimaced. The force was more than her abdomen could take.

Dan immediately sent soothing pulses over her womb, calming the muscles that were protesting their recent assault. "Tell me what you want to wear. I think the stairs are going to be tough for a day or two, so we'll just stay down here until tonight, and then I'll carry you to bed. And apparently my mother did all of your laundry, so whatever you'd like should be clean," he offered wryly.

"I almost fell off the couch when I saw her pick up that G-string." She squeezed her eyes shut.

"Yeah, I'm going to try not to think about the fact that my mother's hands were on those the next time I put my hands on them." His slight shudder made her laugh again.

She stopped abruptly with a delighted grin. "It doesn't hurt to laugh anymore."

Her excitement over being able to laugh with him soothed Dan's soul. "Adeline is pretty amazing."

He donned a ragged pair of sweat shorts and brought Fionna down an assortment of T-shirts for her to choose from.

"Will you bring me those black sweatpants with the Angel wings on the booty, the ones that are too big? I've really missed wearing pants for the past few days, but these jeans are squeezing me funny."

He wanted to get her out of any pain first so he rushed to the couch. "I know I'm not allowed to take this any further, but I do consider myself an expert on taking off your jeans."

The sweet sounds of her laughter had been absent from the house for so long, every time he heard them it mended his fractured heart.

She managed to get up off the couch with just a little help. Each thing she did on her own seemed to thrill her. Dan helped her change into her requested outfit.

He turned up the heat and queued up several of her favorite movies. He lay behind her and cradled her back to his chest.

Pillow Talk with Doris Day began, and Fionna sighed contentedly.

"Best fiancé ever," she whispered.

~

Crown Governor Stephen Haydenshire

"How's Fionna doing, son?" Stephen was trying to put off the information the men standing in his office had come to tell him.

"She has her moments." Garrett sighed. "She's getting there, but it's gonna take a while. When Dan leaves the room, she panics. I'm not even sure she knows she's doing it. She's a little better if I'm there but not for long. I think it's going to take several weeks of him staying right by her side for her to really pull through this."

"Daniel didn't seem to be faring any better when he was at the diner for a grand total of forty-five minutes yesterday for breakfast."

Fitzroy and Portwood both nodded their agreement.

"Dan's not okay, and don't let him tell you that he is. Whatever's going on, I think it would be best if we left Dan and Fionna out of this." Fitz's commanding tone bled through his words, though he seemed to try and rein it in for Stephen, which was something Dan rarely did.

"You're planning on going by tonight and telling them about the other trial?" he asked Fitzroy.

"Yes, sir, but I'm not planning on sharing anything we've noted in the past two days."

Portwood had been working his chiseled jaw since he'd entered the office. Stephen was certain his molars ached. "I get that we need to let Dan and Fionna heal, sir. But I can't figure this out, and I swear, Dan probably could. Someone has access to Interfeci accounts. Ones we've already frozen. How are they still drawing money? And in odd amounts? It has to be someone with either top level banking credentials or someone with some serious clout. And there were two cameras in the Angels' locker room, but it doesn't appear they ever worked. I may be missing something though."

"Don't doubt your own abilities, Landon." Stephen appreciated that Landon Portwood was both an outstanding officer and was a deeply humble man, but at that moment he would have preferred Dan's pompous assurances that he could get anything done.

"We'll figure it out. Leave Dan alone," Fitz ordered.

Garrett nodded. "Nic said Bridgette's help was ineffective. I bet the cameras never worked. You're not missing anything there. You've got this. I agree with Fitz. You can't push Dan out and then suck him back in, Dad." Garrett reminded his father of his decision.

"How much money is missing? And how many men working with the Interfeci in any capacity have we arrested?"

"Ramier found four accounts that whoever this is was pulling from every few hours. He was taking small amounts. I shut them down, and another four pop up. I assume he hoped we wouldn't notice. Just a few thousand dollars at a time. All routed to accounts all over Europe. Half of them are fakes. We just shut down another one in Switzerland. It's so methodic. I honestly wonder if Wretchkinsides set it up to happen if he was killed." Portwood's frustration colored his tone.

Fitzroy stepped in. "French Iodex has successfully rescued all of my undercover officers and they've arrested everyone with known affiliation. We're trying to get that done here as well, but we've run into a few snags. The press has been reporting on the takedown endlessly which gave anyone with half a brain enough warning to get the hell out of town before we could get to them," Fitz huffed. "Spain, Italy, and Britain are working as well. They're having a little more success, but there weren't as many operatives there. Only Russia and Belarus have held out on my orders."

CHAPTER 47

FITZROY'S CREPES
DAN VINDICO

Dan awoke several hours later to someone banging on the front door. He rubbed his eyes and checked his watch as he took in the darkened skies out the window and the blank television screen.

Fionna was sound asleep. She was clinging to his right arm that he'd cradled underneath her hours before. He didn't recall them even seeing the end of *Pillow Talk*, and that was three movies ago.

He gently extracted himself from her grasp and shook out his arm. He tried to get blood and his energy to return to his fingers. He extended his spine and rolled his head side to side as he tried to stretch out the crick in his neck.

With a deep yawn, he flung the door open. "Geez, why don't you just break it down?" He gestured to Fionna's sleeping form on the couch.

"Sorry, I've been out here for twenty minutes." Fitz was carrying several file folders and numerous grocery bags. He headed to the kitchen.

"What's all that?"

"This is the dinner I'm making for you two," he informed Dan as he began loading things into the refrigerator. "And that is the work slash bad news I was nominated to come and tell you about. How long has she been asleep?" He peeked in the living room with deep concern already etching his face.

"We got home around eleven this morning. I kicked my parents out a little after that and turned on all of her favorite movies. I think we were out before the opening credits."

"Maddie slept a lot for the first week after she miscarried." He choked slightly which Dan politely ignored. He'd nearly forgotten Maddie had miscarried a baby. She'd been further along than Fionna, and it had been horrible for both of them.

Dan had flown out and looked after Alex and Alfred while she was in the hospital.

"I don't think either of us really slept much in the hospital," Dan explained.

They both stared at Fionna sound asleep on the couch. They were both relieved she didn't appear to be in any pain.

"Your parents were here when you got home?" Fitz went back into the kitchen. He chuckled at Dan's expression.

"Yes," Dan sighed.

"So that would be your mother's famous rubberized ham in the fridge?"

"The one and only."

They both laughed quietly, but Fitz seemed to be debating something.

Dan was about to tell him to spill it when he heard Fionna call. He raced back into the living room.

She sat up, blinking heavily, and stared up at him like she couldn't quite get his face to come into focus.

"Hey, baby doll, how are you feeling?"

"I have to go to the bathroom," she fussed sweetly. "And I'm really thirsty."

Dan helped her up and lambasted himself. One of the instructions from Adeline had been to make sure she drank plenty of water throughout the day.

"I can do it. Just stay close by in case I get stuck somewhere."

"Fitz is here, sweetheart." He didn't want her to say anything that might embarrass her.

"Oh." She rubbed her eyes still trying to fully awaken. "What time is it?"

Time did seem oddly variable.

He glanced at his watch. "Uh, it's almost six."

Fionna walked almost normally to the half bath downstairs, and Dan waited right outside the door.

"Is she okay?" Fitz joined Dan in the living room. He handed over a large glass of water with a straw.

"Thank you." Dan accepted the glass on Fionna's behalf. "And that's the best I've seen her walk so far."

Fionna emerged from the half bath looking very proud of herself. Dan bit his lips together to keep from laughing over how adorable she was. "I'm so proud of you," he teased.

"Why, thank you," she drawled as he was unable to contain his laughter any longer. He handed her the water which she downed readily.

"Hey Fionna." Fitz winked at her.

"Hey Fitz," Fionna came right back with a broad grin on her face.

"You sit. I'm making you dinner unless you wanted to eat the shoe leather in your refrigerator."

Still laughing, Fionna looked impressed. "I didn't know you cooked."

Dan rolled his eyes. "He learned to make crepes so he could get Maddie to come back to his flat in Paris."

Fitz chuckled as he nodded his admittance of that.

Dan continued with a smirk. "As I recall, he settled on crepes because he could make her crepes for dinner and then again for breakfast."

"But they're damn good crepes."

Fionna was still laughing. She seemed to have missed doing it as much as Dan had missed hearing it.

"Crepes sound amazing," she assured Fitzroy.

Without warning, Fionna decided to stand up off the love seat where she'd seated herself after her bathroom trip.

"Whoa." Dan and Fitz leapt as she wavered. Both of them caught one of her arms and held her upright.

"Sorry," she whimpered dejectedly. "I wanted to watch you make them. I've always wanted to learn how."

"No problem," Fitz agreed. "Just maybe learn from a seated position."

"Here." Dan hoisted her back into his arms. He settled her on one of the bar stools in their kitchen. "Does that feel okay? Do you want me to get you a pillow to sit on?"

"No, I think I'm all right."

As Fitzroy began teaching Fionna how to make French crepes, Dan was entranced watching her. Her laughter, her teasing, letting him cradle her for hours on the couch, there being nothing between them that they weren't discussing, and her eagerness to learn a new cooking technique had his heart swelling rapidly.

He hadn't realized how far into the depths of depression she'd sunk until he saw her a little closer to normal. He recalled her father deciding to move her all the way from Hawaii to Texas on a whim after her mother's death.

She was Maylea. Dan understood more in that moment than he ever had before. Fionna was a beautiful wildflower capable of taking even the darkest of places and making them bright and beautiful. Her smile lit his entire world. She could find the good in the worst of people or the most awful of situations.

When she could no longer do that, when the depression had swallowed her whole, her father couldn't stand to watch her fade away any more than Dan had been able to.

He stood there watching her quiz Fitz on the best way to make batter for crepes and vowed to himself to never again let her fall so far. He would either leap with her or reach out and catch her in his arms.

~

Jean Paul Fitzroy

As they ate, Fionna studied Fitz. "I'm really feeling a lot better. I can tell you're worried." It appeared she not only read him with ease but that she wasn't going to hide that fact from him. She didn't want him to worry over her. Dan grinned, but Fitz's face formed a scowl.

Dan just had to fall in love with a Receiver. He debated his available excuses. Some semblance of the truth was likely all that would work with a Receiver as powerful as Fionna. He ground his teeth and went on with it. "Well, you got shot on my watch, but that's not what has me worried." She may have known he was worried, but even the strongest Receiver of their generation couldn't name the worry, only the emotion.

"How exactly was that on your watch?" Fionna looked shocked by his statement.

~

Dan Vindico

Dan knew Fitz would take responsibility for everything that happened. It was Wretchkinsides's doing. It was their job to end him. They didn't work fast enough.

"I'll let Dan explain that, but here's the deal. Governor Haydenshire asked if I'd mind hanging out over here for a week or so and helping Iodex tie up all of the loose ends with Wretchkinsides."

Dan was certain that Governor Haydenshire would offer the position of Chief to Portwood. Garrett was next in line, but he had no interest in being Chief of Iodex. It didn't surprise him that he'd wanted Fitz to help out for the interim, but he was certain there was something Fitz was leaving out.

"We all want you to go on your trip and not have to worry about what's going on here. The problem is that the governing board wants to get through Pendergrath's trial and all of the Interfeci members that were arrested Saturday relatively quickly. Governor Haydenshire wants it put to rest."

"That sounds like a good thing to me," Fionna said.

Dan nodded and continued inhaling the blueberry and lemon crepes, which he had to admit were outstanding. He was starving.

"I agree. It's just the logistics of everything," Fitz explained.

Dan's brow knitted as he set his fork down to listen. He assumed this was what Fitz had been avoiding.

"Logan Haydenshire has been given two weeks mandatory vacation per his father's orders," Fitz allowed hesitantly.

"That's only going to make him miserable, but I get why his dad wanted to do that," Dan pointed out.

Fitz served Fionna another crepe before she'd even asked. He nodded. "I tried to tell him that, but I didn't get very far. Pretty sure you have to be a Shield to think like a Shield. Logan will still be allowed to testify at the trials, so that's not the big problem. The problem is that you two are supposed to leave on Thursday morning and will be gone until late next week. Obviously, Dan, you have to be at the trials, so you're going to have to be up at the Senate quite a bit because I get the distinct impression that hell would freeze over before Governor Haydenshire agreed to work the days before his baby girl's wedding. Then we have the Lawson slash Haydenshire two-week lovefest after that."

Dan and Fionna chuckled.

"And there is one other slight problem," Fitz finally confessed.

Dan had known there was more. He could read Fitz like the back of his own hand.

"What?" He felt Fionna's uneasiness as she laid her hand on top of his. She was visibly reading Fitz's emotions, and she drew from Dan suddenly. He turned his hand over, grasped hers, and pushed his soothing energy into her. The feeling was absolutely exquisite.

Fitz politely ignored the two of them gazing at each other with pleading eyes both hungry for so much more.

"Uh…" Fitz grimaced. "Eric Kent's lawyers are demanding that the board hold his trial bright and early Wednesday morning. Because he was arrested long before any of the Interfeci members, they're demanding precedent."

Fionna broke the energy stream. Dan, who'd almost begun drooling in his plate from feeling her heady energy combine with his own, shook as his rhythm stream sizzled.

"I sort of forgot about that," she admitted fretfully.

"Me too." Dan drew a long sip of water, trying to calm his fraying streams. "With everything going on, it just slipped my mind."

"It's okay. We don't have a choice, do we?" Fionna asked.

"The trial could be postponed and reset if you don't feel up to testifying," Fitz assured her. "But, his father is being an asshole, pardon my French, so to speak," he chuckled.

Dan bit his tongue to keep from ordering Fitz to watch his mouth. Fionna was giggling, so he allowed it.

"He's gone from pushing the trial off to demanding that it happen now. I suspect that his lawyers plan to use what happened and your injuries from it to discount your testimony." Fitz shook his head in disgust.

"That's not going to work," Dan assured Fionna.

"No, it's not, but I'm assuming it's the best his lawyers can offer up. They're taking any perceived advantage they can find. The good part though"—he turned to Dan—"is that...you did it. You ended Wretchkinsides, and that means she's safe."

He said the very things he knew Dan so desperately needed to hear.

"You can get up on the stand and tell the truth. Tell them why you were at her house. Tell the entire story, fact to fact, without putting her in any danger at all. That has to mean something."

Fionna beamed. Neither of them had really considered any of that until that moment.

"He's right." She gazed deeply into Dan's eyes. "You ended him. You ended all of them, and now I am safe. We're safe, and everyone can know. I can hold your hand in public. And you can lean me up next to the Ferrari and kiss me just like we always wanted."

Fitz laughed, clearly thinking Fionna was adorable.

"Yes, I can," Dan allowed the words to exit his lips. His lungs drew fresh breath and his heart beat anew. "And believe me, I plan to every chance I get."

He turned back to Fitz with a wry grin. "I might not get up on the stand and tell them all of the reasons I was at her house, but I really appreciate the sentiment."

Fitz and Fionna chuckled, and this time Dan kept Fionna's hand in his own.

CHAPTER 48

CONFIRMATION

Bright and early Wednesday morning, Dan pulled the Ferrari into the Iodex parking deck. He and Fionna had been given permission to enter the courtrooms through Iodex instead of her trying to climb the stairs on the front of the building.

The press had spotted his car, and they were beginning to swarm.

"Are you sure you're ready for this?" Dan quizzed for the fourth time in a ten-minute period.

Fionna giggled. She gazed at him like she couldn't possibly love anything more. His heart skipped several beats.

"I have been peeing on my own for a couple of days now, and this morning I even scrambled my own egg, so this seems like the next logical step."

Dan cracked up. He'd never deserve the woman sitting beside him wearing his ring, but he would never give up trying to earn her.

"Yes, but you weren't supposed to make your breakfast. You snuck and did it while I was in the shower. I'm supposed to take care of you."

She rolled her eyes. "You have been waiting on me hand and foot for days. Plus, I'm really excited about our plan."

Garrett and Fitzroy appeared along with Rainer and Portwood. They tried to back the press off, but after they'd been robbed of shots of Fionna leaving the hospital, they were even more determined.

Although Dan knew Fionna was still rather swollen, and he still saw remnants of the desperation and sadness that seemed to have permanently affixed to her eyes, she looked stunning.

She'd spent a great deal of time fixing her hair and makeup, donning a conservative silk top and a gray pencil skirt, and a pair of her favorite black heels. The skirt was a few sizes too large and gave her rapidly healing muscles the room they needed.

"All right then, let's do this. I can't wait to show the Realm that I'm somehow lucky enough to belong to Miss Fionna Styler."

"Not Styler for too much longer."

With a broad grin, Dan threw open his door to dozens of flashbulbs. He stalked around the car and ignored the annoying chants of his name.

He opened the passenger side door and offered Fionna his hand. She stepped and smiled for all the cameras.

"How are you feeling, Fionna?" chanted a female reporter near the front of the crowd.

"Much better, thank you. Dan's taking good care of me."

"Will you continue your Summation career?" shouted from sports reporters all around them. Fionna smiled but refused them an answer.

"Were you ever dating Garrett Haydenshire?" called another.

Fionna shook her head. "No, Dan and I have been together for quite a while."

"How did you hide the relationship?" called several others.

"Very carefully," Dan quipped. Fionna and Garrett laughed.

"Is that an engagement ring?" sang from everyone on the front row.

"It is an engagement ring," she informed them with a broad beaming grin.

"We need to get in there," Garrett urged.

Dan nodded and then winked at Fionna. He turned and gazed into her eyes. He willed away the clicking sounds of the cameras and the flashbulbs in his face.

He backed her slowly to the door of the Ferrari. Still being very gentle with her, Dan put one hand behind her back and cradled her face with his other. He leaned, and they kissed heatedly for several long seconds. The press went wild.

Garrett, Rainer, and Fitz all whistled and applauded. They offered a wave to the crowds and hurried inside the building.

~

"Ms. Styler, please tell the Senteon, in your own words, what happened on the night Eric Kent was found in the kitchen of your home," Jack Stariff guided Fionna.

Dan noted that he gazed at her tenderly. He wanted to take care of her too. He'd called several times over the past two days to make certain she was up to this trial.

Pendergrath's trial was being held at one that afternoon. Dan was taking Fionna home and returning to testify. Her parents were coming over to stay with her.

Fionna's brow pulled into deep concentration. "Dan and I were asleep upstairs." Heat flooded her cheeks, but when she began to see that no one was going to rebuke her, she moved on. "I woke Dan up because I could feel the extra energy near my house. We heard glass shatter." She shuddered from the memory. She went through the story from her memory down to Dan telling her to move the trunk in front of the door and to call Garrett.

"And did you ever tell Eric Kent that he could come by your home uninvited or show any interest in seeing him again?" Jack asked.

"No! I told him never to come over again, repeatedly. I signed a restraining order when he kept showing up. He was stalking me. He even showed up at the arena where I work and refused to leave."

Dan was put on the stand next. He recounted the same scenario, only he informed the Senteon that Eric was intoxicated, belligerent, abusive, and had lunged at him with a knife.

He narrowed his eyes in on Eric, who sat in his seat scowling for most of the trial, and he spoke the words, "I cannot even allow myself to think of what might have happened if Fionna had encountered him alone."

His lawyers objected, but Governor Haydenshire allowed the statement to stand.

Garrett took the stand, retelling the story yet again, starting from what he'd found when he arrived at Fionna's.

Dan held Fionna's hand which allowed her to draw from him as Eric took the stand and shot a hateful glare at Fionna. Dan's shield sizzled. He returned the glare on her behalf.

She was exhausted. This had been too much. Dan could feel it as soon as he touched her.

He tried to think of some way to get her out and back home before the trial ended. He seriously debated getting Jack's attention and demanding a recess. Fionna had given her testimony. She should be able to leave.

Fionna shook her head as she realized what he was considering.

"Mr. Kent, could you define your relationship with Fionna Styler?" Eric's lawyer drawled.

Dan's eyes narrowed.

"She was my girlfriend," Eric supplied confidently.

Fionna's eyes burned with fury. Dan shook his head and pushed soothing energy into her.

He went on to inform the Senteon that Fionna had invited him into her home whenever he desired to be there and that they'd discussed marriage.

Fionna was on the verge of using her newly resuscitated body to lunge at Eric and choke the life out of him.

Jack stood, and Dan wrapped his arm over Fionna's shoulder. "Just watch, baby."

Jack was vibrating in his desperation to attack Eric on the stand. "Mr. Kent, I think it is fairly obvious to the entire courtroom that Ms. Styler seems to be rather attached to Dan Vindico. He is currently seated beside her with his arm around her. I also believe that most everyone in the room has taken in the large diamond engagement ring on her finger."

Eric rolled his eyes.

"I was informed that several months ago you were waiting at

Fionna Styler's home when she arrived with Mr. Vindico. Is that true?" Jack demanded.

"Yes," Eric huffed indignantly.

"Could you tell the Senteon how many dates you and Ms. Styler went on together?"

"Let's define date, Jack," Governor Haydenshire ordered.

"Okay," Jack nodded his agreement. "Let's go with you picked her up from her home, and she went out with you for an evening of entertainment."

"We attended Crown Governor Haydenshire's inaugural ball together," Eric announced proudly.

Dan's stomach turned. That damned ball. He tried to let the panic work through him. He'd stupidly allowed Bridgette to insist that she be his date. He couldn't even stand to be around her. He used her to get to Wretchkinsides, and she'd ranked him right beside his mortal enemy, perfectly happy to play them against each other. Dan would never forgive himself for his own stupidity that had ultimately cost her life.

"Okay." Jack looked pleased. "The inaugural ball was held on October 31st. Mr. Vindico and Ms. Styler found you in her driveway awaiting her return on December 7th. She'd actually been on vacation with Dan Vindico for a week before. I have her plane tickets and boarding passes here, Governors." Jack held up a file. The governing board nodded their understanding.

"So between October thirty-first and December third when they left for Sydney, you and Ms. Styler were in a committed relationship, but she didn't tell you that she was going to Sydney with her current fiancé?" Jack's tone said that was highly unlikely.

Fionna grinned over Dan being called her fiancé. Dan squeezed her tighter into his embrace.

Eric fumed, "I was busy with my campaign, so we hadn't been able to go out as often as I would have liked."

Fionna rolled her eyes.

"But you took her out once, to the inaugural ball, and you discussed marriage?" Jack demanded. "That's all it took. One date and you two were sold?"

Dan and Fionna tried not to smirk as Governor Haydenshire raised his eyebrows to the two of them. Sometimes one date was all it took. Fionna's warmth and peaceful serenity flowed through Dan's hand. Forgiving himself for what had happened to Bridgette, what had happened to her, would be a long time coming, but she was the only way through.

Jack hammered home the fact that Fionna had only gone on one date with Eric, but that he'd then begun stalking her, culminating with his showing up drunk at her house and breaking in.

"Both of them threatened me when I was arrested for being at Angels Arena," Eric announced stupidly as he threw his finger out to Dan and then to Garrett.

Governor Haydenshire stepped in. "Call me old-fashioned, son, but if someone showed up demanding that Lillian go with him somewhere and refusing to leave if she didn't, I can guarantee you I would have done a lot more than threaten." He stared Eric down in his most harrowing infuriated expression. "I would also like to add that I was witness to the scene at Angels Arena that day."

"And yet none of this really matters," Jack leapt back in. "The point of this entire trial is that Eric Kent, after showing rapidly escalating anger issues, showed up intoxicated at Ms. Styler's home. He broke in and then attacked Mr. Vindico and Officer Haydenshire when he was confronted."

An hour later, Eric Kent was sentence to ten years in Felsink with option for early release after seven years if he joined a prison work force out in Montana. He was also ordered to three years of in-prison counseling from the Auxiliary Department.

CHAPTER 49

A CHILD OF THE LAND

"I'm so excited! I can't believe we're going to land in twenty minutes, and you'll be there with me." Fionna was vibrating in her seat as a Senate flight attendant handed her another bottle of water.

Dan was thrilled she was so happy. "So do I get laid when we get off the plane?" he teased.

She rolled her eyes, but she was beaming broadly.

"You know the flower thing?" He gestured to his neck, effectively cracking her up.

"That is not called being laid, Mr. Vindico."

"It sounds pretty damn good to me."

"You sound like Garrett."

Dan laughed. "Guilty as charged."

"And, according to Adeline's rules, we could have done that last night, but you turned me down. So I might just lay you when we get to my grandparents' house."

Dan growled in her ear and planted a kiss on her cheek.

"We'll see, and that might not give your grandparents the best impression of me."

"Well then, maybe after I get you to the guest cottage."

"Maybe. But only if you're up to it, and only if we take things nice and slow."

She sighed audibly. She was weary of Dan's relentless worrying. He'd fought the need and the desire that had turned to desperation, and tapped into the terrorizing fear of accidentally hurting her.

But he could think of little else. He wanted to hold her with nothing between them. He wanted to touch her. He needed to feel her energy flow into his mouth, around his fingers, and then around him. He wanted desperately to hear the sweet sounds she made for him. He wanted to feel the heavenly pulse of her body as it tightened around his like she was made for him alone. He wanted her as much as he wanted to draw his next breath. He watched the plane touch down on the lush green island of Kauai.

Dan carried the suitcases into Lihue Airport, the smallest airport he'd ever seen. He drew a deep breath of cleansing, floral-infused air.

He had to get it together. She still wasn't okay. Her voracity to be with him again might've been nothing more than another hormonal surge. He couldn't hurt her.

He was weary, and his muscles still ached with the haunting memories of everything that had happened.

As they made their way to baggage claim, "Maylea," shrieked from their left.

Fionna squealed as a woman Dan assumed was Malani raced toward her. They embraced, nearly jumping up and down.

"How are you? Oh, are you okay? I shouldn't have squeezed you," Malani fussed as soon as they broke apart. She looked terrified.

"I'm all right. Just still a little sore." Fionna gestured to her abdomen, the approximate location of the bullet wound. "But I have to introduce you. Malani, this is Dan, my fiancé."

"Good job, Maylea. He's cute." Malani giggled as she threw her arms around Dan as well.

She stopped and Dan watched as Fionna leaned forward and Malani did indeed place a lei around her neck. She stood on her tiptoes and Dan knelt as she performed the same for him. The deep respect for the tradition was apparent in both Malani and Fionna. Dan was moved by it all.

"Come on. I parked close, so you don't have to walk far." Malani linked her arm through Fionna's and pulled her away from Dan. Fionna glanced back at Dan.

He winked at her and followed the ladies to Malani's Jeep.

"Can you surf?" Malani asked hesitantly.

"No." Fionna shook her head and took Dan's hand as he helped her into the back of the Jeep. He seated himself beside her.

"I figured."

"Everyone here knows me as Maylea, so if you say Fionna they won't know who you're talking about," Fionna whispered.

Dan had assumed as much, given the past five minutes and the fact that he'd never heard her own parents refer to her as Fionna.

"I know you're supposed to be recuperating and chilling with your ku'u ipo," Malani sassed.

Fionna rolled her eyes but then giggled with Malani.

"What does that mean?" Dan whispered.

"Several things, but lover, in this case." Fionna raised her eyebrows at Malani. "Would you behave? How's Kai?"

"He's good. We were hoping you two would come over for dinner in a few days."

"We'd love to." Fionna looked thrilled with the idea.

"Tutu is pretty insistent that you rest and that you let her restore your rhythms. You do feel off, Maylea. She's been cooking up oils and potions ever since we heard about what happened. Of course, I knew something horrible was going to happen. She'd been chanting for days. She'll probably have you and Dan in a bathtub as soon as I drop you off."

Fionna nodded. "I'm sure."

Dan knew that Fionna called her mother's mother Tutu, and that her grandparents ran a large farm. They used most everything they raised for oils and herbal remedies that they sold.

Several of the tinctures stayed in Dan and Fionna's bathroom. He loved the way they smelled, and Fionna seemed to calm and re-center whenever she used them.

They were heading south from the airport when Malani abruptly gasped, "Do you want me to take you to…?" The car slowed. Malani turned to study Fionna while blinking back tears.

Fionna shook her head. "I'm not up to that today. Maybe later. Malani and I usually go to Hanakāpīʻai Beach before I go to my grandparents'," she explained quietly.

Dan wrapped his arm around her. "If you want to go, baby, I'll take you."

She forcibly willed away tears. "I don't think I can do the hike yet."

Hanakāpīʻai Beach was the beach where Fionna's mother had drowned. She'd told him that she always made a lei and took it out to the waters there whenever she visited.

Dan kept his arm wrapped around her shoulders as he studied the landscapes. It was astounding. Lush green trees, grasses, and shrubs filled the roadside. To his right were majestic, rippled mountains that shot upward and stabbed the azure blue sky. To his left was the mighty Pacific. Teal blues mixed in with the sandy waves as they crested against the shorelines, chased by the breeze. Beauty surrounded him, and most importantly his beautiful Kauaian baby was nestled against him with a broad grin spread across her face. Her eyes danced in elation as she took it all in. She seemed to be studying every tree and every flower like they might disappear if she looked away.

Traffic slowed as they drove through a bustling town with antiquated storefronts, artsy boutiques, surf shops, and cafes. Fionna sighed contentedly. Her entire being soaked up the town. "This is one of my favorite places in the world. Malani and I used to take the bus up here and hang out all day." She pointed out her favorite coffee shops and walk-up restaurants.

Malani turned down a gorgeous road encased in a canopy of trees. Fionna's energy soothed. The houses and few small shops gave way to expansive pieces of land covered with trees and crops.

Dan smirked as Malani halted the car to allow several roosters to pass in front of them. Neither Malani nor Fionna seemed to think this was odd, so he didn't comment.

They continued down a one-lane dirt road, and then they traveled through a large gate. At least a mile passed before they stopped at a small, teal, one-story home with a low pitched roof. An expansive porch ran the length of the house on all four sides. Roosters and hens pecked around the home that was set off by the most astounding floral display Dan had ever seen. It was truly beautiful.

Dan guided Fionna out of the Jeep and reached for their luggage.

"Just set those on the front steps. We're staying on the other end of the farm in one of the hales. Tutu believes that everyone needs their own piece of heaven, and she says no one should have to hear Papa snoring except for her," she giggled. "They have several all around the farm."

"Maylea, e komo mai, my aloha." A woman Dan knew instantly must be Fionna's grandmother beckoned them as she glided from the swinging screen door.

Her island heritage showed in the graceful lines that etched her face. She was beautiful, and Dan felt he was somehow looking into his future as he stared at a seventy-five-year-old version of Fionna.

"Tutu," Fionna sighed blissfully as she embraced her grandmother. "This is Dan, my fiancé." She stepped away from her grandmother's embrace and took Dan's hand.

He felt her rhythms soothe just being on the island. It seemed to restore and calm her.

"Dan." Fionna's grandmother embraced him tightly.

"Hi, it's so nice to meet you. Thank you for having us," Dan offered distractedly. He was astonished at the lands and the way Fionna seemed to bloom when she stood amongst the flowers.

"Where is my grandbaby?" A man with a broad chest, round stomach, and one of the kindest smiles Dan had ever seen sauntered onto the front porch, beaming at Fionna. "Maylea, get over here. Let me look at you," Fionna's grandfather ordered.

She rushed into his arms. Her entire being glowed with his love. "Prettier every time I see you, just like your mama." He offered Dan his hand. "This the one, Maylea?"

Fionna nodded as Dan shook his callused hand. "All right, as long as he makes you smile, that's all your Papa wants." Fionna's grandfather acquiesced much quicker than her father had.

"Come inside. I've made you tea that will have you on the path to becoming you again," her grandmother commanded cryptically.

Fionna smiled. "All right, Tutu, but I want to show Dan the farm and the guest houses."

"Dan, this,"—Tutu gestured out to the surrounding land covered with beautiful indigenous trees and shrubs, numerous gardens that extended much farther than Dan could see, along with several outbuildings—"is the farm. The beach a mile or two that way." She pointed back out the front door as they made their way onto the porch. "The guesthouses, we call them hales, that way." She pointed to the west end of the farm. "There, now you can have my tea. I've been brewing it since this morning," she instructed Fionna.

Dan chuckled as Fionna shook her head at her grandmother.

"Oh, take off your shoes," Fionna instructed as she slipped off the sandals she'd worn. Dan followed suit and made a mental note to always remove his shoes before entering a home on the island.

"Maylea, this will ease any pain and let you heal, my precious keiki." Her grandmother fussed over her as they entered the rustic kitchen.

Malani giggled. "I told you, and I'm going to run before she makes me drink any. Call me whenever you want to get together." She kissed Fionna on the cheek and did the same with Tutu.

"I will." Fionna settled at her grandmother's ancient laminate kitchen table. "I'm okay, Tutu. I'm much better actually."

"Yes, well, you never did want anyone to worry about you, but you are not okay. Do you no longer feel your own energy?"

Fionna's eyes cast downward. "Fine, I'm not okay."

Tutu nodded. "I have several remedies I put in the hale where I want you to stay for Dan to help you with," her grandmother informed her as she poured a large mug of tea and added lemon and honey and set it down in front of Fionna.

Shrugging, Fionna sipped the tea. "She's pretty much always right, so..."

Dan gazed at her adoringly as she drank with more vigor. When the mug was empty, she looked impressed with the restorative effects the tea had and requested a second mug.

"She always argues. I'm always right," Tutu informed Dan, who chuckled as he sipped a glass of spring water he'd been supplied.

"Now, Dan," Tutu began, "Maylea needs to be given baths each day she's here. Morning and night. I've put all of the oils and salts I want you to add to her baths twice a day in your cottage. I added massage oils as well, along with a few compresses I'd like you to heat and apply wherever she experiences pain."

Fionna blushed violently. She squeezed her eyes closed.

"Uh, okay," Dan agreed, not certain what else to do.

"Maylea, I made you and Dan a fresh batch of 'Ōhi'a lehua." Tutu turned back to Fionna.

Dan watched Fionna's expression turn horrified. "Okay, please don't talk about that. I'll explain it to Dan later."

"Maylea, it is part of your healing," Tutu scoffed. "If you use it, it will help."

"I know, but just please."

Tutu shook her head. "On the mainland far too long again, I see. The tea, you feel better, yes?"

"Yes," Fionna begrudgingly agreed.

"You need to heal, Maylea. Dan needs to heal. I can feel it in his spirit as well." Her grandmother reached and patted Dan's hand. "He is carrying something he longs to rid himself of. Let the island heal you both. It always has before. Let us help you. Go sit by the waves, walk the farm, swim in the spring waters, and breathe in the air. Your spirit is choking. I cannot let you go on like this." Fionna's grandmother spoke from depths of wisdom that had Dan instantly mesmerized.

Papa came into the kitchen just then. He kissed Fionna's cheek. "I went out and got Maylea's coffee this morning just for my girl." Her grandfather clearly wanted to spoil Fionna. That was a feeling Dan understood only too well.

Her eyes danced. "Thank you." She hugged her grandfather.

"Let us get you to your hale," Fionna's grandmother urged.

"You be okay in my truck, Maylea?" Her grandfather looked concerned.

"I'll be fine. I promise."

Dan and Fionna were crammed inside the cab of Fionna's grandfather's ancient truck with both of her grandparents. Dan pulled Fionna into his lap which delighted both her and her grandmother.

"That's the waterfall." Fionna pointed to a lush water spring with a small waterfall that was surrounded by tropical vegetation. It did look idyllic. Dan winked at her.

"Four baths before the falls, Maylea. You cannot accept this spring water yet. And Salt Pond tonight." Each time her grandmother spoke, wisdom seemed to permeate the air. *I should have brought her here days ago. This is the only thing that will make her well.* His own realization shocked him. It was as if he'd heard someone else explain this.

With another turn down a tree-lined path, Fionna's grandfather halted the truck.

Dan took in the small, weathered cottage home with a green roof surrounded by local vegetation. He helped Fionna out of the truck and grabbed their suitcases from the back.

The cottage was simple. It contained two enclosed rooms. One half of the house was a living room with a couch and mismatched chairs that seemed to fit perfectly. The other end of the open room was a tiny kitchen.

Dan noted a very nice coffee maker on the counter and stacks of bagged Kauai coffee beans nearby. Fionna's grandfather had taped a small piece of notebook paper on one of the silver bags declaring the stash to be Maylea's coffee.

Fionna beamed as she led Dan into the other half of the house. There was a queen-sized bed, a dresser, two bedside tables, and an antique washstand that contained several brown bottles closed with droppers, compresses, and numerous screw top jars and containers.

They all had white labels with handwritten information on them. Dan recognized a few of the ones Fionna's grandmother mailed to her each month.

There was a screened-in porch off the bedroom that took up a fourth of the small cottage. In the center of the porch was a massive bathtub. Rolling curtains in floral patterns could be pulled over the screens, but currently the bathtub was exposed to anyone who might wander up to the house. The large windows between the porch and the bedroom were wide open.

"Dan," Tutu called as he was setting their luggage in the bedroom.

"Yes, ma'am?"

"When we leave, place seventeen drops of this, fourteen drops of this, and a cup of this into Maylea's bath. Then add one container of the salts here. Sit with her. Hold her against you. She needs you. She needs to be worshipped, and the bathtub is big enough for even you." Her grandmother seemed to find no issue with the fact that she was ordering Dan to take a bath with her granddaughter.

He listened intently.

"Tell her to breathe deeply and relax. She is chaotic. You feel this, yes?"

"Yes, ma'am." He saw no reason to lie.

"Relax and feel the rhythms of the island. Those are her rhythms. Let it move you. Let it heal you. Maylea is kama'āina. Let it heal her," she concluded.

"I'm sorry, Ms. Iona. I don't know what that means."

Fionna's grandmother patted Dan's cheek. "A child of the land. A child of that which sustains her. And the land will not only heal her. It will heal you both. My island is the healing island. It will bring you together if you allow it. And you must call me Tutu—everyone on my island does." She pointed to a large glass jar with a screw top lid. "She will tell you what this does. For me, try to get Maylea to relax and listen to her own rhythms, the rhythms of our family, and the rhythms of the island. You will be surprised," she offered wryly.

Dan wondered if he should have taken notes on the prescribed remedies. "I've written it on the labels." Fionna's grandmother seemed able to read his mind.

"Thank you." He wasn't certain why he was suddenly so willing to follow instructions from what he would have called nonsensical drivel a few months before.

But as Fionna moved to him from the kitchen and Dan wrapped his arm around her, he knew why. She was so much stronger. She was already less chaotic, as her grandmother had pointed out. They'd been there less than an hour, and Fionna's energy was already beginning to heal.

"The lands are yours. You know this, Maylea. Pick anything you want and feast. I put a pot of my chicken long rice in the refrigerator. Your Auntie Agnes sent you half of the bakery. So relax and enjoy." Tutu chuckled, and Fionna's energy lilted in excitement.

"We are off. We'll be working on the other end of the farm for most of this week, taking in a fresh crop of awapuhi for Maylea's hair oils, but if you need us you know where to find us."

"Thank you, Tutu, for everything!" Fionna clung to her grandmother fiercely.

"A bath, Maylea, very soon."

"Yes, ma'am," she placated. Dan and Fionna waved to her grandparents as they drove away.

CHAPTER 50

THE MAN BENEATH

"So, do you think my grandmother is crazy?" Fionna looked terrified that Dan was going to tell her yes.

"No." He shook his head.

"You don't?" she quizzed incredulously.

Dan sank down on the sofa in the living room and guided Fionna beside him. He was shocked at the comfort of the mismatched furniture.

Fionna smiled. "Tutu doesn't see any point in furniture matching because she says all that matters is your comfort and ability to relax. She thinks once you sit down you can't see if what's under your rear end matches anyway." She blushed again and rolled her eyes.

"Makes sense." Dan earned himself another incredulous glare. "She reminds me of you." He gathered her long hair gently with his fingers and brushed it behind her shoulder.

"You think I'm crazy too?"

"I don't think either of you are crazy," Dan corrected her. "And she is very obviously where you got your exceptional Receiving abilities."

She nodded her begrudged agreement. He understood that Fionna was caught up in two very different worlds. What he hadn't gotten until they'd arrived was that they were pulling her apart at the seams.

She lived in one of the busiest cities in the world. Where things like comfort of furniture and natural remedies were laughed at and scoffed over. High price tags and high wages were the cures for whatever might ail you even if earning them killed you.

But so much of her was a simple farmstead in Hawaii where life was much slower, and the remedies may not cost much, but they actually worked. He knew the rest of the world would laugh heartily if she professed any of that.

"All of the stuff she makes really does work." It seemed Fionna suddenly felt the need to prove her grandmother's worth. "Like the kukui oil she sends me."

"Baby doll, I think most everything she said makes a lot of sense, and I would really like to try out everything she told us to do. I don't think it could hurt, and like you just said, it might just work."

"Tutu is big on baths," she explained hesitantly.

"Bathing is generally thought to be a positive thing."

Fionna laughed, but she still seemed caught somewhere between elation to be where she was and embarrassment that Dan might think her family was insane.

She drew a deep breath and tucked her head under Dan's chin, hiding away for a few minutes before she continued. "Tutu believes that just about anything can be cured if you eat lots of island food, take long walks in the waters of Kauai, take long baths with her prescriptions, drink the teas she prepares, take long naps, and have long lovemaking sessions."

Dan could feel her cheeks burn against his neck.

"Sounds like a hell of a vacation to me." He was certain Fionna's grandmother might be one of the wisest people he'd ever met. "Hey," he lifted Fionna's chin and gazed into her frightened eyes. "Baby, everything they did at Georgetown healed you physically," he allowed.

Fionna's brow knitted and she nodded.

"But you're not okay. I'm not okay. We're kind of a walking collective disaster. So how about if we give Kauai and Tutu a try?"

"You're amazing." Fionna looked overwhelmed.

"That's you, baby doll, and how about a bath?"

Dan started to lower the curtains on the screened-in porch, but she shook her head.

"Breathing in the island air will help heal us. No one will come over here. They all know I'm in Tutu's infirmary."

Dan immediately recalled one of their many conversations when they were in Sydney. She'd been frightened to tell him that she slept naked. She'd been afraid he would judge her. He began to understand that she was meant to exist in a natural world, not in a concrete jungle of smog and belligerence. She'd sought to hold on to her authenticity in any small way she could.

He left the curtains open and began studying the porch instead. There was a large double swing on one corner and a flat mattress suspended on a wooden frame that hung as a swinging bed on the other.

"Tutu believes sleeping outside is good for you too. More breathing in the island air," Fionna explained about the bed as she filled up the massive bathtub with hot water.

Dan went back into the bedroom and returned with the bottles Tutu had shown him. Fionna grinned and began adding the prescribed formula to the water. He noted that she didn't have to read the instructions. She knew the remedy.

"Come here to me, baby." Dan guided her into the sanctuary of his arms. Her breath panted as he brushed a tender kiss across her lips.

"I love you, and I want to take care of you always," he whispered as he began unbuttoning the sundress she was wearing.

"I love you too." Her chest rose and fell rhythmically. Her eyes closed. She reveled in the sensation of him undressing her. She trembled in his arms as he eased the straps off her shoulders.

He popped the clasp of her bra and devoured her mouth. He let her breasts fall in swollen mounds into his hands. They were still so fevered and tender. He knew they ached. He massaged them gently, adding to the pressure, until she was moaning, arching her back, and pushing them into his hands.

Dan lowered her panties and then guided her into the tub. He pulled off everything he was wearing and stepped in behind her. He cradled her body between his outstretched legs.

Fionna drew a deep breath and let her entire body relax against his. He lay back against the tub, amazed as he felt the tedious ache of his own muscles begin to ease. His shoulders lowered as he held her to him.

They lay there in the peaceful serenity for several long minutes. Dan concentrated. He was astonished by how much of Fionna's energy was evident in the very air around him.

Her rhythms were of the island. He could hardly believe what he was feeling and seeing once he began to relax. *She is a child of the land, and the land will heal her.* Dan heard her grandmother's adamant vow in his mind as he began massaging her body slowly with his hands.

He considered Fionna's stepmother's somewhat insistent suggestion that he bring Fionna to Kauai to see her grandparents. She could feel it as well. She'd brought Fionna back numerous times growing up, even though she was bringing her stepchild to see her maternal grandparents, because she loved Fionna and knew that her energy needed to feel the rhythms of the island often.

The air around them was permeated not only with spectacular floral perfume but the heady scent of her.

"What's the stuff in the glass jar that you didn't want Tutu to tell me about?" He slicked his hands with the oil Tutu had prescribed for massage and rubbed his hands over Fionna's neck and shoulders. The muscles that had been knotted for weeks began to unfurl.

Fionna drew a deep breath and sighed. "Here, please," she finally begged and drew his hands to her breasts. She gave in to the ache and knew he held the cure.

He tried to order away the fierce erection he knew she felt press tightly against her backside as he gently rubbed the oil into her breasts. The fever began to abate at once.

"There's a Hawaiian legend about the ʻōhiʻa tree and the lehua flower," she whispered.

Dan listened intently. He'd almost forgotten his own question in light of being asked to give her an in-depth breast massage. He tried to refocus. He wanted to hear the legends and understand her heritage. He wanted all of her, each and every piece.

"One day Pele met ʻŌhiʻa. He was a handsome warrior. She fell in love with him, but he was pledged to another beautiful woman named Lehua. When ʻŌhiʻa turned down Pele's marriage proposal, she was furious and turned him into a twisted tree. Lehua was devastated and begged the gods to return ‘Ōhi‘a to her. Instead of turning him back into a man, they turned Lehua into a beautiful flower that grows on the ‘ōhi‘a tree, so they're always together. The legend says that if you pick the lehua flowers, it will rain because the lovers weep when they're parted."

The tale poured from her in the hallowed voices of her past. Generations of love and care, of her heritage, echoed in the legend. It was a vital part of her, one Dan hadn't fully understood until that moment. Like a beautiful wildflower that somehow grew in the choking cracks of concrete, she'd managed to survive. Maylea indeed.

Curiosity coursed through Dan as he listened. "Does Tutu grow those trees or use the flowers in something? Is that what is in that jar?"

"Tutu uses the sap from the tree and the flowers so that the lovers are always together. They must never be parted. She mixes them with coconut oil and aloe leaf juice. She alters them, and enhances them, then spins them into a kind of creamy ointment. She thinks the ointment will, uh…" Fionna seemed to choke in her explanation.

"I'm sorry, baby. I would try to help you out, but I'm not sure where this is going." He felt badly he'd asked.

Fionna laughed and turned suddenly so that the side of her face was against his collarbone. She instinctively kept her body submerged in the deep water.

"It's a lubricant. It's very healing." Her body trembled as he kept up the massage. "Tutu thinks that if you were to rub it inside of me before we had sex, that it would ease any pain or discomfort I might have. It would also heal there as well."

The answer to his gut-wrenching fear was in a jar in the bedroom. "Baby, why didn't you want to tell me that?"

"I don't know. It does actually work." Her body gave a slight shiver against him. "I've used it before. That summer I stayed here when I was nineteen. It's actually kind of amazing."

He kissed the top of her head but had no interest in thinking about her with anyone else.

"Malani and Kai always use it. They say it makes everything feel more incredible, but I don't know. I only ever used it afterwards when I hurt. I had to sneak it out of Tutu's workshop that summer because I didn't want to tell her what we'd done, but she knew anyway. She left another jar on my bedside table." Fionna blushed violently as Dan chuckled and kissed her again. "But, I understand that it sounds totally nuts."

"You just said it worked, and that your best friend since you were born uses it with her husband."

"I know." It seemed she still wasn't certain what to make of Dan's willingness to use products her grandmother cooked up in her tiny workshop. But he knew it was her. She'd chipped through the callused, caustic, cynical shell that he'd worn like his shield since the day Amelia had been killed.

When Dan had reheated the water with his hands a second time, he kissed her cheek tenderly. She was almost asleep. "Ready to get out, baby doll?"

With a heavy nod, she let him help her out of the tub. He pulled the drain plug and took the large towel she handed him. He haphazardly ran it over his body, heated it, and then moved to dry her off thoroughly.

"I'm kind of tired." Her admission was cut off by a deep yawn. That was the first time since she'd been shot, hospitalized, undergone intense emergency surgery, and had summarily miscarried their baby that she'd admitted to being tired.

He wondered if she was beginning to listen to her own rhythms, like her grandmother had urged her to do. Dan smiled at her. "I believe another of Tutu's requirements for healing was a long nap."

"You really don't think this is all crazy?"

Dan chuckled as he followed her back into the cottage. He pulled the quilts and blankets back on the bed and held his hand out to her. She glided to him as he lay down and cradled her on his chest.

The bed was heavenly. He'd never lain down and instantly felt like he could sleep for hours. It had simple white bamboo sheets. They were soft and smooth. They smelled of lavender and jasmine. His eyes longed to close. A thin comforter was covered with two handmade Hawaiian quilts. It enveloped them in a soothing cocoon.

"You know,"—he forced himself to say all of this before they drifted into a deep sleep—"six months ago, I would have said it was crazy. But I've already told you how much you changed me all for the better. And, sweetheart, you've been here for a few hours, had two cups of tea, taken one bath, and you're already moving so much better. You're less swollen. You don't seem to be hurting." He rubbed his right hand tenderly up over her abdomen and then back to her breasts, astonished at how the fever had all but disappeared. "Your rhythms feel so much healthier." He willed her to feel it as well.

Fionna brushed her lips over his bare chest. "So do yours." A minute later, she was sound asleep. Dan cradled her closer to him, and he let his heavy eyes close as he drifted into a deep, dreamless sleep.

CHAPTER 51

CERTAIN

JEAN PAUL FITZROY

"You're certain he's dead, right? I mean, you were standing there when Dan killed him?" Fitz demanded of Garrett.

"I was there. He's dead. Dan fucking drained him in a matter of seconds. I felt his energy in the air. I've never felt sicker. So who the hell is doing this?"

They stared down at a grainy street cam video of two men discreetly being handed Halliburton cases in the streets of Brussels. The same cases had been found at a home in Roubaix, France—the home of Niles Marcheau, one of the undercover agents that Fitz had placed in the Interfeci. One that had taken some time off after Wretchkinsides had fallen. He'd gone to visit family in Roubaix. They were now planning his funeral. The cases were left. The guns they'd contained were gone.

"Is Pendergrath getting orders out from Coriolis?" Fitz asked again.

"He's buried in the last chamber. He's probably barely breathing at this point," Portwood huffed. "And who would he be giving orders to? We've arrested half the planet."

Fitz's head fell into his hands. "Who the hell is doing this?"

"We could…" Portwood started again.

"No." Fitz and Garrett were adamant. Dan was not to know any of this.

⁓

Dan Vindico

It was late afternoon when Fionna stirred against him. She moved into the water closet off the bedroom and then crawled back in the bed. Dan was mesmerized. She was really truly relaxed.

Her eyes were calm, her shoulders lower, and her gait was smooth and languid like nothing had ever hurt her.

"Are you hungry, baby doll? We never had lunch." Dan ran his hands up and down her back.

Fionna gave him one of his smiles, and the effect of her cheeks glowing a healthy pink, her eyes no longer red and swollen from crying with regularity, and of his smile lighting her beautiful face had him short of breath.

"Do you want to go into town and go to my favorite taco place of all time, and then go watch the sunset on Salt Pond? Salt Pond is actually the beach. I mean, there is a Salt Pond where we get salt as well, but I'm talking about the beach park. We can take Papa's truck."

"Anything you want, I'm there."

Fionna phoned her grandfather after they were dressed. The truck pulled up a few minutes later.

"Your Tutu said to give you this and to tell you to use it." Fionna's grandfather handed Fionna more brown bottles and small screw top jars.

Fionna studied them. Another round of relief soothed her face before she laughed. "Tell her I will, but she's getting awfully bossy."

Her grandfather scrubbed her hair and laughed heartily. He kissed her cheek and promised to give her grandmother the message.

"What's that?" Dan asked after he thanked Fionna's grandfather for the keys to the truck. If there was something either of them needed to use to heal, he wanted to do it.

"Just about the best stuff to clean and moisturize your face with ever. She noticed that I broke out after the miscarriage." Fionna pointed to her chin and forehead.

Dan hadn't really noticed until that moment, but there were several red bumps on her face.

"And this is for your lips. It's amazing. It makes them so soft. Mine have been chapped for a while. I haven't been drinking enough water." She immediately unscrewed the lid and applied a shea butter balm to her lips with her finger.

Dan kissed her lips quickly. He was careful not to remove the balm. "And it tastes good," he teased.

A half hour later they were devouring fish tacos from a hot pink and neon green concrete shack with a tie-dyed sign that declared them to be the best ono tacos on Kauai.

"These are incredible." Dan couldn't recall a better meal. He was genuinely surprised that something that delectable had come out of a shack.

"I know." Fionna seemed thrilled he was so pleased. They ordered another round and consumed them as they drove out to the beach Fionna wanted to show him.

"You sure you're okay? This is a lot of walking." Dan helped Fionna out of the truck. It was several yards over grass and a parking lot to get to the shoreline.

"I feel okay. I really want to go. I need to. Please. It's one of my favorite shorelines. It's so calm and steady," she begged.

"I wasn't going to take you back, honey. I was going to carry you."

She smiled as she led him down to a rocky shoreline. It certainly wouldn't have made a postcard or magazine cover, but as Dan studied it, he smiled. Salty tidal pools surrounded them, and low-lying rock jetties were situated about thirty feet back in the water. They protected the shore. They made the waters serene. Waves would occasionally crash against the jetties, but the water remained controlled and the shoreline thoroughly protected by the shield of the rocky seawall.

She sank down in the sand and stared out at the beautiful waters of her island.

He sat beside her. He was more entranced watching her than the rhythmic lapping water as it made its slow, steady return to the sands. He noted that her rhythms matched the tides of her island. The rise of the moon seemed to draw her magnetically to the shore, just like the water.

She turned to him as the sun began its descent into the water. She stared up at him intently.

"What is it, sweetheart?" He played with her hair as she reclined in his lap.

"What would happen if I quit the Angels?" Her eyes locked back on the water.

Dan considered his words carefully. "I assume we would get married, and I would eventually get a job. I have no idea what I'm going to do, but something. I was going to ask you if you want me to sell my shares in the team. You just won them the cup, so the price for the stock skyrocketed. The returns on the investment are already quite good, but if you'd feel more secure with the money in the bank, that's what I want to do. But I want you to do whatever you want, whatever makes you smile."

She drew a deep, steadying breath and sat up again. "When I was pregnant..." The tears began again. They flowed rapidly down her face and cut Dan to the quick.

He started to embrace her, but she shook her head. "Just let me get this out, please."

He settled for holding her hands as she continued. "I was so scared all the time, but every now and then, I guess I let myself pretend that everything was different. And in those moments, there were things that I'd always thought were important that just weren't important anymore. It was all so confusing, and I wanted to talk to you about it, but I just couldn't.

"One afternoon while you were at work, I made myself some of my tea that I used to have with my mom and Tutu. I just let myself imagine that I could tell you, that there wasn't any Wretchkinsides, that we were already married so your mom wouldn't have been mad, and that when I told you I was pregnant, you were really happy."

Dan's shield tensed like he was being stabbed brutally, but he let her talk. She needed to say this, and he needed to hear it. This was part of the process.

"Anyway," Fionna went on as her tears continued to cascade down her cheeks, "when I dreamed that or whatever, I kind of realized that what I wanted most in the world was to be your wife. I wanted to have your babies. I wanted to stay at home and take care of them just like Tutu took care of me. It was like, all of a sudden, partying in Vegas with the Angels, or joining the mile-high club, or hanging out in Anglington's and letting some guy I don't even know drink liquor out of my navel seemed so pointless and stupid. Now, I just kind of wish I didn't have to be a part of all of that anymore." She removed her right hand from his grasp and began moving it through the sand. She let her island slip through her fingers.

"Fi," Dan whispered and waited on her to raise her gaze back to his. He blinked back tears of his own as he cradled her face in his hands. "If you want to get married soon and start a family, then I'm ready for that too." He kept his eyes steady with hers. He wanted her to know he had no hesitation. "And if you don't want to challenge for the Angels anymore, even if we don't have a family for a while, then I want you to quit, sweetheart."

"Really?"

"Really," he pledged.

"Dan." She linked their hands and drew from him heavily as she willed repose. "I want to have a baby," she choked convulsively and then began to sob.

He let the words wash over him like a soothing balm, like the rhythmic healing tides of her island. He wrapped her up in his arms as tears fell from his eyes into her hair.

As she quieted, he leaned back and wiped the tears from her cheeks. "Me too," he assured her.

A smile spread across her face as his words seeped through her tear-filled plea. She let what Dan assumed was their decision set firmly in her mind.

"Adeline said she thought it would be okay if I get pregnant again. She said everything was healed, just that there would be scar tissue she would have to watch. It might take longer because of that," she choked.

"I know, sweetheart. I just don't want you to get upset if it takes us a little while." Dan gazed at her, certain he could never love anything more. "Do you want to get married first?"

"Yes, but just something quick. I don't want anything elaborate. I just want to be married to you. I don't want to do the whole Senate thing Rainer and Emily are doing even though your dad's a governor." She shuddered at the very idea.

The warmth of her own tidal waters washed through Dan again. She baptized his weary soul and cleansed his lungs for fresh breath.

He kissed her forehead. "My mother will be devastated," he teased through his tears.

Fionna laughed as she leaned and brushed a kiss along his jaw.

They watched the salty waters kiss the sands and then turn to an inky black as the sun sank slowly into their depths.

Dan noted that their tears felt different here as well. They were healing and productive as if there might be an end to them at some point.

"Do you wanna go back to the farm and practice getting pregnant?" she whispered with a mischievous grin.

He tried with all of his might to hide his desperate desire with a chuckle. It proved a futile effort. Every cell in his body propelled him toward her. His body ached and sent the pain surging fiercely to his groin.

He helped her up as they brushed the sand off and walked hand in hand back toward the truck.

"Are you sure you feel all right?" Dan studied her rhythms more than he listened to her words.

"I think so. Maybe just kind of take it slow." Her voice was low and breathy in need all her own.

Dan helped her into the truck and held her hand as he drove back to her grandparents' farm. "Baby, I want to be with you so badly I hurt, and I know you can feel that. I know you can feel my desire. But if we're gonna do this, then you have to promise me if I do anything at all that..." he stammered, trying to think of the best way to phrase everything, "doesn't feel the way it's supposed to, you'll stop me. I'll wait as long as you need. I just need you to promise me you're not doing this because you can feel what I want. I only want this if it's what you want right now."

"I promise, but I need you. I need us." Her energy spun in desire and elation over their oceanfront confessions and decisions.

CHAPTER 52

THE COTTAGE

Dan drove slowly along the winding lanes. There was no rush. Though he longed to be with her, he knew they had all night, and he needed to move with tenderness, to worship her beautiful body, and soothe her soul.

He needed to work her over slowly, to make certain each and every move brought her healing and restored the two of them as he made them one.

The rhythms of the island soothed him and gave him cues as to how to really love and adore the woman he was going to make his wife. If he listened closely, he could hear the steady thrum of the ocean telling him how to allay her every fear and the whispered melody of the breeze guiding him on soothing her every ache.

They moved into the cottage. Fionna's grandmother had lit and heat casted a few candles in the living room and bedroom. It gave the cottage a soft, luminescent glow.

Dan pulled Fionna gently toward him as he stood outside the bedroom door.

"Sweetheart," he whispered as he cradled her head to his shoulder and wrapped his other arm loosely around her back, "I can't wait to be your husband, to make you my wife, to make babies with you, and to have a real life. I'm so sorry that I made you wait for all of that."

"No." She shook her head as she whispered the word. "I told you everything happens in its own time," she quoted her grandmother.

Dan cradled her face in his hands and stared at the hesitant fire glowing deep in her sienna eyes.

He leaned and laved her mouth with his own. He let their lips form together and bond them. Their souls melded as their breath mingled.

"I'm going to take you to bed, baby," Dan soothed as she began to pant. Her body trembled against his.

He lifted her into his arms and carried her to the bed. He stood her beside it, still unmade from their nap.

She watched as he slowly unbuttoned her sundress yet again. He let his hands glide over her silky, fevered skin as he worked his way down.

"You are so beautiful, sweetheart. Just so damn beautiful," he whispered softly as he slid the dress away from her and took in her swollen curves.

"I hurt for you." She let her eyes close, feeling the energy around them as it began to spin and dance. "I ache to feel you move against me, to feel you inside of me."

She let the confession pour from her soul without hesitation and distress. She let down every armament she'd erected to safeguard her heart and let him in.

He groaned from the realization of what she was allowing him to see. "I won't let you hurt, baby. Never again. I'm gonna make everything feel better. I promise. I'll make it stop hurting, every single thing."

Her entire body shook as he released her bra and let it fall away and reveal her to him. Unable to stop himself, his desire simply too great, he leaned and dragged his tongue over her left nipple. He primed its timid swell. She gasped and cried out for him. It had been so long since he'd soothed their tender need, she writhed from the sensation.

While trying to remember to be gentle, he suckled at her right breast.

"More," she begged. He tugged it deeply into his mouth and bathed her with his tongue and his energy.

Her rhythms pulsed and quaked. With a heady groan, he felt them begin to permeate his body through his lips. He moved to the left, starting slowly and working steadily until her moans were unending.

Dan lifted her into the bed, cradling her tenderly in the soft sheets as he pulled her panties away from her. Another hungry groan shook from his lungs. He gazed at her, swollen and wet, the soft folds of her so needy the wet heat shimmered in the moonlight.

He reminded himself to move with precise gentleness, as he pulled off his clothes and rushed to the washstand. He grabbed the jar they'd discussed in the bath and climbed into the bed beside her.

A breathy moan lit the air. Her rhythms flew as she felt the mattress lower under his weight.

"I'm gonna set the cast, sweetheart. Tell me if anything hurts or feels tender at all."

She nodded and watched his every move. Her eyes were dark and pleading. Her energy was fraught with need.

Dan summoned from the erotic energy spilling from her pores. He added in heavy doses of his own calming and soothing energies as he slowly let the orb move up her, and he closed her off.

"Are you okay?" he whispered.

"Perfect." She reached her hand down and slowly tracked her fingers up his cock. She moaned as he hardened in her hand. Desperate for her touch and for her attention, he groaned from the heavenly sensation of her fingers tracing the throbbing veins that ached for her.

The air held their energy, spinning slowly, sensuously all around them. The night breeze carried her scent over him. He reveled in the serenity of her skin next to his.

He took his time and let his tongue and his touch soothe her silky skin, fevered from need. He kissed her deeply. Their tongues danced in perfect motion inside of her mouth.

She pulled away gasping for breath. "Dan, please," she pled, "just please."

"I know you're needy, baby. I feel it. Just relax for me. We're gonna go nice and slow." Her body rolled as a frustrated whimper echoed from her lungs. The pulse of her body beckoned his.

He dipped his fingers into the jar and then began tracing her slit. Slowly, his fingers worked the healing salve into her lips.

She cried out for him and begged for more. He gently eased her apart and coaxed her opening with one finger. Her moans grew desperate and frantic.

He added another finger and delicately worked them inside of her.

"Oh, yes," gasped from her in heated desire.

Rhythmically, following her natural ebbs and flows, he coated her with the salve. He could feel it working. It carried her energy to his fingers much easier than he'd ever felt it before. The energy he supplied her flowed through her body quickly. The lube seemed to amplify the tender sensations.

He clenched his jaw and prayed nothing would hurt her, as he dipped his fingers deep and then gently pulled them back.

She writhed and begged for release.

"Does that feel good, baby doll? Tell me." He had to make certain.

"Oh god," she moaned fervently.

Unable to hide his grin, he added slightly to the friction and force. He stroked the spot she preferred so deep within her. He felt her muscles relax from the salve and then coil and tighten against him. She clenched around his fingers and pulled him deeper.

Her breaths were quick and constant. "That's it, baby. Can you come for me? I know you need to. Can you let it go?"

Her body contorted. She writhed and called out his name, and then she lost it all. She gave up the tension and the fear. The need overtook her, and she unfurled in crashing waves all around him.

The orgasm stole her breath. She quaked against him as he held her tight. It had been so long.

As she eased, she reached and dipped her fingers in the jar and then coated his cock in the salve. He was hung so thick he ached. A moan thundered from him. The sensation was overwhelming.

"Take me," she pled, "please."

Desperation churned in his veins. His body thrummed to the cadence of her rhythms. He gave himself over to her needs.

"Turn over on your side for me, baby doll." He guided her, unwilling to lie on top of her and accidentally cause her pain, and

400

certainly not about to flip her on her stomach and pull her back over him forcefully.

He positioned himself behind her. He cradled her close and allowed no space between. There had been enough space, and he wouldn't allow the chasm to exist any longer. She melted into his powerful embrace.

"You sure you're ready, baby?"

"Please," she whimpered again.

Dan eased her legs apart with his knee, and then spread her folds tenderly as he pushed inside her. Her energy began to consume him as he halted, barely inside her.

"What do you feel, honey?"

"You," she writhed. "More, please more."

He pushed another inch, and then, unable to fight it as her muscles cinched around him and her energy devoured his own, he placed his hand over her mound and pushed soothing energy into her. He made certain that she felt nothing from him but all-encompassing pleasure.

As he began to thrust, he pushed his shield out over them. She moaned and writhed as she felt him permeate the air around her and the tender, exquisite paradise between her legs that was all for him.

He pushed rhythmically into her and then pulled away, coated in her heavenly nectar. It was utter perfection. She bound and healed his broken heart and his weary, ragged soul. Her warmth and her love filled him and restored each and every broken piece. Her body milked him, satiating every need of his soul.

She cried out his name as he slowly circled and teased her clit. The climax began to take hold of her. Her muscles trembled around him as he buried himself in deep and lost it all. They came together. Their rhythms fused rapidly. Their releases mixed in heady waves of ecstasy and bliss that gave them reprieve from all that the world had taken away.

Dan watched over her as she fell into a gentle slumber. He was still afraid. He was still worried the energy he'd taken on with so little thought might affect her. But she seemed to experience nothing but his all-consuming love and joy that they'd reunited and that together they were going to heal.

CHAPTER 53

TOIL THROUGH THE PAIN

Dan awoke to the distant sound of cawing roosters as the sun poured its warmth into the bedroom. He inhaled the fresh floral air that permeated the room. He blinked and tried to recall the last time he'd slept so well. He reached across the bed but found it empty. He leaned up on his elbows to study the space around him.

He heard her. Through the large window screens that looked out onto the porch, he could see her. She was humming. He sat up and rubbed his eyes.

She was sitting cross-legged on the bed swing, sipping coffee and doing something with her hands. Dan pulled on a pair of sweat pants and moved to the porch. His body still required hers constantly. His very survival depended on being near her.

She was surrounded by dozens of different kinds of flowers that he assumed she must've picked from around the farm that morning. She smiled up at him, but her eyes were red-rimmed and swollen again. She'd been sobbing.

"Hey, baby." He cleared the sleepy gravel out of his throat. His heart ached that she hadn't awoken him when she'd clearly needed the sanctuary he'd been trying so hard to construct for her in his arms.

He picked up a pile of delicate, white and purple orchid blossoms and seated himself where they'd lain. Dan watched her work.

"I want to go to Hanakāpīʻai today." Her voice was strained and hoarse from her tears.

"Of course," he agreed.

Still waking up, it took him several minutes to determine that she was making an intricate lei. Her hands moved in steady rhythm, just like she'd been taught. He watched her work. She gracefully laced the blooms in a beautiful, patterned oval.

His eyes drifted to the left. He saw that there were already two completed leis lying on the mattress. The lei she was working on contained numerous colored large hibiscus and orchid blooms in yellows, pinks, and whites.

The smallest of the completed leis, only a few inches around, consisted of tiny, five-petal pink flowers. The very center of each flower was yellow. Beside that was a full-length lei made of beautiful pinks and purples.

Like there was a brutal fist crushing his heart and threatening to rip it from his chest, Dan could only surrender to the pain. He swallowed back emotion so forceful he wasn't certain his body could contain it. His throat closed. His soul shattered. His shield tried to sustain him, but it was weaker than the consuming tidal wave of emotion.

"Malani and Kai are coming, and Tutu and Papa," she stated firmly.

Dan nodded his understanding. He was unable to speak as he forced himself to study the lei she'd made for their baby which she must have felt was a little girl.

The other lei was made for Amelia, and his body convulsed as sobs overtook him.

As she worked methodically, tears flowed down her face. She never stopped, and Dan was unable to do anything but sit beside her and watch her toil through the pain and devastating heartbreak with her bare hands.

Perfectly willing to carry his pain when it was more than he could bear, she completed the lei for her mother and drew a deep breath. "I want to go now."

Another nod was all he managed. They dressed quickly. Dan pulled on a dress shirt and tie. Fionna donned a long, flowing sundress.

Dan drove the truck, and Fionna's grandparents rode with Malani and Kai. No one spoke as they trekked the miles to the beach. He helped her take each step. The hike was part of the process. They came to an enclosed basin surrounded by the mountains.

Dan had never seen ocean water so turbulent. The tide ripped harshly and beat against the rock walls. Everyone standing on the beach that morning in the tightly knit circle had tears flowing rapidly down their cheeks.

Fionna moved to the water. She held tightly to Dan's hand. She placed the tiny lei inside of the ones for her mother and Amelia, their little girl's protectors. She wound them together and whispered a long prayer in Hawaiian.

He knelt with her, and they released the leis out into the ocean. They stood there for several long minutes, watching the ocean take them away. Pieces of each of their hearts finally released, though the scars would forever remain.

Dan held her tenderly. They sobbed together as he whispered how much he loved her, and how sorry he was for every hurt she'd had to live through, for every heartbreak she'd had to endure.

After a quiet lunch that included several restorative bowls of chicken long rice and another nap, Dan and Fionna stood outside of the Blue Tiki Tattoo shop in Kapa'a.

"You don't have to do this with me," Fionna vowed again.

"I want to do this. It's perfect actually."

"Okay." She smiled, pleased with their plan. As they entered the Gifted tattoo shop, Fionna supplied a picture of the symbol of Hapai, a twisted, cylindrical, scrolling shape with an enclosed loop at the top. It symbolized pregnancy and meant *to carry* in Hawaiian, a reminder that they no longer had to carry burdens alone. They had each other.

Dan pulled off his T-shirt and pointed to his left shoulder blade across from the large Celtic cross he'd had done for Amelia.

Fionna kicked off her flip-flops and supplied the inside of her left ankle opposite her Maylea tattoo. After the sketches were completed, they held hands. As the artists worked steadily, they soothed each other's pain.

It was late afternoon when they made their way out of the shop. The tattoo brought remembrance and a way to work emotional pain into physical, which could be dealt with. It seemed to give both of them a place from which to start again.

They headed to a coffee shop bursting with local delicacies. They stood in line outside, enjoying the breeze coming off the ocean. When they stepped inside, Dan decided the smell alone was more than worth the wait.

"The coffee here is amazing," Fionna vowed. She seemed so much lighter. The healing processes she'd finally allowed herself had soothed her rhythms. Dan couldn't bear to let go of her hand. The feeling of her was far too addictive.

"Okay, so what do we order here, Miss Styler?" He thoroughly enjoyed the sensation of flirting with her again.

She giggled. "Well, the future Mrs. Vindico gets a tropical chicken salad sandwich and a lilikoi kumquat cupcake, and a one hundred percent kona coffee drip, and she sits outside,"—she pointed to the tables in front of the coffee shop that were tucked along the bustling main street—"and she very seriously considers moving back to Kauai."

Dan grinned and nodded his understanding. They moved up in the line, and he placed a double of her usual order. He added two large bags of kona coffee beans that they could take home.

He joined her at her selected outdoor table and handed her the bag of coffee beans as they waited on their order to be supplied.

"Best fiancé ever." She leaned across the table and kissed his jaw.

"Now you can sit at our kitchen table, and we can decide if we're moving to Kauai." Wherever she wanted to be, he would go, and he wanted her to understand that.

The large sandwiches, cupcakes, and cups of coffee arrived. Fionna thanked the waitress in Hawaiian before turning back to Dan. "I need to come back more often. I've been away far too long."

As Dan had already determined this, he smiled. "Yes, you have. So how about whatever we decide we might want to do with the rest of our lives, we make sure that we take time to come back out here on a regular basis."

They ate the delectable sandwiches and then he fed her a bite of one of the cupcakes, then took one himself.

He almost moaned aloud. "Okay, if we move out here, baby doll, I'm going to have to find a gym quickly and stay there most of the day."

"Nah, see, you just surf all morning, then work the farm, and then swim in the evening and you can pretty much eat whatever you want, and you have an amazing tan."

Dan squeezed her hand. "I'm sorry you can't surf yet." He was sorry for so many things.

Fionna shrugged. "It's okay. We're coming back soon, right?"

"You just say the word, and we'll be on the next plane."

Papa and Tutu had declared no work be done that day on the farm. It was to be a day of remembrance of all that had been lost.

Malani and Kai had gone to the beach. They spied Dan and Fionna at their table.

"We don't want to interrupt," Malani hesitated. "We just saw you, and I wanted to give you another hug."

Fionna grinned. "You can have a hug, and you can join us."

"You sure, Maylea?" Kai asked concernedly.

"We would love that."

They ordered and joined Fionna and Dan at the table.

"Let me see it." Malani peeked under the table, trying to see Fionna's ankle. She supplied her newly tattooed left foot.

"That's perfect." She touched the tattoo lightly.

"Yeah, I really like it." Fionna's gaze traveled from her own foot to Dan's eyes.

"You got the same thing?" Kai quizzed Dan.

"Yeah, it's on my back." He gestured to his shoulder blade.

"Very cool, brah." Kai let just a little Hawaiian slang slip. The tattoo seemed to be all the proof he needed that Dan would take care of Fionna.

"You know what I was thinking about?" Malani scooted closer to Fionna along the bench seat so that their thighs were touching.

Fionna smiled and shook her head. "There are so many, many things."

"That time when we were eleven." Malani giggled.

"Oh my gosh! I'm surprised we survived."

Malani turned to Dan. "You know how Tutu is always talking about letting the island rhythms guide you, and move you, and everything?"

His breath came up short as he recalled those very rhythms thrumming out of Fionna while he'd taken her the evening before. The rhythms of her that set the very cadence of his heart. Yeah, he knew the rhythms, and he'd follow them anywhere.

He managed a half nod and waited on Malani to continue.

"Right, so, we were only eleven, and we couldn't really access our energy just yet." A slight heat formed in her olive cheeks. Kai chuckled and gazed at his wife like he could never love anything more.

"We didn't really understand what that meant entirely. I mean we did but we didn't."

Fionna laughed and shook her head at the memory. Dan was very intrigued to see what they'd done.

"So Maylea and I decided that we were going to spend the night at her house and sneak out and come into town all by ourselves, because there was this huge island wedding for some rock star or something."

"No," Fionna smirked, "it was for Representative Kalakona after all of that crazy stuff had happened. But she was just head of the Molokai Consul then."

"That's right!" Malani gasped. "The guy she's married to, his family is really weird and super wealthy and his dad committed suicide or something right before the wedding. It was crazy, and we wanted to see the big, huge wedding."

Dan reached and held Fionna's hand across the table.

"Anyway, so we snuck out, headed toward where we thought the wedding would be, but we couldn't find it," she lamented.

Fionna nodded. "But we did find ourselves very, very lost in the dark."

A smirk had formed on Kai's kind face. He was shaking his head at both Malani and Fionna.

"Papa found us the next morning, and I thought Maylea's dad was going to explode when we told him that the island rhythms told us to do it."

Dan laughed as he envisioned just how Fionna's father would've reacted. Fionna was giggling over the memories, the angelic melody that sung to his soul.

"When they finally let us out of the house again, we found out the wedding was actually on Molokai, which is where Representative Kalakona lives." Fionna rolled her eyes.

Dan listened intently to Malani and Fionna recount stories from their childhood, but the story of the two of them sneaking out for the wedding stuck out in his mind.

CHAPTER 54
CONFUSION

As the sun set after Dan and Fionna had eaten at her grandparents' home, Dan kept the swing on the screened-in porch of the guest cottage gently gliding.

Her grandmother had insisted on another bath for Maylea before they went to bed, and he was looking forward to it.

She'd spent some time alone in the waterfall spring just before their supper, letting the waters heal her. It was part of the process, but Dan had missed her. His rhythms still frayed and spun in chaos when she was away from him. But in those moments when he'd sat outside alone, his shield seemed to home in on the island. He knew what they needed to do next.

"Dan?"

"Fionna?" He grinned over her slight giggle.

"My abilities still aren't working quite right, but something feels off. Something is different about Malani. And something far away feels dark. I think, but I can't quite tell. I'm still not myself. Normally, things are much more clear. Something still feels dangerous."

"Didn't Tutu say that it was going to take several weeks for you to really stabilize? I think it's probably normal. What happened to you was…" he choked.

"I'm okay. I promise. I just wish I could figure it out. It's scary, but I'll be able to eventually. I hope."

He continued to swing them softly as the evening breeze whispered through the canopy trees. He went on with his plan.

"Can I ask you something, baby doll?"

She was lying on the swing with her head in his lap. Her energy had tensed with her confession, but with a few more sways of the swing, it calmed again. He kept his fingers stroking softly through her hair.

"Of course."

"I know this might be a little rushed," he admitted hesitantly.

She picked up on his trepidation and sat up to study him. She linked her fingers through his, and he felt her soothing energy move out of her and into his hand.

"You know, if I'd never made love with you, I would think that was the most incredible feeling in the world," he groaned from the sensation.

She beamed and then closed her eyes. As she began to draw from him, she worked her rhythms magically so that she drew his energy in and then supplied him with her own. It was precisely how it felt when he thrust himself inside of her.

His entire body shuddered from the heavenly perfection traveling through him. He wrapped her up in his arms and devoured her mouth. He needed more. He needed it all. She was panting and writhing in his arms when he finally pulled away.

"I want to be married to you." He'd been planning on broaching the subject with a little more finesse, but it poured from his mouth without calculation. "I don't want to wait anymore. I want to get married now, here, please. No parents, no invitations, no press, just us."

Her energy spun in frenzied euphoria. "Really? You want to get married here?"

Dan nodded and tried to steady his heartbeats. "If you want to."

"Are you kidding me? I've always wanted to get married here. I just never thought I could."

"You could teach me, or your grandparents could show me all the things I need to know for a Hawaiian ceremony. I want you to have that. You should get married here. This island is…it's just where we should do this. It's where you belong."

"If it didn't hurt to jump up and down, I would. But what about your mom?" She deflated suddenly.

"I'll call and tell them before the ceremony." He wondered if he should feel bad about cutting their parents out, but he was unable to access any guilt.

"You need a best man for the exchanging of the leis." Her exuberance delighted him. He let that information settle on him. He needed to make a few phone calls.

"You really want to do this now? You really want to get married before we go home?"

"Yes, I don't want to wait anymore. I want to marry you right now, but I'll wait a couple of days and help you plan whatever you want the ceremony to be. I'll do anything you want, just please. Let's do this. Let's start over. Let's really live a life outside in the daylight instead of hidden away in the dark."

"I have to call Malani!"

～

Dan and Fionna spent the next two days deep in preparation. Tutu would stop them occasionally and have Dan give Fionna baths or make them walk in the waters of Kauai, which made each day perfect by Dan's estimation.

Tutu also provided Fionna's mother's diamond wedding band, which fit underneath her engagement ring perfectly. Fionna was ecstatic.

Malani and Fionna flew to Oahu the following morning and located a dress.

After a dinner of poke nachos, Dan and Fionna shopped the stores near Hanalei Bay and located a wedding band formed of island palladium and koa wood with intricate scrollwork throughout. The design was unending but not a repeating pattern. Each picture was different but then bled to the next image.

To Dan's shock, it fit him perfectly. He was certain he would need something custom made. His hands were rather large, but the ring seemed to have been made for him. They purchased it immediately.

∼

Garrett Haydenshire

"Uh, here." His father was flustered as he signed his name on the marriage certificate. Garrett wasn't certain if it was due to the fact that money was still disappearing from Interfeci accounts or that Dan had asked the governor not to tell the Vindicos.

"I'm not going to say anything to them," Garrett vowed. "They're getting married. They need a real life. Fi was dying, trapped the way they were. We can figure this out without Dan, and then I'm going back to the precinct. Rainer and Logan can handle this now."

His father sighed. "Nothing like being between a rock and a hard place. No one knows more about the ins and outs of the Interfeci than Daniel, and he's the one guy I don't want to call. You're right. He and Fionna need a fresh start. I offered him one, and I'm not going to take it away now."

As his decision became resolute, his father's gaze locked on Garrett's. He shifted uncomfortably and glanced at his watch. He needed to get out to the planes. He'd have several hours between DC and Lihue to figure out how to keep his worries and fear from Fionna. She could read him like a freaking book.

He'd just focus on her. She was finally getting what she wanted, and that delighted Garrett. According to Dan, she was happier than he'd ever seen her. So the Interfeci or whatever remnant of them was doing this could just go to hell.

"Are you sure you're okay with this wedding, son?"

Garrett rolled his eyes. *Not this again.* "Dad, come on, how many times do I have to swear to you that I am not now nor was I ever in love with Fionna? I do love her, but I love her like I love Emily. Nothing more. She's my best friend, and she's marrying one of my closest friends. I'm thrilled."

Governor Haydenshire held up his hands in surrender. "I believe you. I just wondered if this might be difficult for you."

"I'm really, really good. Flying to Kauai tonight, Brazil day after tomorrow, and then I'll be back a few days later. If we can manage not to lose any more money or operatives between now and then, I'll be even better."

"Agreed." The governor rolled up the marriage certificate, casted it, and handed it to Garrett.

∾

Dan Vindico

"Aww, Maylea, you brought us sex salad." Malani and Fionna dissolved into a pile of giggles. Dan and Kai both shook their heads.

"Uh, what?" Dan finally asked.

"Tutu made me bring it. I had to eat it last night too." Fionna set the large bowl full of baby spinach leaves on Malani's kitchen table.

"It's full of island ingredients that are good for reproductive organs," Malani explained. "Did you bring...?"

"Maca dressing, of course." Fionna held up the oily brown dressing in a glass jar. "She's been slipping maca in my tea and coffee too. She's not even trying to be sneaky about it anymore."

Dan studied the salad. He'd assumed it must've been one of Fionna's favorites. Tutu had prepared it several times since they'd arrived. He wasn't aware that it had other purposes.

It was quite good. He'd enjoyed several bowls himself. He'd usually skip over the seaweed pieces, but the rest was delicious. It was loaded with island fruits and vegetables, almonds, macadamia nuts, and was covered in acai juice. Fionna loved avocado and it was loaded with it.

"Tutu prescribes it all the time for women who have any kind of reproductive issues. So when we were teenagers, we started calling it sex salad." Malani giggled again.

"I'm not allowed to go back to the farm until we finish this," Fionna teased.

"I'm so excited about tonight." Malani was moving around her house throwing things into duffle bags. She and Fionna were having one last slumber party for the two of them with Tutu before Fionna walked down the aisle the next morning.

Dan's heart thundered in his chest each time he tried to picture it. It always seemed just out of reach. He'd ended Wretchkinsides. He told himself he was being insane, that he'd lived so long in a constant state of terror that something would happen to her, he couldn't believe that they were really safe now. Whatever was plaguing his shield and whatever had her rhythms tensing oddly was imaginary. It had to be. Nothing else could go wrong.

After their lunch of sex salad, Fionna and Dan had returned to the farm for a nap. A massage therapist had visited the farm at Tutu's request. He'd worked on Fionna. Dan bit holes in his tongue to keep from ordering the guy to get his hands off his fiancée.

Still wary of his own temper and that damn remnant of energy, he ordered himself to remain calm. To his shock, when the guy was finally finished, Fionna was glowing and seemed to feel even better.

The spirituality of it all, and those heady island rhythms, soothed his irritation.

He held her hand and guided her out to the truck. They headed to the airport.

As the Crown Governor's jet touched down, Dan kept his arm wrapped over Fionna. Passengers began to disembark. Garrett made his way down the corridor, sporting his broad, mischievous smirk.

Fionna laughed as he hugged her fiercely. He slapped Dan on the back while shaking his hand.

"I'm supposed to give you this." Garrett chuckled as he unrolled the marriage certificate signed by Governor Haydenshire. "Dad says, you know, to tell you how thrilled he is, proud, yada yada yada."

Dan laughed. He was certain the governor's actual statement

hadn't gone quite that way. Fionna all but leapt in Garrett's arms. He embraced her readily.

"You look amazing, baby. So much better." Garrett studied Fionna while they walked to the truck.

Dan and Fionna shared a knowing grin. "Yeah," she agreed. "It's been quite a trip. But what's wrong with you?"

Garrett tried to hide his grimace. Panic churned in Dan's gut. "Just tired. Long flight, and I got in a disagreement with Dad. I want to leave Elite and go back to the precinct now that the deed is done, so to speak, but Dad wants me to stay on."

"I really appreciate your coming out for this." Dan suspected the story Garrett had just spun was highly fabricated, but he had no intention of calling him on it. Nothing was going to worry Fionna. She'd been through enough. But she seemed to sense that he was lying as well. Her powers weren't that diminished despite everything she'd been through.

"Are you kidding me? I wouldn't have missed this for anything. Although I do really want to be in the room with you tomorrow when you call your folks and tell them what you're doing."

Dan laughed. "You're my best man. I was thinking maybe you'd call them."

"Right." Garrett pulled his cell from his pocket and mocked a phone call. "Hey Mrs. V, it's Garrett Haydenshire. Yeah, that Garrett Haydenshire," he continued as Dan and Fionna cracked up. "Uh-huh, I'm in Kauai with Dan and Fi, and he just kissed the bride. Just wanted you to know, and by the way, Dan says to tell you to suck it up your Jell-O mold," he concluded as they all laughed raucously.

Dan drove the roads back to the farm with ease. He'd done it many times since their arrival.

"So there will be hula girls at this shindig, right?" Garrett was doing quite a job of hiding whatever was bothering him. Dan clenched his jaw shut, but Fionna was studying him intently. He wondered what she was picking up on.

Fionna rolled her eyes. "Yes, and they are all my friends from when I was a little girl, and most of them are married, so could you please be good?"

Dan reached and laced his fingers through hers. He let her draw strength from him.

"I'm always good, baby. Don't worry about that." He winked at her as she shook her head.

Dan felt her rhythms forcibly resist the emotion she picked up on from Garrett. She didn't really want to know what had gotten to him any more than he wanted to tell her.

CHAPTER 55

RUSSIAN WINTER

The next morning, Dan lay in the bed watching the clock tick slowly toward six. It was only the second night in many months that he'd slept alone. The last time had been the night Fionna had stayed with Garrett. The night he'd hunted down Wretchkinsides. That felt like a lifetime ago. It *was* a lifetime ago, he told himself. Everything was going to be different now. She was all that mattered.

While lying there breathing in the sweet Kauaian air and watching the daylight begin to vanquish the dark, he knew he never wanted to sleep alone ever again.

He heard Garrett and Kai stir in the kitchen of the hale that they'd been moved to the night before. The call of the roosters alerted them to the dawn of a new day.

Fionna and Malani were sleeping in the cottage that Fi and Dan had been sharing. They would be getting up soon to get Fionna ready to become Fionna Kalani Halia Styler Vindico.

Dan's cell phone chirped from the nightstand.

I miss you. I can't sleep without you. Malani doesn't cuddle me right, and I can't wait to be your wife.

Dan chuckled. His heart swelled. He couldn't wait either.

419

I'll meet you on the beach in three hours. I'm counting the minutes. He typed his confession and sent it back quickly.

He stretched and yawned as he moved into the kitchen.

"Coffee?" Kai offered kindly.

"Yeah, thanks." Dan sank down in one of the mismatched chairs at the small kitchen table.

Garrett joined him. "Man, what the hell do they do to the beds here? That's the best I've ever slept in spite of those fucking roosters."

Kai laughed. "It's the Hawaiian bamboo in the mattress. Maylea's Papa builds all the beds so they're made to help you relax. Tutu has a bamboo supplier on the Big Island that makes the sheets too. It all makes the beds here better than anything anywhere else. The roosters you just learn to live with."

Garrett looked impressed, but he began studying Dan's back without his shirt on.

"You and Fi get those inked together?" He must've noticed Fionna's ankle the evening before.

Dan nodded. "Yeah, we got them done several days ago."

"It's cool looking," Garrett immediately complimented.

"Thanks, it means a whole lot."

They drank the delectable Kauai coffee that was grown just a few miles from where they were currently sitting.

"So since you're getting married here without anyone at home knowing, save Mom and Dad, does that mean that you'll be Dan and Fionna Vindico or Dan and Maylea Vindico?"

Dan smiled. "They are one and the same. Trust me."

"Okay, I get that you two have this whole thing no one else knows about going on. I want you to have that, but tell me what Maylea means? I've heard her dad and stepmom call her that for as long as I've known her, but she never seemed to want to talk about it. I never wanted to push."

"It means wildflower, and if you think about it, it's the perfect description of her."

Garrett grinned. "I don't even have to think about it. She is that, and you are one lucky son of a bitch, my friend."

"That I am," Dan agreed as they all laughed.

Papa arrived with breakfast for the men. He explained the meanings of everything that would be happening at Dan and Fionna's traditional Hawaiian wedding. His tone carried the wisdom of generations that had come and gone, but they'd left their traditions to be carried on.

Dan listened intently as did Garrett. He seemed fascinated with what was taking place.

Papa left after giving Dan advice on how to care for Maylea's spirit, which according to Papa, was the combination of Fionna's energies and her soul.

"One cannot exist without the other, and they must flow in equal parts. If one is off, the other is also," her grandfather had elaborated.

Dan knew that everything he spoke was the absolute truth, and he made a vow to himself to care for all of her, to take care of her spirit, not just her energy.

Fionna had phoned her parents several days ago. She'd invited them out for the wedding. Gretta told her that they couldn't afford to close the bakery but that they were happy for them. Fionna knew the bakery was an excuse. Her father couldn't bear to return to Kauai even to see his only daughter be married.

Dan glanced at his watch and sighed. He doubted the phone call to his parents would go as smoothly as Fionna's, but the deed had to be done. He sank onto the sofa and stared at his cell phone like it had fangs.

Garrett offered him a sympathetic gaze as he joined him in the living room with another cup of coffee. He was right by his side, just like he'd always been, just like he'd always be. He slapped Dan on the back.

They needed to get ready, so with a deep breath, he called his parents' home.

The Senteon wasn't hearing trials that day, and Governor Haydenshire wasn't working at all. They were preparing for Rainer and Emily's wedding.

There was a decent chance his father would work from his home office instead of going into the Senate. Dan prayed his parents would be together. He didn't want to have to do this twice.

His mother answered on the second ring. "Daniel, is everything all right? I knew you shouldn't have taken Fionna off to Hawaii so soon after her surgery. Is she sick? Do we need to fly you home? You should have taken her to the Poconos like I told you," she demanded without stopping to breathe.

Garrett gave Dan a sympathetic head shake as Dan tried to get a word in edgewise. His father, presumably having overheard his mother's freak-out, must've casted her cell phone and brought the signal to his own.

"What's wrong with Fionna?"

"Nothing. Fionna is fine. She's amazing actually," he insisted. "Well, I assume she is. I haven't actually seen her since last night," he confessed as Garrett chuckled.

"Why haven't you seen her? Are you fighting?" The governor sounded devastated.

"No, Dad." Dan tried to remember that no one in DC had lived through the journey of healing they'd embarked upon since they'd arrived in Kauai.

His face pulled into a broad grin. "I'm actually not allowed to see her until the wedding." He listened to the deafening silence. No one spoke for several uncomfortable moments.

Garrett laughed hysterically in whispered guffaws on the sofa.

"What did you just say?" Governor Vindico finally demanded.

"Uh," Dan swallowed, "I'm not allowed to see Fionna until she walks down the aisle at our wedding, which starts in about an hour and a half," he allowed with a quick glance at his watch.

"Marion, sit down," the governor soothed. "You and Fionna are getting married in an hour?"

"Yeah, it's just something we need to do. I'm sorry you and Mom aren't here, but we didn't want the big Senate affair. We need this to be just us. We don't want to wait anymore." Dan willed his parents to understand.

"But I've already picked out Fionna's gown—long sleeves, high collar, with a navy velvet bow—and I've just finally gotten Lillian to tell me which florists Emily and Rainer used," Mrs. Vindico spat.

"We're going to have a Russian Winter theme. I'm ordering brocade fabric!"

Garrett rolled his eyes and shook his head. Dan knew instantly that having the wedding on South Shore that morning had been the perfect decision. He had no idea what *Russian winter* looked like to his mother, but he knew beyond a shadow of a doubt that it wasn't Fionna.

She was his island girl, with sunshining warmth and the breath of the palm trees coursing through her veins. The pahu drums set the cadence of her heart. Her rhythms were those of the mighty Pacific surrounding them. The island permeated her very essence. It was her spirit.

"Sorry, Mom, but we're doing this here, now, and honestly, I couldn't be happier."

"Well, I'm just so glad you're happy!" his mother shrieked in furious resentment.

"Marion," the governor sighed, "if this is what they want...."

"What about what I want for them?" Mrs. Vindico demanded.

"I'm sorry you're upset," Dan admitted carefully, "but right now I need to take care of Fionna, and we need to do what's right for the two of us, not anyone else."

"Arthur, make him stop," Mrs. Vindico ordered. Dan tried to hide his chuckle.

"Marion, he's almost five thousand miles away, not to mention the fact that he's thirty-two years old. I can't stop him."

"Mom, if you want to be mad, be mad at me. This was all my idea," Dan stated calmly, more and more pleased with his decision with each passing minute.

His mother made an odd, muffled, screeching shriek before she ended the signal on her cell.

"Was that your mom?" Garrett gasped after hearing the disconcerting noise. Dan nodded as they both tried hard not to guffaw.

"Well, I guess I'm happy for you. Tell Fionna how pleased we are, and I'll try to talk to your mother." The governor sounded thoroughly put out.

"We'll see you when we get back," Dan managed as he ended the call.

"Wow." Garrett shook his head as Dan doubled over. "Wait 'til she finds out I was here for it."

"Yeah, you might not ever want to mention that."

CHAPTER 56

THE FIRE AND THE WATER

Dan shrugged into a white, button-down dress shirt and white slacks appropriate for the beach, the traditional attire for the groom in a Hawaiian wedding.

"Hell of a lot better than a tux," Garrett complimented as he pulled on a pair of khaki shorts and a polo.

Fionna's Papa arrived to take the men to the ceremony. Dan's heart stuttered as emotion settled thickly in his throat.

"Hey, can you let him in? I just need a minute," Dan pled to Garrett.

"No problem." Garrett closed the door to the bedroom and allowed Dan a moment with his thoughts.

He tapped into the rhythms of the island again. He closed his eyes in deep concentration and tried to discern how to let go and how to hold on. His phone rang in his pocket.

"Hey," he offered Fitzroy.

"Just wanted to check on you, man," Fitz explained.

"Thanks, I'm okay. I wish you could be here." He'd called Fitz first, explaining that though Fitz was certainly welcome to come out that Dan really thought with everything that had happened, Garrett should be his best man.

Fitz had adamantly agreed, and his only request had been that Dan and Fionna make a trip to Paris to visit with Maddie and the boys.

"You know she would have wanted this for you." Fitz said the words Dan so desperately needed to hear.

"Yeah, I think in a whole different life she would have loved Fionna, you know?"

"Yeah, I do know, and she would have. Fionna's an amazing woman, and you deserve a real life."

A real life. It just still didn't seem possible. "I guess I better go."

"You have to let *her* go, Dan."

He knew Fitz was right. He had to let Amelia go just like he'd watched the leis disappear into the water so many days before. A part of the earth, always a part of his spirit, forever in his soul.

"Don't freak out now. You're almost there," Fitz urged him on.

"Yeah," Dan choked, "I really am."

He exited the bedroom and took the first of many steps toward life.

"Are you okay?" Garrett grasped Dan's bicep in a gesture of holding him up, even if it was metaphorically.

"I will be as soon as I see her." Dan kept his march toward the front door. He needed Fionna, and as long as he kept putting one foot in front of the other, he was going to get her.

He stopped to allow Fionna's grandfather to tie the red sash around his waist. It was the very sash he'd worn when he'd married Tutu, and that Fionna's father had worn when he'd married her mother.

"You have fire in your soul, Daniel," her grandfather stated knowingly. "And my Maylea is the water who can tame the fire and soothe its burn. You were meant to be together, to live in accord so the fire does not consume you, but rather glows brightly to give her light and protection. It keeps her warm. Neither can exist without the other, and yet you must understand that fire can never quell the water."

Dan nodded. He was astonished at the truth as it settled on his conscience and soothed his soul. She was the only thing that could ever have doused his vicious flame, the only thing strong enough to tame the blaze. She was always the stronger force.

∼

They drove the short distance to the beach. The breeze blew through his hair as he walked beside Garrett down to the waters. He swallowed harshly as he took in the soothing sounds of the ukuleles playing and noted the circle of Hawaiian blooms set in the sand.

He shook the minister's hand, the same man who had performed Fionna's blessing when she was a baby.

"Are you ready, Daniel Arthur Vindico, to marry our sweet Maylea?" he asked in his deep, drumming intonation.

"Yes, sir," Dan nodded, "I am." He stood there on the beaches of Kauai and knew that he was ready to move on. He was ready to start again.

Malani's parents were standing in the small area for guests along with a few of Fionna's other family friends.

There were three women dressed in traditional hula skirts and leis ready to perform the dance of the wedding.

Garrett studied Dan intently. "I don't know how, man, but somehow this is gonna work. All of that shit is gonna be worth it."

"As long as I get her," Dan agreed in a choked whisper.

"Then let's do this." Garrett slapped Dan on the back and disappeared with Papa.

Kai took his place in the audience and the ukulele music lowered slightly.

"Let us begin," the kahu soothed. Dan tried desperately to will his heart to remain inside of his rib cage as he walked beside the minister as he chanted up the aisle.

Dan kept his gaze and his body facing the ocean and away from the guests. He saw Fionna's grandmother take her seat from his peripheral vision and glanced to his left to see Garrett walk Malani to her place on the other side of the minister before he stood solidly by Dan just like he'd always done.

Dan's hands trembled, and he focused on drawing breath. His

stomach clenched and sweat dewed on his neck but was cooled by the soothing ocean breeze.

He closed his eyes in a fervent prayer that he would be everything Fionna ever needed and that what he was doing wouldn't hurt Amelia in any way.

Suddenly the conch shells sounded in a triumphant roar, and Dan's lungs begged for air.

"Damn," he heard Garrett whisper. Dan turned, finally allowed to gaze out.

Fionna was breathtaking. She kept her gaze locked on his as she glided over the sand on the arm of her grandfather. She was dressed in a long, billowing, sleeveless wrap gown with a slit up her right leg.

Her head was adorned with a dizzying crown of Hawaiian wildflowers, and tears swam in Dan's eyes. She was stunning. Her grandfather kissed her cheek and then placed her trembling hands in Dan's.

"My Maylea," he whispered. "Take care of her. For you hold her spirit, and she holds your fire."

Dan nodded but was unable to take his eyes off the most beautiful sight he'd ever beheld.

"My God, you are so beautiful," he whispered as she smiled sweetly with tender tears beginning to form in her eyes.

"Fionna Kalani Halia, our sweet Maylea, will now exchange leis with her bridegroom Daniel Arthur. The lei with no beginning and no ending symbolizes their eternal love," the kahu explained.

While drawing a deep breath and feeling the warmth, the serenity, the life flow through him from her hands, Dan kept one clasped tightly in his own as he turned to Garrett, who supplied him with an all white lei created the evening before by Fionna, Malani, and Tutu.

Dan breathed deeply of the white ginger lei as it combined in the steady billowing breeze that carried Fionna's scent to his nostrils. She lowered her head, and he delicately placed the lei around her neck as he continued to blink back tears.

Fionna gazed up at him with all of her love and adoration as she turned and took the lei she'd made for him out of Ti leaves. He lowered his head in a bow to her as she draped it over him.

428

The ukulele began again, this time joined with a slack key guitar and pahu drums to play the Hawaiian Wedding song in soft soothing tones. The hula dancers began to sway.

As they danced, Dan and Fionna pledged to love each other and care for one another for the rest of their lives and to let nothing come between them. *Not ever again,* Dan vowed to himself as he pledged his love and devotion to her.

They watched as the kahu dipped a deep brown bowl formed of koa into the mighty Pacific and then placed their rings inside the bowl. Another Ti leaf was also dipped, and the rings were sprinkled with the ocean water three times as the kahu began to chant.

They slipped the rings on one another and then closed their eyes, holding each other's hands, joining their energy, letting it pass between them.

"Daniel Arthur, you have pledged to care for Fionna, for Maylea," the minister urged. "You have alerted the earth, the sea, the air, and the fire to bear witness today to your vow to one another. So Daniel Arthur, as the elements of the earth celebrate with you, so do we, and I will now grant you tide to kiss Fionna Kalani Halia, your bride and our sweet Maylea."

Dan swallowed down the rock-like enclosure in his throat as he tenderly wiped away the tears streaming down Fionna's beautiful face.

"I love you so much," he whispered.

She nodded as he cradled her face in his hands. He leaned and brushed a tender kiss across her lips before he turned and devoured her mouth. He dipped her back in his arms and held her safely in his embrace.

Garrett and Kai wolf-whistled as the small crowd applauded. He stood her back up after several minutes. She was laughing and giving him his smile.

They turned to her friends and family. "Maylea tells me I must now say, their spirits are tied and formed as one, I present to you Mr. and Mrs. Daniel Vindico," the minister announced proudly. "But I think they are forever Dan and Maylea."

They walked back down the aisle. Dan knew he had every single thing he would ever need clinging tightly to his arm.

~

They sat out on the sands, devouring kalua pig, poi, lomi salmon, and other island delicacies. Tutu had prepared plenty of sex salad, and it was all delicious.

"Seriously, best wedding ever. I'm in a polo and shorts, barefoot on the beach in Hawaii," Garrett vowed.

Fionna laughed. She hadn't stopped smiling since she'd walked down the aisle, and Dan couldn't keep his eyes off her. Her hair whipped in the breeze, which occasionally lifted her dress off her legs.

She'd pulled off the large crown of wildflowers and had handed Dan a single pink and yellow orchid bloom. "You're supposed to put it over my left ear because that means I'm taken."

"Oh, baby doll, you are most definitely taken," he assured her. His trousers tightened as he slipped the flower in her hair and brushed a tender kiss on her cheek. "I can't wait to make you my wife."

She'd trembled beside him with her breath stuttering deliciously.

They'd eaten the meal prepared in their honor but kept in constant contact.

"Do I want to know what your mom said when you called?" She wrinkled her nose as she devoured the food on her plate.

Garrett cracked up. "She made some kind of horrible choking sound. I figured that corn cob she's had shoved up her ass her whole life finally blew, or that she was trying to beat the governor with her tennis racket in lieu of Dan."

Dan nearly choked on the piece of papaya he'd placed in his mouth as he joined Garrett's hysterical laughter.

Fionna looked stunned for a split second before she began laughing as well. "Wow! I guess the next time we go to their house will be fun."

"Because it's always been so fun before now," Dan pointed out.

They finished up their meals off the recycled cardboard plates that Tutu had located in her pantry.

Dan tried to envision his mother sitting leisurely on the sands of

Kauai, eating off of cardboard plates, and drinking out of plastic cups and beer bottles pulled out of coolers at their reception picnic, after attending their wedding which had consisted of less than twenty people.

"Apparently my mother saw our wedding theme as Russian winter," he informed Fionna wryly.

She grimaced. "Freezing cold, gray, and run by a deranged dictator?"

Garrett laughed. "That and she knows how much fun Danny had the last time he was in Moscow. She wanted to recreate it for him."

They laughed until Dan couldn't catch his breath. It was an extremely cathartic sensation.

"Papa told me you were taking me off somewhere tonight," Fionna whispered as she leaned against Dan's chest as he lay on his side in the sand propped on his elbow. He'd been tracing his index finger slowly over her exposed shoulders.

"I am," Dan assured her.

"Where are you taking me?" Her eyes sparkled in a dance that made him ache.

"That is for me to know, and you to find out."

Malani and Kai joined them on the patch of sand. "Tutu's making me go with her to prepare your love nest, so do you need me to have the talk with you before I leave?" Malani harassed.

"Yes." Fionna giggled. "Tell me everything I need to know."

Dan and Garrett laughed heartily.

The girls began giggling and suddenly they were embracing.

"I'm so excited for you two. Please come back more often. I miss you every single day!"

"I promise we will, and I miss you every day too!"

Malani released Fionna and threw her arms around Dan. He sat up to embrace her.

"I love you because you love her, and because she loves you. But if I ever find out that you don't love her, I'll push you off a volcano."

He laughed and nodded. "That won't be necessary but sounds entirely fair."

"All right." Garrett leapt up and brushed the sand off of his hands.

"That Hawaiian hottie looks like she needs some help with her suntan lotion." He waggled his eyebrows and gestured toward a woman sunbathing on the beach nearby. "Then I'm heading to Rio."

Fionna's mouth fell open. "Oh my gosh. I forgot all about that. I'm sorry. You're going to be flying forever."

"Hey." Garrett grabbed her hand, guided her up into his arms, and hugged her tightly. "I take total credit for this." He gestured from Fionna to Dan. "And I'm about to make my little sister and Miss Aida the two happiest girls on the planet, minus hottie in the bikini over there if she takes me back to her place, of course."

"Thank you for everything." Fionna hugged Garrett again. "Even if you are a total man whore."

Dan and Fionna hugged Kai and Malani goodbye as they listened to Garrett sweet-talk the bikini-clad woman.

Fionna rolled her eyes. "Did he really just tell her that she looks like Miss Hawaii?"

"He did." Dan chuckled.

"And she bought that?"

"Since he is now rubbing her down with some kind of oil as she sits between his knees, I assume she must've."

"Something is up with him." She broached the trepidation they'd both picked up on.

"I know, but right now I need to take care of you. I let you down. I have to try and make up for what happened to us. We need to let everything else go for a little while including whatever is worrying Garrett."

"You didn't let me down, but that sounds perfect." She grinned as he drew her into his body and held her close.

"Maylea," Tutu beckoned from farther down the beach. Dan and Fionna walked hand in hand to her grandmother. They climbed in the truck and were driven out to the mountaintop villa that Kai had recommended to Dan.

"May the fire of the islands burn for you both this evening," Tutu

432

wished them as they carried their luggage up to the villa that had been prepared for them. It was built on one of the rocky island cliffs that overlooked the stunning crystal-blue waters.

"Tutu." Fionna blushed and shook her head.

"I love you both, and Maylea, I have packed you boxes and boxes of oils for your baths, lotions for your skin, and ointments for your ails. There is a box in there that you will need soon enough. Use them, Maylea, and come back soon, my precious keiki," her grandmother pled.

"I will. I promise. I'm not staying away anymore. This is where I belong." Fionna cried and hugged her grandmother fiercely.

After deciding that he would bring Fionna back for the summer when she could surf to her heart's content, Dan hugged Tutu as well.

Papa cradled Fionna's face in his rough callused hands. "My precious Maylea, even wildflowers need the sunshine. You can't stay in the dark. You have to live in the light."

Fionna swallowed back more emotion. She didn't want to think about her very recent time in the darkest of depths.

"You see, Dan, if you let the island rhythms move you, you might just end up married," Tutu teased.

"I should have listened to them a long time ago." Dan reached back and laced Fionna's fingers in his.

"Have a good night, and we will see you soon. I feel it," Tutu stated wisely.

Fionna and Dan waved as they drove away. Fionna sighed as she walked into the villa.

It was rustic, but she seemed very pleased. There was a king-size four-poster bed hung with white gauzy curtains, a small kitchen with a coffee pot that already had Maylea's coffee perking, and a large double hammock hung on the wooden front porch, along with numerous cushioned chairs.

There was a massive tub full of heat casted water that had lotus blossoms floating on its surface, along with Tutu's oils swimming in the depths. There were indeed wooden boxes full of oils, lotions, and treatments situated near the kitchen to be taken home with Dan and Fionna the next day.

CHAPTER 57

MAYLEA

"This is beautiful." Fionna stared out to the setting sun, swimming in replicated perfection on the softly rolling sea.

"I'm glad you like it, but I've never seen anything more beautiful than my wife."

Heat climbed seductively up from the swells of her breasts. She gave him an abashed grin.

"Want some coffee, baby doll?"

Fionna shook her head. She began gliding toward him slowly with her eyes darkening and her breath picking up pace. Dan shuddered as he watched her walk.

"What do you want?" he whispered. The love and lust swirled rapidly between them.

She paused just inches away from him. "I want to be your wife." Her hot breath caressed his neck. "I want you to take me to bed. I want you to lay over me. I want to feel you pressed against me. I feel so safe in your arms. I want you to suck me, and touch me, and take me. I want you to open me. I need to feel full of you. I want to really be Mrs. Daniel Vindico."

A shuddering growl echoed from Dan's chest as he listened to her pleas. He pulled her to his body. "I'm going to make you mine, sweetheart. I'm gonna take good care of you, but we have all night long. This is our wedding night, baby. I want you to relax for me.

"I want to touch every square inch of your beautiful body. I want to lick you and drink that sweet honey you make for me. I want you to let me touch each and every hidden-away place that all belong to me now. And then I'm going to lay you in that bed, and when I know you're ready, I'm going to make you my wife. I'm gonna own you, baby doll, all night long." His voice rasped low and reverent as he gazed at her longingly.

She panted and quaked in need and desire. Threading his fingers through her long, soft hair, he kissed her tenderly and then gently removed the flower he'd placed over her left ear.

He worked his lips down her neck and spun his tongue in the dip of her collarbone. She liked that, he knew.

He took her hand and gently spun her around in a dance. He halted when her back was to him. His lips worked from her shoulder blade down. They followed his hands as he unzipped the wedding dress, letting it fall in a pile of billowy white at her feet.

A bra had been sewn in the dress, and suddenly she was bare. She'd worn nothing under the layers of soft cotton and organza. She'd allowed her body to feel the ocean's breezy caress, the warm sand on her bare feet, the cool waters of the sea, the rhythms of the island, the rhythms of her.

A greedy moan sounded from low in his chest. The humid air between them filled with their voracious desire. Their rhythms pulsed, eager to be united. The stunning display of her in nothing but the delicate white lei that he'd placed around her neck hours before hung him with searing need.

Her deep olive sun-kissed skin glowed enticingly. The lei set off her swollen breasts. Her nipples were peaked, beckoning him like a sweet confection that needed to be sucked and licked and consumed.

"My god, you are the most beautiful thing I've ever seen."

Her energy tensed. Her rhythms begged for relief.

"Come here to me." He removed the lei and hung it from a low-lying tree branch off of the front decking. He was still learning, but he wanted always to honor the island and the people that had given them back their life.

He turned, lifted her into his arms, and carried her to the tub. Gently, he lowered her into the water and then unbuttoned his shirt. He pulled it off quickly. He knelt beside her and watched her gaze up at him as the water lapped around her curves.

"Lie back, sweetheart." His hands slicked down her body. He massaged and caressed her. He groped her breasts as she moaned. He dipped them lower, unable to help himself.

She let her legs fall open and made him ache to plunge her depths.

"Close your eyes. Just feel me touching you," he commanded as her body fevered from the warmth of the water. She begged for his touch.

He traced her opening, letting the water enter and soothe her. She writhed. The water rippled and sloshed as he dipped his fingers deep inside of her.

She craved more. She swelled rapidly, eager for him to claim her. Her body tensed. She began to pant as he swirled his fingers and the water to the places she was most sensitive. He coaxed her body, still priming her to release. They didn't come quite as easily as they once had, but he had plans to rectify that in time.

Her body tugged rhythmically. Her walls pulled his fingers deeper. She shuddered and gasped for breath.

"Just let it go for me." He had her. She sang out his name as her energy unfurled for him. It spun around him, engulfing him in her love and her sweet tender spirit.

Her body went lax in the water. She stared up at him, still so needy and desperate all for him.

After she regained enough strength to continue, she stood. The water poured down over her gorgeous curves. Dan groaned from the sight of her.

"Please, please. I want it. I've wanted it for so long." Desperation perforated her tone. The flames in her eyes lit explosively.

Unable to fight it, unable to deny her anything at all, he tried to order himself to remain in complete control. It was a ridiculous order. She held all of his cards. He'd willingly handed them over, and he lived to fulfill her.

He heated a large towel from a nearby shelf and wrapped her up inside of it. He tended to each swell, to each luscious curve, and to every perfect hollow of her body as he dried her thoroughly.

"Go get in my bed, baby doll." He watched her move gracefully into the waiting four-poster.

He shed his trousers. His heart flew and his body burned. Seeking the water, he lay beside her. His body was at war with his mind. He wanted this night to be everything she deserved for it to be. But her pleas for him to own her, for him to permeate all of her, to fill her body and soul, were more than he could deny.

He laved her mouth with his own, dipping his tongue between her kiss-swollen lips, sucking them until he was dragging his teeth over them. Her energy poured into his mouth like the nectar of heaven.

His lips traveled down her beautiful body. He sucked her breasts in rhythm and bathed her skin with his tongue.

"I want to taste all of you, honey. I want to drink you before I make you mine." He settled his shoulders between her legs and coaxed her open with his thumbs. "Watch me."

"Yes," she urged as he revealed her folds and the pink entrance to that perfect column of rippled silk that drowned him completely. She was already swollen. Her inner lips begged for his care.

He began at her inner thigh, kissing and then nibbling his way to the heart of her. Slowly, he spun his index finger between her lips at her opening, gathering the liquid heat, and then tenderly teasing her clit until it swelled all for him. He coaxed the silk from her and then leaned and surrounded that swollen, throbbing pearl with his mouth and began to suck. He eased her legs over his shoulders and tended her thoroughly.

Her body shook. He held her gently, still cautious of her injuries. She went wild as he sucked and then dipped his tongue between her folds, feeling her give way a moment later. She convulsed as a powerful orgasm broke in heated waves over her. Her thighs tightened against his jaw. He drank her.

Simply unable to drag it out any longer—his need was too great and her desire too strong—he glided up over her body. He carefully kept his weight on the mattress below her.

"Look at me," he commanded. Her eyes flashed in fevered voracity. Her body gave needy writhes against his. She was so damn hungry he indulged her by prodding her with his head, rubbing it between her folds, priming her clit, making her quake.

"You are mine. All mine forever. And I'm about to make you my wife."

A stuttered moan escaped her, and she rolled like the waves underneath him, desperate for him to fulfill his promises.

"Look at me, baby." He waited until her eyes locked on his again. Her chest rose and fell in reedy desperate gasps. "Do you want me to cast you?" He was perfectly willing to do whatever she wanted, but he wanted a child. He wanted her to carry his baby. He wanted it all with her.

"No." She hadn't even had to pause and think. He studied her energy. It was unwavering and strong. She wanted it as well.

Holding her gaze, he dropped low. "All mine," he groaned as he prodded and then pushed himself inside of her perfection.

She'd wanted it badly. Her body inhaled his. He'd wanted to wait after their time together in the cottage on their first night to make certain she wasn't going to hurt, and she'd stayed with Malani and Tutu the night before. They'd only been together a few times on their trip. Her body craved his just as he longed hungrily for her.

He pushed farther, claiming her, understanding the gravity of what it meant this time on this night.

She bucked underneath him, needy and expectant.

"Can you take more, baby doll?" He gasped for breath. The feeling was indescribable. She was perfection.

"Oh god, yes," she pled.

"I've got all you need, just take it." With a demanding thrust, he plundered her depths. Their energy spun in tantric accord, none all hers or all his. It existed as one together. Her hips undulated like the wild tides of her ocean. He plunged deep into her waves, baptizing himself in her waters as he gasped for breath.

He was stunned. It was different. Of all the women he'd been with, and each magical time he'd been with her, it had never felt so perfect, so complete.

She was his and he hers in entirety, and as he made them one they could never be broken apart. Nothing would ever feel as heavenly as this, he knew.

"I'm gonna..." she gasped, but couldn't quite get the warning to pour from her breath as another wave washed from her body.

"I feel it, baby. Open your eyes. Look at me when I bring you. You're all mine." His order gasped from him as he continued to pump.

Her eyes flashed open and a pleading whimper escaped her.

"It's coming. I know. I've got you. Just let it go for me," he urged and she shattered. The waves were much stronger this time. Her energy flew in utter fulfillment and elation.

"I know you have another one for me, baby doll. I want them all. They're mine." He kept his thrusts rhythmic, pumping her full of him.

She swelled tight as he built her again. His release churned and throbbed in his groin. The heavenly peace washed through him as she permeated his entire being. Her energy flooded through him as he pushed his into her.

She cried out for him, and he wrapped her up in his arms. He buried himself deeply as he spilled all of himself inside of her, feeling their releases mix in heady ecstasy. His seed exploded inside of her with nothing to keep it from her womb. He groaned from the thought, and he pumped deeper into her.

He withdrew but kept her body wrapped safely in his arms.

He leaned away from her and managed to reach a larger jar of the healing ointment that they'd used several nights before. Tutu had placed it conveniently near their bed for the night.

He dipped his fingers inside of it and began to gently rub it on her lips and inside her.

"I'm not hurting," she assured him. Her deeply satisfied smile completed the absolute perfection they'd just experienced.

"I want to make sure, sweetheart. I can't ever let anything hurt you again." He continued his task, soothing everything he'd just done. "And I need more. I'm not finished. I want you full of me, so fucking full of my seed you're overflowing."

"Oh god, yes," she groaned.

They eventually moved from the bed and ate the dinner Malani had left them in the kitchen. Dan held her on his chest as the ocean breeze swung them gently in the hammock. They cuddled under several quilts and watched the sunset.

She fell asleep against him. Her energy still waned much faster than it used to.

As the moon began its dance on the ocean waves, Dan eased her out of the hammock and carried her to bed. She never stirred. Content and finally safe, she slept peacefully in his arms.

He closed the hangings around them and cradled her tenderly. He was so thankful for all he'd been given. He offered a fervent prayer of overwhelming gratitude for his precious Maylea.

CHAPTER 58

RELUCTANT LEADER

CROWN GOVERNOR STEPHEN HAYDENSHIRE

"Sir, I don't know. I can't seem to figure this out. Maybe I'm not the guy for this job." In his dress uniform, Landon Portwood made a very sharp looking chief. Julie stood steadfast by his side. She gazed up at him with a great deal of pride and adoration. Stephen appreciated his hesitations, but he had no doubt in his choice.

"You have an outstanding team, Landon, and you are an extremely capable officer. I don't know what's going on, but we've lost two undercover operatives, one here and one in France. There are hundreds of thousands of dollars missing. We need a chief, and you're the man for this job. I have complete faith in you."

Stephen stepped back before he could argue again. He held up his right hand. Portwood copied his motion. All of Iodex, weary and worried, looked on to the swearing in of their new leader.

"Just repeat after me. I, Landon Portwood, do solemnly swear to uphold the justice of the American Gifted Realm, to well serve the people, both Gifted and Non-Gifted, faithfully and to the best of my ability, without favor, or affection, malice, or ill will. I will uphold the law in every capacity as the Chief of Elite Iodex."

With a harsh swallow, he began, "I, Landon Portwood…"

About the Author

J.E. Neal (aka Jillian) vastly prefers coffee to tea, guac to salsa, the beach over anywhere else, and the world inside her head over the one outside her front door. She also loves not having to choose.

Driven by the question 'what if,' J.E. Neal's world began to manifest. What if there were people with powers the rest of us couldn't see? What if the energy of our world could be summoned and used at their will? Characters with these amazing abilities took shape in her mind. She created—and continues to create—an endless number of stories full of delicious escape from our reality where emotions are visible, desire is palpable, and danger is universal.

Learn more about J.E. Neal at JillianNeal.com

facebook.com/jilliannealauthor
twitter.com/JillianNeal_
instagram.com/jilliannealauthor

ALSO BY J.E. NEAL

ENERGY OF MAGIC

Shield and Shattered Cages (Book 1)

Shield and Faltered Steps (Book 2)

Shield and Splintered Oaths (Book 3)

Shield and Humbled Crown (Book 4)

Shield and Vile Serpents (Book 5)

Shield and Coveted Splendor (Book 6)

Shield and Guarded Shadow (Book 7)

Shield and Worthy Sinner (Book 8)

Shield and Sacrificial Heirs (Book 9)